This book is dedicated to my husband, John, and my brother, Tim, for their editing contribution and helpful advice. I would also like to thank my friend, Solveig, for her proofreading skills and our lifelong friendship.

Chapter One

On Patrol

Commander Lapin, leader of the Noble Rabbits from the Eighth Regiment, had been out on patrol when he heard loud banging in Witch Zeldar's backyard. The sound was coming from a small garden shed behind a rickety, foul-smelling house on Dead End Street. Something larger and stronger than a rabbit was pushing against the bolted shed door. Before investigating the shed, the commander scanned the backyard because Witch Zeldar, who lived in the house, was very wicked and devious. Suddenly, the back door flew open. Lapin crouched down beneath an azalea shrub with pink flowers and watched the crone storm across the backyard to the small shed and threaten to harm whomever was locked in there. After the witch returned to her house in a huff, the commander crept across the yard. He noticed that there were a couple of knotholes near the foundation of the old, wooden shed. He balanced on his hind legs as he peeked through one of the peepholes. He was stunned to see two distraught girls in disheveled clothing. The younger one was crying. He immediately sprinted back to the safety of the forest to report his findings when he came upon Skit and Kreen patrolling the night sky.

Skit and Kreen were Little Peepers. All Little Peepers were trained to ride birds and guard their forest from trespassers and the banished magi who intended to harm them. Skit and Kreen, the youngest and newest of the owl pilots, had been assigned to patrol Commander Lapin's territory tonight. They had just been paired with their new owl companions earlier that day. After a year of flight patrol training, Skit was proudly riding a barred owl named Peck, while Kreen was whizzing through the air on top of Trill, a western screech-owl.

Commander Lapin felt a great sense of relief when he spied the patrol owls swooping above his head. This meant he would not have to travel deep into the woods to sound the alarm. Although the forest had been cleared of witches, warlocks, sorcerers, and sorceresses for the past thirteen years, he always remained alert. The Noble Rabbits from the Eighth Regiment, or any of the other rabbits of the forest, did not have the luxury of dropping their guard against their enemies. With his long ears raised high, he flagged down Skit and Kreen and waited for their owls to land near him.

As expected, Trill and Peck touched down gently, as if landing on a fragile bird's egg. Skit and Kreen did not pitch forward even the slightest bit, which was a good thing since pilots never strapped themselves to their birds. As soon as they reached the forest floor, the two Little Peepers jumped off their owls and greeted Commander Lapin by touching his brownish-gray nose. This was a sign of respect. Everyone in the entire forest held great admiration for the commander. For countless generations, his extensive family lived on the edges of Hidden Forest to help the Little Peepers guard their enchanted forest. In return, the Little Peepers protected the rabbits from their predators, except for the Black Dragon, who lived on the highest point in all of Hidden Forest.

"I came here to alert the inhabitants to an imminent danger," said Commander Lapin. Like all the animals in Hidden Forest and the rest of the world, Lapin spoke Tiere, an ancient language that consisted of plenty of twills, chirps, twitters, growls, and clicks of the tongue. He also thumped his hind leg when he became excited, nervous, or agitated. He was currently pounding his left rear leg.

"What great danger do you speak of?" questioned Kreen. The Little Peepers spoke fluent Tiere as well as their own language called Peep, which originated from the elf tongue. Elves and Little Peepers spoke to each other in either Peep or the Elfin language, or Tiere if animals were among them. No creature in their forest was human or spoke a human language. On the off-chance humans ever encountered Little Peepers, they would describe them as ugly fairies who made peeping noises. However, Little Peepers were not related to fairies. They did not sport wings or cast spells with wands. Nonetheless, they had a supernatural ability. They had the capacity to "bend" other creatures' minds to their will, which was the reason the other beings in the forest often referred to them as mindbenders. They could persuade a hot-tempered witch to lower her wand or force a stubborn dragon out of its den. Although they were no taller than four inches, their strength was in their numbers. If they combined their mindbending abilities, they could outmatch any other woodland creature. This had frightened the nine witches, warlocks, sorcerers, and sorceresses of Hidden Forest, known collectively as the Malum, which meant evil in both the Elfin and Peep languages. Once the Little Peepers made their appearance in the forest, the magi's prominent status was diminished. Because it was unacceptable for the Malum to lose their influence, they decided to get rid of the Little Peepers for good.

"Witch Zeldar has imprisoned two children," Commander Lapin said to Kreen and Skit and their patrol owls. "I'm afraid this can only mean one thing. She is growing old and desperate and needs to drink the children's blood under a full moon to restore her magical powers."

Everyone in the forest knew that the Malum lost their magical powers after they had been expelled from the Hidden Forest. Unfortunately, the banished magi had the ability to regain their magic with a blood enchantment, or they could return to the magical forest to replenish their magic. The patrols kept them from returning. The threat of the Malum returning was the primary reason the rabbits, the owls, and the Little Peepers conducted regular patrols around the forest borders. For centuries, the rabbits kept a steady watch on intruders. But the Malum had become the biggest danger of all after they were kicked out.

"It seems that Zeldar and probably the rest of them are intending to perform a ritual under the next full moon," continued Lapin, his hind foot rapidly beating against the ground. He had not forgotten how the witches cut off rabbit paws for good luck and then placed the rabbits in a stewpot to eat. "I won't allow their return. I will not let the Malum capture us rabbits again."

Trill and Peck hooted from outrage, recalling how the magi had trapped owls and used experimental magic on them. They were never freed from their cages. Eventually, most owls succumbed to their sorcery.

"My ancestors spent most of their lives in cages," said Trill. "We must notify the queen at once."

"We shall warn others, as well," added Skit, climbing on top of Peck's back. The barred owl had mottled brown feathers and a large, round head and dark eyes. He had a barred throat, hence its name, barred owl.

Kreen followed Skit's lead and clambered up Trill. She sat down right behind her owl's neck and positioned her arms and legs in a way to grip Trill without pulling on her feathers. Unlike Peck's coloring, Trill had the typical gray plumage of a western screech-owl. There were dark brown crossbars scattered across her feathers. She also had ear tufts while Peck did not. Her huge, round eyes were amber in color. Although Trill was half the size of Peck, both were equally competent at flying.

Commander Lapin had not moved from his spot and his hind leg was still beating the ground. "Will you save the captured girls from Witch Zeldar?"

Kreen and Skit had no immediate answer. Little Peepers typically did not get involved in the affairs of humans, unless a person unwittingly trespassed into Hidden Forest. Luckily, humans were relatively easy to scare out of the forest. A blood-curling scream usually did the trick. A barred owl can produce a hair-raising, catlike scream and a screech-owl can emit the eerie wail of a ghoul. If shrieking did not frighten off the trespasser, a Little Peeper could use their mindbending ability to instruct the human to leave the woods.

"The children will die without our help," Lapin reminded them.

"We will bring your concern to Queen Wista," said Kreen. "She will decide what to do."

Lapin watched the owls take flight. Then, he returned to his warren to alert the others to what he had seen tonight on Dead End Street.

Chapter Two

The Garden Shed

Ruby and her younger sister, Shauna, had been imprisoned in the garden shed for three days. Even if they managed to escape, they had no home to return to because their stepfather had kicked them out. After their mother died a week ago, their drug-addicted and drug-peddling stepfather sold them off to a male stranger. They assumed they were traded for money and drugs. After the deal was brokered, the man put them in the back of a windowless van. For what seemed like hours, they rode. Their silence was only broken by Shauna's crying. Since Ruby was twelve years old and three years older than Shauna, she kept her emotions in check for her sister's sake. During their time in the van, she planned their escape. She realized that nobody would come looking for them because she and Shauna were poor and brown-skinned and from the inner city. If they had been rich, white, suburban girls, she was certain their sudden disappearance would be posted on social media and their story would make national headlines. The police and caring strangers alike would frantically search for them. A national hotline would have been set up for all the incoming tips. Alas, Ruby knew that she and her sister came from the wrong part of the city. Furthermore, her stepfather would lie about their absence if anyone in the neighborhood or from their school inquired about them. She decided that it would be up to her to snatch the handgun from her abductor, who concealed it in the deep pocket of his black cloak. She would fatally shoot him, if it came down to that. Life had taught her to be street smart and tough. Or so she believed until she met the old woman who tricked her and Shauna, imprisoning them in her garden shed.

After a half-day of driving, the man with the gun had dropped them off at the old woman's house. The woman gave the man a large, heavy duffle bag. At this point, Ruby was certain they were being traded for cash, drugs, or weapons, or a combination of them. *In exchange for what?* However, she did want to think of all the terrible things an adult can do to a child. The old woman told them that her name was Zeldar and she had no intention of hurting them. She fed them food that resembled canned cat food. After they finished eating, she lured them into the shed by offering to show them a litter of kittens born there a week earlier. Ruby and Shauna fell for one of the oldest tricks in the world. Ruby was still kicking herself.

Zeldar only came to the shed to threaten their lives if they made loud noises or called for help. These threats were made through the locked door. Zeldar never opened the door. Before they were imprisoned, food and water had been stored in containers in the shed. Evidently, their abduction had been carefully planned out. Once, Ruby asked Zeldar what she intended to do with them. The woman cackled like a witch and checked the lock on the door. Shivers ran up Ruby's spine while Shauna burst into tears.

During the third night of their imprisonment, Ruby was awakened by the sound of scraping and digging. The noise came from below the shed. She glanced over at Shauna, who was still sound asleep. Her sister's body was curled up in a fetal position toward the back of the shed, wedged between a huge bag of pesticide and a sack of rat poison. The floor was made of cheap plywood and covered in stains. There were no blankets. Fortunately, it was nearing the end of May and the weather remained warm at night.

Ruby scanned the garden shed for a makeshift weapon to protect her and her sister. However, the only items in the shed were the giant bag of pesticide and much smaller containers filled with water and food. The water was nearly depleted. Her anxiety rose when the scratching noise became louder and closer. Someone was clawing their way through the floorboard. She crouched in the corner of the shed near Shauna. She was debating if she should wake up Shauna when a pile of dirt and a furry head burst through the plywood floor. She gasped while Shauna jolted wide awake.

The head belonged to a mole.

"Do not be frightened," said the mole in Tiere to the wide-eyed girls. His name was Rooter. "I have come here to rescue you." He shook the dirt from his face and then pushed himself through the hole. Two more moles trailed behind him. All three moles were covered in short, velvety, black fur. Their pink snouts were long while their pink tails were short and almost hairless. Their muscular forelimbs were equipped with shovel-like claws, which were designed for digging tunnels. Working as a team, the three moles began digging a tunnel under the shed as soon as they received the urgent request from Queen Wista to free the two human children.

Ruby and Shauna were speechless as the three moles appeared to be speaking amongst themselves. It sounded like grunting and snorting.

"They cannot understand us," said Erde. She was the second mole to emerge from the hole. She was squinting at Rooter because moles had poor eyesight. "Where is Golden Belle? I cannot see her." Just as she posed the question, a golden fairy flew out of the hole. She soared over the children while waving her golden wand. The fairy dust gave the children the ability to understand Tiere and the other forest languages. The golden fairy disappeared back down the tunnel as quickly as she had first appeared. Fairies did not like to be confined in tight spaces, such as garden sheds.

"Come quickly, children. You must not dawdle," said Snoot, straining his eyes at Ruby and Shauna. "You must make your escape before the witch is awakened."

"I believe we have made the tunnel wide enough for your escape," Rooter said proudly, as he sized up the girls the best he could with his limited sight.

"Hurry now. The rabbit guards are waiting for us," said Erde encouragingly. "We can make formal introductions later."

The sisters looked at each other, flabbergasted. They comprehended every word the moles had said since the fairy dust was sprinkled on them.

Shauna rubbed her sleepy eyes. "Is this a dream?"

"Of course not," said Erde, giving the younger girl a baffled look. "Why would it be a dream?"

"It's not possible that animals can talk," said Shauna.

"Certainly, you have heard animals talking before tonight. It was your ears that were not working properly until Golden Belle fixed them," pointed out Erde. "No more talk until we reach the safety of the forest."

Ruby and Shauna went with the moles because there was no better alternative. They did not want to discover what the witch would do to them once she awoke from her sleep. Besides, they wanted to meet the rabbits of the forest.

The tunnel was extremely tight for Ruby, who was half a head taller and a few inches wider than her sister. Despite both girls being slender, they had to maneuver through the tunnel on their bellies like snakes. It was pitch-black in the tunnel and the soil was damp. It smelled of earthworms. They could hear the moles, who were in front of them, urging them on. Luckily, it was a short tunnel, ending a couple feet from the back of the shed. Ruby was the last to emerge. She had not seen the sky for three days. The moon was nearly full and stars shone brightly overhead, casting dark shadows on the yard.

To make up for their poor eyesight, moles have superb hearing. They stood still and listened carefully for any sign of danger. As soon as the moles directed the girls to follow them, they heard a door slam shut. The noise came from the direction of the house.

"It must be the witch," gulped Snoot.

"You must follow Golden Belle to the Hidden Forest," said Rooter, addressing Ruby and Shauna. "We cannot outrun the witch."

"When Zeldar figures out what we have done, she will set out traps," Erde said worriedly.

"More likely, poison," countered Snoot.

In the meantime, Golden Belle had swooped down from a nearby tree when she heard her name. The moles wished them luck and jumped back into the tunnel for protection.

The tip of the fairy's wand glowed in the dark like a candle flame. "Come with me," said Golden Belle. Her voice was light and airy.

The girls had to run to keep up with Golden Belle. The golden fairy zipped around in the same manner as a hummingbird. When she got too far ahead of Ruby and Shauna, the golden-haired fairy hovered in one spot until they caught up with her.

They only had to run across the large backyard to reach the border of Hidden Forest, which was not hidden at all. They could easily see the silhouettes of the tall trees of the forest in the moonlight.

"The forest will protect you from Witch Zeldar," said Golden Belle, as she perched herself on top of a low hanging evergreen limb. "She would not dare enter the forest without her magic, especially alone. The patrols will nab her as soon as she crosses the boundary line."

Ruby glanced around, puzzled. "Where are the rabbit guards?"

"Here we are," said Commander Lapin. He popped out behind a tree along with another gray rabbit named Poppin, who was First Officer of the Eighth Regiment of the Noble Rabbits. She was slightly smaller than the commander.

"The rabbits talk, too!" exclaimed Shauna.

"The moles told us that all animals talk," Ruby reminded her sister. "It was our ears that needed repairing."

"Zeldar is approaching," said Poppin with her ears erect.

"I hear her footsteps, too," said Lapin. "We will not greet her upon her arrival. Come, children, we will take you to Queen Wista and she will decide your fate."

"Our fate?" Shauna said nervously. "Will she kill us?"

"Certainly not. She is not an evil queen," said Poppin, appalled by such a gruesome thought. "The creatures of the forest do not go out of their way to harm humans, except for the Dark Shadow. Maybe the frog-snakes are dangerous to humans. I do not know. Nevertheless, the queen will determine where you should belong. We must go now before the dragon begins his hunt."

Ruby and Shauna traded a fearful look of uncertainty. They were worried that they were being tricked again.

"We don't belong to anyone," Shauna stated defiantly.

"My sister and me only belong to each other now," said Ruby. "Nobody else wants to take us in."

"Surely, there has to be someone who will care for you," said Poppin. At last count, she had six hundred forty-two cousins. Commander Lapin was one of them, although he had been adopted into the eighth regiment. He was discovered as a frightened kit by Poppin's great-grandmother. His parents were nowhere to be found.

"You can explain your circumstances to Queen Wista," said Lapin. "And I am sure that you have plenty of questions to ask the queen. But, please, we must go now. I do not want to lay eyes on the witch. She's a troubling sight."

"She is homely to look at," admitted Shauna.

"It is not her physical looks I dread," said Lapin. "She has the heart of a monster and she will attempt to seek revenge upon the rabbits if she sees we have participated in your rescue. The magi have always sought out rabbits to put in their stewpots and cauldrons."

"But you told us that she can't enter the forest," said Ruby.

11

"She *won't* enter the forest without the protection of her magic," said Lapin. "That is why she is after the two of you. In fact, all of the Malum will be looking for you. But I do not have time to explain it. Please no more talk!"

From above, Kreen and Skit and their owls spotted the human girls. Even though the children would be accompanied by Lapin and Poppin, the two Little Peepers and their owl companions also kept an eye on them as they circled overhead. For the past few days, there was something in the forest that made them uneasy and set their teeth on edge. Whatever it was, it prickled their skin as they rode their owls. They could tell the other forest creatures were also sensing something was wrong, especially the nymphs and the trees. The laurel tree, inhabited by a nymph, was shaking its leaves, even on windless days. Tree nymphs, or dryads, had the ability to know things others did not because their trees held onto ancient secrets.

Golden Belle excused herself from the group because the other fairies were expecting her return soon. They would be concerned for her well-being. Even the fairies, who were usually carefree, had been growing uneasy lately. They, too, were anxious about the return of the magi. They helped to expel the Malum, who would not forget the part the fairies played in their expulsion.

Exhausted and half-starved, Ruby and Shauna trudged through the woods, as if each foot weighed a thousand pounds. Sometimes they staggered. Shauna almost fell asleep on her feet. Although only a week had passed since their mother's death, it had been a long journey since then. Tonight's walk just made the journey longer. The rabbits did not push them to go faster as they continued to follow a well-trodden path made by unicorns over thousands of years. Hence, its name, Unicorn Trail.

"Do we have to go much further?" questioned Ruby, drowsily.

"Only a little ways from here," replied Poppin.

Ruby sighed. "You said that a long time ago."

"We've been walking all night," whined Shauna. "My eyes and legs are tired."

"The Little Peepers live in the middle of the forest," explained Poppin. "Since we do not have wings, we must walk to get there."

Ruby yawned again. "Who are these Little Peepers? And what does the queen have to do with the Little Peepers?"

"Queen Wista is the leader of the Little Peepers," replied Lapin, who was hopping alongside Ruby, full of energy. "A few centuries ago, a sorcerer turned eight frogs into little humanlike forms, closely resembling short gnomes. They received the name Little Peepers because of the peeping sound they made as frogs. They still occasionally peep when they become excited or agitated."

"Little Peepers are like fairies without wings and wands," added Poppin. The brilliant moonlight illuminated her glossy gray fur. The Noble Rabbits of the Eighth Regiment were known for their shiny coats. They were also swift and cunning.

"The eight Little Peepers escaped from Sorcerer Spellbinder and began to populate the forest by magical means. Sometimes his spells had an unpredictable outcome," continued Lapin. "Their numbers grew over many years. Now, there are a thousand of them residing together in treehouses in their hamlet, Arborville. They have bird companions that fly them around the forest." He glanced up at Skit and Kreen and their patrol owls swooping back and forth over the trail, keeping an eye out for them. "The pilots and their bird companions have been trained at a flight school. They are excellent flyers."

Ruby wrinkled her nose. "Bird companions? What kind of bird companions?"

"During the day, they get around on hawks, falcons, and eagles. At night, they ride owls," explained Lapin. "Sometimes they ride owls during the daytime, depending on the owl's mood on that particular day."

"Aren't owls nocturnal?" asked Ruby.

"Not all of them," answered Poppin. "Sunlight doesn't affect their eyes, in the same manner as the moles."

"Will Little Peepers turn back into frogs someday?" asked Shauna. Her eyelids were becoming as heavy as her feet. Both of them weighted down by a lack of sleep and nourishment.

Lapin looked over at Poppin before replying. "The Little Peepers fear that the Malum will return to Hidden Forest and change them back into frogs in retaliation for evicting them. Actually, all the forest dwellers are worried that the Malum will put a curse upon them or outright kill them."

"The magi were banished from the forest in the first place because they were wreaking havoc upon the rest of us," said Poppin. "They had become too wicked and they knew the Little Peepers had the ability to remove them from Hidden Forest. So, they attacked the Little Peepers. The rest of the woodland creatures struck back, except for the ravens and the Black Dragon. It was the Little Peepers who finally drove out the fiends with their mindbending abilities."

"*Mindbending abilities*?" repeated Ruby, wrinkling her nose. "What is that?"

Her question remained unanswered because a white unicorn stepped out onto the trail in front of them, regarded them for a few seconds, and then vanished into the woods.

"A unicorn rarely reveals itself to others," said Lapin, sounding surprised. He had only seen a unicorn six times during his lifetime. He was born centuries ago. The magic of the forest kept him from dying, just like many of the other forest creatures.

From above the treetops, Skit and Kreen and their owls also spotted the unicorn. This was the first time they had ever seen a unicorn, even with the advantage of having an aerial view of the entire forest.

"The unicorn has to be sending us a message," Kreen said to Skit. "Otherwise, it would not have shown itself."

"I agree," said Skit. "But what is it telling us?"

"It might be warning us of danger," interjected Peck. "Let's fly ahead and scout the area before us." He flapped his wings harder.

Lapin and Poppin caught sight of the owls taking off toward the village of the Little Peepers. The sudden departure of Kreen and Skit and their owls concerned them. They wondered if they rushed off to seek help for them. Two Little Peepers could not fend off the Black Dragon. It would take dozens of Little Peepers to tackle an obstinate dragon. Nor did two rabbits and two human girls have the physical strength to fight off a fire-breathing dragon with its voracious appetite for small creatures.

"They should have told us where they were going," muttered Poppin. "Sometimes rabbits don't get the respect we deserve."

"Unfortunately, this is true," Lapin agreed unhappily.

"Who left us?" questioned Ruby, her eyes searching the dark shadows between the trees.

"The two Little Peepers who had been watching over us the entire time," replied Lapin. "Did you not see their owls sweeping over us? The barred owl is a rather large bird."

Ruby shook her head and said she was too tired to look up at the sky. "I barely have the strength to keep my eyes open."

"Me, too. I don't feel well—" Shauna stumbled forward and collapsed to the forest floor. At last, exhaustion, thirst, and hunger had overcome her.

In a state of panic, Ruby crouched down by her sister and shook her. "Get up, Shauna! We're almost there, according to the rabbits." She shot Lapin and Poppin a look of doubt. "Don't you die on me!"

"Is she on her way to the next world?" Poppin asked Ruby, confused. "Is this how humans die? As if they are sleeping?" She was leaning over Shauna with her ears cocked, inspecting the young girl. The girl was the same brown shade as the Noble Rabbits from the Second Regiment.

Ruby put her hand over Shauna's beating heart. "She seems alive. I guess she just needs rest. Some food and water might be helpful, too." She licked her dry lips. "It was hot in the shed. And we haven't slept much since our mom died. Was murdered, I mean."

"Murdered? How tragic and ghastly!" gasped Lapin. These girls were in more danger than he had originally anticipated. "In Hidden Forest, you cannot die naturally. But you can suffer an unfortunate death if you are not careful. Once the heart quits beating, it cannot start up again, even if the rest of the body is immortal. Please be vigilant at all times."

"Thank you for the warning," Ruby said, sounding a little short. She was cranky because of all the things she had been through lately. "But I'm mortal. I will die no matter how careful I am."

"You are immortal as long as you remain in Hidden Forest," said Lapin. "Or, at least, I think so. I don't know much about humans. You are human, right?"

"I believe so. But even if I was immortal, I can still be killed, right?"

"If you're not paying close attention to your surroundings, then yes." Lapin gazed up at the sky, apprehensively. "The Black Dragon hunts at this hour. He usually preys on rabbits, but his hatred for humans might change his appetite." The early morning light was returning once more to the forest. "We cannot stay here long."

"She is too heavy for us to carry," fretted Poppin. Her gaze was on Shauna. "The poor girl is in a deep sleep, as if hibernating like the Black Dragon when the temperature falls below freezing."

Ruby gazed up at the sky, searching for this dragon of theirs. "It's well above freezing."

"There is a gnome community close by," said Lapin. "I could go fetch the gnomes. They are incredibly strong for their small size. I've seen them pick up rocks ten times heavier than they are. They live in little houses made of heavy stone," he explained to Ruby. "They don't pick up rocks and throw them at each other for sport. The gnomes are not mean-spirited, but they can be mischievous."

Poppin's ears shot up, listening intently. She had extraordinary hearing even for a rabbit. "Do you hear that noise?" She scanned the westward sky and spied a small squadron of Little Peepers on their owls. Kreen and Skit were leading the way. "Thank goodness, our help has arrived."

Ruby counted seven owls of various size and appearance. She did not know it at the time but Little Peepers, who were rather superstitious, consider the number seven to be exceptionally lucky and a symbol of celestial harmony. Then again, they also believed the numbers three, five, six, and ten also signified universal goodwill. Nor did Ruby know that all the owl species in the world could be found in Hidden Forest. She also was not familiar with the names of the seven owl species before her eyes—barn owl, long-eared owl, great horned owl, barred owl, western screech-owl, spotted owl, and the largest of them all, the great gray owl—because she had never seen an owl until today. There were no owls to be found in her neighborhood. Her mother had been too poor to take her and Shauna to the city zoo. Nonetheless, she could not imagine that any of the owls in the nonmagical world carried riders. After dismounting, the pilots quickly introduced themselves and their companion owls. She noticed that the Little Peepers were about the length of her hand and had a faint greenish skin tone. Their amber eyes bulged out slightly, like a frog. Other than that, they looked like miniature humans with potbellies.

"Your friend appears to be out like a candle in the wind," said Herona, eyeing the sleeping girl. She was the tallest, oldest, and perhaps the wisest, among the Little Peepers gathered on Unicorn Trail. She was also Queen Wista's chief advisor. "We will have to quickly call upon an elf to carry her to our village. We cannot linger on the trail for too long."

"What is wrong?" asked Lapin, sensing the counselor's anxiety.

"The Dark Shadow was spotted earlier tonight in the forest," replied Herona. "Once again, it has risen from its pit. I prefer not to encounter it."

"That is most likely the reason the unicorn showed itself," Poppin said in a breathless tone. "I suspected that she was warning us of danger."

Ruby noticed that all of them were scowling, including the two rabbits. "What is the dark shadow?" This place was nothing like the inner city. There, the residents were afraid of gang members, drug dealers, immigration officials, landlords, and sometimes, the police. People were terrified of gun violence. Not once could she recall anyone mentioning they were scared out of their wits by a dark shadow.

"Flycatcher and Hummer, please go retrieve a couple of elves and bring them back to us," said Herona, ignoring Ruby's question for the moment. "This one looks too worn-out to carry on much longer." She was looking at Ruby, whose clothes were soiled. She had never seen anyone looking as ragged as the girl, except for her sister, equally as filthy, passed out on the ground. It was a terrible sight.

"Should I first speak with the elf queen?" questioned Flycatcher.

"Yes, follow proper protocol," answered Herona. "Or else Queen Rossen will be offended. Also, request medicinal herbs. These girls will require them to regain their strength."

Flycatcher nodded and then she climbed aboard Tuft, her long-eared owl. Meanwhile, Hummer mounted his spotted owl, Dots. The owls took flight.

Next, Herona turned her attention to Ruby. "You should rest while we wait for the arrival of the elves."

"What about the dark shadow?" Ruby was so overly tired that she was swaying on her feet. "Don't I have to be awake to run away from it?"

"The Dark Shadow no longer hunts in Hidden Forest," replied Herona. "You can safely close your eyes without worry."

"And the black dragon?"

"The Black Dragon will not attack us. We have the ability to control his mind," said Herona. She knew that this wasn't entirely true. There weren't enough Little Peepers in their party to fend him off. Commander Lapin and First Officer Poppin also realized this, but did not contradict Herona. They understood the counselor did not want to upset Ruby more than she already was. In this case, reminding everyone that the dragon could easily set them on fire would not be beneficial to anyone.

Ruby lay down by Shauna, who did not stir in her heavy slumber. "And the witch?" she asked drowsily.

"She will not enter the forest without her magic. Close your eyes," said Herona. "We will protect you."

"No one is ever completely protected," said Ruby, thinking of her murdered mother. She shut her eyes and drifted off to sleep. She dreamt of a man arguing with her mother. He wanted her to hand over the children to him. Her mother refused. There was a loud bang and then her mother's voice fell silent.

Ruby jerked in her sleep.

Herona gazed up at the girls. The older child slept fitfully while her younger sister was out cold. "They must be the children of one of the magi."

"I know," said Commander Lapin. "It's the only explanation for their capture. The magi would not waste their time on humans."

The rest agreed. And then, their voices also fell silent as they waited for help to arrive.

Chapter Three

The Treehouses

When Ruby awakened, she was no longer on Unicorn Trail. She was in what appeared to be a large tree cavity hollowed out by tools. It was not an animal burrow. A scratchy, but warm, blanket was thrown over her. It appeared to be roughly patched together with bits of cloth. A pile of little, soft, brown pillows was beneath her head. She noticed that there was a flap covering the entrance for privacy and, most likely, to keep out bugs. Shauna was not with her. She scrambled to her hands and knees and crawled out of the hollow tree. She was surprised at what she saw next. There was Shauna sitting cross-legged as two Little Peepers were fixing her hair. Other Little Peepers were bustling across a green meadow. Dozens of them were clambering up and down on little, wooden steps leading to the entrances of their treehouses situated high in the trees. Their homes were carved into the tree trunks of evergreens. Later, Ruby would discover that their treehouses had three or four levels, containing even a rustic kitchen and a bathroom without plumbing. Next, Ruby noticed that some of the treehouses extended out on sturdy branches. Perched on many of the tree limbs were large birds. Most of them were various species of owls but there were several eagles, hawks, and falcons. What was most shocking of all were the Little Peepers riding on the birds. They zipped from tree to tree or from a tree limb to the forest ground and vice-versa. The Little Peepers and the birds cheerfully chattered to each other. Meanwhile, several birds were just returning from hunting in the nonmagical world. Their sharp talons held fresh prey.

Ruby's attention returned to her sister. There were now three elves who were speaking to Shauna. They had long, flowing, white hair, pointed ears, high cheekbones, and eyes the color of a glacial lake. Their clothing appeared to be spun out of white silk. In comparison, the clothes of the Little Peepers were made from cedar bark and other woodland plants. Even more noticeable was the size difference between the two species. The Little Peepers were squatty and had little potbellies, resembling portly leprechauns, while the elves were slightly taller than the average human and had the athletic build of a competitive swimmer.

Ruby approached her sister. The three woodland elves and the two Little Peepers grooming Shauna greeted her. It looked as if Shauna had taken a bath and her clothes had been washed and dried. How long had she been sleeping?

"You are the older sister who suffered at the hands of Witch Zeldar," said Auralia, a young, female elf who carried her to the hollow tree. Ruby had slept peacefully as she was cradled in the safety of the elf's arms. "I am sorry for your recent troubles."

"Thank you for helping us. Is this Arborville?" Ruby put a hand over her eyes to shield them from the blazing noon sun. Overhead she spied a hawk circling high in the sky. She could not tell if the hawk was being piloted by a Little Peeper.

"Yes. You are in the home of the Little Peepers," answered Auralia. "Arborville is situated in Emerald Valley. Is it not beautiful?"

Ruby's gaze swept past the treetops and spied the high hills in the distance. "It is certainly a green place. The place where I come from is mostly gray—gray buildings, gray roads, and gray sidewalks. But the people come in different colors."

The elves and the Little Peepers smiled at her.

"The inhabitants of Hidden Forest come in different colors, too," said Auralia.

"We shall fix you up to look presentable for Queen Wista," said one of the Little Peepers. "As soon as you are ready, the queen will meet with you and your sister."

"We get to meet a queen! Can you believe it?" gushed Shauna. "It's like we are in one of the fairytales that Mom used to tell us at night."

"This is not a Disney fairytale where the mom dies."

"Our mom was killed just like Bambi's mom," Shauna reminded her.

Ruby rolled her eyes. "Okay, fine. We're living in a fairytale." She did not share her sister's enthusiasm. She sensed that there would be a price to pay for their rescue. The queen would want something from them. Back home, nothing came without a cost, including her mother's life.

"I do not know of this Bambi you speak of," said Auralia. "But I do know that our world is not a fairytale. It is real to us. And it will become real to you, unless you decide to leave our forest. That would not be a good idea. Queen Wista will soon explain your current situation."

Meanwhile, Queen Wista was already in the midst of a meeting with another queen. Queen Rossen was the ruler of the elves. The elves of Hidden Forest were shapeshifters. Aside from the ability to take on new forms, they had no other magical abilities. However, they were skilled at making curative medicine out of herbs and other plants. Many times, their medicinal potions had saved forest inhabitants, including the animals. For the elf queen to fit into Wista's tiny treehouse, she had shapeshifted into a field mouse, which was one of her favorite animals. The two queens were sitting across from one another at a table carved out of birch wood. Its three wooden legs twisted like tree roots from the center of its tabletop to the floor. They were drinking tea made from nettles and eating roasted mushrooms. Lavender honey sweetened the tea.

"Early this morning I received a message from the three moles, Rooter, Erde, and Snoot, that the two human girls carried the scent of the Malum," said Queen Wista to the elf queen, who had arrived with her chief advisor, Nirva. The two elves, Auralia and Tark, who carried the human children to Arborville had remained overnight in the hamlet, awaiting the arrival of their queen.

Queen Rossen clumsily set down her teacup on its saucer, almost breaking the clay cup. The elves drank from gold and silver cups. "Drinking from a teacup with paws is no easy feat," she said. "But drinking with bird talons is more difficult."

"I have never tried it."

"Do you suppose the scent of Witch Zeldar rubbed off on the girls?"

"No, I do not think so."

The elf queen looked quizzically at Wista. "Are you suggesting that the girls are magical beings?"

"They can see us. Ordinary humans cannot see the magical creatures in Hidden Forest. Hence, the name of the forest."

"Perhaps it was the fairy's gold dust that gives them the ability to see us."

"I do not believe so," said Wista. "This morning the younger sister, Shauna, told Counselor Herona that her mother seemed quite ordinary. Never wore a black robe or anything remotely resembling the magi's attire. In fact, her mother wore bright floral prints. From the girl's description of her mother, we can safely assume that her mother was not one of the Malum."

At this point, Wista had Rossen's full attention. The elf queen did not twitch her nose or tail. Instead, she remained frozen in her tiny chair but her eyes were alert. "Who was their father?"

"The girl stated that she did not know her father. She had never even seen a drawing or a portrait of him."

"So, you think her father is a wizard or a sorcerer? And he had children with a human?"

"Yes. But I have no evidence of it, except they can *see* us." Wista took a bite from her favorite mushroom—the chanterelle. It used to be her son's favorite, too. "Are the elves aware that a magus can drink the blood of one of their own kind under a full moon and his or her magical powers will be restored? It would enable them to return to Hidden Forest."

"No, we are not familiar with black magic potions," said Rossen. Unlike the elves, the Little Peepers were familiar with all sorts of magical potions because their frog ancestors had once been used in them. "We prepare herbal potions, not blood potions."

"I am more familiar with herbal teas than anything else," said Wista, smiling. "So far, a cup of tea has fixed most of my ailments."

Rossen did not return the smile. "What does this blood potion require, aside from a family member's blood?"

"A full moon. The magi's victim must be sacrificed under the moonlight. It is a cruel and gruesome ritual." She visibly shuddered. "I believe a sorcerer or a wizard, or perhaps both, sired children with the intent to drink the blood of their offspring after the bodies grew large enough to provide for all nine magi."

"If it's true what you have just said, then these girls are half-magical beings. Perhaps the potion requires a full magus."

"I don't believe so. Two half-magical beings would make a complete whole. The spell would work if enough blood is drunk." Wista took a sip of tea while waiting for Rossen to fully grasp their dire predicament.

"It seems that the Malum have been planning this since they were expelled," said Rossen.

"It appears so," answered Wista. "It does not surprise me, though."

"What else have you learned from our new visitors?"

"Shauna told Counselor Herona that an unfamiliar man had driven her and her older sister to Zeldar's house. I believe this man to be her real father. I think that all the Malum were planning to gather at Zeldar's house on the night of the next full moon to kill the girls and drink their blood. It is the most logical conclusion." Wista knew how much the elves valued logic and disproving allegations. They loved logic and order as much as their lovely clothing and jewelry. "As you know, the moon will be full tonight."

The elf queen sat back in her chair, twitching her whiskers. She could hear the hummingbirds whirring outside the open window. One or two of them might have been elves in bird form, making it possible for them to visit the Little Peepers in their homes. "It has been a number of years since the Malum were exiled and lost their immortality. They must be growing old and weak in the human world. I imagine they are growing desperate to return to the forest and revive themselves."

"I suspect they set this plan in action the day after they were banished," said Wista. "The older sister, Ruby, is twelve years old. The Malum have just been biding their time until the girls grew big enough to provide blood for all of them to feast on."

Rossen wrinkled her black nose in disgust. "It is quite possible there were other half-magical children that were sired for this purpose, as well. Perhaps a sacrifice will still be made under the full moon tonight."

"That is my fear, too," admitted Wista. "To make matters worse, the Dark Shadow was spotted last night. Both of us know that it arises when it is disturbed from its sleep."

"I recall the last time the Dark Shadow cast its shadow upon us." Rossen squeezed her eyes shut. She did not like to think about that time.

Wista noticed that Rossen's pale face had gone paler. "I remember it all too well, too. Fortunately, we were able to retrieve most of the souls from the Pit of Despair."

"Not all of them were freed," pointed out Rossen.

"I have not forgotten nor shall I ever forget." Wista frowned deeply. "Unfortunately, to save the souls that we did, we struck a terrible bargain. We cannot rid the forest of the Dark Shadow."

"Yes, it was a horrible bargain. But we had no other choice but to agree to its terms. We could no longer afford to have it continually preying upon us," Rossen reminded her.

"I know. But the deal was made in such haste," Wista said regretfully. "It has never sat well with me."

"The Dark Shadow has kept its end of the bargain. It only captures human souls not worth anything."

"We can only assume that it chooses worthless human souls." Wista reached for her queen-size teacup, which was the size of a toothpaste cap. "We know nothing about the humans that it has dragged to its pit." She took a couple of sips and returned the cup to its saucer.

"I prefer not to deal with it ever again. Once was enough."

"I am sorry that you had to confront the Dark Shadow alone. I wasn't strong enough after losing my son. You, on the other hand, forged ahead, despite your husband being trapped along with my son in the pit with the Dark Shadow." Queen Wista's eyes were nearly brimming with tears, remembering how her son, Rossen's mate, and another elf named Rowl still lingered to this day in the Pit of Despair.

"Elves are trained to set our emotions aside, when it is necessary." The elf queen took another drink from her tea and finished her mushroom. All the while, she was pondering their circumstances. "I suppose that I could assign one of my best spies to observe the Malum and report back to us. I think it would be best to keep a close eye on Witch Zeldar since the girls were held prisoners in her shed."

"That would be a splendid idea!" said Queen Wista excitedly, as if the thought had not occurred to her until now. Actually, the idea had been sitting in her head since Commander Lapin spotted the girls imprisoned in the shed. "We need to have a closer look and see what the Malum are up to. Our patrols can only get so close to them. And with Warlock Highbrow living in the big city, it's hard to keep track of his doings. It makes me wonder if the girls are his."

There was a knock on the door.

"Come in," said Wista.

Kreen opened the door and entered. "Queen Wista," she said, as she gave a quick curtsy of respect. Mostly, she bowed because the elf queen was there. The Little Peepers were generally informal. "Both girls are prepared to meet with you."

"I will come down at once to speak with them," said Wista.

"If you don't mind, I would like to accompany you," said Rossen. "I am very curious to hear what they have to say."

"You are very welcome to join me, Queen Rossen."

Wista stood up from the table and Rossen followed suit. Both of them headed for the doorway while Kreen clambered on top of a waiting taxi falcon, which flew her to the forest floor. The Little Peepers had their own assigned birds for patrolling, but they also had available taxi birds to fly them back and forth from their treehouses to the ground. Sometimes they climbed up and down ladders to reach their homes, but it was exhausting to do that more than twice a day. Their houses were built high in the trees for their own protection. The hooves of foraging animals would trample their homes on the forest floor. Also, the frog-snakes in Hidden Forest liked the taste of the Little Peepers, but did not like to slither up trees because the eagles could easily snatch them off high branches. Mostly, though, when Little Peepers were still frogs, they lived in trees. Little Peepers had not forgotten their ancestors' old ways.

Queen Rossen changed herself from a mouse to a chickadee. After she landed, she turned herself back into an elf. Ruby and Shauna watched in amazement as the elf queen transformed herself from a tiny bird into a full-sized elf. The size of her clothing and jewelry changed with her. They were so impressed by her performance that they were hoping the elf queen would repeat it. In the meantime, the taxi falcon flew Wista to a low branch of an oak tree. She wanted a better view of the girls.

The subjects of both queens bowed their heads and stepped back, while Ruby and Shauna were nudged forward by Nirva. The counselor's long, white hair was almost the same length as the queen's. Supposedly, elves never cut their hair, which grew throughout their immortal lives. Sometimes, though, they trimmed it on the sly to make the ends neater. Elves were vain about their physical appearance. They wore jewelry and gold chains, mostly around their long necks and on their slender arms and ankles. Sometimes, they weaved thin, gold chains through their long, thick hair. They traded with the Black Dragon for gems and other riches, especially gold.

"Ruby and Shauna, I am pleased to make your acquaintance," said Wista. "Welcome to Hidden Forest. I am Queen Wista." She gestured to the elf queen. "And this is Queen Rossen, leader of the elves."

"I am delighted to meet you," said Queen Rossen. She did not sound delighted. She came across as stiff and stern.

"You are lovely girls," said Wista.

Ruby and Shauna were nearly speechless. Since they had never been to Disneyland or England, they had never met a queen until this moment. Furthermore, no one had ever called them "lovely" before now. Usually, the drug dealers and the gang members taunted them and called them obscenities. Their stepfather insulted them when their mother was away. Their mother had worked odd hours at a convenience store, which explained why she was shot out on the streets at three in the morning. She was on her way home from work when the bullet pierced through her right temple. No one was arrested for her murder.

Queen Wista looked out at the gathering crowd. Her subjects totaled around a thousand. Among the Little Peepers were the elves Auralia and Tark who assisted in the rescue of the girls. Queen Rossen made it clear to Wista that Auralia was only chosen to go because she was available to lend a helping hand. The elf queen emphasized that Tark was selected because of his superior espionage skills. "Queen Rossen and I need to speak privately with Ruby and Shauna. I will politely ask all of you to give us the space that we require. Later on, I will inform you of our predicament. I promise that I shall not keep you in suspense for long since we are all in this together." For the most part, the Little Peepers were a classless society and made joint decisions, chiefly about collecting food for the winter. Collectively, they even decided which days they would remove the frog-snakes from the meadows or invite the gnomes to their hamlet for trading wares. However, having two newcomers in their midst threw their egalitarian system off-balance. Queen Wista decided it was best for her to step in until things settled down, as she did during the Great Banishment. It was no secret that Queen Wista was adored among the Little Peepers because they rarely kept secrets amongst themselves. In fact, since they were so terrible at keeping secrets, they made no effort to try anymore.

The Little Peepers and the elves dispersed, but they occasionally stole glimpses of the queens and the new arrivals. Unlike the elves, Little Peepers were never punished for eavesdropping on their queen or her only advisor, Herona. Living close together, the Little Peepers were always in each other's business.

The two leaders asked Ruby and Shauna all sorts of questions. They wanted to know about their life in the human world, how their mother died, and how they wound up in Witch Zeldar's garden shed. Shauna had already revealed parts of her life to Counselor Herona, but she repeated her story about how her mother was killed on her way home from work. After their mother's funeral, their stepfather sold them off to a stranger.

"And neither one of you has ever seen your father?" asked Wista.

"Our mom told us that he disappeared after Shauna was born," said Ruby. "She said that she didn't even have a photo of him because he refused to have his picture taken. He said that he was too old for such nonsense."

"I wonder if he was a vampire or a ghost," said Shauna.

"As I told you before, vampires and ghosts do not exist," Ruby reprimanded her sister.

"Ghosts do," said Wista. "Once in a while, one of them will pass through the forest. They are mostly harmless."

"You see, I was right," Shauna said triumphantly.

"Anyhow, we thought our father might be embarrassed by his looks," said Ruby. "Mom said he was old enough to be our grandfather."

"Mom also said that he dressed like an old person, too. He wore a black cloak, like a *vampire*," said Shauna, looking knowingly at her sister.

"Our father was not a vampire," refuted Ruby. "He just dressed like one."

"Do you know your father's name?" questioned Queen Rossen.

"Mom said it was Sean Smith. I searched for him on Facebook and other media sites, but the name is too common," replied Ruby.

"'*Facebook*'?" repeated Wista. "What is that?"

"A good place to find people," replied Ruby.

"A good place to find missing people," Shauna added.

Ruby shrugged her shoulders. "Apparently, our father didn't want to be found. Or, at least, by us."

"You mentioned that your stepfather handed you over to a man who took you to Zeldar's house. Can you describe this man?" questioned Rossen.

"He wore a baseball hat and sunglasses, so we didn't get a good look at him," answered Ruby. "He was white . . . but not as pale as you." She gestured at the elf queen. "He was tall and lanky—a few inches over six feet, about your height, and had a long, gray beard. He was *really old*."

"His long, black coat came down to his calves," added Shauna. "He was dressed too hot for the weather. But he wasn't sweating . . . which seems rather odd now that I think about it. Do vampires sweat?"

Wista raised an eyebrow, astutely. "Do you suppose he was your father?"

Ruby and Shauna sucked in their breath at the same time.

"But he was so old!" said Shauna. "Like a hundred years old!"

"The nonmagical world takes a toll on magical individuals," explained Wista. "Their bodies deteriorate faster."

"Did this man say anything to Witch Zeldar?" asked Queen Rossen. Her expression was as frozen as the Ice Age.

"I couldn't make out what they were saying because they spoke in a different language. I thought it might be Russian," said Ruby. "But I did see the witch handing over a huge duffel bag to the man and he left with it."

"She tricked us into following her into the shed," Shauna said bitterly. "I think that she was planning to kill us. Are you going to destroy her with magic?"

"At the time being, only the fairies have magic in Hidden Forest," Wista replied. "They do not practice dark magic. They will not harm another." She was unsure how to exactly answer Shauna's question at this point. She had no idea how to combat the Malum if they regained their magical abilities and made allies with other woodland creatures, such as the Black Dragon, the ravens, or the frog-snakes. "There are many of us here in the forest to protect you and to tend to your needs. However, you will have to make the difficult choice of how you want to be protected. The fairies can cast a spell upon you to shrink you to the height of a Little Peeper. Or, you can go live with the elves and stay at your present size."

"What if we want to return to the human world?" asked Ruby.

"Someday you may return. However, you cannot go back to the human world until matters are settled with Witch Zeldar and the other magi." Wista smiled kindly at them. "I realize that this is a big decision for you to make, but you will have to decide by sunset. Or, if your mind is already made up, please share your thoughts with us now."

Without discussing it, the sisters both knew that they would never go back to the human world if their stepfather and the rest of the people who wanted to hurt them were still there, including Witch Zeldar.

Shauna locked her big, brown eyes on Queen Wista's bulging, amber ones. The shadow of a large hawk passed over Wista and then Rossen. "Would we learn how to ride birds?" she asked tentatively.

"I don't see why not," replied Wista.

Like Shauna, Ruby was also staring at Wista, trying to imagine being the same height as her. She supposed that it would not matter being so short if everybody else in the community was of a similar stature. "Could we change back to our regular size later on?" Ruby asked in a tone that was almost as timid as Shauna's. She did not want to push her luck. If she and her sister were thrown out of the enchanted forest, she suspected Witch Zeldar would take a knife to their throats.

"The fairies have the ability to undo their spells," said Wista with confidence. "Later on, you might decide to live with the elves at your full height. As I said, the choice will always be yours."

Queen Rossen cleared her throat, as if it was her turn to speak. "Keep in mind, fairies do not have the capability of turning you into shapeshifters. You can never be like elves, but we would be willing to accept you as our own. You could certainly become a beekeeper or a gardener in our community. Extra pairs of hands are always needed."

"They show a talent for other things, as well," Wista interjected. "Their minds appear to be quite sharp. Since they can speak a human language, they could spy on the human world and report back to us—"

"Very well," Rossen interrupted. "We could examine your abilities and decide your fate by the outcome of your test results."

Since Ruby and Shauna hated taking tests, they gave each other a knowing nod. They had made their decision.

"We want to be shrunken down and fly on top of birds," declared Ruby.

"Then, the matter is settled." Wista appeared elated by their choice. She called out in a merry voice for a couple of Little Peepers to notify the fairies that their services would be required. The two Little Peepers whistled for their peregrine falcons. The falcons would take them to the fairy village of Tinsel. Traveling by peregrine falcon was the fastest way to get around in Hidden Forest.

Ruby and Shauna were dismissed as the queens gathered together their closest advisors. They needed to devise a plan to stop the Malum from returning to Hidden Forest. They also sent word out to the far reaches of the forest that the Dark Shadow had once again risen from its pit. Everyone in the forest was put on high alert, just as they were during the Great Banishment. The Black Dragon and the frog-snakes were not notified. Nobody dared approach the Black Dragon because he had a terrible temper when disturbed. The dragon might strike down the messenger with fire, while a frog-snake might use venom. Frog-snakes were created by the Malum to kill Little Peepers.

It did not take long for Golden Belle to arrive in Arborville along with four of her closest cousins, Glitz, Dazzle, Sparkles, and Flicker. They danced around Ruby and Shauna as they waved their golden wands. Flecks of gold dust shot out of the tips of their wands. Ruby and Shauna felt themselves shrinking while a thousand Little Peepers witnessed their transformation into Little Peepers. It did not hurt to shrink, as Ruby and Shauna had expected. When the fairies completed their magical spell, the girls were three inches tall. The same size as Little Peepers of their own age. They did not quite wind up looking exactly like Little Peepers because their skin remained brown instead of the greenish tone of a Little Peeper. Their eyes did not bulge, either. They also kept their lean shape. Nevertheless, their new appearance was close enough to the Little Peepers that the other forest creatures would describe them as such, even though they were closer in resemblance to fairies, who were also no taller than four inches.

"Do you suppose they might have the ability to bend minds?" Skit whispered to Kreen after observing the girls' transformation.

"Probably not," replied Kreen. "They are still themselves—human. Or half-human."

"The queen has ordered the girls to be enrolled without delay into Aviation School. She wants to keep their minds occupied, so they do not think about their poor dead mother or their father, who wants them dead."

"I suppose Aviation School is a good way for them to meet others of their own age," pointed out Kreen.

"And their own size," said Skit. "They will have to make new friends in our world."

"And learn the ways of the forest," added Kreen. "I imagine it will not be easy for them to adjust."

"I suppose not. But I imagine they will. They have no choice with the Malum breathing down their necks."

"At least, their little necks will be harder to find now," jested Skit, grinning at Kreen. They had been friends as far back as they could remember.

"But still, we must be vigilant as we watch over their tiny necks . . . and ours, as well. The trees are still whispering amongst themselves. Something is upsetting them."

As soon as the two sisters had completed their transformation, the crowd applauded with approval. Subsequently, the girls were given clothes to fit them. No one had seen them naked because their human clothes were piled on top of them. It was the five fairies that rescued them from their mound of clothing and helped them dress in garments worn by the Little Peepers. The girls' clothes were made from the plants, Indian hemp and spreading dogbane. While the girls were changing into their new garments, the spectators dispersed and carried on with their own lives, including gossiping about the newcomers. They were very curious about the humans and their customs.

Shauna wanted to have a wand like the fairies, but Golden Belle reminded her that Little Peepers had no magical abilities. "Little Peepers' only skill is mindbending. But it is an extremely useful skill."

"What exactly are the Little Peepers?" questioned Ruby. "Are they related to fairies?"

"No, they are not related to fairies in the least bit. In fact, they descended from frogs—" Before Golden Belle could finish her explanation, the wand flew out of her grasp and into Shauna's hand.

"I was just wishing that I could hold the wand," explained Shauna, startled. "I never intended to take it away from you." Wearing a sheepish expression, she gave it back to Golden Belle.

"I want you to do it again," said Golden Belle, looking just as astonished as the rest of them.

Shauna silently commanded Golden Belle's wand to come to her. As the wand began to tug in her hand, Golden Belle gripped it tighter. Then, she let go of her wand and it zipped over to Shauna, who snatched it out of the air. She had always been quick with her hands.

"Let me try," said Ruby, excitedly.

"Try to disarm me," said Sparkles.

Ruby trained her mind on Sparkles' wand. Within moments, Sparkles' wand was in Ruby's grip.

"That is amazing," said Flicker, firmly clutching her own wand. "Let's see what else you can do."

Queen Wista and Counselor Herona were peering out the window of the queen's treehouse, watching the interaction between Ruby, Shauna, and the fairies. It was just the two of them in the treehouse since the elf queen and her company had already parted for their village. Wista and Herona looked on as the sisters were making the wands shoot out golden flecks. The fairies appeared impressed.

"There is our proof that their father is a Malum," Wista said to her advisor. "Though, I was confident that they were. Otherwise, there would be no reason Zeldar would keep children in her midst. All the magi hate children. Just look at what they did to my son."

"They must be told the truth about why they were held captive in the shed."

"It will not be easy for them to hear that they were brought into the world to be sacrificed." Wista looked at Herona. "Nevertheless, it must be done for their own safety. We cannot leave them in the dark. Have the children brought here after the fairies leave. I will tell them myself."

Herona took a half-bow, backed out the door, and hailed a taxi bird.

As Herona retrieved Ruby and Shauna, all sorts of questions floated around in Wista's mind. But she could not anchor any of her questions to a single answer. Not yet, anyway. It would take time to sort it all out. But time was not on their side. She could sense the

Malum had other tricks up their sleeves. They would not give up so easily. And Queen Rossen might be right about the Malum having more offspring ready to sacrifice under a full moon. If so, they would have to rescue them before tonight. If not, the Malum would have to try to find a way to get the girls out of Hidden Forest. She hoped the elf spy would come back with the answers she needed from the nonmagical world.

Chapter Four

The Malum

There were nine magi expelled from Hidden Forest. Their names were Witch Zeldar, Witch Mortify, Witch Blackheart, Warlock Highbrow, Warlock Gloominus, Sorcerer Spellbinder, Sorcerer Serpentine, Sorceress Hexla, and Sorceress Underhand. Between them, they had committed the most heinous acts against the forest creatures. For instance, they made potions out of rabbits, frogs, and owls and cast horrible, sometimes fatal, spells on unsuspecting passersby, including fairies and Little Peepers. The only species they did not torment were the elves, the Black Dragon, and the Dark Shadow. Even so, the Malum did not befriend them either. The Malum had never made friends, even amongst themselves. That is, until they were banished. At first, they went their separate ways, angry and embarrassed by their defeat. They had to beg for handouts from humans or steal food from trashcans. After a few months of isolating themselves from the other exiles, they noticed that they were beginning to age at a rapid pace. Not only had they lost their magic, but their immortality was slipping from them faster than they had anticipated. Therefore, the nine Malum banded together and hatched a plan that would save them from dying from old age in the mortal world. The Malum knew of an ancient spell that would return their magical powers by drinking their own slain child's blood under a full moon. However, the witches and sorceresses were well past childbearing age. The warlocks and sorcerers would have to produce children with human females. They also agreed they would have to wait until the half-magical children were big enough to provide enough blood for all nine of them. It would take all nine of them to defeat the Little Peepers and the other creatures of the forest. But still, they were worried one of their own would run off with an offspring of theirs and perform the blood ritual without the others. A magus could never be trusted.

According to the spell, each of them would be required to swallow enough blood to fill the horn of a one-year-old ram to regain their magical abilities. But they would have to drink twice as much as the spell called for, since they would be drinking the blood of a half-magical child. Hence, they required enough blood to fill eighteen horns. Years earlier, Highbrow got ahold of a horn of a juvenile big horn sheep and measured its capacity. It held a cup or half a pint. They needed nine pints of blood. After conducting research on the matter, they learned that a forty-pound human child had between two and three pints of blood, a one hundred ten-pound youngster had about seven pints. In comparison, the average adult contained approximately ten pints. After thirteen years of exile, Warlock Highbrow's two daughters, ages twelve and nine, were determined to be of adequate size to provide the necessary amount of blood since the children were tall for their ages.

Because the girls escaped last night, the Malum would have to sacrifice Sorcerer Serpentine's three offspring. They were a bit younger and smaller than Highbrow's two daughters, but they were fairly confident they could drain enough blood from them. The problem was that Sorcerer Serpentine's offspring lived with their mother, who had a restraining order against Serpentine. The children's mother would have to be eliminated to wrench the kids away from her.

"Once I learn which moles helped the little imps escape from the shed, I will personally cut off their heads," Witch Zeldar muttered to the others. They were gathered around her large dining table, its wood spotted by glass rings. All of their meetings were held in her white, two-story house that resembled an old farmhouse. Or, as the neighbor kids described it, a haunted house. To obtain the house, she killed its previous owner, a very old man, who was buried in the backyard. She explained to the neighbors that the house belonged to her older brother, who was suffering from dementia. He was currently under care at an assisted living facility in another city. No one doubted her story.

"You should have been more careful," Sorceress Underhand scolded Zeldar. "I warned you that your house was too close to the forest's edge and the patrol rabbits. We should have hidden the children somewhere else."

"None of you offered to guard the children," Zeldar retorted. She was a decade older than the youngest among them, but looked decades older than all of them. "I will also punish the patrol rabbits upon our return. I'll poison every last one of them." Poison was Zeldar's weapon of choice and her solution to anything that annoyed her.

"We should round them up, cage them, and put them in our stewpots and cauldrons when needed," said Sorcerer Spellbinder. He was given his name because his spells were incredibly binding, including the one he put on the original eight Little Peepers. Even if all the fairies combined their magical powers, they could not break his spells. Neither could he. "We will need to spare some of the forest creatures for food and magical potions."

"We are getting ahead of ourselves," said Witch Blackheart, who was quick to cast black magic upon her enemies. She also had blown up numerous cauldrons due to potions that had gone awry. "We first need the other children. The moon will be full tonight." She was looking at Sorcerer Serpentine.

"The brats are just across town," said Serpentine. "I will bring them here as soon as the moon can be spotted in the night sky." His children's ages were eight, six, and four. He could not remember their names. "As I have mentioned on numerous occasions, their mother has a restraining order against me. I will have to murder their mother and steal the children out of their beds. I cannot risk retrieving them too soon. We do not want the police involved in this matter. Without our powers, we cannot defend ourselves against their weapons. They could imprison us for the rest of our lives. And I guarantee you that we would die in prison."

"You would die in prison," shot back Blackheart. "I am not going to prison with you."

"Let's not argue about this," said Warlock Gloominus in a gloomy tone. "I just wish that we had more spare children. What if they don't have enough blood for all of us?"

"We can't wait any longer," said Zeldar. "I'm afraid that I won't last much longer out here in the human world."

"What if we're short on blood?" Gloominus grumbled again. "Who will remain behind?"

"Don't be so pessimistic. There will be enough blood for all of us because we'll squeeze the last drop out of each one of Serpentine's brats. Besides, where are your offspring, Gloominus?" asked Blackheart in an irritated tone. Gloominus had no offspring. "You didn't do your part."

Gloominus' face flushed. No matter how hard he tried to convince himself to produce a child, he could not enter into a physical relationship with a human. Being near humans made him queasy. "What about Spellbinder? He didn't sire any children, either."

"It's not my fault that humans in this world are beneath me," sniffed Spellbinder.

"How quickly you forget that it was you who turned away, or rather turned off, females," said Sorceress Underhand. She was known for her underhanded ways and cutting remarks. "How many singles clubs did you join, Spellbinder? Six or seven? And how many females did you meet?"

"I was on seven useless dating sites, which resulted in a single, horrid date," he replied in a disdainful manner. "And the date was not the least bit magical, as the Magical Dating Site falsely advertised. The disgusting female only spoke of her ex-mate who left her for another. She stated that he was a monster. So, you see, even humans view each other as repulsive." He gave them a triumphant look, as if he had just scored a great point.

"It does not matter now," snapped Witch Mortify. She was so named because of her way of mortifying others with embarrassing incidents that occurred centuries ago. She never forgot them nor did she let them go. In fact, she relished bringing up embarrassing incidents that happened to others. "Just bring your three brats here, Serpentine. In one piece. Don't repeat what you did with those owls."

"That happened three hundred years ago," snapped Serpentine. He had inadvertently blown up fifty owls when he attempted to transport them via magic from his hut to Mortify's hut. "This is an entirely different situation. I will drive them over here in a car."

"Will you miss your children, Serpentine?" questioned Sorceress Hexla, sarcastically. "Will you mourn their deaths? Shall we have a funeral for them after we drink their blood?" Hexla was merciless. She put hexes on others just to see them writhe in pain.

Serpentine smirked cruelly. "I could barely stand to be around my human family, their mother included. All of them whined and demanded too much from me. It was a relief when I was kicked out of the house and it will be a bigger relief to put an end to their lives, especially the youngest. He's weak."

"As long as the child has blood in him, we don't care about his strength," said Mortify, chuckling to herself. No one else joined in her laughter.

"I have to agree with Serpentine. It was not a pleasant task to be around humans," said Warlock Highbrow, making a repulsive face. He received that name because his forehead comprised half of his face and he had a superior air toward the rest of them. "I have intentionally forgotten the names of my daughters. Unfortunately, I do remember that their mother was intolerable and revolting. Thank goodness, she is no longer among the living."

"How did you kill her?" Witch Mortify asked Highbrow. She appeared eager to hear the grisly details.

"I killed her quickly," he replied snidely. "Before she could scream."

The rest of them agreed that it was a good way to kill a human.

"I have finished creating our new wands," announced Sorcerer Spellbinder, changing the topic. "Tonight I will give them to you." Right before the magi were expelled from the forest, the Little Peepers forced them to snap their wands in half. The Little Peepers confiscated them. "I made the wands from the strongest oak tree I could find in the nearby parks." In the magical world, oak symbolized physical strength, endurance, and triumph. It also represented a long life. He made certain that all nine wands would be of equal strength by carving them from the same tree. However, he fashioned himself a spare wand, which was made from an olive tree. The olive tree was even older than the oak tree. In the dead of night, he removed a limb from an olive tree at the arboretum. There were no olive trees in Hidden Forest. With his new, more powerful wand, Spellbinder planned to outlast his fellow magi if any of them ever challenged him to a duel. He was aware no magus was trustworthy, including himself.

"Once we enter the forest, we can use our wands to strike down our foes," said Witch Mortify.

"The test will be if our oak wands are powerful enough to fend off the mindbending abilities of the Little Peepers. That was our weakness last time. We did not have enough magical power to block out their mindbending," pointed out Warlock Gloominus, sullenly. He lived up to his name because his tone always sounded glum.

"If we stick together, we can defeat the Little Peepers' mindbending," Zeldar assured Gloominus and the rest of them. "I will poison them later."

"We also need to entice the Black Dragon to join us," added Witch Blackheart. "His fire-breathing should come in handy. That is, if he doesn't burn down the entire forest."

"We should never have gone after the Little Peepers without reinforcements," mumbled Gloominus. "I clearly remember calling for backup before our attack. And we certainly should've slaughtered the Little Peepers before retiring to our beds."

"But it was late and we were exhausted!" protested Sorceress Hexla. "I had every intention of hexing them first thing in the morning."

"You needed the rest of us!" huffed Zeldar. "Not one of us can singlehandedly defeat the Little Peepers!"

Highbrow snorted haughtily.

"Gloominus and Zeldar are right," snarled Blackheart, frowning at Highbrow. "We shouldn't have waited until morning before finishing the Little Peepers off. In the middle of the night, while they were sound asleep in their beds, we should've burned them alive in their treehouses."

"We will be prepared this time," Zeldar reassured them again. "The Little Peepers are not entirely without their weaknesses. They can be subdued by black magic if we combine our powers. Last time we split up after our initial attack on King Hoppit and his little band of owl pilots. This time we will remain together, like we did with—"

"Don't mention that horrid name to me right now!" snarled Witch Mortify. "I am in no mood to hear it." This was the only incident from the past that she would not bring up to the others.

"Don't fret, I have a few tricks up my sleeve that will stop the Little Peepers cold," muttered Sorceress Underhand. "I can sic the frog-snakes on them. They are terrified of them."

"No tricks on our own, though! We must work as a *team*," Witch Zeldar repeated impatiently, "and strike as one. Our enemies greatly outnumber us."

Sorceress Underhand glared at Witch Zeldar, but held her tongue. She considered witches to be bossy and snooty. Warlocks were even worse.

Sorceress Hexla turned her head to address Sorcerer Serpentine. "But first, we need to drink the fresh blood of your three offspring to regain our powers," she emphasized. "Otherwise, we cannot finish what we started. Will you need help fetching them?" Aside from her enjoyment of causing pain to others, she was also known for her hot temper. If she did not like what was said to her, she would attempt to hex the offender in the blink of an eye. Fortunately, the slowest wand could block her spells. Hexla's temper was quicker than her mind. She had trouble recalling spells, particularly as she aged in the human world.

"Hexla, may I remind you, that you can't steer a broomstick, much less a car," replied Serpentine, who did not like to be challenged by another. "I promise you that the brats will be here tonight to serve their purpose. After their arrival, you can watch me slit their throats. Would that make you happy?"

"Very much so," Hexla replied, her dark eyes dancing with excitement. She lifted her mug of mead over the center of the table. "I would like to make a toast to our return to Hidden Forest. May we reclaim our magic and immortality!"

"Here, here!" said Witch Blackheart. "I can't wait to be young and powerful again."

"We will torture and obliterate our enemies. We will make them pay for what they have done to us," chimed in Sorcerer Spellbinder.

"For devil's sake, let us drink our mead," muttered Warlock Gloominus.

They raised their mugs and drank to their future. They spoke excitedly of the blood that would fill their cups and which creatures of Hidden Forest they would annihilate first. Most of them leaned toward the Little Peepers. They took great pleasure in plotting their revenge before returning to their homes, except for Witch Zeldar, who spent the rest of the day sharpening her kitchen knives. If truth be told, the magi lived for retaliation because they had nothing else to live for.

Chapter Five

The Shapeshifters

Unbeknownst to the Malum, there was a mouse, hidden in the wall, eavesdropping on their conversation. But this was no ordinary mouse. It was the elf spy, Tark, in disguise. Queen Rossen had directed him to go to the house of Witch Zeldar to spy on her. Tark uncovered more than he had expected. He lucked out that all nine magi were gathered in one place. He also learned that they were intending to drink the blood of three half-magical children fathered by Sorcerer Serpentine. Moreover, he learned that Warlock Highbrow was the father of the two girls who were rescued from the garden shed. It was challenging to slip into Zeldar's house without being detected. His next challenge was to sneak out of the house without being spotted. He headed back to the crawl space, trying to be as quiet as a mouse.

Zeldar's company had already departed from the house when the witch heard a scratching sound in the wall. "Hell's Bells!" she swore. "I knew there were mice in the house! I am going to kill you and your little friends with poison." She pounded on the wall and then stormed out to the garden shed to retrieve the sack of rat poison. Frequently, she had used rat poison on neighborhood pets that had trespassed into her yard. Although the neighbors suspected her, they had no evidence to prove it. The pets returned home and died a painful death.

After emerging from the crawl space, Tark transformed himself into an elf owl and flew directly toward Hidden Forest. Although there was a headwind that slowed him down, he was long gone before Zeldar returned with the rat poison.

The patrols were put on high alert to watch out for intruders and the Dark Shadow. Commander Lapin was in charge of his regiment this afternoon. He caught sight of a little owl heading toward the forest. The Little Peepers did not ride owls that small. Lapin signaled the alarm with the thumping of his hind leg. "Incoming owl!" he warned.

First Officer Poppin raced over to Lapin. "Do we have a trespasser, sir?"

Lapin gestured at an owl that sped past them. "We have an owl with no rider."

Poppin squinted upward. "It appears to be an elf owl. And it looks to be in a hurry."

"It might be an elf." Sometimes the patrols spotted riderless owls coming and going from Hidden Forest. Though, typically, at night. They assumed that they were elves spying on the Malum.

Both of them watched the brown owl, with its very short tail and lack of ear tufts, veer sharply left. "Should we follow it?"

"It appears to be traveling toward the elf village." Lapin was still tracking the owl with his eyes. He pulled his gaze away from the sky and peered at his first officer. "Just in case, we should notify the Little Peepers on patrol."

Poppin nodded. "I will get right on it, Commander."

In the meantime, Tark was keeping a sharp eye out for the Black Dragon. He did not want to become today's meal, although the dragon generally fed on rabbits. Out of the corner of his eye, he spied two nearby owl patrols. They were Skit and Kreen, who normally patrolled at night. The patrols were working extra shifts because of the Malum's recent threat.

"I wonder where that elf owl is going," Kreen said to her screech-owl, Trill. She was pointing at the petite owl which was passing by. She knew that an elf owl was too small to be used as a rider companion.

"That's an elf," huffed Trill, as if insulted. "A true owl flies without making a sound. I can hear its wings flapping from here."

"Should we follow it?" Skit asked Kreen.

"No, there are other patrols that will most likely track it," answered Kreen. Just a little while ago, she had caught a glimpse of Flycatcher and Hummer patrolling in the area on their owls, Tuft and Dots. "Besides, we must hurry back to Arborville. We promised Queen Wista that we would be back in time to give the newcomers a tour of the forest."

Skit was still watching the elf owl. "I am curious what news the owl is bringing back to Queen Rossen."

"It's an *elf*," Trill insisted. All owls had the ability to hear a mouse crawling under a heavy pile of leaves or snow. "I can still hear it."

"Trill is right. That owl is an elf," chimed in Peck. "Probably an elf spy."

Even though Skit could no longer see the passing owl, his eyes were still looking in the direction where it had vanished into a cloud. "The elves spy on the Malum almost every night. Yet, they seemed unaware of the magi's offspring. Don't you find that curious?"

"Very curious," said Kreen, narrowing her eyes. Trill and Peck agreed with them.

Kreen and Skit and their owls had been on patrol since midday. Queen Wista had ordered the patrol units to triple their numbers until the situation with the Malum calmed down and the Dark Shadow had slunk back into his pit and fell back into a deep slumber. Unfortunately, the Dark Shadow would need to collect a few more souls before returning to a state of hibernation. Earlier today, Wista had gathered her subjects and reminded them of the bargain that Queen Rossen had struck with the Dark Shadow the last time it rose from the Pit of Despair. It had promised to seek only human souls that had been rotted by hatred and cruelty. Kreen and Skit had never been entirely confident that the Dark Shadow would keep its promise to the forest residents. Last night, they spotted the Dark Shadow slipping out of the forest and returning with a human soul at first light. Was the soul of its victim rotted out? They had no idea since no one dared approach it. It lived in solitude, as did the Black Dragon.

Tark noticed two patrol owls on his tail, but he did not slow his pace. He made a beeline for his village, Glenhaven. The instant he landed in the royal courtyard, he switched back to his elf form. The riders on the patrol owls waved at Tark as they passed over him. They turned around and returned to their post. Tark recognized them. They were Hummer and Flycatcher and he knew they were given those nicknames for their piloting skills. He became good friends with Little Peepers after his father, Rowl, was imprisoned in the Pit of Despair. Not a day went by without Tark imagining his father suffering in the pit.

Tark was greeted in the courtyard by Rupin, his fourteen-year-old brother, and Prince Massen, Queen Rossen's son, who was the same age. Rupin and Massen had been inseparable since the Great Banishment. Both of them shared the tragedy of their fathers never returning from the Pit of Despair. The two friends had been anxiously awaiting Tark's return. After Tark calmed their worries, the two young elves tagged along with him to the queen's private quarters.

Queen Rossen was speaking with Counselor Nirva when there was a knock on the door. "Is that you, Tark?"

"Yes, my queen. I am also here with the prince and my brother."

"Let them in, Nirva."

Tark's heart fluttered when Nirva opened the door. He'd had a crush on her ever since they sat in the same classroom, learning how to make herbal potions. He nearly failed the class because he had spent too much time focused on her instead of the textbook. Typically, elves were quick learners and only spent two years of their lives in the classroom. After that, they were assigned their occupations by Queen Rossen and her small group of advisors. Rossen handpicked Tark to be her personal spy and Nirva as her first counselor.

Massen, who favored his father's looks, went over to his mother and respectfully kissed her jeweled hand, while Rupin and Tark bowed to the queen.

"Massen and Rupin, thank you for seeing Tark safely to my quarters," said Queen Rossen. "Show yourselves out and have a good day." She tended to show her guests the door quickly when there was no reason for them to remain, including her own son.

"They seem rather fond of you," Nirva remarked to Tark after the boys left.

"It appears so." Tark, who was ten years older than either boy, had been a surrogate father to Rupin and like an uncle to Massen since they were little. "I am afraid that I bring back disturbing news from Witch Zeldar's house," he said to both Rossen and Nirva. He reported everything that he had seen and heard at the witch's place. "If the Malum are not stopped, three human children will be dead later tonight—"

"And the Malum will return to the forest with their magic, bent on destroying us," concluded Rossen.

"It appears so," he repeated. He looked at them and then around the queen's quarters. It was a beautiful, silky-white room. All of the drapery was woven from the finest silk. This silk was produced by the silkworm caterpillars that lived in the mulberry trees, which the elves grew in a nearby grove. The mulberry trees also provided fruit, timber, and rubber for the elves. They made ropes, baskets, and textiles from their bark and medicine from their leaves. The rich brown furniture in the queen's room was carved from a red mulberry tree. It had deep engravings of the sun and the moon and a single eye between them, symbolizing knowledge. Elves prided themselves on knowing things. But they also kept secrets.

"We must retrieve these children and bring them here," declared Rossen. "Did you learn of their location, Tark?"

"Unfortunately, the magi did not mention their names or whereabouts. Nevertheless, Sorcerer Serpentine did say that he would fetch them and bring them to Zeldar's house for their ritual tonight. Therefore, they must be nearby."

"They are just as vile as the day they were expelled," snorted Nirva. "They have learned nothing from their banishment."

"And what about the children's mother?" Rossen asked.

"I imagine she will be murdered just as Ruby and Shauna's mother had been," replied Tark. "Warlock Highbrow showed no remorse for eliminating his mate. In fact, he was gloating about her murder."

Queen Rossen put a hand on the back of her high, commanding chair, as if bracing herself for the next wave of bad news. "The children will probably be sacrificed at the witching hour. The magi are loyal followers of black magic. They're most likely sharpening their knives as we speak."

"But they are not loyal to each other," Nirva reminded her queen. "They might end up taking their sharpened knives to each other's throat before the night is over."

"Serpentine seemed terrified of the 'police' getting involved," said Tark, continuing with his report. "I don't know who they are. They might be criminals or thugs. Or chubby cherubs, for that matter."

"These *police* could also be a danger to us," pointed out Rossen. "I am aware that humans have dangerous weapons that can cause great bodily harm. I shall send word immediately to Queen Wista and let her know what we have recently learned of the Malum's latest scheme. Meanwhile, we must spy on Serpentine. He must be stopped from killing his three children and their mother. The Malum cannot come back here."

"I will have the Little Peepers notified at once," said Nirva. She bowed her head at the queen and took her leave.

Rossen pretended not to notice Tark's gaze lingering on Nirva as she made her departure. Nirva came from a household of high-ranking officials while Tark's parents were potion-makers and alchemists. Typically, the two classes did not intermarry. Thinking of young love brought up memories of her first encounter with the future king whom she wedded a year later. It was an arranged marriage. Not once did Koning look at her as Tark had just looked at Nirva. She shook her memories of King Koning from her head. She had to keep her focus on the Malum.

Chapter Six

The Lay of the Land

Ruby and Shauna were shocked to hear what Queen Wista was telling them. They couldn't believe that their father was, in all probability, a warlock. Though, it would explain their ability to command wands to come to them or shoot golden sparks from the fairies' wands. The queen also told them of the specific reason for their capture because she did not want them to hear it from another source.

"Gross!" exclaimed Shauna. "The Malum want to drink our blood like vampires!"

Ruby opened her mouth but nothing came out. She wanted to remind her sister that vampires did not exist. Or did they?

"I realize it is quite disturbing to hear this," said Wista, "especially since you have been through so much lately." On her round table were three mugs of tea and a big plate of mushrooms. She always offered tea and mushrooms when she had to break bad news to her dinner guests. She also set tea and mushrooms out on the table when she had good news to share.

"It's so much to take in at once," said Ruby. "There are magi who want to harm us, moles and rabbits who talk and rescue others, Little Peepers who fly on birds and live in trees, elves who are shapeshifters, fairies who perform magic. And now, Shauna and I can perform simple magic because our father is a warlock, who wants to kill us no less." She shook her head in disbelief. "How can this be possible?"

"Have you ever imagined another world existing?" asked Wista.

"I often dreamt of a magical world," interjected Shauna.

"Of course, you have," replied Wista. "You have magic in you. It affects your dreams."

Ruby often had recurring dreams about talking forest animals, fairies, elves, and so forth. Come to think of it, her dreams looked awfully similar to Hidden Forest. There was even a dragon in them.

"It will take time to absorb all the newness in your lives," continued Wista. "Meanwhile, I will have the newest members of our patrol pilots, Kreen and Skit, show you around Hidden Forest, including Aviation School. Class will begin bright and early tomorrow morning."

Ruby arched her eyebrows. "Tomorrow?"

"Yes. It's necessary that you know how to take a taxi bird on your own. Unless, of course, you want to spend your time climbing up and down trees," said Wista. "Also, I have arranged for you to learn magical spells from the fairies. You need to hone and control your magic. Little Peepers cannot help you in that department."

"We don't have wands," said Shauna.

"The fairies will eventually outfit you with your own wands. In the meantime, you can borrow theirs." Wista gave her an encouraging smile. "It will be nice to have you repelling frog-snakes instead of always depending on the fairies to clear the area for us."

Ruby wrinkled her nose. "Repelling frog-snakes?"

"Periodically, the fairies clear Jade Meadow of frog-snakes, but the frogs eventually come back." She wagged her head in disdain.

Ruby winced. "But what are frog-snakes?"

"They are very pesky, venomous creatures that Sorcerer Spellbinder created to eliminate us. As I had mentioned, the fairies can't undo his spell or any of the magic spells, for that matter. However, they can remove the snakes from the vicinity with their wands."

"How?" asked Shauna.

"First, a wand senses a frog-snake. Then, the fairy shrinks the snake to the size of a worm and transports it away from the meadow using magic. The snakes remained unharmed because the fairies do not hurt others." Wista scooted her chair backwards. "Skit and Kreen will give you an aerial view of Hidden Forest and also an overview of our way of life."

To reach the queen's treehouse, Ruby and Shauna had ridden on taxi birds with Kreen and Skit, who were currently waiting outside for them. The flight was exhilarating and terrifying just like they had imagined. Unlike paragliders, they wore no safety harnesses nor had any control over the wings. However, they felt much safer with Kreen and Skit holding on to them, even though the taxi hawks were very smooth flyers. They were never in danger of falling off.

Queen Wista promised Ruby and Shauna that she would regularly check up on their well-being. "After your tour, Kreen and Skit will show you to your new accommodations."

Shauna looked alarmed. "Will we be living on our own?"

"Certainly not. You are too young to be on your own. A little while ago, Vorte and Berruga offered to be your guardians. They lost their only child tragically to a frog-snake many summers ago while he was picking huckleberries." Wista noticed the sudden alarm on the girls' faces. "This is why it is so important that you learn magical spells from the fairies. To protect yourself from danger."

"Wasn't there anyone else around to protect him?" asked Ruby.

"He wandered off too far from his berry-picking group. He was a good boy. It's heartbreaking to lose one of our own, especially when the frog-snakes are the handiwork of the Malum." She looked sadly at them. "I know what it feels like to lose a child, too." She sighed deeply, as if it came from the depth of her soul. It was still hard to speak of that tragic day. "I had a son. His name was Cobias. Sorcerer Spellbinder kidnapped him. When Cobias' father, King Hoppit, went to rescue him, the Malum shot down his owl and the other members of his party with their wands. The king and his owl were killed."

Ruby heard herself gasp. "And your son?"

"The magi threw him and the rest of their captives into the Pit of Despair, turning them over to the Dark Shadow." Wista blinked back her tears. "King Koning, the elf king, attempted to rescue Cobias and the others from the pit. The magi attacked the king and his rescue party. They were also tossed down into the pit. Since the Dark Shadow was awakened from its long nap, it claimed their souls, trapping them below earth. Queen Rossen made a deal with the Dark Shadow. If the Little Peepers did not use mindbending to chase the Dark Shadow out of the forest, it would free the captured souls, except for three. It needs the energy source of others to sustain itself, according to Queen Rossen. I have never spoken to the Dark Shadow. As far as I know, only the elf queen has attempted to communicate with it. We prefer to give it a wide berth as it passes through the forest. I advise you to do the same."

"King Koning was the husband of Queen Rossen?" asked Ruby.

"Yes. Since both Queen Rossen and I had lost our family members, we banded together and, with the help of the other woodland creatures, we were able to expel the Malum from Hidden Forest. And now you know the reason for their banishment."

Shauna appeared both mesmerized and saddened by the queen's tale. "Can't the souls escape when the Dark Shadow isn't there?"

"We assume the souls are too weak to climb out of the deep cavern because the Dark Shadow has sapped their energy. Or, possibly, the Dark Shadow keeps them in a trance. We don't fully understand the Dark Shadow. It did not come from our world. To be honest, we never attempted mindbending on the Dark Shadow because we feared getting inside it. We're not certain what we're dealing with. But that's enough information for one day. Kreen and Skit are waiting for you."

It was apparent to Ruby and Shauna that this magical place was not a perfect paradise.

Wista went to retrieve Kreen and Skit, who were currently waiting on a nearby tree limb with their patrol owls. The taxi birds that brought the girls to Wista's treehouse were shuttling other passengers. Since the window was wide open, the young patrol pilots had overheard the entire conversation between the queen and the girls. In spite of their eavesdropping, they heard nothing new. Nearly everyone in Hidden Forest knew the stories of the Malum and the Dark Shadow. They were told how the magi used the Pit of Despair to their advantage and how three souls were still trapped down there.

As the girls approached the patrol owls, Trill and Peck bade Ruby and Shauna a good afternoon. The girls were still surprised when animals addressed them. Kreen and Skit helped them get on the back of the owls. Kreen sat behind Shauna, and Ruby was seated behind Skit. Both sisters clung on to their pilot. When the owls launched from the tree branch, the girls tightened their grip. Once they soared above the tall evergreens, Kreen and Skit pointed out the more notable landmarks.

Skit gestured at a small lake below. "We call that the Lake of Smoke because it is frequently shrouded in morning mist."

"How big is Hidden Forest?" asked Ruby. Her hands gripped the back of Skit's shirt.

"As far as the eye can see," Skit replied. Unbeknownst to all of the creatures of Hidden Forest, the land was claimed by the U.S. Forest Service. Since the forest creatures were unfamiliar with human languages, they could not read the faded sign nailed to a pine tree indicating they inhabited federal land. Since it was in a remote area, humans never came to that part of the forest. Needless to say, no one had ever read the Forest Service sign after it was posted on the tree.

"It's quite beautiful, isn't it?" said Kreen, beaming at the land below them.

No one could argue that it wasn't. It had everything—trees, meadows, hills, rivers, and waterfalls. Far off in the distance, there were snowcapped mountain peaks.

"If you squint hard enough, you will see the town where eight of the nine Malum reside." Skit motioned toward the small town. "Warlock Highbrow went off to live by himself in the big city."

"Where Shauna and I are from," noted Ruby.

"Yes," Skit replied. "We did not know of you and your sister's existence because he didn't live with you."

Ruby could make out the buildings beyond the trees. She also could see a row of houses bordering the forest. One of them appeared to have a shed in the backyard. "Is that where Witch Zeldar lives?" Holding her breath, she pried a hand from Skit's shirt and gestured at a two-story white house with a red-bricked chimney.

"That is, indeed, Zeldar's home. It's apparent that she could not bear to leave Hidden Forest far behind."

"How do you keep tabs on the Malum in the human world?" questioned Ruby.

"Our owl squadrons, elf spies, and patrol rabbits regularly check up on them. There are ten rabbit regiments." Skit stifled a yawn. He was short on sleep ever since the girls were found in the garden shed. He and the other patrols were rarely off-duty.

"Where do all the rabbits live?"

"Their rabbit warrens ring the entire perimeter of Hidden Forest," replied Skit.

"There must be lots of rabbits," said Ruby.

"Yes, Hidden Forest has a huge population of rabbits," he said, "despite the Black Dragon's ravenous appetite for them over the many years."

"The rabbits must want to banish the dragon from the forest," said Ruby. "I would, if I was a rabbit."

"The rabbits are unhappy about being preyed upon," he replied. "The Black Dragon is not originally from Hidden Forest. But he has lived here a long time."

"And where does the Black Dragon live exactly?" asked Ruby.

"In a cave by a waterfall. Peck, let's fly over to Misty Falls."

"Isn't that dangerous for us?" gasped Ruby.

"The Black Dragon prefers to sleep during the day and hunt right before dawn. Sometimes he will hunt at dusk. Though, on occasion, he's been spotted hunting in the middle of the day."

"He hunts like an owl," said Peck. "Only owls are quieter."

"He uses his sharp talons to kill his prey," explained Trill. "He doesn't roast his quarry with his fiery breath."

Trill followed Peck as they changed course toward the lair of the Black Dragon. As they headed toward the cave at Misty Falls, Skit and Kreen continued to point out the lay of the land. They showed them Unicorn Trail, Bear Mountain, the villages of the elves and the fairies, the molehills created by Rooter, Erde, Snoot, and the rest of the moles who resided underground, and the other well-known sights of Hidden Forest. They also spotted the wooden huts which the Malum used to inhabit. All nine huts were within a mile of each other. For the most part, the magi lived solitary lives, not counting the animals they kept caged inside their huts.

"Do not go anywhere near the huts of the Malum," Kreen warned the girls. The owls were flying side by side. "They might be booby-trapped with dark magic. Not even the fairies will enter this section of the woods."

"Ruby and I can perform magic," said Shauna with a touch of boasting.

"I have heard," replied Kreen. "But your magic is no match for the dark magic of the Malum."

"Not even the fairies dare to take on the Malum," said Trill. "The Malum are only afraid of the Little Peepers' mindbending abilities. Without the Little Peepers, the Malum would have taken control of Hidden Forest. We are forever grateful for the Little Peepers." The western screech-owl turned his head and gave a respectful nod to Kreen.

"The owls have saved us numerous times, too," replied Kreen. Her sparse, windblown hair swayed in the wind like cattails. "We could not survive without them flying us from place to place, especially to our treehouses. We are grateful for them, as well."

"There is Misty Falls." Skit gestured at a giant hilltop. A gushing waterfall spilled from its very top to its bottom, where it emptied into a river. "The Black Dragon lives in a cave at the top. On the bottom is a deep cavern. That is where the Dark Shadow resides."

"So, the dragon and the shadow share the same hill?" said Ruby.

"And waterfall," replied Skit. "Over the years, the pounding water carved out the rocks to make caves and caverns."

"Basically, the water made holes in the rocks," said Ruby.

"That's correct," said Skit.

"What water creates the waterfall?" asked Shauna, clearly mystified. "It's not raining . . . there's no river or snowbank on top of the hill—"

"Magic provides the water for Misty Falls," explained Kreen. "This is another reason we don't allow humans to enter our forest. They would tear the waterfall apart in search of its water source."

"And Queen Wista's son is down there?" Ruby pointed to the bottom of the hill. "Living with the Dark Shadow?"

"Yes. He is also with King Koning and an elf named Rowl. He is the father of Tark. You have already met Tark."

Ruby nodded. Tark was hard to forget because he was tall and handsome and had pointy ears.

After their sightseeing tour, Trill and Peck dropped down in front of the Aviation School. The class was finishing up for the day. The birds, mostly owls and hawks, were dropping off their last passengers.

"The students are not called pilots, yet," Kreen explained to Ruby and Shauna. "Little Peepers began flight school at the age of ten. For a year, the pupil learns how to fly on different types of birds and navigate the skies. If a rider shows a knack for flying, then he or she has a good chance of being accepted into the one-year patrol pilot program upon turning eighteen. Skit and I just recently graduated. That is why we are given the night patrol. You have to work your way up through the ranks to be on day patrol. The most experienced pilots fly on a falcon. Falcons are too fast to handle for most pilots." She looked over at Trill and winked at her screech-owl. "I prefer riding owls, though. They are silent flyers. The hawks and falcons are quite loud in comparison."

"Owls are also chosen on their flying skills and how well they keep a passenger onboard," noted Trill. "Not all birds are accepted as patrol birds. Some will wind up as taxi birds," she added in a quiet voice, as if worried about being overheard by the other birds. "Taxi birds are good at what they do. But they are not good at patrolling for long stretches of time. It takes dedication and stamina."

"Even though you are only nine years old, Shauna," said Kreen, "the queen and the flight instructor have made an exception in your case to enroll you in Aviation School a year earlier." She looked past the girls. "Here comes your instructor now. His name is Oide. He has been teaching aviation for such a long time that he should have sprouted his own pair of wings by now."

"He could teach birds how to fly," added Skit.

"That's a bit of an exaggeration," hooted Peck, as if mildly insulted. "Not even fairies can teach birds to fly." He lowered his voice. "Or, at least, they can't demonstrate how to fly silently. They are as noisy as a swarm of bees."

"How wonderful! There are my new pupils!" croaked a male voice. "And my most recent patrol pilot graduates!"

"Hello, Oide," Kreen and Skit replied together.

Oide was slightly greener in skin tone than most Little Peepers that Ruby and Shauna had seen so far. Later, they would learn that Oide, along with King Hoppit and Queen Wista, was one of the eight original frogs turned into Little Peepers. He approached them with a cheerful grin. His mouth was as wide as a bullfrog's. "I am always excited to receive new students." He was grinning from cheek to cheek. He usually wore a broad smile. "We have fewer and fewer new pupils nowadays."

Ruby and Shauna gave him a puzzled look.

"Is it because of the frog-snakes eating them?" questioned Shauna.

"Oh, no! A frog-snake only gets about one student every ten years or so. Usually, that happens because the offspring wanders off on his or her own." He shot her a warning look. "Nope, frog-snakes are not the problem for our declining student population." He peered pointedly at Kreen and Skit. "Hasn't anyone told them yet?"

Ruby lifted her brow, fearful of the answer. "Told us what? Does the Black Dragon snack on the children of Little Peepers?"

"Nope, that's not it, either. We are having a difficult time reproducing since the Great Banishment. Some of the babies are born with two heads or three or four legs. They die shortly after birth," Oide's smile faded. "Some of us think it is because of the water. Our lakes and ponds are not the same as they once were a century ago. There are fewer fish in our rivers and streams. Others believe that the Malum put a hex upon Hidden Forest before being expelled from it. The fairies have not been able to fix the problem."

"Do the elves have the same problem?" Ruby asked.

"Everyone and everything in the forest is showing a sharp decline in growth, even the rabbit population has recently plummeted," replied Oide. A small peep escaped from his mouth. His serious expression suddenly became as bright as the sun. "But we shall not concern ourselves with the matter at this time. I am just pleased to know that soon I will have new students soaring high above the earth. Perhaps by the end of summer you will be able to wheel above the clouds on your own."

Shauna gazed upward at the single cloud in the sky, which was shaped like a coffin. "Do any of the young students die from falling off their birds?" she questioned nervously.

"Surely not," interjected Peck. "We owls would catch our riders before they splattered on the ground . . . unless, of course, we were struck down first." The barred owl was remembering what happened to King Hoppit and Greystone, his great gray owl, on their way to rescue Prince Cobias from the magi. He had seen the entire incident unfold because he was trailing behind Greystone. He, too, had taken a hit to his right wing from a blow produced by a magus's wand. He managed to stay upright long enough to get his pilot safely to the ground. However, as soon as he landed, Sorcerer Spellbinder attacked again, striking Peck's pilot, which paralyzed him. Peck could not put up a fight because his wing was badly injured. His pilot and the other wounded Little Peepers were snatched by the Malum and dumped into the Pit of Despair. Although Peck's pilot and the others were quickly freed from the Pit of Despair, most of them never patrolled the skies again. It was the elves who healed Peck's injuries with their herbal salves. Skit was Peck's first patrol pilot since that awful night. Physically, he healed quickly. Mentally, it was a long journey to recovery.

"In all my years of flight training," said Oide, "I have not lost a single student to a fall." He smiled proudly.

Ruby and Shauna looked instantly relieved.

"We have to get going, Oide," said Kreen. "Skit and I have night patrol and the girls still need to move in with their new guardians, Vorte and Berruga."

"Ah, that is good. Vorte and Berruga will take excellent care of you," Oide said to Ruby and Shauna. "I will see you bright and early and bushytailed tomorrow morning. Perhaps you will become my top students and soon be riding a peregrine falcon. Falcons can outfly a tornado and strike their prey like lightning."

"Riding a dragon sounds less dangerous," stated Ruby.

"I would like to go as fast as an airplane," said Shauna.

"That's the spirit," Oide said, widening his smile. "I've seen falcons zip past those flying machines."

"And we don't wear parachutes?" asked Ruby.

"Parachutes?" Oide wore a puzzled look.

"Never mind," said Ruby.

While they said their goodbyes, Ruby wondered if Little Peeper children learn how to read and write and do math equations. There was no mention of learning subjects, other than flying on top of birds. *Hidden Forest was a strange and hazardous place, indeed.*

Vorte and Berruga were waiting eagerly for the girls' arrival. It had been a long time since there had been a child in their treehouse. It was still difficult to speak of their son who was devoured by a frog-snake many years earlier. Ever since that tragic day, Vorte and Berruga took on the role of patrolling Jade Meadow for snakes. With the aid of the fairies, they had managed for the most part to keep the snakes out of Arborville.

Kreen and Skit did the formal introductions and left soon afterwards to get some needed rest and eat before their patrol shift. Trill and Peck also needed to rest and eat. After Kreen, Skit, and their patrol owls departed, Ruby and Shauna stood awkwardly in the living room, waiting for direction from their hosts.

"Would you like something to eat?" asked Berruga. "Earlier today I traded a tart pie to the gnomes for the best toadstools in all of Hidden Forest."

Both Ruby and Shauna were famished, but eating toadstools did not sound appetizing to their ears. Nonetheless, they needed food to survive. They accepted Berruga's offer and seated themselves at the kitchen table. Vorte and Berruga joined them after piling their plates with a variety of food. As it turned out, the meal was delicious. They feasted on mushrooms, toasted nuts, beetroots, nettles, currants, honey, and blackberry tart for dessert. While eating, Vorte and Berruga told them fascinating stories about the woodland inhabitants. Some of the tales were so hilarious that Ruby and Shauna were doubled over from laughing so hard. None of the diners could recall being this happy in a long time. Their sad memories vanished with their meal.

After dinner, Vorte and Berruga showed the girls their shared bedroom. They would be sleeping on a bunkbed because the rooms in the Little Peepers' homes were small.

Berruga opened a large, wooden trunk, made from a chestnut tree, sitting at the foot of their bunkbed. It was chockfull of clothing that Berruga had collected for the girls from other Little Peepers. "I took the liberty of getting you some new clothes, especially for flight school. I hope they fit you properly."

Ruby and Shauna noticed the drab clothing looked exactly like what they currently were wearing. The Little Peepers did not vary their wardrobe very much. They graciously thanked Berruga and Vorte for the clothes. Back in the city, they rarely received gifts.

"I will make new clothing for you as soon as I collect some cedar bark," said Berruga.

Vorte, who was standing at the doorway, was watching the girls' reaction to their new bedroom. He beamed when he saw the pleased smiles on the girls' faces. He had spent all day building the bunkbed and the trunk. Aside from Berruga gathering the girls' clothing, she baked two tarts and then took a taxi bird to the gnomes' village. She bartered for an hour with the gnomes, returning with the most scrumptious toadstools in all of Hidden Forest. They wanted to make the girls comfortable and happy in their new home.

Shauna yawned loudly, which was a habit of hers. She also sneezed noisily. Ruby always covered her ears when Shauna yawned or sneezed. Ruby yawned, too. Although the sun had just set, they were tired from their ordeal of the past days.

"Oh, dear," said Berruga. "You girls must be exhausted."

"It has been a long day for us," replied Ruby. "So many changes."

"I imagine so," answered Berruga. "Your nightclothes are in the trunk." She cast a glance at her husband. "We should let the girls get some rest." She turned her attention back to Ruby and Shauna. "We will be just outside your door. Call if you need anything."

Ruby and Shauna thanked them again. After their new guardians closed the door, Shauna curled up into the bottom bunk and began to cry quietly. Fortunately, Shauna did not cry as noisily as she yawned or sneezed. Ruby lay down alongside her sister and rubbed her back, like their mother used to do when they were upset.

"It'll be all right," Ruby said gently.

"I know. I just need to get all the sad tears out. Berruga and Vorte seem nice enough. Don't you think?"

"I guess so."

"I miss Mom, though," Shauna said, her eyes still brimming with tears. "I think she would've liked it here. It's nothing like the inner city. It's peaceful. Except for the frog-snakes."

"And the Black Dragon and the Dark Shadow," added Ruby.

"And, if the Malum return, it'll be even less peaceful."

"I don't know if we should laugh or cry."

"Me, either," said Shauna. "At least, we have some magic in us to protect ourselves."

"That's true. We will have to learn how to use our magic, though. I don't know a single spell."

Shauna closed her eyes and within minutes she had fallen sleep.

Ruby did not get up and change into pajamas. Instead, she remained on Shauna's bed and drifted off to sleep. Before she knew it, she felt herself being shaken awake.

"Wake up, Ruby," whispered a voice. "The elves want to speak to you."

For a second, Ruby did not know where she was. As soon as she remembered, she bolted upright. Luckily, Shauna was a heavy sleeper and did not stir when Ruby bumped against her.

Berruga noticed that the girls were sharing the same bunk but did not comment on it. "Come with me to the main room. The elves are waiting there to speak with you."

Ruby slid off the bed and followed Berruga down the stairs to the bottom level of their treehouse. When she entered the room, she saw two chickadees speaking with Vorte. At once, she realized the chickadees were elves in disguise.

"Sorry to bother you at this hour," said an elf. "However, it is of utmost importance we talk to you at once."

"What is it?" asked Ruby in a frightened voice. "Have the Malum entered the forest?"

"Not yet," answered the elf. "Earlier today we learned from one of our spies that Sorcerer Serpentine has fathered three children. The Malum intend to harm them tonight, as they had planned to do with you and your sister."

Ruby's pupils were enlarged in the dim lighting. Vorte was scurrying around the room, lighting beeswax candles as fast as he could. "You mean, sacrifice them?"

"Yes," replied one of the elves.

"Are you going to rescue the children?" asked Ruby. "If so, why wait so long?"

"We will attempt to do so . . . under the cover of darkness. Unfortunately, we do not know of their whereabouts. All we know is that they live with their mother, most likely in town," replied the second elf.

"It will be difficult for us to mount a rescue since we do not know how to find them," admitted the first elf. "Our spy also informed us that the Malum are afraid of the police. Who are the police?"

Briefly, Ruby was speechless as she grasped the seriousness of the situation. Those three children and, most likely, their mother would die without her help. There was no way the elves would be able to track them down in time if they cannot speedily navigate their way through the human world. To make matters worse, if the Malum returned to the forest, she strongly suspected they had no intention of letting Shauna and her live, either.

"Are you feeling okay, Ruby?" asked Berruga. "You have not said another word."

"I'm fine," replied Ruby, though she did not feel fine at all. "When are you planning the rescue?"

"We are leaving as soon as we finish speaking with you and organizing our rescue crew," answered the first elf. "Queen Rossen sent us here to persuade the older girl to join—"

"I am coming with you," interrupted Ruby.

"No, you must not!" said Berruga, alarmed. Her bulging eyes were nearly popping out of their sockets.

"You won't be able to find those kids and their mother without me," insisted Ruby. "I know how the human world functions. I know how to find people on the Internet. I know how to use GPS. I know how to avoid the police." She noticed that the others wore blank faces. "The police are like your patrols."

"Oh, that makes sense," declared the first elf. "That is why the Malum want to avoid them."

"I think it would be wise of us if we avoided the police as well," said the second elf.

The two elves peered at Vorte and Berruga, as if asking their permission to take Ruby with them. Everyone in the room realized that it was true what Ruby had said. The inhabitants of Hidden Forest could not quickly locate the three children of Serpentine without her assistance. The world beyond Hidden Forest was too foreign to them. Possibly too dangerous as well. The elf spies and patrols only tracked the Malum, always avoiding humans as much as possible.

Berruga cleared her throat and then spoke up. "Ruby, I see that you must go with them. The thought of that poor mother and her children being killed by the Malum . . ." Her voice cracked and she began to cry, thinking of her own son who was taken from her.

"We cannot allow those horrible magi to murder another," added Vorte, as he went over to comfort his wife.

"But I want you to watch out for Ruby's safety," said Berruga, choking back her tears. "Can Kreen or Skit or another patrol pilot go with her? I want someone to hold onto her as they are whizzing through the air."

"If Queen Wista approves of it, we will take one or two patrol pilots with us," said the second elf. "We will also bring along our best spy with us."

"Tark," said Ruby. "I want Tark to go."

"We would have to ask Queen Rossen," said the first elf.

"Nonsense," said Berruga. "There is no time for your formal rules and customs when three children's lives are on the line."

The elves didn't look so sure.

"I recommend you receive Queen Wista's approval. She only lives a short flight away," Berruga emphasized. "Queen Rossen will approve of our queen's decision. They are good friends."

"We will go speak with Queen Wista," said the second elf, nodding with relief. The elves did not want to fly all the way to their village and then come back to Arborville with Rossen's reply. "Stay here until we return from Queen Wista's treehouse."

"Where would we go?" asked Vorte. "We live here."

It did not take long for the elves to return with Wista's permission. Even though it made Queen Wista anxious, she understood that Ruby would need to go with the rescue party. Skit and Kreen would be accompanying their group. She also recommended that they add a fairy to their rescue party. They would need someone trained with a magical wand. As a result, the search party included a shapeshifting elf, a couple of patrol pilots and their owls, a fairy and her wand, and Ruby, who was a human shrunken down to three inches high. They would leave at once for the riskiest mission taken since the Malum were exiled. The two messenger elves did not join the rescue mission because they were under strict orders to report back to Queen Rossen. The patrol rabbits and most of the other forest animals, who were already on high alert, intensified their border security. All ten rabbit regiments, the elves, the fairies, and the Little Peeper patrol squadrons were out in full force. Once Serpentine's children were located, the others from the forest were prepared to swoop in and help with the rescue. There would also be two hundred Little Peepers waiting to descend on Zeldar's house, if Serpentine eluded the search and rescue team and made it to the witch's place with his offspring in tow. Everyone who was awake in the forest was on pins and needles, even the woodland nymphs were whispering nervously amongst themselves.

As they were preparing to leave, Ruby tried her best to muster her bravery. Nevertheless, she did not have the courage to wake up Shauna and say goodbye. It would have broken her resolve to go at all.

Chapter Seven

The Search

Ruby was with Tark, Golden Belle, and Skit and Kreen and their owls, Peck and Trill. Tark had shapeshifted into a western screech-owl. They were standing on a large branch of a weeping willow in the town square, utilizing the tree's thick foliage to conceal themselves. The willow's long, arching branches hung over them, its leaves stirring gracefully in the wind. All sorts of ideas ran through Ruby's head. She reflected on the best way to locate individuals without knowing their names or home address. If only she had a last name to work with . . . There was a chance that one or all three children had their father's last name—Serpentine. She suggested they could sneak into a public library and use the computer to look up the name Serpentine. The others stared at her as if she had just petrified them with a spell. Even Tark, who was the most familiar with human ways, gave her a strange look.

"What's a computer?" Tark asked her.

"A computer keeps a list of all the humans who live in the area," explained Ruby. "It also lists people's addresses. I mean, where they live." She had already discovered that the inhabitants of Hidden Forest did not have specific home addresses. For instance, Queen Wista lived in the tallest pine tree in Arborville. No other detail was required because all one had to do was look up at the trees and find the tallest one.

"Sorcerer Serpentine might have used a different name among the humans," pointed out Tark.

"He is vain, though, like all the magi," said Golden Belle. "I think he would keep using his original name."

"It's not a very nice name," said Ruby.

"I imagine the magi named each other," said Peck. "They could even be cruel to one another."

"Nonetheless, they're aptly named," said Trill. "Serpentine was as sneaky as a snake. He played nasty tricks on others, including trapping animals."

"We must prevent him from committing further cruelty," said Kreen. "Where do we find this *public library* to look up names?"

"It's probably somewhere near the town square," replied Ruby.

"What's a *town square*?" asked Skit.

Ruby gestured at the buildings surrounding the town park. "The library should be one of these buildings around the park. We will have to sneak in because the library will be locked up at this hour." It was well past closing time. "However, most of us could slip through a narrow slot in the building wall where the books are returned." She shot a glance at Trill and Peck. "I'm afraid that you'll be too big to squeeze through the slot."

"I can shrink them to a smaller size," offered Golden Belle. "I have enough magic to shrink small animals in the human world."

Queen Wista was smart to suggest they include a fairy in their rescue party, thought Ruby. "Once, inside the library, I hope that I can pull up the names and the whereabouts of Serpentine's children from a computer."

The others peered at one another, studying each other's expression.

"I think it is worth a try," spoke up Tark. "Besides, what other options do we have? We must locate the children before the witching hour. That's the time the magi will most likely perform the blood ceremony."

"Is the witching hour the same as midnight?" asked Ruby.

"When is midnight?" asked Tark.

"Never mind," said Ruby.

"We must find this library since we don't know where Serpentine lives . . . and we can't go door to door, looking for the children," said Golden Belle. "But I do find it odd that none of the elf spies knew the sorcerer's residence." She was looking pointedly at Tark. "The elves were supposed to be keeping track of him."

The others waited for an explanation, but Tark had no answer. He was assigned to spy on the ravens and the other less than trustworthy woodland creatures, who had aided the magi in the past. His first spy mission outside of Hidden Forest was at Zeldar's house earlier today.

"I don't believe Kreen and I have enough combined mindbending power to make any of the Malum reveal the whereabouts of

Serpentine's offspring," spoke up Skit. "I agree with Tark and Golden Belle. Our best bet is this library."

They elected to go to the library. Ruby rode with Kreen on Trill, and Golden Belle sat behind Skit on Peck. Golden Belle was conserving her strength. There would be many miles of flying tonight. The owls had more flying endurance and were swifter than fairies. The owls were also quieter in flight. The fairies' wings droned like dragonflies. Since Tark was inexperienced at carrying passengers on his back, he flew solo.

As they searched for the library, something disturbing caught their sight. There was a dark shadow the size of a city bus moving across a vacant street. Or, at least, the street was empty of vehicles. On the sidewalk was a pedestrian who appeared to be a man stooped over from old age. Without warning, the Dark Shadow grabbed the elderly man before he could scream for help and dragged him away. It happened so fast that there was no time for the search party to react.

"Was that the Dark Shadow?" gulped Ruby.

"Yes," replied Kreen. Both she and Trill glanced over at the living shadow. "It has begun taking human souls."

"Shouldn't we help the poor man?" asked Ruby, her eyes wide. Even though she was at least fifty feet away from the Dark Shadow, she could feel its coldness.

"There is nothing we can do for the man now," said Tark. "We have to find this library."

Hoping the Dark Shadow remained on the ground, Ruby pulled her gaze away from it. Nevertheless, she now saw dark shadows looming everywhere. "How many souls does the Dark Shadow need to take before it falls asleep again?"

"When it snatched souls from Hidden Forest, it usually took three or four," said Kreen. "I don't know how many souls it will take from the human world."

"That hardly seems fair to people. The Dark Shadow is the problem of Hidden Forest."

"The Dark Shadow is originally from the human world." Before she could finish her explanation, Trill did a quick nosedive to avoid a huge group of incoming bats that were feeding on mosquitoes and other flying insects.

"Bats," Trill huffed. "They never look where they are going."

They continued their flight. They flew past a general store, a hardware store, a shoe store, a bakery, a bank, two diners, and a hair salon, which also advertised manicures and pedicures on its storefront. At last, a white building had large letters above a set of double doors, spelling out "PUBLIC LIBRARY."

"There's the library!" Ruby gestured at the two-story building. The rescue party set down in front of the entrance. "Over there!" she pointed to the book return slot. The slot was no higher than three inches and not quite a foot in length. "We can slip through there."

Golden Belle pointed her wand at Trill and then Peck. In the blink of an eye, the two owls shrunk to the size of Kreen and Skit. Tark changed himself into a fairy, which clearly impressed Golden Belle. As they slipped through the slit in the wall, an orange cat named Miss Whiskers was waiting on the other side for them. Miss Whiskers had been the library cat for the past five years. She took it upon herself to greet every library patron, especially the children. So, when the rescuers made it inside the library, she was there to greet them. They froze in their tracks upon seeing the orange cat staring, if not glaring, at them.

Momentarily, Miss Whiskers was startled by the physical appearance of the strangers. "Hello," she said calmly. "The library is closed right now. You will have to come back in the morning. The library hours are from nine to five, except on Sunday."

"Aren't you curious to know why we are here?" said Ruby.

"I am more curious to know *who* you are," replied Miss Whiskers. Among the local cats and library patrons, she had a reputation for being unflappable.

"Do you have any intention of harming us?" questioned Trill, backing away from the cat's fangs. He was aware that cats killed small birds with their sharp teeth and claws. Currently, Trill was smaller than a pygmy owl.

"I have no intention of hurting anyone. I am a library cat. Cat librarians do not dine on birds and mice. We have an appetite for knowledge. And my meals come out of cans. Not from the local streets or the woods. Now, who are you? And where did you come from?"

Tark changed himself back into an elf. "We are from Hidden Forest. It's a magical place. We came here because we need your help finding a mother and three children who live in this town."

Miss Whiskers sat down on her haunches, observing them closely. "Who are you precisely looking for?"

"The father's name is Serpentine," interjected Ruby. "Maybe they came here to check out books."

Miss Whiskers eyed all seven of them, suspiciously. "Do you intend to harm these humans?"

"Of course not!" said Kreen. "We intend to save their lives." She proceeded to tell Miss Whiskers the quick version of the Malum and how they hoped to regain their magical abilities by the most contemptible means.

Miss Whiskers listened intently because she took her responsibility as a librarian very seriously. "I am familiar with the name Serpentine. He comes here frequently to borrow books on magic, particularly dark magic. A few years ago, he brought a child with him. I clearly remember it because he didn't seem the type to have a child."

"What do you mean?" asked Golden Belle.

"He had no patience for children," replied Miss Whiskers. "Come with me. I can look up his name in the computer file."

The rescuers grinned. This lucky break made their mission seem less daunting. They watched as Miss Whiskers hopped onto the desk of the head librarian and plopped down in front of the computer. To all but Ruby, the computer was a strange contraption. Odd sounds came out of it. As Ruby watched Miss Whiskers tapping on the keyboard, she wished her old school had a cat librarian. It would have added a little excitement to the place.

"Here you go!" said Miss Whiskers, beaming. "With a little research, I was able to find the home address of an S. Serpentine." She glanced at them. "You won't have far to go to find him. He lives in a house on Druid Street."

"Were you able to find the names of his children?" asked Ruby.

"There are no other Serpentines in our records. However,"—she squeezed her eyes shut as if recalling a past incident—"I remember Mister Serpentine speaking heatedly with a woman in the fantasy section. She walked out of the library without checking out any books. That happened about six months ago."

"Do you remember the woman's name?" asked Skit.

"Of course. Nothing goes unnoticed while I am on duty. And I am never off-duty," replied Miss Whiskers matter-of-factly.

"She is like a patrol," Skit remarked to Kreen.

Miss Whiskers gave the Little Peepers a look that said a patrol was nothing like a librarian. "The woman's name is Jackie Jubilee. She and her three children used to come here quite often before that encounter with Serpentine. Neither she nor her children ever came back here again after the incident."

"I overheard Serpentine say something about the mother having a restraining order against him," said Tark. "I am not sure what that means."

"It means that he isn't allowed to go anywhere near her," said Ruby. "It would also explain why Jackie Jubilee quit coming to the library. She was frightened of him. We need to go to Jackie Jubilee's house, and not Serpentine's place."

"Most likely, she feared that he would also harm their children," added Miss Whiskers, who was very familiar with the peculiar nature of humans. "Let me pull up Jackie Jubilee's file."

Ruby looked out the front window of the library. The full moon hovered above the town park, giving it an eerie glow. She wondered whether the black dragon had gone hunting, and, whether all the patrol rabbits survived his hunt.

"Jackie Jubilee resides at 1598 Hickory Lane," said Miss Whiskers. "Hickory Lane is on the other side of town, near the cemetery. The graveyard is a spooky place. Most of my cat friends refuse to go there, except for the black ones. I don't know why black cats are drawn to cemeteries, tales of sorcery, or cheesecake."

"You have cat friends?" Peck assumed cats were mostly solitary creatures because they hunted alone and not in packs like dogs.

"Why wouldn't I? Once a month, we hold our book club here, no matter the weather. Typically, twelve or thirteen of us show up for the club." She began printing out the map and directions to Jackie Jubilee's residence. "Someone usually brings an appetizer and a carton of cream. The stray cats have a different perspective on books than housecats, making for a lively discussion."

"Do you read cat books?" questioned Ruby.

"We read books about cats. Sadly, none of them are written by cats. Someday I intend to write a book series about cats, though," added Miss Whiskers. "I've already come up with the premise and title of the first book, which is *Miss Tails and Her Tales*. Miss Tails travels through time, meeting all the famous cats throughout history. Its sequel would be *The Nine Fabulous Lives of Miss Tails.* Parts of my life will show up throughout the pages."

"I didn't realize that cats could even read, much less write," said Ruby.

Miss Whiskers peered sideways at Ruby and said dryly, "All cat librarians know how to read and write. And all cats live interesting lives—all nine of them."

"I didn't know there were famous cats, either," said Trill, hoping there was a book about famous owls. Screech-owls, in particular.

"The adventure stories of that suave, swashbuckling Puss in Boots were based on my great-great-great uncle," Miss Whiskers replied matter-of-factly. "Now, who among you can read a simple map?"

"Are the words on the map written in Tiere?" asked Peck.

"No," answered Miss Whiskers. "Humans are not familiar with that particular animal language. Humans can only make a few improper animal sounds, like *moo and baa.*"

"If it's not written in Tiere, I cannot read the map," admitted Peck. He always wondered why humans were incapable of learning Tiere. They were surrounded by animals that regularly spoke the language.

"I think that I can figure out the map," said Ruby, who sounded tentative. She had never looked at a paper map. Before yesterday, she had never ventured beyond her own neighborhood. Nevertheless, she could read street signs.

Miss Whiskers pushed a sheet of paper toward Ruby. The sheet was much too big for Ruby to carry, so she had to memorize the directions. There were ten street blocks between the public library and Jackie Jubilee's home.

"We should be on our way," said Skit. "Time is of the essence, as the owls often say, particularly the wiser ones like barred owls." He winked at his barred owl companion.

"We do say that a lot," acknowledged Peck. "But we say it in a timely manner."

Miss Whiskers glanced at the time. It was a little past nine-thirty. Even though there was plenty of time for her to show the visitors the way to Jackie Jubilee's residence, she was reluctant to leave her library post. As soon as she turned her back, she imagined the mice in the basement would sneak upstairs to gather paper for their nests. It was a constant struggle to keep them from chewing through books. The mice produced new offspring faster than humans produced books.

Ruby stifled a yawn by pinching her lips tightly together. She felt quite tired from the events of the past few days. She hadn't even recovered from her mother's death. "Are you sure you can't shrink Jackie Jubilee and her children, Golden Belle?" She was hoping that all of them could fly home. In that way, she could be back in her bunkbed in a couple of hours.

"No, my magic is not as strong in the nonmagical world as it is in Hidden Forest. I cannot shrink a full-sized human being while I am here. It's the reason I could not shrink you and your sister back at the garden shed." Golden Belle waved her wand and tiny sparks sputtered from its tip. "I can feel the human world pressing down on my magic. I am afraid that the children and their mother will have to travel by ordinary means."

"Let us take our leave before Golden Belle grows too weak to fly home," said Kreen.

"If that happens, I will carry you home, Golden Belle," offered Trill.

"Do not worry, my magic will last for a full day in the nonmagical world," said Golden Belle, smiling gratefully at the screech-owl. Fairies and owls had always been fond of each other.

"Thank you, Miss Whiskers, for your assistance. Library cats are very helpful and quite intelligent," said Kreen.

Miss Whiskers was beaming from the compliment. She would have invited them to the next book club meeting, but she was doubtful that any of them were serious book readers. Or read books at all.

The search party thanked Miss Whiskers once again. They were about to slip through the library slot from whence they entered, but Miss Whiskers told them that they could exit through the cat door, which was located in the head librarian's office. Miss Whiskers considered herself and the human named Ms. Forks, the head librarians. Golden Belle used her wand to return Peck and Trill to their original size while Tark transformed into a screech-owl once again. Ruby requested that Trill fly low to the ground, as Golden Belle lit up the street signs with her wand. The rest of them watched for any sign of the Malum. They did not want to encounter a magus before rescuing

Jackie Jubilee and her children. However, the possibility that Serpentine had already captured his children weighed heavily on their minds.

It so happened that Jackie Jubilee lived directly across the street from the front gate of the town's only cemetery. When the members of the search party reached Jackie's house, they spotted a couple of ghosts lurking in her front yard. Actually, the ghosts appeared to be pacing. Typically, Ruby would have been afraid of ghosts. However, in the company of an elf, a fairy, two Little Peepers, and a couple of owls, she was not scared at all. Besides, the ghosts appeared to be so worried about something that they barely paid any attention to the approaching strangers. The male ghost was attired in a black suit from the mid-nineteenth century while the female ghost wore a white wedding dress with a gaping hole in its bodice. Upon closer inspection, the male ghost had a hole in his forehead. Ruby surmised that the two ghosts had been shot on their wedding day.

"I don't know if ghosts can understand Tiere," said Golden Fairy. "Let me sprinkle some fairy dust on them." She flew over the ghosts' heads and sprayed them with gold dust.

"Is that a hummingbird or a dragonfly zipping around us, my love?" the male ghost asked his female friend.

"I thought it was a wasp or a bumblebee," she replied, appearing baffled. "Perhaps a hornet."

They had no fear of being stung. They just found insects pesky.

"Hello, there!" Skit called out to the ghosts.

The male ghost looked at his female companion, perplexed. "My dearest Opal, there are strange things addressing us!"

"Oh, my word, my sweet Edward!" said Opal. "Shall we take leave?"

"Please don't leave," Ruby pleaded. "We are from a magical place called Hidden Forest and we are looking for Jackie Jubilee and her three children. They supposedly live here. We have come here to rescue them from the terrible magi." She further explained their present situation to the ghosts to clear up the confusion.

"We are having a most unsettling day," said Opal. "Aren't we, dear?"

"We truly are, love."

Opal was biting her bottom lip, clearly upset. Ruby imagined that it did not hurt ghosts to chew on their lips or any other body part. In that sense, they were like zombies. "Where could they be, Edward?"

The ghosts were shocked when Tark turned back into his original elf form.

"Oh, goodness gracious, my love! What strange creatures they are!" expressed Opal. "If I still had a beating heart, it would've popped out of my chest."

"Who are you looking for?" Kreen asked them.

"The same people that you are seeking," replied Edward, motioning to the two-story house behind him. "Jackie Jubilee is the caretaker of our cemetery."

"She tidies up the place," added Opal. "She does such a lovely job of cleaning the moss, dusting off the gravestones, and picking up leaves and branches from the ground. Sometimes she sings to us. We just adore her."

Ruby gazed across the street at the graveyard, imagining that Jackie sang to herself to pass the time. "Are you sure she sings to the ghosts in the cemetery?"

"Oh, yes. She has a lovely singing voice," replied Opal. "My aunt also had an enchanting singing voice. She was in the church choir . . . until she was kicked in the head by a mule. She was a little daffy after that. My aunt, not the mule. Both of them were equally stubborn, though. Do you remember her, my sweet love?"

"I do, indeed, my darling. It is not every day you see a woman wear a flowerpot as a hat to church." He winked at Opal, as if they were sharing an amusing joke.

"You stated that you came from Hidden Forest," said Opal. "Why is it called Hidden Forest? Is it concealed?"

"Humans cannot see the magical beings in Hidden Forest," explained Skit. This was the first time Ruby had heard the reason for the forest's name. Suddenly, it occurred to her that she and Shauna must be something other than human because she could clearly see everyone in Hidden Forest.

"Nevertheless, we scare off trespassers from our woods," tacked on Kreen. "We cannot afford to have outsiders cut down our trees or pollute our land."

71

"For centuries, we have heard rumors of an enchanted forest near here," said Edward. "I wasn't sure if it was true or not because we ghosts are rather susceptible when it comes to the spiritual world. We can believe anything out of the ordinary since *we* are out of the ordinary."

"We have seen many strange things over the years." Opal floated over to the group of peculiar-looking creatures, except for the owls who appeared quite ordinary to them. Her gaze fell on Ruby, Skit, and Kreen. "You are so little that there isn't much of you to hide, is there?" Next, she eyed Golden Belle. "And a real fairy! If only my mother was alive to see this day! She was a true believer in the supernatural and a regular participant in séances. I was more skeptical of spirits until . . ."—she glanced down at herself—"I became one myself."

Golden Belle was growing a bit impatient. She flew over to Opal and hovered near her nose. "Do you have any notion of where Jackie Jubilee and her children could be?"

"I'm afraid not. We saw them pack up their car with suitcases before dawn and they drove off in a hurry." Opal would have been in tears, if she could have produced them. "Edward and I became concerned because she wouldn't leave us for long without telling us." She gestured once again at the cemetery. Everyone turned to look at the graveyard. Ruby spotted *Hillside Cemetery* spelled out in metal letters above the wrought-iron entrance gate. The metal bars reminded her of the long spikes where the decapitated heads of criminals were placed as a warning to others. Needless to say, the cemetery did not look like an inviting place. From the corner of her eye, Ruby swore that she saw a black cat crossing the street and heading toward the cemetery.

Kreen slid off Trill and stood at the toes of Opal's wedding slippers. "So, do you think Jackie has the ability to see ghosts?"

Opal looked down at Kreen. "Jackie seemed to be an ordinary human with a sense for the supernatural. She couldn't see us, but I believe she could feel our presence. Yesterday, we left flowers on her doorstep to show our appreciation for her. We assumed that she would know they were from us."

"Or, she could have thought they were from Serpentine," Ruby pointed out. She glanced over at Jackie's front porch and saw that it was completely covered with dead flowers, including dandelions. "If so, it might have freaked her out and she decided to disappear from here."

"It was her birthday yesterday," explained Opal. "We gave her extra flowers for the special occasion." Her face fell. "Oh, sweet, dear Edward, whatever have we done! We scared away our poor Jackie!"

Edward rushed over to her side and held her in his arms. "Please don't fret, my darling."

"Oh, drat, I cannot help it! I was born with this sensitive soul."

"Your flowers may have saved the lives of Jackie and her children. If she had not run away, Sorcerer Serpentine would have murdered her and their children under the full moon tonight," pointed out Tark.

"Murder! How horrible! I know what that feels like! To have all of your hopes and dreams taken away from you with a single bullet." Opal clutched the hole in her bodice.

"My Opal truly possesses the sensitive soul of a poet," Edward explained to them. "And a heart of gold. This is truly difficult news for her to bear."

"Is Sorcerer Serpentine the one who wears a black cloak and stinks like a dead fish washed up on the beach?" asked Opal, regaining her composure.

"Most likely," said Golden Belle. "All of the magi dress in black cloaks and have an unusual fishy odor."

"Oh, my dearest Opal," said Edward, "this evil sorcerer has the scent of a rotting corpse and a murderer!"

"He stinks because his soul is rotted out," exclaimed Opal. "Whatever shall we do, my love? We must do something!" She was searching Edward's face for an answer. "We must bring our Jackie back to us."

"In one way or another, our Jackie will find her way back to us, my love," said Edward. "We shall not abandon her or her children."

"Do you have any idea where Jackie could have taken the children?" asked Peck.

The ghosts were surprised upon hearing the owl speak.

"You understand my words because of the gold dust," explained Peck. "All owls are eloquent orators and lecturers, when it is required."

73

When the ghosts recovered from their shock, they recalled Jackie mentioning several living relatives but could not recall much about them.

"They were ordinary and boring," explained Opal. "However, her nonliving family members were far more interesting. Most of them are buried in the cemetery with us. You could speak with them. The tombstone of Jackie's grandfather is three rows over from ours. Isn't that right, dear?"

"You are always right, dear." Edward clutched Opal's right hand to his heart. Or where his heart used to be. "We weren't willing to be parted in death. Our graves lie right next to one another."

Ruby peered inquiringly at Opal. "Who shot you?"

"A former suitor," she replied. "In the end, he wound up in a far worse place than this graveyard."

"Did he go straight to hell?" asked Ruby, enticed by their tragic story.

"I'm not sure. However, my father shot him and threw his body down a well," Opal explained. "My father told me that he had avenged my death as he stood over my grave. Then, he shot himself. It was a terrible time for all of us."

"How sad," said Ruby.

"You are very kind to say so," said Opal. "My father did not stick around as a ghost. He went on to join my mother in the afterlife. But Edward and I remained ghosts even after our murders were avenged. There must be a reason for it, but we do not know what it is. Isn't that right, my truest love?"

"It is so, sweet Opal."

"Do you think it is worth our time to speak with Jackie's family in the graveyard?" asked Tark, ignoring the kiss Opal planted on Edward's cheek.

"If you are in a hurry, then I would not venture into the cemetery," said Opal. "Some of the ghosts are chatterboxes. Though, I have been unfairly accused of the same. Haven't I, my dear Edward?"

"Yes. A terribly unfair accusation, I might add. You are the life of the cemetery and take out the 'grave' in graveyard."

"And you, my sweets, turn the cemetery into a carnival," replied Opal.

Edward and Opal were beaming at each other.

"What should we do?" Kreen asked the rest of the group. She was ignoring the ghost couple who were praising each other's good company.

"We cannot search for days to find Jackie Jubilee and her offspring," said Tark. "I suggest we go back to Hidden Forest at once and regroup. A scouting party, consisting of long-range flyers, could be sent out."

"Aren't owls long-range flyers?" asked Ruby.

"Owls can fly a long way, but we cannot fly when it is raining," Trill explained to Ruby. "We don't have waterproof feathers. Albatrosses, geese, and ducks are better suited for longer scouting missions. However, in a pinch, we're willing to go the distance."

"But what about the magi?" Ruby asked.

"I doubt if they know the whereabouts of Jackie, either. I sense they will not be drinking the children's blood tonight." Tark observed the moon climbing above a wispy cloud. "It will be a race between us and them to find Jackie and the children before next month's full moon."

"A race that cannot be lost," noted Opal. "A single bullet can change a life forever." She gripped Edward's hand. "Is that not true, my love?"

"It is true, my precious." In return, Edward squeezed her hand. "If Jackie and her children return home, we will notify you . . . How do we find our way to Hidden Forest?"

"It is behind Witch Zeldar's house," replied Tark. "Ask the librarian cat, Miss Whiskers. She is good with directions."

"Though, be careful of the magi. You will recognize them by their black cloaks and grim faces," warned Kreen. "Do not approach them. Although they have no magic, they still have terrible tempers and evil ways."

"We cannot be killed twice," Edward reminded them. "These vile magi cannot harm us."

"Let us embark for home. Time is of the essence," repeated Peck. He rotated his head the full two hundred seventy degrees to peer at Skit, who was climbing onto his back. Then, he turned his head to regard the ghost couple. "The ravens were the messenger birds for the magi. Watch out for them, too."

"Did you hear that, Edward?" remarked Opal. "From now on, we must be careful what we say around the ravens in the graveyard."

"We must warn the others since we can't keep the ravens out of the cemetery," said Edward.

"We will have Mister McCurry sing to the ravens, dear. His voice can scare away the devil himself!" Opal looked at the others. "Mister McCurry does not have Jackie's angelic vocals."

The group of seven searchers thanked Opal and Edward for their assistance. In return, the ghost couple invited them to come back and visit them and the others in the cemetery. Once more, Tark transformed into a screech-owl and all of them flew back to Hidden Forest. Right away, Opal and Edward began to miss their company, as well as Jackie Jubilee and her lovely singing voice.

Chapter Eight

Weighing the Options

Commander Lapin spotted the Dark Shadow slithering out of Hidden Forest that evening. It disturbed him to know that the Dark Shadow would be preying on a human soul. On the other hand, he was relieved that the shadowy spirit would not be capturing anyone from the forest. He was aware of the bargain Queen Rossen made with the Dark Shadow. Lapin just wished that a bargain could be made with the Black Dragon to spare rabbits. It seemed incredibly unfair that the dragon fed on the rabbits. The rabbits had lived longer in Hidden Forest than the dragon. Consequently, he and his fellow rabbits were debating how to deal with the Black Dragon. Among all ten regiments, there were whispers of slaying the dragon once and for all. In the past, the other woodland creatures argued that the Black Dragon maintained balance in the forest. It was easy for them to make that argument for their lives were not in danger of being plucked from the ground by dragon talons. He felt soon that there would be an uprising among the rabbits if the dragon wasn't removed in one way or another. He did not know if he would even attempt to contain the revolt. In fact, he might even lead the charge to kill the Black Dragon. He despised the fire-breathing beast.

"Commander," said Poppin, interrupting his cousin's thoughts. "Both the Dark Shadow and the Black Dragon have been seen ready to prey on others."

"Just keep an eye on the Black Dragon. The Dark Shadow will not harm us."

"Yes, Commander." Poppin seemed reluctant to leave Lapin.

"Is there something else, Poppin?"

"I was hoping to get your opinion on the rescue party. Do you think they will succeed?"

Lapin sniffed the night air. It was this natural instinct that kept him alive for the past centuries. His intuition and wisdom were greatly valued among the other rabbits. It was he alone who had sensed Ruby and Shauna locked up in Zeldar's garden shed. "Something is very wrong, Poppin. My whiskers tell me so."

"Do you know what it is?"

"Not exactly." He sniffed the air again while his ears stood tall. "Get word out to the other regiments that the Dark Shadow will return tonight to the forest with a human. Under the agreement made by Queen Rossen, we cannot stop it."

Poppin looked dismayed. "Can it not be destroyed?"

"It has one great weakness. But if we attempt to annihilate it and fail, it might retaliate against us. We know nothing about its temperament."

"What is its one great weakness?"

"If the Dark Shadow appears at midday, it is a death sentence. The sun will destroy it."

"How many souls do you think the Dark Shadow is made of?" Poppin's parents had once told her that the Dark Shadow was actually the dead souls of murdered victims seeking retaliation against the world. Over the many centuries, they joined together and became a moving shadow on earth, always searching for revenge. And then, the dead souls grew tired. They needed their rest. So, about a hundred years ago, the Dark Shadow moved into Hidden Forest to regain its strength. But it needs the energy of new souls to sustain itself. However, no one knew this for certain. It was only one of several theories.

"The Dark Shadow must be comprised of a dozen souls or so. I can feel its coldness three hundred feet away. It leaves a trail of sorrow behind wherever it goes." At a very young age, the rabbit offspring were warned not to get too close to the Dark Shadow.

"I wonder why it cannot go off to the afterlife."

"That's a good question. No one knows how to make it move on from here." Lapin had not forgotten the day the Dark Shadow appeared in the forest. It darkened the forest floor as it drifted toward the Black Dragon's lair, leaving a deep chill behind it. The residents watched as it sank into a cavern below Misty Falls. At the time, no one considered it dangerous as it seemed to disappear permanently into the earth. However, forty-one years later, it reappeared and began dragging off the local inhabitants. As soon as an attack was mounted, it vanished once again into the protection of its cavern. This cavern became known as the Pit of Despair. Another thirty-eight years passed before the Dark Shadow suddenly reemerged again. Once more, it snatched innocent bystanders. Before the locals could capture and destroy it, it escaped deep into its pit again. It reappeared thirteen years ago because the Malum had awakened it from its hibernation when the magi dumped their captured souls into its pit. That's when Queen Rossen went alone to confront the Dark Shadow.

As Poppin stood guard alongside Lapin, the three moles, Rooter, Erde, and Snoot, surfaced from one of their countless tunnels throughout Hidden Forest. If the moles had better eyesight, they could have seen the house of Witch Zeldar from where they stood. The patrols were keeping a close watch on it.

"Ah, Commander Lapin, have you heard any recent reports of the rescue party?" questioned Rooter, rubbing his almost blind eyes. "You know how long it takes for news to reach us underground."

"We are still waiting for the rescuers' return," said Lapin. "If the children and their mother have to walk here, it will take a while."

"They probably own one of those loud contraptions with four wheels," said Erde. "It makes the ground shake. What are they called?"

"Deathtraps," said Poppin. "They make crossing the road dangerous to one's health."

"That's why traveling underground is the best way to go," said Snoot.

"The elves have told me that humans have vehicles that go underground, too," said Lapin. "It is not safe for us to be out in the human world for too long."

"I find it interesting that the elves know about underground vehicles. Yet, they knew nothing about the existence of the Malum's offspring," Erde pointed out. "They were supposedly spying on the Malum, were they not?"

"I have spotted elves leaving Hidden Forest at night to spy on the Malum," said Lapin. "What they bring back from the human world, I do not know."

"Are you worried about the rescuers, Commander?" asked Erde, noticing that Lapin was thumping his back foot.

"Somewhat." Lapin wriggled his small nose. "There are many things out there that we do not know about."

"We heard that the older girl whom we rescued from Zeldar's shed is with the rescue party. She will know what to do," said Rooter, trying to sound encouraging. "We also heard that she has inherited her father's magic. And so has her younger sister."

"Is that why you have come here tonight?" said Lapin. "To learn the status of the girls?"

"Well, it would be nice to know if we have something more powerful in our midst than the fairies," said Erde matter-of-factly. "We smelled the poison in Zeldar's shed. Right then, we realized that Zeldar will use it on us as well as the rabbits if the Malum return."

"This is the first I have heard of the poison," said Lapin. His hind leg was beating faster than his pounding heart.

"The Malum are monsters," said Poppin. "I hope the Dark Shadow drags back the magi and dumps them into the cavern."

"Unfortunately, it was agreed that the Dark Shadow can only capture *human* souls," said Lapin.

"Queen Rossen did not negotiate well," muttered Erde.

Lapin and Poppin were aware that the moles and the elves had occasional conflicts. The elves would become upset when the moles dug tunnels below their orchards and gardens.

"Nonetheless, I am glad that Golden Belle went along because she is trained in magic," said Snoot. "Unlike the girl."

"Even if the girls have magical abilities, they will not stand a chance against the Malum if they return," said Erde, her thoughts still focused on Ruby and Shauna. "Not even the fairies can put up a good fight against the magi."

"Thank goodness for the Little Peepers and their mindbending skills," said Rooter.

"Yes, thank goodness for the Little Peepers," agreed Lapin. He gazed upward and spied the Black Dragon flying overhead. Maybe it was time for the Little Peepers to make the dragon go, too, he thought. Lately, their rabbit population was beginning to decline on its own. Their litters were smaller. Something was amiss in their magical forest, but he couldn't quite put his paw on it.

The moles decided to remain with Commander Lapin and his eighth regiment patrol unit because nothing exciting was happening belowground. Because of their poor eyesight, they did not stand watch. Mostly, they chatted with the rabbit patrols while they waited for the return of the rescue party. They wanted to be the first to bring the most recent news down to the other moles.

The moon was well above the treetops when the rabbit patrols spotted the rescue party. Sorcerer Serpentine's three children were not among the rescue group. The rescuers intended to fly over the rabbit patrols without stopping, but Commander Lapin flagged them down by hopping up and down and waving his forelegs, which rabbits considered to be arms. His gray ears and white tail were high in the air.

"I'll update the patrols on the situation," offered Golden Belle, spotting Lapin waving at the rescue party. "The rest of you can keep going." She leapt off the back of Peck and flew down to the rabbit patrols, who wore anxious expressions. The thought of the Malum returning to the forest weighed heavily on the rabbits' minds. The rabbits would pay a heavy toll if the magi came back to the forest.

The remaining six searchers headed straight for Arborville, where Queen Wista, Queen Rossen, and their advisors were awaiting their arrival. Ruby, who was nodding off from lack of sleep, was dropped off at Vorte and Berruga's treehouse. The rest of them continued on their way toward Wista's home. While Ruby's new guardians were overjoyed to see her again, Shauna was in a deep slumber, oblivious to the impending danger to Serpentine's three offspring.

"Why don't you go straight to bed, Ruby," said Berruga. "After you wake up, you can tell me all about tonight's outing."

Ruby nodded sluggishly. Her leg muscles were stiff and sore from her ride on Trill. Her legs had been pressed into the western screech-owl. She had struggled to remain on the owl's back. She imagined that it would take some time getting comfortable riding a bird.

Meanwhile, both queens and their top counselors had been anxiously waiting in Wista's treehouse for the return of the search party. Rossen and Counselor Nirva had changed into chickadees. Counselor Herona was fixing herbal tea and toasting flower seeds for the four of them when Flycatcher notified them that the searchers had been spotted from the sky.

"They are almost here," said Flycatcher, who delivered the message at the door. "There are no humans among them, other than Ruby . . . who isn't with them anymore. They just dropped her off at Vorte and Berruga's place. The poor girl was exhausted."

"The rescuers are almost at your queen's doorstep and we're just hearing of their arrival?!" Rossen huffed to Flycatcher. She turned toward Wista. "What kind of security system are you operating?"

"If we had been in danger, the patrols would have notified us earlier," Wista said quietly, keeping her temper in check. She turned away from Rossen and gave her attention to Flycatcher. "Tell them we will come down to meet them." She attempted to remain composed but her trembling voice gave her true emotions away. She was clearly disturbed by the recent news. All of them in the treehouse were wondering if Serpentine's children were already in the hands of the Malum. That frightening thought put everyone's nerves on edge.

At once, Flycatcher clambered onto his companion owl, Tuft, who was waiting on a nearby tree limb. They flew only a few feet to deliver Wista's message to the incoming searchers. A few moments later, Queen Wista and Counselor Herona took taxi birds to reach the forest floor while Queen Rossen and Counselor Nirva fluttered down on their own as chickadees. The elves did not transform back into their original selves, knowing the members of the search party were rather short in stature.

Upon hearing the news that the search party had returned, the Little Peepers began to assemble on the forest floor to find out what had been discovered. It was a bit unsettling to Rossen and Nirva that the ordinary citizens of Arborville would receive the report at the same time they would. Unlike the Little Peepers, the elf community followed a strict chain of command.

The party of five remaining searchers landed near the two queens and their counselors. Seeing that Queen Rossen and Counselor Nirva were in bird form, Tark stayed as an owl. Kreen and Skit hopped off their companion owls and nodded respectfully to both queens. Trill and Peck rested on a nearby tree branch. It had been a long night of flying for them. Tark explained that Ruby was safely at her guardians' home and Golden Belle was addressing Commander Lapin and his patrol unit.

"But where are Serpentine's children?" asked Rossen, looking around as if they might be invisible or shrunken to the size of an ant. However, she was keenly aware that Golden Belle could not have made them invisible because of her limited magical powers.

It was Kreen and Skit who took turns recounting what occurred during their expedition, including their encounters with Miss Whiskers and the graveyard ghosts, Opal and Edward. They also expressed how Ruby had helped them.

"She can read maps and street signs and locate a library," noted Kreen. "She also explained to us that Sorcerer Serpentine has a restraining order against him. This means he cannot get near Jackie Jubilee without being arrested by the police." The crowd wore blank faces. "The police are like our patrols, except they can legally lock people up in cages. Something like what the Malum did to our owls in the past. In both cases, it's against the prisoner's will."

The blank faces began to nod knowingly. The owls hooted with contempt for the Malum.

"So, the mother of Serpentine's children vanished in the wee hours of the morning," cut in Queen Rossen, while gesturing at the owls to be quiet. "Did the ghosts have any idea of their whereabouts?"

"No," replied Tark. "However, I highly doubt the Malum know where to find Jackie and the children, either. They are probably in hiding."

"Perhaps the wise cat in the library could assist our search," remarked Counselor Herona. She stood alongside Wista, peering out at the throng of Little Peepers. She sensed Queen Rossen did not like the crowd gathering around them.

"Even if we could track down the four humans, how do we bring them back here?" questioned Queen Rossen. "None of us can transport them to Hidden Forest if we cannot shrink them. Even if a couple of elves shapeshift into dragons, we would not have enough endurance to fly a long distance, especially with the added burden of a rider."

Queen Wista's eyes wandered over to the highest point in Hidden Forest, where the Black Dragon had his lair. "Perhaps we could convince a real dragon to bring them here."

"Using our mindbending skills, we are capable of doing so," added Herona. The onlookers nodded in agreement.

"I would prefer the Black Dragon do it out of his free will," said Wista. "Forcing it to heed our instructions will cause resentment."

The Little Peepers nodded their heads again.

"We still have the issue of locating the humans," said Rossen. "What if the cat at the library cannot help us?"

"We have Ruby and Shauna," said Wista. "They know more about the human world than any of us. We could employ their help."

The Little Peepers were leaning against one another and craning their necks to hear how the elf queen would respond to their own queen's advice.

"The other alternative is to eliminate the Malum altogether in the human world," said Rossen. "Then, we would never have to worry about the Malum returning to the forest. Furthermore, we would not have to track down Jackie Jubilee and her offspring and bring them back here."

"It would also prevent the Malum from producing more children," spoke up Counselor Nirva.

"The Little Peepers could make the Black Dragon kill the Malum," Rossen said cleverly.

The crowd broke out in murmurs and Queen Wista quieted them down by raising her hand. "May I remind you, it was Sorcerer Spellbinder's magic that created us. If we destroy our creator, would his spells be broken? Would we disappear along with Spellbinder? We do not know the answer."

"Maybe the girls' magic will protect us," said Flycatcher, standing alongside Hummer. They had been friends since Aviation School. Both of them received high marks from Oide. "Their magic is different than the fairies."

The onlookers looked encouraged, but the elf queen appeared worried.

"Is the girls' magic a danger to Hidden Forest?" asked Rossen. "Will the sisters turn on us if they have inherited Warlock Highbrow's dark magic?"

This time the spectators began murmuring amongst themselves. They had not considered the possibility that the girls might become like the Malum.

Queen Wista silenced the crowd again. But it was Berruga who rushed to the girls' defense. She had been standing on her balcony, listening to the public discussion. She hopped onto a taxi owl and the two of them made a beeline for the tree branch where Queen Wista stood. She leapt off the boreal owl and planted herself beside Wista. The spectators grew silent because they had never seen Berruga so determined before or so red in the face.

"There will not be another word spoken about these young girls having a dark side! They are kind and thoughtful. Not once have they complained about their new circumstances, even though they recently lost their mother to the Malum. Just as important, we might need their magic to save us. So, why are we attempting to alienate them? Why make enemies out of our friends? Let's give them our support and protection. Moreover, show them kindness because it's the least we can do."

The Little Peepers applauded and the owls hooted. Berruga acknowledged her audience's approval with a simple smile.

Wista looked over at Rossen before addressing the crowd. "I guess the matter is settled. The girls will continue to remain with us and learn their magic from the fairies. Meanwhile, we will send out another scouting party to find Jackie Jubilee and her children."

"Where will we look for them?" asked Counselor Herona.

"We will begin our search with the cat librarian and the ghosts in the cemetery," replied Wista. "Someone will know something about where the missing have gone."

Tark and the rest of the searchers turned in for the night. They were bushed. As they rested, the two queens put together a list of potential rescuers. They saw no choice but to add Ruby to that list. They needed someone who was more familiar with the ways of the human world than the elves, who didn't seem particularly knowledgeable about humans at all.

□□□

Shortly before eleven o'clock, Sorcerer Serpentine parked his rental car in the cemetery, across the street from Jackie Jubilee's residence. The house was dark. Jackie and the three brats were probably sound asleep, he thought. He placed a handgun in his cloak pocket. It started raining. The splattering of the raindrops against the car windows made it difficult to see Jackie's house. The windows began to fog up. He opened the car door.

The ghost couple, Edward and Opal, noticed a man emerging from the black sedan. He was attired in a black, calf-length cloak. The type of cloak that Edward wore while he was alive.

"That's him, my love," Opal whispered to Edward. "Shall we follow him?"

"Most certainly, my sweet."

Unbeknownst to Serpentine, the two ghosts were silently trailing behind him. The other ghosts watched all three of them leave Hillside Cemetery and cross the street. They were not concerned about Opal's and Edward's safety because the ghost couple were incapable of dying twice. Instead, the other ghosts were very interested in his car. They would make sure that Serpentine would suffer a panic attack when his car alarm went off, alerting the neighbors on Hickory Lane to the sorcerer's presence. Everyone in the neighborhood, including the graveyard ghosts, knew that Jackie Jubilee had a restraining order against Serpentine. They also knew that Jackie had moved to the house across from the graveyard right after filing the restraining order against him. Secrets and private matters leaked out into the neighborhood and into the graveyard.

As the ghosts tinkered with the rental car, Opal and Edward watched as the sorcerer walked to the back of Jackie's house and peeked through the sliding glass door. Serpentine was straining his eyes to cut through the darkness. Every light in the house was turned off. He cursed under his breath. Where were they? He needed the blood of his offspring tonight. He had to make good on his promise to bring them to Witch Zeldar's house tonight. The other eight magi were already there, waiting for him—waiting to regain their magical powers. He swore again. Opal and Edward traded a look, disgusted by his ill manners.

"Let's frighten him, darling," Opal whispered to Edward.

Edward replied with a mischievous wink.

Opal floated over to Serpentine and knocked off the strange-looking hat from his head. She was not familiar with baseball caps. People did not wear baseball caps to the graveyard. After Serpentine was exiled to the human world, he traded his pointy sorcerer's hat for a baseball cap and his wand for a gun. He wanted to fit in with the humans. Opal vanished before Serpentine spun around to see who knocked his cap to the ground. Then, a patio chair slid across the back porch. A good-sized flowerpot floated in the air near him and then crashed into the side of the house. The noise was loud enough to startle the neighbors.

"I am not frightened of spirits," Serpentine said aloud, sensing the ghosts' presence. It was true that he was not easily spooked by ghosts, but he was scared of the police. He had to get out of there before the neighbors called them. Nothing terrified the Malum more than the thought of being locked up behind bars.

"Go away and never come back," Opal hissed. She showed herself to him. "I do not care for your kind."

Serpentine noticed the bullet hole in the bodice of her wedding dress. "You most likely deserved your death."

Edward picked up a small flower pot and aimed it at Serpentine's head. Serpentine ducked but the clay pot shattered the window. Jackie's elderly neighbor, Louisa, who had been sound asleep, heard the sound of breaking glass coming from the direction of Jackie's home. She looked out her window and noticed that the house was pitch-black. She assumed that a thief was attempting to break in and called the police.

"What did you do with Jackie and my children?" Serpentine spat at Opal.

"They left you for good." Opal indicated to Edward that it was time for them to leave. They vanished into mid-air, as all ghosts were capable of doing.

Serpentine rushed back to his car. He did not want to stick around any longer. As he drew nearer to the cemetery, he heard the wailing of a police siren in the distance. He quickened his pace. The ghosts watched him as he removed the car keys from his cloak pocket. As soon as he pushed the button to open the car door, the car alarm went off.

"Hell's Bells!" Serpentine swore. Behind him, he heard chuckling. He turned around and saw dozens of ghosts laughing at him. "I curse all of you!" he yelled at the ghosts. He followed that with a platitude of profanities that he learned in the human world. If he still had his magic, he would have vaporized every last one of them with his wand. Then, he remembered Spellbinder had made new wands for the Malum. His brand-new oak wand would be waiting for him at Zeldar's house, if Spellbinder kept his word. Once more, he cursed. He could not go to the witch's home without the three children.

The police sirens were growing louder. He jumped into his sedan and sped off with the car alarm still blaring. All the neighbors on

Hickory Lane heard both the car alarm and the approaching police siren.

While Serpentine was evading the police, the other Malum were waiting for him. The full moon was hanging above Hidden Forest. They were so close to returning there.

The Malum were growing more impatient as time ticked by and Serpentine still had not arrived.

"What if Serpentine decided to use the blood of his three brats just on himself?" questioned Witch Blackheart, suspiciously. "What if he betrayed us? He would be the only one among us to regain his powers." Her accusation triggered an outburst in Zeldar's living room.

"If Sorcerer Serpentine is not here by midnight, we must go and look for him," stated Warlock Gloominus. "Personally, I've never trusted him."

"But where do we look?" said Sorceress Underhand. "He might be miles from here." Her comment prompted another flare-up among them.

Dismayed, Warlock Highbrow shook his head. "If only we had our powers—"

"But we don't!" snapped Sorceress Hexla. "If you and Zeldar had done a better job of keeping the two girls in the shed, we would not be in this terrible fix."

"That's enough!" snarled Witch Mortify. "We don't know if Serpentine betrayed us. But there is a way to search for him without having to leave here."

"How?" questioned Witch Blackheart.

"We will call for the ravens of Hidden Forest. If we provide them with something they want, they will do our bidding," replied Mortify.

"They might want magical powers," said Sorceress Underhand unhappily. "I'm not willing to share mine with a bunch of birds."

"The ravens don't want magical powers," countered Warlock Highbrow. "All they'll want is food to get them through the brutal winter."

"It's too bad the ravens are not strong enough to carry humans," mused Sorcerer Spellbinder. "They could bring Highbrow's brats to us from the forest."

"I have already thought of that," said Mortify. "It would only be possible if the brats were shrunken to the size of Little Peepers."

"We should still call for the ravens to come here tonight," said Sorceress Underhand. The ravens of Hidden Forest were capable of flying well in low light, unlike the ravens in the human world. Sorcerer Spellbinder had put a spell on them many years ago as an experiment. Naturally, he could not undo the spell. "We should request that the ravens first look for Serpentine. And, if we learn Serpentine has deceived us, then there might be a way for us to force a fairy to shrink the girls. Then, the ravens can carry them to us with their claws."

"But remember, we must change the girls back to their original size in order to provide us with enough blood," Warlock Gloominus reminded them.

"Then, the ravens would also have to bring us a fairy," said Sorceress Hexla, "to change them back."

"Stop being fools!" snarled Witch Blackheart. "A fairy's magic isn't strong enough to regrow a human being in the nonmagical world. This world drains their energy just as it did ours."

"Witch Blackheart is right," said Witch Zeldar. "Witches are always right."

"Bah!" Gloominus scowled.

"Enough! I will go contact the ravens. We need to speak with them." Sorcerer Spellbinder walked out to the backyard and called in a low-pitched, drawn-out croak for the ravens to come to him. He also emitted a high-pitched squawk, telling the ravens to hurry. Zeldar's neighbors on Dead End Street heard the sorcerer's cries, but assumed it was just feisty ravens squabbling with one another. The ravens, in both the human world and Hidden Forest, often fought among themselves as if they were longtime foes, though they continued to flock together as if they were inseparable friends. Needless to say, the ravens behaved like the Malum.

After Sorcerer Spellbinder returned to Zeldar's house, the magi plotted their revenge against Serpentine, in case he had tricked them.

Outside, Commander Lapin was keeping watch behind Zeldar's backyard. His gray hair still bristled from Sorcerer Spellbinder's raven call. Numerous times he had heard this beckoning call. He would never forget the sound of the magi calling for a raven to deliver their messages when they inhabited Hidden Forest.

"That is the voice of Spellbinder," Lapin said to Poppin. "I remember it well. Perhaps, too well."

"What do you suppose he wants with the ravens?"

"He probably wants the ravens to search for Ruby and Shauna and report their whereabouts to him," replied Lapin. "This can only mean one thing—the Malum have discovered that Serpentine's three children are missing. They might still need the blood of Ruby and Shauna."

"Or they want the ravens to find Serpentine's offspring," countered Poppin.

"Either way the magi are up to no good."

"What should we do?" asked Poppin.

"Notify Queen Wista. We need the owl squadrons to trail the ravens." Lapin flagged down the owl patrol circling over them.

Flycatcher and her owl companion, Tuft, alighted before the two rabbits. "I heard the call for the ravens. Do you know which magus summoned them?" she asked. The Little Peepers did not have the well-honed hearing of the rabbits.

"That was Sorcerer Spellbinder," said Lapin. "I would suggest that Ruby and Shauna be kept out of sight because the ravens will soon be searching for them."

"I will report back to Queen Wista immediately."

"I recommend that you first relay the message to the sky patrols on your way to Arborville," said Lapin. "They need to keep a sharp eye out for the ravens, particularly their leader Gavran. Most likely, they will be heading toward Witch Zeldar's house."

"I will pass on your message to the patrols and the queen," Flycatcher replied.

"I will inform the ground troops, as well," said Lapin.

"The ravens might decide not to help the Malum," said Flycatcher.

"We will soon see where their loyalty lies," Lapin said, wearing a grim face. His hind leg was pounding the forest floor.

Flycatcher leaned over Tuft and touched Lapin's nose to show her deep respect for the commander. Next, she and her long-eared owl took to the air.

Lapin directed Poppin to relay the newest information to the other rabbit regiments and to the other animals of the forest.

Chapter Nine

Flight School

Vorte held onto Shauna as they took a taxi bird to Aviation School. Their bird was a semi-retired falcon named Swift, who once was King Hoppit's favorite daytime ride. Before his death, King Hoppit was regularly seen soaring high above the clouds and over Hidden Forest on Swift. After the king died from his fall, Swift fell into a deep depression. It was Vorte and Berruga who eventually pulled him out of his gloom. Afterward, he worked part-time as a taxi bird and kept company with the other falcons.

Aviation School was located in a pine tree between two limbs shaped like outstretched bird wings. Swift landed on the branch to the right. Both Vorte and Swift gave last-minute instructions to Shauna.

"While riding, do not lean too far to one side," said Swift.

Vorte helped Shauna get down from Swift. "Always be polite to your bird companions. Your life is in their hands."

"You mean, their wings," Swift corrected Vorte.

Oide was standing at the entrance to his school, heartily greeting his students. "Oh, what a fine day for flying! Oh, there is our new pupil! Watch your step on the branch, Shauna. Morning dew sometimes makes the bark slippery."

Shauna peered down at her feet. She had on wooden shoes. Vorte had stayed up late last night to carve shoes out of red mulberry wood for the girls. He traded huckleberries to an elf for the mulberry wood. He wanted to make them sensible shoes. Red mulberry wood was resistant to decay. But wooden shoes were not the most comfortable on the feet.

"Where is your sister, Shauna?" Oide called out to her.

"She was out last night, chasing down Sorcerer Serpentine's kids," said Shauna. "She's catching up on sleep this morning."

"Oh, my, crickets! I had heard she had gone with the search party. I was here until late last night, preparing flight lessons. Is she all right?" said Oide. His bulging eyes were about to pop out of their sockets.

"Ruby is no worse for the wear. She just needs some rest," Vorte replied, who was right behind Shauna. "However, the search party did not locate Serpentine's offspring. But the searchers discovered the mother's name. Another scouting party will be sent to search for them as soon as possible."

Oide cast a baffled look at Vorte. "We could bend Serpentine's mind to tell us. He should know the location of his own children."

"The mother hid her children away from Serpentine," explained Vorte. "I can't blame her for that."

"The human world is a big place to search," noted Oide. "Luckily, we have birds that can fly a long way, if need be."

"True," agreed Vorte. "But only a dragon can carry three children and their mother back to Hidden Forest."

"Jackie and her kids could be driven here by car," suggested Shauna.

"The rabbits have told me about those contraptions with four wheels made by humans," said Oide. "But I have only seen their flying machines."

Shauna scrunched up her nose. "Airplanes?"

"Yes, airplanes," said Oide. "We have seen them flying numerous times over Hidden Forest, but no one from the forest can figure out how these *airplanes* can stay up in the air without flapping their wings. It's best we stick with birds."

Vorte wished Shauna a good day in school and then he reluctantly left with Swift. He kept looking back at Shauna, who was talking with Oide in the doorway.

"Do not fret, Vorte," said Swift as soon as they landed on the ground. "I will watch her during her solo flights. If she falls, I will snatch her from the air. However, no student has ever tumbled off a pilot bird. The pilot birds have lots of experience with novices."

"I never want to lose another child again," Vorte said sadly. "The pain nearly killed me. It was just as hard on Berruga, too."

"I know the pain of loss and suffering," said Swift. "We birds will never again let the Malum strike us down from the air or put us into cages. We will always be on the side of the Little Peepers, no matter what."

Briefly, Vorte put his hand on Swift's beak to show his appreciation. "I have heard the ravens are remaining neutral if the Malum go on the attack again."

"I have my doubts. A raven's word cannot be trusted," Swift said bitterly. "The Malum have never caged the ravens as they did the other birds."

"The next time it might be different for the ravens, if the Malum return. They might become caged birds."

"Let us hope we never find out," replied Swift.

Vorte gave Swift a smile of gratitude. "Thank you for the lift. I don't know how Berruga and I would manage without your services. And friendship," he added, widening his smile.

"Do you need a lift to your treehouse?"

"No, thank you. I have business to conduct on the forest floor. Have a good day, Swift."

"You, too." Swift took flight to hunt for his morning meal. He was hoping to quickly grab a mouse or a vole to eat while Shauna was in the classroom. Unlike the Black Dragon, the falcons and the other local birds did not hunt in Hidden Forest. They entered the human world to catch their prey. They did not want to make enemies in the forest, except with the magi.

In the meantime, Oide was introducing Shauna to her classmates. There were twelve pupils and twelve birds, evenly split between owls, falcons, and hawks, squeezed inside a giant tree cavity. Oide stood before them as he explained the four forces of flight—weight, lift, drag, and thrust. There would be no assigned homework. The final test would be to stay upright on a great gray owl at full speed. Initially, Shauna felt a sense of relief. But suddenly, it saddened her. Her mom wanted her to become a pilot, astronaut, or some sort of aviator because both of them dreamed of flying. Shauna was certain that flying on top of a bird wasn't exactly what her mother had in mind. She felt a hand nudging her. It belonged to the classmate to her right. Shauna couldn't recall the classmate's name.

"Don't be frightened," the girl said kindly. "Father says that new students never fly solo their first time out."

Shauna forced a smile. "I'm okay. I flew on a bird yesterday."

The girl pretended to be impressed, even though Little Peepers flew on birds even as infants in their parent's arms.

"The newest pupils will fly with experienced pilots," announced Oide. "Once again, no student of mine has ever fallen off a bird. Now, let's head outside. To learn how to fly, one must take to the air. No somersaults or nosedives on your first day out, either," he warned his pupils. "Don't be the first student to fall from the sky."

Shauna gulped and trailed behind her classmates as they filed out the door. Oide assigned each student to a veteran pilot and an equally accomplished bird. They had been waiting on a tree limb for the new students.

Oide gestured at Hummer and his spotted owl, Dots. "I want the two of you to accompany Shauna. First, take her for a spin around Emerald Valley and then out to the territory of the Second Regiment of the Noble Rabbits. While you're there, take a look below and see if the ravens are holding a meeting in their fir tree. Queen Wista asked us to check it out for her."

"Will do," replied Hummer, saluting Oide.

"The ravens cannot be trusted," muttered Dots under her breath.

"Have a safe flight," Oide said to Dots. "And, if the ravens give you any trouble, Luna and Chase will be nearby, patrolling that section of the forest." Luna was the veteran patrol pilot and Chase was her peregrine falcon, who won last year's speed contest. If Little Peepers had a way to measure speed, they would have discovered that Chase clocked an impressive two hundred twenty-three miles per hour. Oide was also in charge of scheduling all the flight patrols and flying contests for Hidden Forest.

"All aboard," Hummer said to Shauna, extending her a helping hand. "Let me assist you onto Dots' back."

"Thank you." Shauna sat in front of Hummer. "I went out for a ride yesterday with Kreen and Skit."

"So, I heard. Today we will fly a little faster, as if we were chasing after a witch on a broom," said Hummer.

"Do witches fly fast?"

"About the speed of a spotted owl. Right, Dots?"

Dots hooted, as if insulted. "Hang on!" She took off without making a sound. Shauna jerked backward. "Hey, there's Specks over there by the big cloud. Abruptly, she let out a *cooo-weep*. Specks answered with four doglike barks.

"What are they saying to each other?" Shauna whispered to Hummer.

"They are greeting each other," said Hummer.

"Specks is a Southwest spotted owl. I'm from the Northwest. That's why her feathers are lighter in color than mine, but not in weight," explained Dots.

Shauna had not noticed the color difference, but their hoots were completely different from one another. "How come there are so many types of owls in the forest?"

"The various kinds of species have always been here in the forest," replied Dots.

"Can a desert owl live in the forest?" asked Shauna.

"Of course. Hidden Forest is magical. Anyone can survive here if they remain alert."

Immediately, Shauna sat up straighter and widened her eyes.

"Oh, look, the fairies are clearing the meadow of frog-snakes." Dots gestured by tilting her head. "Yesterday morning, a snake was spotted just outside Arborville."

Shauna spotted dozens of fairies fanned out across Jade Meadow, waving their wands. "How often do they get rid of the snakes?"

"Whenever one is spotted in the meadow," replied Hummer. "The fairies will shrink the snakes down to the size of inchworms and take them to another part of the forest. But eventually, the fairy's magic wears off and the snakes grow back."

"And then they come back to the meadow to look for a Little Peeper to snag," added Dots.

Shauna scanned the world below her. "Why can't you get rid of the snakes by killing them?"

"The snakes were created from black magic. They cannot be destroyed, not even by fairy magic," said Hummer. "Trust me, we have tried various ways of killing them. We even chopped off one snake's head, but it just grew back within a day."

"Did you try chopping the snake up into tiny parts?" asked Shauna.

"Yes. All the pieces just grew back together," replied Hummer. "Only black magic can destroy black magic."

Dots veered left toward the territory of the Second Regiment of the Noble Rabbits. She explained to Shauna that the ten rabbit regiments encircled the Hidden Forest in numerical order. "It makes it easier to locate them."

"Why are they called Noble Rabbits?" mused Shauna.

"They gave themselves that title because their self-sacrificing nature allows the Black Dragon to live here," explained Hummer. "In other words, the dragon preys on them."

"The dragon eats them?" Shauna made a repulsive face. "That's horrible! Why don't you make the dragon live somewhere else?"

Dots rotated her head to exchange a look with Hummer. "At one time, there were too many rabbits for the forest to support. The dragon kept their population in check. But now, the rabbit population is on a decline. I do not think the commanders of the rabbit regiments will tolerate the Black Dragon's presence much longer."

Shauna gazed at the seemingly endless forest interrupted by open meadows, lakes, and ponds. "Why didn't the rabbits leave the forest when there were too many of them?"

"They would have died from old age," said Hummer. "The magic of Hidden Forest keeps them young. Some of the rabbits are over a hundred years old, like Commander Lapin, who rescued you from the garden shed."

"Will I get old someday?"

"Only if you leave Hidden Forest," replied Hummer.

"Then, I will never leave . . . but will I grow older than nine?"

"I imagine so. Our offspring grow into adults, then they stop growing older," said Hummer.

"Our young, too, grow into mature adults," said Dots. "But we never get old."

"But, keep in mind, years in the human world are not the same in the magical world," said Hummer. "For instance, I am twenty-five years old in my world and will remain so for a long time."

"So, you will still look twenty-five when you're a hundred?"

"Yes. Time is very different for us. We don't even start our families until we're hundreds of years old."

"Are you a thousand years old when you first become a grandparent?" asked Shauna, looking perplexed.

"Maybe so. None of us are old enough to be grandparents, yet . . . except for the rabbits. There are many generations of them."

Shauna whistled under her breath. Some of her neighbors in the city were grandparents before they had gray hair and wrinkles. "I think I'll need more time to absorb all of this."

"Take all the time you need," said Hummer, smiling. "We have time to spare in the magical world."

"Am I nine years old right now or some other age?" asked Shauna, still appearing confused.

"You're nine," said Hummer. "You take your age with you to Hidden Forest. But if you remain here, you will age the same as the rest of us."

Shauna felt a sense of relief remaining her current age.

"Even though the Great Banishment occurred only thirteen years ago, the Malum have aged greatly. The magic of the forest had protected them from aging," said Hummer. "Before they were banned from Hidden Forest, they were young and handsome. They never aged a single day in the forest."

"But their hearts were shriveled up before their banishment," muttered Dots.

"Who knows if they even have hearts," Hummer replied.

"If you look yonder, you will see that the ravens have congregated together in a large number," said Dots. Below them was a gigantic tree with a black scorch mark on its trunk. Its branches were chock-full of ravens.

"We will report this back to Queen Wista," said Hummer, squinting his eyes as he counted the number of ravens. There were fifty-eight of them convening in the fir tree. "Ravens were messenger birds for the Malum," he explained to Shauna. "Queen Wista wants us to keep a close eye on the ravens, in case the Malum will need them to locate Serpentine's children."

"How can the Malum call them all the way from the human world?" asked Shauna.

"Some ravens live near the forest's edge, not far from Zeldar's place," said Hummer. "All ravens report to their leader, Gavran."

"Have the rabbit patrols been notified of the situation?" Dots asked Hummer.

"Flycatcher and Tuft notified the regiment commanders this morning," answered Hummer. "But the rabbits were already aware of the situation."

"Swift is nearby. He has been following us ever since we passed by the big cloud that resembles a giant bumblebee." Dots directed her gaze at the peregrine falcon. "He must've been assigned to watch the ravens, too."

"Swift is watching out for me," said Shauna. "He told Vorte that he would do so."

"I will let Swift know that we are heading back." Hummer pointed in the direction of Arborville.

On their return flight, both Hummer and Dots helped Shauna adjust her weight for a better balance.

"Shift your body weight in the direction of your owl companion," instructed Hummer. "Or else you could lose your balance and be knocked out of your seat."

"Tuck down and lean in during a strong headwind," said Dots. "If you lean back, the wind will blow you backward and off your bird."

Shauna reacted by gripping Dots tighter. But not too tight. She did not pull on the feathers. According to Hummer, that was the worst thing to do to a bird, aside from caging it.

"Eventually, you will have to learn how to fly through storms," said Hummer. "But owls cannot fly in the rain. That's why it's so important to learn how to fly on various bird species, like ducks and geese."

"Sometimes Little Peepers are reluctant to fly on other birds because owls are such smooth flyers," explained Dots with a touch of pride. "We do not have to flap our wings as much as other birds in order to fly and we can glide for long stretches." She shook her head. "Poor ducks. They really have to get their wings flapping to achieve lift. Nonetheless, you must master flight on all bird species, except for the ravens. Do not ride on top of a raven. Ravens cannot be trusted," she reminded her.

"I'll remember and I'll tell Ruby, too," said Shauna. She had forgotten that she had been mad at her sister for leaving last night without telling her.

Clouds were beginning to bunch up on the horizon. The wind was becoming stronger and hotter. Shauna's leg muscles were aching from the flight. And they were only halfway back to Arborville. When they reached the edge of Jade Meadow, Dots noticed trouble brewing beneath them. A frog-snake was sneaking up on a fairy, who was oblivious to the danger. The fairy was engrossed in a deep conversation with a tree nymph, also known as a dryad. The snake was coiled on a nearby tree branch, poised to strike the fairy from behind. Dots dropped down from the sky as fast as she could. Just as she landed, the snake attacked. The tree nymph screamed as the fairy attempted to jump out of the way. The snake knocked the wind out of the fairy and the wand out of her hand.

Shauna recognized the fairy. It was Flicker. She had been one of the five fairies who reduced Ruby and her to their present size.

The dryad escaped by hiding in her oak tree while Hummer leapt off Dots and dashed toward Flicker, who was sprawled out on the ground. Seeing that he would never reach Flicker before the snake struck again, he used his mindbending ability to tell the snake to leave the fairy alone and go away. Since there was only one of him to get inside the snake's mind, he could only temporarily confuse the frog-snake. In a moment or two, the snake would be able to shake Hummer out of its head. The snake would regain control of its own mind.

In the meantime, Dots was cautiously inching her way toward Flicker, who appeared too frightened to move. The snake was baring its fangs at her. As this was unfolding, no one was paying attention to Shauna. She ran over to the fairy's wand and picked it up. As the snake flicked its tongue at Shauna, she pointed the wand at it and shouted, "Go away!"

No one had expected it, especially the snake. A stream of gold flecks sprayed out of the tip of the wand. The snake was tossed through the air and slammed against the wide trunk of an evergreen tree, twenty-five feet away. Not even the most powerful fairy could fling a full-sized snake that far. Before anyone could react, Swift dropped down from above at top speed. He landed in front of Flicker. The peregrine falcon was the first to notice that Flicker was bleeding from the shoulder. Apparently, the tip of the snake's fang had sliced open her flesh.

"The snake venom will kill her," said Hummer in a panicked voice. Flicker moaned before she lost consciousness. "We need to take her to the elves. They have an antidote that will save her life."

"I will fly her there," said Swift. "Who will hold her? I cannot carry her with my talons because of her fragile state."

"I will go with you, Swift," offered Hummer. He looked over at Shauna. "Can you fly solo on Dots?"

Shauna nodded because she had not regained her voice yet due to the frightful experience. She was still clutching Flicker's wand.

Hummer removed the wand from Shauna's hand and picked up the lifeless Flicker. He placed her on the falcon's back and then climbed aboard. Swift took off in haste.

The tree nymph reappeared from her oak tree. "You are not a Little Peeper," she said to Shauna. "Only a Malum can toss a snake that distance using only a wand."

"Actually, I did it with my mind. I imagined the snake hurling through the air . . . and it just happened."

"The wand read your mind and obeyed you. That is worrisome." Abruptly, the tree nymph vanished into her tree once more.

"Tree nymphs are known to be shy," Dots said, explaining the dryad's sudden disappearance. "They do not stick around for long."

"Why is it worrisome?"

"Because your magic is more powerful than the fairies. And you are so young to have such magical ability."

"I would never hurt anyone."

"I know. You will have to learn how to control your magic. A badly aimed wand could kill someone." *And reacting before thinking could also kill somebody*, thought Dots. More than once she had seen an ill-tempered magus harm another. Magic seemed to have gone straight to the Malum's heads and poisoned their hearts.

"Will Flicker die?"

"Certainly not. The elves will revive her with their herbs and potions."

"Will the snake come back?"

"I am afraid so. A snake like that always does," Dots replied in a frustrated tone.

Shauna glanced at the horizon and saw dark clouds as thick as sludge. "You can't fly in the rain."

"All the more reason to hurry home. Also, Vorte and Berruga will be worried about you."

The first drops of rain began to fall. Dots flapped her wings harder, increasing thrust.

Chapter Ten

The Missing

Due to her short stature, Ruby asked Counselor Nirva to tug on the library door. It was locked despite it being the middle of the day.

"It won't open," Nirva said. "What shall we do?"

"The library must be closed. I bet it's Sunday." Ruby had lost track of the days. In Hidden Forest, there were no names for specific days. Besides Nirva, Counselor Herona was with her along with her companion bird, a great gray owl named Rings. Nirva had transformed into a whiskered screech-owl and flown to the library. She changed back into her elf form as she stood in front of the building.

"We'll knock on the door and see if Miss Whiskers is here," replied Ruby. Nirva rapped loudly on the door.

A good thirty seconds had passed before a large, orange cat inspected them through the glass door. She opened the door by pressing a button on the wall.

"Welcome back, Miss Ruby," said Miss Whiskers. "Would you like to introduce me to your friends?" She was surprised to see Ruby return so soon.

"May we please come in first?" whispered Ruby, nervously peering over her shoulder. "The Malum might be out in full force. By now, they probably are aware that Jackie Jubilee and her children skipped town."

"I can assure you that none of the magi are here," replied Miss Whiskers, composed as ever. "But please come in and inform me of your circumstances. And why you have come here."

It was Counselor Herona who made the introductions and explained that they needed to stop the Malum from locating Jackie Jubilee and her offspring. In the middle of her explanation, her amber eyes began to shine like a couple of spotlights. "Is that a spellbook I see over there?" She pointed to a gray cart piled high with books ready to be shelved. On the top of the stack was a book titled, *The Top 100 Magic Spells for Beginners.* A drawing of a gnarled wand ran down the book's spine.

Miss Whiskers nodded without looking at the cart. She made it her job to know the whereabouts of every library book. "Magic books are popular amongst certain library patrons."

"If we could find a spell that would make the Malum forget who they were in the first place, such as an amnesia spell, they would die from old age," Herona said excitedly.

"I didn't realize fairies could cast spells like magi and deity," said Miss Whiskers.

"We might have a couple of individuals in our midst that can," replied Counselor Nirva. She did not tell the cat librarian that one of them was Ruby.

"How many books about magic does the library have?" asked Ruby.

"Forty-eight books," Miss Whiskers replied without hesitating.

"Do you know of a spellbook that might help us?" asked Counselor Herona, who was amazed by all the books on the library shelves.

"Most books are helpful in one way or another," said Miss Whiskers.

"Perhaps we could take a look at them," said Counselor Nirva.

"What you are looking for is not in an ordinary library book," said Miss Whiskers. She noticed the disappointment on their faces. "But I might be able to help you." Their disheartened expressions swiftly changed to hopeful looks. "Mister Barnaby lives with a Wiccan, Madame Papulose. He says that she has all sorts of books pertaining to spells and potions. In fact, it is a hobby of hers to collect spellbooks."

"Does she live near here?" asked Counselor Nirva.

"It's within walking distance," replied Miss Whiskers. "Mister Barnaby will be arriving here shortly. He is a member of our book club and is picking up next month's book selection, *The Master and Margarita* by Mikhail Bulgakov. It's about a vodka-swilling, gun-crazy, wise-cracking cat who pals around with the devil. You've never heard of it? Why it's a classic among Russian cats," she said, after noticing their blank stares. "Never mind. Mister Barnaby can show you to the home he shares with Madame Papulose."

"Does this Mister Barnaby hang out with people in black cloaks?" said Ruby, nervously. It was possible that Madame Papulose was actually one of the magi.

"Madame Papulose wears a black cloak," replied Miss Whiskers. "She's kindhearted. I have heard others describe her as peculiar, though."

"We will wait for this Mister Barnaby," Counselor Nirva said matter-of-factly to the others. "In the meantime, I am still interested in seeing your books on magic."

"The books are written in a human language," said Miss Whiskers. "But Ruby and I could translate them for you."

"Yes, I would like that very much," said Nirva, bowing respectfully to Miss Whiskers.

"We will accept all the help you have to offer," Herona said politely.

There was another knock on the door and Miss Whiskers went to open it. She was astonished to find two ghosts in old-fashioned wedding attire at the library door. "Would you like to come in?"

"Yes, thank you," replied Opal.

Miss Whiskers opened the door wider while wondering if the ghosts would walk right through her. But Opal and Edward skirted around the orange cat that stood in the doorway.

"Oh, look, my dear Edward! Our little friend, Ruby, is here!" gushed Opal. She drifted over to Ruby.

"I met Opal and Edward at Jackie Jubilee's house," Ruby explained.

Quick introductions were made before getting down to the reason they came. The ghost couple proceeded to tell them about their encounter with Serpentine in Jackie Jubilee's backyard soon after the search and rescue group departed.

"So, we now have proof that the Malum do not know the whereabouts of Serpentine's offspring," stated Nirva, contemplatively.

"They will attempt to make a deal with the ravens to find Serpentine's children . . . or Highbrow's children," said Rings, peering at Ruby.

"Queen Wista was right," said Herona. "She sent out word early this morning asking the other animals to keep an eye on the ravens."

"I would guess the magi are familiar with computers and cars," said Ruby, her worries increasing. "They have ways of tracking people other than using ravens."

"The Malum are stubborn in their ways," said Herona. "Most likely, they will fall back on their old ways."

"Highbrow knows how to use a gun. He shot my mother in the head with a gun instead of whacking her over the head with a wand," Ruby reminded them.

"He sounds worse than the dastardly villains that I have read about in books," declared Miss Whiskers.

Ruby caught sight of Opal and Edward looking offended. They were standing beside the library suggestion box. Opal picked up a pen and a scrap of paper and wrote, "Ghosts are not entirely invisible. I suggest that you start paying attention to them." She shoved the paper into the suggestion box.

"What's wrong?" asked Ruby.

"Edward and I made a special trip here to tell you something of utmost importance," said Opal, wearing a hurt look. "Ghosts are not hollow beings without hearts and minds. We have feelings and opinions. Don't we, dear?"

"That is correct, my dear Opal."

The others apologized to Opal and Edward because they did forget they were standing there. They *were* hard to see.

They were interrupted by a voice coming from the next room. "I hope you don't mind if I let myself in, Miss Whiskers. But the cat door was left unlocked." A black cat entered the front lobby. "Holy Cat! Who are these individuals? Those two over there look like a couple of ghosts—"

"Mister Barnaby, I would like for you to meet Counselor Nirva. As you can see for yourself, you can tell by her pointy ears that she is an elf"—Miss Whiskers gestured toward her own pointed ears—"which makes her more distinguished, I might add." Next, she motioned to Herona and Ruby. "They are Little Peepers. But the shorter one is Ruby, who is actually a twelve-year-old human transformed into a Little Peeper. The fairies shrunk her to her present size."

"Holy Cat!" repeated Mister Barnaby.

Miss Whiskers nodded toward the great gray owl. "And this is Rings, who flies the Little Peepers from place to place. They are all from an enchanted forest called Hidden Forest. Its location is behind

Dead End Street, where that nasty woman, Zeldar, takes pleasure in poisoning cats."

"I am very familiar with that horrid woman," huffed Mister Barnaby. "Someday I would like to put poison in her food. And see how she would feel about that! That is, if she lives to tell about it."

Lastly, Miss Whiskers introduced Opal and Edward. "These two distinguished guests are from our local Hillside Cemetery. They have come here to assist in the search for the children of a vile sorcerer." She let out a deep breath. "Did I miss anyone or leave anything out?"

"That's about everyone, Miss Whiskers," said Herona, clearly impressed by the librarian cat's attention to detail.

"So far, I have lived seven lives and have seen and heard many unusual things. But this situation is the most unusual of all," declared Mister Barnaby.

"They need to find an amnesia spell that will erase the memory of nine evil Malum who were cast out of Hidden Forest. Zeldar is one of them. All of them have lost their powers," continued Miss Whiskers.

"Serves her right," muttered Mister Barnaby.

"These Malum are bent on returning to the enchanted woods to seek revenge against the forest creatures who banished them. I think I covered most of it," said Miss Whiskers.

"You summed up the situation nicely," replied Herona.

"That's a lot to take in," said Mister Barnaby. "But fortunately, I have a quick mind." He hitched up his tail a little higher.

Miss Whiskers twitched her long, white whiskers, as she fixed her green eyes on Mister Barnaby. "Do you suppose Madame Papulose has a book with an amnesia spell in it?"

"I could look for you in one of her many spellbooks," said Mister Barnaby. "Even if there is a spell for amnesia, Madame Papulose could not perform it. She just pretends to be a witch. She has no real magic in her."

"We might have someone from Hidden Forest who can cast an amnesia spell," said Herona, her eyes darting over to Ruby.

Ruby looked down at her feet. She had her doubts that she could perform any serious magic. What if she is more like Madame Papulose than Witch Zeldar?

"Come with me," Mister Barnaby said. "I will show you Madame Papulose's spellbooks."

Edward caught everyone's attention by loudly clearing his throat. "Opal and I would like to come along to help. We are proficient readers."

"I was the spelling bee champion throughout my eight years in school," Opal boasted. "Besides, Edward and I are growing tired of the cemetery. We want to get out around town more and meet more of the locals who still have a pulse."

"Eight years spent in school is a long time," exclaimed Nirva. "Humans must be slow learners."

"Humans cover more topics than elves," said Ruby, who was as deeply offended as the ghosts. "Nowadays, most people attend school for thirteen years or more."

"Oh, my," said Nirva, still wondering why humans needed so much schooling.

"I am well-educated and didn't spend a single day in school. I learned everything from this library," stated Miss Whiskers.

"Will you come with us to Mister Barnaby's place, Miss Whiskers?" asked Ruby.

"I'm afraid that I cannot leave the library unattended." She was tempted to go along with the others, but she felt an obligation to guard the library books against the mice in the basement. If she took an eye off the library for a second, the mice were brazenly running off with a book. If they didn't like the book, the mice shredded the pages and made a nest out of the paper. They seemed to be always having babies.

Just as they departed from the library, a raging thunderstorm blew in and was upon them. Counselor Nirva put Rings on her right shoulder and placed Ruby and Herona in her pocket. She put a hat on to hide her pointy ears from curious eyes, as well as to keep the rain out of her face. She kept her face toward the ground and hastened to Mister Barnaby's home. In spite of the driving wind, Ruby and Herona kept mostly warm, dry, and out of sight. Once they arrived at their destination, Mister Barnaby opened the door, shook out his drenched fur, and let them in. Madame Papulose was not home. She was attending a Wiccan event.

None of them realized that Sorcerer Serpentine lived across the street from Mister Barnaby's residence . . . or, that Serpentine had returned home to collect his belongings before skipping town.

Chapter Eleven

The Black Dragon's Surprise Visit

Prince Massen and Rupin, Tark's brother, were in the royal courtyard when the Black Dragon circled over their heads and then landed with a heavy thud. The dragon was the size of an elephant and its snout was twice as long as an alligator's. The fourteen-year-old boys backed away from the dragon, fearing for their lives.

Most elves were having their midafternoon meal in their homes. They rushed out of their houses to see what caused the commotion, even Queen Rossen.

The dragon was in a fury. From his mouth, he shot fireballs high into the air, lighting up the sky. As soon as he laid eyes on the elf queen, he turned on her. "Someone has been stealing from me! Which one among you is the thief?" He motioned to all of the observers, who kept a safe distance from his fire-breathing mouth.

"I assure you, no one in Glenhaven has been stealing from you," said Queen Rossen. She had never seen the Black Dragon so upset in all of her life, making her wonder which of his many treasures had been stolen from him.

Tark, who had just arrived, crept closer to his brother and the prince. He was hoping to grab them out of harm's way. Presently, they were still in the courtyard, too petrified to run or shapeshift into a swift animal. The dragon continued to accuse the elves of pillaging his loot. Plumes of hot smoke and smoldering ash escaped from his mouth as he called them thieves and scoundrels.

The elves could shapeshift into dragons. However, they would not be able to emit fire. They wouldn't stand a chance against the Black Dragon's fiery breath. They would be charred within moments.

"I want my treasures returned by sunset tomorrow. Every coin, gem, gold sword, silver and gold cup must be brought back to me. If I discover something has not been returned, I will burn down your village!"

Tark was within several feet of Rupin and Massen. As he positioned himself to grab the boys out of the courtyard, the dragon suddenly took flight and snatched Rupin and Massen with his sharp talons. The boys yelled for help. Tark sprang into action, reaching out to yank them free from the dragon's clutch. He missed them by a hair. The onlookers shouted at the dragon, pleading with him to let go of the boys. Rupin and Massen shapeshifted into chickadees, mice, and other sorts of small animals. But the dragon did not lose his grip on the captives.

"I will return them to you once I have my treasures back!" the dragon shouted down at the horrified spectators. He wheeled once in the air and then headed straight for his lair, where he would wait for his stolen loot to be returned.

Queen Rossen faced the crowd. The spectators were staring at her as they waited for her next reaction. She could not consult with Counselor Nirva, who had gone to the human world. However, she did not fully trust her three official councilmembers. In fact, she mostly disregarded them and instead consulted with her own handpicked advisors.

"Shall we go after the Black Dragon, my queen?" asked her second advisor, Baruk.

"We will discuss this matter in my chambers." Rossen motioned for Baruk and Tark to come with her. She considered Tark to be wiser than Advisor Baruk. Unfortunately, Tark was not born into the elite class and his opinion was not considered to be as valuable as Baruk's. Both Baruk and Nirva were related to high officials.

"Are we not going to rescue the boys?" a voice called out from the middle of the crowd.

"The issue with the Black Dragon will be resolved," Rossen promised the onlookers. "Please continue on with your day. I will take care of this matter." The elves obeyed her, though they were clearly disturbed by what had just occurred.

Tark tried to remain composed, reminding himself that the dragon would not dare harm Massen or Rupin. It was just a matter of tracking down the stolen loot and returning it to the dragon.

After entering the queen's private chambers, Rossen requested that Tark and Baruk seat themselves on two silken chairs and then ordered a servant to bring them nectar-sweetened mint drinks. As they waited for their drinks, Rossen seated herself across from Tark and Baruk. "So, who do you think is behind the theft?"

"If one of us did not take the dragon's loot, then it has to be the rabbits," said Tark.

"Or the gnomes," said Baruk.

Rossen regarded Tark and ignored Baruk. "Why the rabbits?"

"There has been talk among them that they could no longer tolerate the Black Dragon preying upon them," said Tark.

"I suppose the rabbits want to cut a deal with the dragon," mused Rossen. "If the dragon no longer feeds on rabbits, what will he eat instead?"

"Hopefully, not elves," jested Baruk.

Rossen rolled her eyes and latched her gaze on Tark. "What do you think?"

"I think the rabbits are desperately trying to save themselves," he replied. "Their population has dropped off while the dragon's appetite has not."

The servant returned with their mint drinks. They did not speak again until the servant left the room.

Rossen shifted in her seat, eyeing Tark. The young elf resembled his late mother. "We need to spy on the rabbits."

"What about Prince Massen and my brother?" asked Tark.

"We should ask the Little Peepers to get involved," said Baruk, who was desperately trying to win favor with his queen. He desired to be her top advisor, replacing Counselor Nirva. "With their mindbending skills, they can either make the Black Dragon bring back Prince Massen and Rupin, or they can make the rabbits simply return the treasure."

Queen Rossen contemplated the matter for a few seconds. "The Little Peepers will not make the rabbits return the stolen goods. The Little Peepers and the rabbits are extremely loyal to each other. They will not betray one another."

"Perhaps we should first speak to Commander Lapin," said Tark. "He will know for sure if his fellow rabbits have stolen the treasure. And, if so, where it is."

"I have no doubts that the rabbits have taken it." Rossen knitted her brow, disturbed by the sudden turn of events. "This is not a good time for the rabbits to start a rebellion."

"They might disagree," said Tark. "We need their numbers more than ever to patrol our vast borders. And they know it. They are taking this opportunity to improve their situation."

"The Black Dragon is no longer needed in the forest," said Baruk. "May I suggest we get rid of him once we have retrieved Prince Massen and Rupin?"

Rossen pursed her lips while listening to them. "We still need to retrieve the boys before we can take action against the Black Dragon. We must convince the Little Peepers to use their mindbending skills to bring the boys back to us."

Tark closed his eyes as he attempted to shut out the scene occurring in his head. Dark figures had entered his mind. He saw their hands fighting over treasure.

Rossen and Baruk observed Tark, who was squeezing his eyes shut as if forcing back a bad headache. One of the main reasons Tark was one of the best spies was his extra-sensory perception. However, his second sight also gave him a throbbing headache whenever he spent too much time with Queen Rossen. His parents had never cared for the queen.

"What is the matter, Tark?" asked the queen.

"It is nothing of importance," lied Tark. He did not want to admit that one of the hands he saw in his vision belonged to the queen.

"We will go speak with Queen Wista," stated Rossen. "We must leave immediately for Arborville."

□ □ □

Prince Massen and Rupin caught sight of a large flock of ravens flying past them as the Black Dragon carried them to his lair on top of Misty Falls. They gave up on shapeshifting because the dragon's talons were like pincers. It was known that the dragon had the ability to clutch a gold coin in his razor-sharp talons. It was also said that he could melt a gold coin with his fiery breath. They did not want to discover if this was true or not. Both boys were hoping to escape once the dragon released his hold on them. It is possible that they could make their getaway as a mouse or a hummingbird. They would have to wait for the right opportunity to make their escape.

Rupin noticed the afternoon sun lighting up the tall trees below him, casting short shadows upon the land. While gazing at the earth below him, he spotted a unicorn on Unicorn Trail looking back at him. Its white coat and ivory horn were illuminated by the sunlight. He hoped the unicorn was a sign of good luck. The unicorn was not the only one who spotted the boys dangling from the dragon's talons. Skit and Kreen and their owl companions, who were returning to Arborville after trailing a flock of ravens, watched in shock as the young elves were carried away by the Black Dragon. They headed straight for the elf village to report their sighting. In the meantime, the fairies were enjoying an all-day festival. They were celebrating the blossoming of the wild roses, which was a symbolic flower to them. Periodically, fairy newborns made surprise appearances nestled in a rosebud. The fairies were in the midst of a show put on by a trio of young fairies twirling their wands when the spectators noticed the Black Dragon flying by with two elves. They immediately went to notify the elves and the Little Peepers. It did not take long for the forest inhabitants to learn about the dragon's capture of the two elves.

All the while, the ten royal commanders of the rabbit regiments were convening with the moles, Rooter, Erde, and Snoot, who had hidden the dragon's loot deep underground. When they heard about the boys' capture, the rabbit commanders were taken aback. They had anticipated that the dragon would immediately suspect them.

More than ever, the entire forest seemed on edge, as if danger was lurking behind every tree.

Chapter Twelve

The Ravens

The raven leader, Gavran, and his flock of a dozen ravens were tailed by the owl patrols. Just as they crossed the border, it began to downpour. The owls would be grounded until the rain stopped. Gavran hoped that the thunderstorm wouldn't let up. He didn't like being followed by the patrols.

The ravens decided to perch in an old apple tree in Witch Zeldar's overgrown yard full of weeds and rat poison, while Gavran spoke alone with the Malum inside the house. The ravens could hear the angry voices of the Malum carry all the way across the yard.

"If the voices become too loud or too quiet," Gavran said to the others, "check up on me." He headed toward Zeldar's back door and knocked on it with his beak.

"For Satan's sake," said Witch Zeldar, "that had better be Serpentine and his three brats."

"It's Gavran at your door," said Gavran. "Not Serpentine."

"I'll open it," said Spellbinder. His knees creaked loudly when he stood up. The others at the table winced.

"I'll get the door, Spellbinder," grumbled Underhand, who was the youngest among them. "You had better sit down before your legs give out."

"Hell's Bells! I can manage to open a door!" snapped Spellbinder.

"You're becoming grouchier in your old age, Spellbinder," retorted Underhand.

Gavran heard a chair scraping against the floor. A few seconds later, the door flew open. "Well, it's about time, Gavran," Spellbinder said testily. "I called for you when the moon was out. Now, it's daylight." He blinked and moved away from the doorway, as though the sunlight was bothering his eyes. But Gavran knew that his late appearance was more bothersome to the sorcerer than the sun.

"It's nice to see you again, too," the raven leader replied sarcastically. He entered the house, circled the living room a couple of times, and perched on the back of an empty wooden chair where

Serpentine was supposed to be. The Malum were sitting around the dining room table, watching him. He glanced around the table. Spellbinder rejoined them at the table.

Gavran noticed that the Malum had greatly aged since the last time he had seen them. Their long hair was grayer and their faces were thinner. They seemed distraught.

"Gavran, were you followed on your way here?" asked Witch Blackheart.

"As you very well know, it is impossible not to be seen by the patrols," answered Gavran. "The patrols have not let their guard down since your banishment. So, why did you call me here?"

"We need a favor from you," said Spellbinder. "As you can see for yourself, Sorcerer Serpentine is not here. We have already conducted our own search for him around town and did not find him. We can only assume that he took his three children and ran off with them. We need your help locating him."

"The children might already be dead," said Gavran. "The moon was full last night." The Malum were slightly taken aback that Gavran knew what they were up to. "All of the creatures of Hidden Forest are aware of your intentions," he added, after seeing their surprised expressions.

"All the more reason we need you to locate Serpentine before anyone else," spat Witch Mortify. "He will be punished if he tricked us."

"If he tricked you, then he will have his powers back," replied Gavran. "How would you be able to punish him? He could easily destroy you with his magic."

"Hell's Bells!" swore Spellbinder. His fist pounded the table. "We need you to find out what Serpentine is up to."

"Is that all you want from the ravens?" questioned Gavran. "To find Sorcerer Serpentine? Or are there others to locate, such as your children, Warlock Highbrow?"

"Are they still in the forest?" asked Warlock Highbrow, sounding both relieved and agitated. He would prefer that they drink the blood of Serpentine's offspring because he wanted to capture his own girls and experiment with spells on them.

Gavran knew the whereabouts of Shauna and Ruby. Earlier today he had seen the younger girl flying on the spotted owl, Dots. He was quite aware that the fairies had shrunken the girls to the size of Little Peepers. He also knew the girls were currently living among them. However, it was too soon to reveal this information to the Malum.

"If Serpentine's brats are still alive, we want to know where to find them," said Witch Blackheart. "There might be a chance that Serpentine lost his nerve and did not sacrifice his children."

"Next time I'll cut their throats," muttered Sorceress Hexla. "If Serpentine's brats are already dead, I will take a knife to your two girls," she said to Highbrow in a helpful tone. Her eyes were fixed on the shiny kitchen knife near him. "It'll be as easy as slicing warm butter."

"No, thank you, Hexla. I can manage to kill my own children. I'm not chickenhearted."

"If the ravens locate all the missing individuals, what do we get in exchange?" asked Gavran, concealing his distaste for the conversation. Ravens took good care of their offspring.

"What do you want?" asked Sorceress Underhand.

Gavran trusted Sorceress Underhand the least of all of them, though he would not dare say so. "We desire seed corn to see us through every winter for eternity."

The Malum immediately accepted his terms. They were in a hurry to find Serpentine. And once they had their powers back, they would break their promise to Gavran and his ravens.

"We will not begin our search for Serpentine until the garden shed in the backyard is stacked full of bags of seed corn," continued Gavran. "The corn cannot be old or moldy."

The magi glanced at one another and nodded.

"It's a deal," said Spellbinder.

"I will keep a few ravens stationed near here."

"Don't you trust us, Gavran?" questioned Blackheart.

"I will trust you when the shed is full of corn." Gavran bade them goodbye and returned to the apple tree, where the ravens were doing their best to remain out of the weather. It was still raining hard. The ravens were hunched under the tree's leafy canopy as Gavran presented them with the magi's offer. On a nearby tree sat a common crow eavesdropping on the ravens' conversation. However, she was not in reality a crow. It was the young, female elf, Auralia, who had carried the sleeping Ruby to the Little Peepers' village. She had shapeshifted into a crow when Massen and Rupin were kidnapped by the dragon. Initially, she followed the dragon until she spied the small flock of ravens heading for the forest's edge. Her intuition told her to follow the ravens because they were usually up to no good. Auralia was one of the best shapeshifters in all of Glenhaven. Not even another crow could tell the difference between Auralia in crow form and a real crow. Her long, heavy bill and fan-shaped tail were perfect. She would have made a superior spy, but she was not allowed to become one. She came from a family of beekeepers. She was expected to follow suit. She desperately wanted to be a spy. More than anything, she wanted to be accepted into the elf spy program, but she was not permitted to enroll. Agricultural workers were on the bottom rung of elf society's ladder.

She tilted her head toward the ravens. She soon learned the Malum wanted the ravens to track down the missing offspring. Because the Malum needed time to stock the shed with corn for the ravens, a search party from Hidden Forest would have a head start towards locating Serpentine's children.

As soon as the thunderstorm passed through, the ravens took flight. Three of them did not travel far. They perched themselves on a high bough of an evergreen tree, which provided a head-on view of the garden shed. Auralia did not follow any of the ravens. She went in search of Tark. She trusted him more than Queen Rossen.

Chapter Thirteen

Madame Papulose's House

While Sorcerer Serpentine was packing his bags across the street, Ruby and the others were searching through spellbooks in Madame Papulose's home. Madame Papulose was at the annual Wiccan convention, which was miles and miles away from there, and she would be gone for the entire weekend. The group was in the basement where books were stacked everywhere.

"If Miss Whiskers saw this mess, she would have a conniption," said Mister Barnaby. "Madame Papulose is a collector, but not much of an organizer."

Mister Barnaby searched through the piles of books, pulling out the spellbooks since they were scattered in different places. He was assigned this task because he knew how to read the book titles. The rest of the group combed through the books looking for an amnesia spell. Ruby had written out the word "amnesia" to aid their progress. Since Opal and Edward had read more books than the others, they were faster than the rest at scanning through the books. Rings, however, kept getting distracted by the drawings of owls. He wanted to know what was written about them and which owls or parts of owls were used in potions.

"Owl eyeballs are used to improve eyesight!" he said in disgust after Opal read the potion ingredients to him.

"We need to find an amnesia spell, not a potion," Herona reminded Rings. "It would be too difficult to make the Malum drink a potion."

Nirva was displeased that elves were never mentioned as the creators of any of the potions. She knew for a fact that half of the healing remedies were concocted by famous elves throughout the world.

Herona had to walk up and down the pages in order to view one in its entirety because of her diminutive size. Her legs and eyes began to grow tired from all the walking and searching. Ruby was capable of standing back and scanning an entire page without moving, but poor

Herona had to walk up to each word to see if it spelled out "amnesia." She swore the words kept moving on her.

"You're the one moving up and down," said Ruby, grinning.

"No, really, the words are moving on their own," insisted Herona.

At first, Ruby didn't believe her. However, after looking closer, Ruby saw some of the words shifting around the page. She closed her eyes and told the letters to hold still in one place. When she opened her eyes, the words no longer jumped around. She did not tell the others that she had made the words stop rearranging.

"I like this place. It reminds me of our graveyard—gloomy, eerie, and damp," Opal announced to Edward. "Perhaps we could move from the cemetery to this basement."

"It would be a pleasant change to have a roof over our heads," said Edward. "And not have the wind whooshing through us."

"Or raindrops falling through us," added Opal. "It's the most unpleasant sensation to feel rain without getting wet."

"I'm not sure Madame Papulose wants ghosts in the basement," said Mister Barnaby, who wasn't sold on the idea.

"How about the attic?" asked Opal. "Is it suitable for ghosts?"

"Spiders and mice already make it their home," said Mister Barnaby.

"Sounds perfect," said Opal, her pale face brightening.

"It gets hot up there in the summertime," Mister Barnaby warned her.

"Didn't you say earlier Madame Papulose was at a Wiccan convention?" asked Opal.

"I did," Mister Barnaby said hesitantly. He was unsure where Opal was going with her question.

"Then, I'm sure Madame Papulose would love to boast about having two ghosts in her house. Don't you think so, my sweet?"

"I believe so, dear."

"Upon Madame Papulose's return, will you please ask her if we could remain here with her, Mister Barnaby?" Wearing a broad grin, she peered at Edward. "I know that she'll say yes! Oh, love, wouldn't that be wonderful!"

"Yes, dear, it would. We would have all these books to read." He gestured at the mound of books nearest him. "And all the time in the world to read them."

"I cannot ask Madame Papulose because she does not understand me," said Mister Barnaby, not at all pleased about having chatty ghosts in the house. He realized putting them down in the basement and locking the door would not keep the ghosts from coming upstairs and invading his peace of mind.

"I guess that we will have to ask Madame Papulose ourselves," said Opal. She continued searching for an amnesia spell. All the while, in her mind, she was redecorating the basement.

Counselor Herona was holding a slip of paper in her hand. Using the broken tip of a pencil, Ruby had written out "amnesia" and "AMNESIA" on the note to aid Herona. For several seconds, Herona compared the words in her hand to the writing on the page. "I think I might have found the word," she said a bit hesitantly. She pointed to the word that caught her attention. "Is that it, Ruby?"

Ruby jogged over to Herona. The thick book smelled musty. She carefully pulled herself up onto the yellowing page because she did not want to tear it. The counselor motioned to the word on top of the page that held her interest. *AMNESIA* "The letters are so squiggly. They look like a jumble of worms. What does it say?"

Ruby's eyes traced the letters. "It looks right . . . I think. The words must have been written centuries ago when people wrote in fancy letters."

"Let me take a look at it. In my day, people regularly wrote in script," said Opal, who was eavesdropping on their conversation. "While courting, people expressed their feelings for each other with poetry and flowers." She sighed longingly. "Those were the days of true romance, weren't they, my love?"

"They truly were, my sweets," said Edward. "But I imagine spellbooks were written by wizards and sorcerers, who did not know true love . . . like ours."

"What a pity." Opal came over to Ruby and Herona and read the description of the spell. "Oh, how wonderful! That's an amnesia spell, all right! And the spellbook looks and smells like it came straight out of the Middle Ages."

"Holy Cat, we've done it!" Mister Barnaby said elatedly.

Opal and Mister Barnaby were beside themselves, as the others looked on. Opal danced a little Irish jig that she had learned from her Irish neighbors when she was a young girl.

"I feel alive again!" Opal declared, grinning at all of them. "We must move out of the graveyard at once, sweet Edward!"

Mister Barnaby suddenly lost some of his enthusiasm.

"Holy Pellets!" hooted Rings. He was perched on the windowsill of the small basement window, keeping a lookout for any sign of trouble. "I believe Sorcerer Serpentine is walking out the front door of the house across the street!"

The others rushed over to the window and saw a man in a black cloak and baseball cap hurrying to a black car. He was carrying a large suitcase.

"I recognize him," said Mister Barnaby with a shudder. "On more than one occasion, he called Madame Papulose a fraud for pretending to be a witch, which is true. But still, it's impolite to say it to a person's face."

"Should we follow him?" asked Counselor Nirva.

"How?" said Rings. "None of us can fly fast enough to keep up with a speeding car. If only we had a peregrine falcon with us."

"Herona and I could hide in the trunk," suggested Ruby.

"It's too risky. What if we were caught?" said Herona. "Serpentine could snap us in half or stomp on us."

They watched as Serpentine tossed his suitcase in the trunk of the car and then slammed the trunk shut.

"He's not being very quiet," noted Rings.

"Despite all the racket he's making, he appears to be sneaking out of town," said Ruby. "If we had some kind of tracking device, we could place it on his car."

"I don't have a tracking device, other than the microchip implanted in me . . . which is solely for identification if *I* need to be found. And I don't want to be *found*, dead or alive, in an evil sorcerer's trunk," said Mister Barnaby, adamantly. "Instead, we should memorize his license plate number . . . Hey, that's not his car! He doesn't own one since he wrecked his last week. Scratch that idea."

"That's probably a rental car," said Ruby.

"A rental car? What's that?" questioned Herona.

"A person pays to borrow a car to go somewhere and then returns it later," said Ruby. "Like a taxi bird, except people have to pay for their rides."

"Do people pay with gold and silver coins?" asked Herona.

119

"Sure," replied Ruby. She didn't want to explain the concept of a credit card to them.

"Even if it was his car, I don't know what a license plate is," said Nirva, straining her eyes.

"It looks like it's too late to tail him, anyway. He is already in the driver's seat," said Mister Barnaby, sounding relieved. He had never felt the urge to chase after the mice in his house, so going after the wicked magi was certainly out of the question.

"I wish we could use that amnesia spell on him right now," declared Nirva.

"But we can't erase his memories until we know for sure if he knows the whereabouts of his children," said Herona. "He might've told the other magi of their location. They will go after them."

"He looks panic-stricken and very old," said Rings, who had better eyesight then the others.

They watched in silence as Serpentine backed the car down the driveway and peeled off.

"It's not surprising that he wrecked his car. He's a bad driver," stated Ruby.

"I wonder if the other Malum are already helping him look for his children," said Nirva, as the taillights of the black sedan disappeared in the distance. "Or will he search on his own?"

"The other magi will definitely search for *him*," said Herona. "They have to be upset with him for allowing his children to escape through his fingers. Or, it's more likely they think he betrayed them. That's probably why he's going away in a rush."

"He might be heading straight for the place where Jackie and her children might be hiding," pointed out Opal.

"What do we do now?" asked Rings, who was still keeping surveillance from the basement window.

"Return to Hidden Forest with the spellbook," said Nirva. "We need to cast the amnesia spell on all the magi. Otherwise, they'll remind each other of who they are."

"Nirva is right," said Herona. "We need Serpentine and the other Malum to permanently forget who they are and what they are capable of doing."

"Another option is to hope the Malum die from old age before they find their children," said Rings.

"Let's take the book back to Hidden Forest since we can't chase after Serpentine in his car," said Herona.

"Madame Papulose has a copier, so there's no need to take the entire book with you. I will make a copy of the amnesia spell and give it to you," said Mister Barnaby.

"Half the time I do not know what you're talking about—a copier, a microchip, a rental car. What are these things?" said Counselor Nirva. "I question how we will ever be able to locate Serpentine and his children in the human world."

"The world has changed for us, too," said Opal with empathy. "When we were still alive, the things that you mentioned did not exist. However, we have learned and adapted accordingly. The younger ghosts introduced us to new ideas and the latest innovations. Isn't that so, my dearest Edward?"

"It is so, my lovely Opal." Edward grinned adoringly at his bride who had not aged a day since their wedding. "But my love for you will never change."

"I am blushing," replied Opal.

Ruby looked at Opal's face, which was as pallid as ever. She did not know what to make of their relationship. Her mother and stepfather constantly argued during their marriage. Not once did they confess their love for each other. Actually, they hated each other and threatened to leave one another. Once, her stepfather pulled a gun on her mother. Shauna screamed for him to leave. Ruby threw herself in front of her mother to protect her. He swore at all of them. Ruby and her mother and sister were crying, assuming he was going to shoot them all. But he put the gun down, kicked over a kitchen chair, and stormed out of their apartment. Although the incident occurred only a few months ago, it seemed like a lifetime to Ruby.

"If someone carries the spellbook upstairs," said Mister Barnaby, pulling Ruby away from her memories, "I will show you to the copier."

Nirva offered her service because she was the only one in the room, aside from the ghosts, capable of carting a heavy book. On the other hand, she wasn't sure how much a ghost could lift. "Just show me what I am supposed to do." She hoped Mister Barnaby knew how to operate the copier since she was unfamiliar with human contraptions.

"It's a simple machine," said Mister Barnaby. "I will show you how to use it."

"Nothing is simple in your world, Mister Barnaby," Nirva replied with frustration.

Mister Barnaby looked at her blankly. "The copier is."

"As soon as we have a copy of the spell, I suggest we head straightaway for home," said Herona.

"The storm has passed over us," noted Rings, watching the sun reappear behind dark clouds. "I'll be able to fly back to Hidden Forest with the rest of you."

"May we stay here until Madame Papulose's return, Mister Barnaby?" asked Opal, tossing a pleading look at the black cat. "I am positive that Madame Papulose will welcome us here. We are the best security guards anyone could require. We can scare away thieves and unwanted guests. Even unwelcome family members, if so desired."

"I must admit that you would be better company than a guard dog," said Mister Barnaby, shrugging. He did not like most dogs.

"Then, it is settled," said Opal, gleefully. "We will remain here with you, Mister Barnaby."

"Let's go make that copy," said Nirva, holding the spellbook in her hands.

"Time is of the essence," said Rings.

"Owls say that a lot," said Ruby, remembering that Peck had said the very same thing.

They were in such a rush that they did not take the time to read the instructions in the amnesia spell. Luckily, Mister Barnaby did read through the spell. Since it was written in Old English, he jotted down the directions in modern English. He suspected that their literary skills were not as sharp as most cats', particularly his.

Shortly after departing from Madame Papulose's home, they caught sight of the Dark Shadow hauling off another human. It was moving quickly, keeping to the protective shade of buildings and trees, as if avoiding people or sunlight. Or, perhaps both.

"The Dark Shadow is out later than normal," mused Nirva. "Prey must be difficult to come by . . . I wonder if humans are hiding in their houses."

"Don't you think we should warn the townspeople that a killer shadow is stalking them?" asked Ruby. Both she and Herona were riding on top of Rings.

"The Dark Shadow only takes humans with corrupted souls," replied Herona. "That is, if it sticks to the agreed-upon bargain."

"Perhaps it will drag off the Malum," said Ruby, her eyes still lingering on the Dark Shadow.

"I don't believe the magi have souls," said Rings.

"What do they have?" questioned Ruby. "And what exactly are they?"

"That's a good question," replied Herona. "As far as anyone knows, they have always been a part of Hidden Forest."

"There is an old owl named Sawwhet who claims to know," interjected Rings. Sawwhet was a northern saw-whet owl. "She lives out in the woods alongside Unicorn Trail. She keeps mostly to herself in a giant western cedar tree. She prefers it that way."

"She is the oldest owl in Hidden Forest. All of her ancestors were slain by the Malum," explained Herona. "Some believe Sawwhet makes up the history of the forest because she does not truly know it."

"Owls never lie," stated Rings. "Most animals in the forest cannot read Sawwhet's scrolls. Or take the time to learn our history."

"Maybe the Malum killed Sawwhet's ancestors because they knew too much," said Ruby. "Knowing too much can be dangerous." She remembered how her stepfather threatened her to keep her eyes and mouth shut while he traded drugs in the house. Her mother was working at the convenience store when the drug deals took place. He sold guns, as well. She speculated that her stepfather had sold guns and drugs to Highbrow. Their stepfather also sold off Shauna and her to their father. She and her sister were just another business transaction.

"It's possible the answer to the Malum's existence might be in one of those books in the basement," said Ruby, recalling the piles and piles of books in the basement.

"Maybe so. But there are too many books for us to read. If I even knew how to read the human language," said Rings. "I can only read owl tracks and pecks." Owl writing consisted of holes made in parchment with their talons and beak. Ruby pictured it to be similar to Braille. "That's how Sawwhet records history."

"Perhaps someday, Shauna and I could look through Madame Papulose's books. Or"—Ruby's face lit up—"Miss Whisker's book club could read through the books for us. Or, Rings could look through Sawwhet's scrolls."

"When the time is right, I will suggest your ideas to Queen Wista," said Herona. "We should learn our history."

"Thank you, Herona."

"You are welcome, Ruby." After a brief pause, she added, "You did well today. Maybe someday you would like to become part of our patrol program."

Just as she spoke these words, Auralia caught sight of the search party. She was returning to Glenhaven to speak with Tark. They did not notice her because she was disguised as a crow. She would have made a good spy, if only given the chance.

□ □ □

Vorte, Berruga, and Shauna anxiously awaited Ruby's return. Shauna and the other trainees had the rest of the afternoon off from flight school because of the snake attack on Flicker. Throughout the remainder of the day, they had all sorts of visitors dropping by. First, it was Swift, the peregrine falcon, who swung by to let Shauna know that Flicker had made a full recovery from her snakebite. After Swift departed, Hummer and Dots paid a visit to also report on Flicker's well-being. According to them, the elves' potion cured her quickly. The next set of guests to appear at the home of Vorte and Berruga was Golden Belle and Glitter. They thanked Shauna for saving their cousin from the snake. They also told her that Queen Wista wanted the fairies to begin teaching Shauna and Ruby how to cast spells, starting tomorrow. While Golden Belle and Glitter were still there, Dazzle popped in. She had to catch her breath before she could speak. "Prince Massen and Rupin have been kidnapped by the Black Dragon!"

"Why?" gasped Berruga, putting a hand to her gaping mouth. "Why would the Black Dragon snatch elves? The elves have never harmed him."

"The dragon's loot was stolen from his cave," explained Dazzle, as she sidled in between her two cousins. All three fairies were standing, their golden wings only slightly fluttering, as if a mild breeze was blowing through the room.

"Did the elves plunder the dragon's treasure?" asked Vorte.

"The elves think it was the rabbits who committed the robbery," stated Dazzle. "We spotted Queen Rossen, Counselor Baruk, and Tark heading this way, probably going to speak with Queen Wista."

"I don't completely understand," admitted Berruga. "Why would the rabbits be involved in this matter? They do not care about possessing gold or other riches."

"It is believed that the rabbits want the Black Dragon to leave Hidden Forest. Only giving back the treasure if he goes," said Dazzle.

"It makes sense that the rabbits have his riches," said Glitter. "They have been wanting to get rid of the Black Dragon for a long time."

The other two fairies heartily agreed with her.

Vorte rubbed the sparse hairs on his chin, distraughtly. "This puts the Little Peepers in a difficult position. Only we can bend the Black Dragon's mind and force him out of Hidden Forest. And the Black Dragon could come after us if we banish him. It will be similar to our situation with the Malum."

"We are making too many enemies," noted Berruga. "We are too small to continually go up against such big foes."

All the while, Shauna was staring at the fairies, trying to block her mind from wanting to hold their wands. She could easily rip away their wands by using her mind. Suddenly, Glitter's wand flew across the room into Shauna's hand.

"Sorry," Shauna apologized, appearing astonished at the wand in her grip. "I was trying to stop myself from wanting to hold yours. But I couldn't control it."

"It cannot be helped. Our wands call to you," said Golden Belle. "The youngest fairies have the same problem. They want to use our wands, too. Instead, we give them toy wands until they are old enough to use them responsibly. Also, we don't want them chewing on our wands while teething." Every so often, a newborn fairy will emerge from a rosebud. Its petals fold around the infant like a blanket. Since fairies have no parents, the entire community shares the responsibility of caring for its young.

"Do not fret, Shauna," added Dazzle. "We will teach you over the next few days how to properly handle a wand."

Glitter fluttered over to Shauna to fetch her wand back.

Berruga was peering curiously at Shauna. "I do not mean to be intrusive. But I am curious about your mother."

"She was just an ordinary person. She had no special powers," said Shauna. Her large, brown eyes began to well up. "My father murdered her."

"The Malum have brought considerable pain to many over the years," replied Berruga. "Both boys, who were captured by the dragon, lost their fathers because of the Malum. You are not alone in your grief."

Shauna found some solace in her new guardian's words. "I might be able to bring back those boys, if I had a wand . . . I was able to toss a snake with a wand."

"A dragon is quite a bit bigger than a snake," Berruga reminded her.

"Down the road, you might have to stand up to a dragon," said Vorte, wearing a sober expression. "However, Queen Wista has a special task for you and your sister that's more pressing. Your magic must become strong enough to cast a spell on the Malum."

"You're kidding me, right?" Shauna looked at the others in disbelief.

"I wish we were," said Vorte, shaking his head no. The fairies were also shaking their heads.

"I don't have that kind of magic," said Shauna, her eyes enlarged. "Confronting a dragon is dangerous enough, don't you think?" The desire for her own wand suddenly faded away.

"We fairies do not contain the magical means to produce powerful spells. You have that capacity, Shauna," said Golden Belle. "But it requires training and the right spell to combat the Malum."

"How can I put a spell on the Malum? I am only nine years old and three inches tall! And there are nine of them and only one of me!"

"The Malum won't be expecting two human girls to have magical powers," said Vorte. "We will have the element of surprise. You will sneak up on them and strike when they are gathered together in one place. Besides, we would never let any harm come to you."

"No, we wouldn't," chimed in Berruga. "The Little Peepers would be right there with you and your sister." In spite of her words of confidence, she looked worried.

Shauna wasn't completely convinced, either. "How exactly did the Malum get their magic?"

"I don't know," replied Berruga. "No one knows where they came from."

"There is an ancient owl named Sawwhet who claims to know," said Glitter. "But no one believes her. She isolates herself from others. Therefore, no one seeks her out or her words."

"Maybe the magi are like gods," said Shauna. "They were just here from the very beginning."

"If that is true, then they are gods who went horribly bad," said Golden Belle.

"Lucky for the humans, the Malum lost their powers once they entered the nonmagical world," said Vorte. "Otherwise, the Malum would attempt to rule over the humans."

"The Malum would be at each other's throats if they still had their powers in the human world," pointed out Glitter.

"If they ever did figure out a way to regain their powers in the human world," said Vorte, "it would be devastating for everyone on the planet. They would destroy the entire world with their treachery."

Shauna sat down on a kitchen chair. Her legs felt wobbly from fatigue and the thought of confronting the Malum.

"Queen Wista and the others are still pondering other solutions to combat the magi," said Berruga gently. "Maybe there is another way."

They heard the sound of movement outside and then a knock on the door.

Everyone stopped.

"Is that you, Ruby?" called out Berruga.

"Yes. Rings dropped me off here."

"Come in!" said Berruga, as she rushed toward the door. She did not want to show it in front of Shauna, but she had been worried sick about Ruby.

Ruby was turning the knob as Berruga swung the door open, yanking her inside. A gust of wind also entered the treehouse.

"Where is the rest of your search party?" asked Berruga. She poked her head out the door, scanning the area.

"They let me off here and then made their way to Queen Wista's home. They have official business to conduct."

Meanwhile, Shauna ran to Ruby and hugged her. "You have the windblown look. Your hair is sticking straight up."

Ruby tried to flatten her disheveled hair with her hands.

"We can fix you up in a jiffy," said Glitter. Ruby noticed that the fairies liked braiding hair and crowning their heads with fairy rings.

All of a sudden, Glitter's wand zipped through the air and Ruby caught it with her right hand. "I didn't mean to do that—"

"It's quite all right," said Glitter. "Your sister did the same thing. But don't worry, there's a cure for wand envy."

"What's the cure?" asked Ruby. She returned the wand to Glitter while Golden Belle and Dazzle tightened the grip on their wands.

"Having your own wand," replied Glitter. "But you cannot have a wand until you know how to properly use one." Her sparkling blue eyes darted over to Berruga and Vorte. "With your permission, we would like the girls to come tomorrow to Tinsel for wand training."

Both Berruga and Vorte nodded.

"Swift will take us there," said Vorte. "The girls should not go off on their own."

"Swift was King Hoppit's falcon, wasn't he?" questioned Golden Belle.

"The very one," answered Vorte. "Swift is finally taking passengers again after the king's passing. He took the king's death hard."

"We all did," said Berruga, wiping a tear from the corner of her eye. "That was a terrible time."

"Yes, it was," all three fairies said in unison.

"Before you begin your grooming session, tell us what happened on your mission, Ruby," said Vorte. "Did you find Serpentine's children?"

"No, but we found Serpentine!" Ruby grinned proudly. The bulging eyes of Vorte and Berruga nearly popped out of their heads. "We were in the basement of Madame Papulose's basement—" She cut herself off and headed back to the beginning of the day. She told them everything that had happened since she left that morning. In return, they shared the story of the Black Dragon kidnapping Prince

Massen and Rupin, and how the dragon was demanding his stolen treasure back from the elves.

"But we think the rabbits took his treasure," said Dazzle.

"So much has happened over the last few days—from the reawakening of the Dark Shadow to the attempt by the Malum to reenter our forest. And the rabbits want to change their lot in life," said Vorte. "Things are moving too quickly. I wish things would slow down."

"Sorcerer Serpentine is slowing down," said Ruby. "He looks really old. Counselor Herona said we might not even have to use the amnesia spell on the Malum. It was just a matter of time before they expire."

"If we keep the Malum from retrieving their magic, they'll die from old age very soon," said Golden Belle. "In the meantime, however, they are extremely desperate and dangerous."

"They'll take riskier chances," Dazzle said nervously.

"I think it's best if you girls stayed away from the edges of Hidden Forest," Vorte warned them. "I don't want you to be snagged by a magus. There are not enough rabbit patrols to guard every square inch of the border."

"I would feel much better if the magi died from old age than having the girls cast a spell on them," Berruga stated.

"But the demise of the magi could come at a hefty price," said Glitter. "It could cost the Little Peepers their—"

"It'll cost us very little," interrupted Berruga, stopping Glitter from finishing her thought. She did not want to burden the girls with another worry.

Baffled by Berruga's remark, Ruby and Shauna traded looks.

"Will you lose your mindbending ability?" asked Ruby.

"I don't believe so," replied Berruga.

"If we did," said Vorte, "it's a small price to pay for ridding the forest of the Malum once and for all."

"I think it's all going to come down to who finds Serpentine's offspring first—the Malum or us," said Golden Belle.

They nodded grimly because it was true.

Chapter Fourteen

Treasure

The moles, Rooter, Erde, and Snoot, were responsible for guarding the Black Dragon's treasure. At the moment, they were rummaging through the dragon's loot and admiring the various jeweled necklaces, silver bracelets, gold goblets, and so forth.

"Now, here's a real beauty," said Erde, putting on a ruby necklace. "Check it out. Do I look like an elf?"

Rooter and Snoot had to squint their eyes to make out the rubies, even though they were the size of plump cherries. The cavern was very dark and they had such poor eyesight.

"It makes you look absolutely glamorous," said Rooter. "You probably look like the elf queen, if I could see her clearly."

"I can clearly see what Queen Rossen has been up to, despite my bad eyesight," declared Erde, gesturing at the gigantic mound of fake gold. "It seems as if she and the other elves have been cheating the Black Dragon for many years. "Apparently, they've been trading fool's gold for his priceless gold and precious gems."

"Gold that he stole from the humans before they had the ability to shoot him down," Rooter added. The moles had heard that the Black Dragon no longer ventured beyond the boundaries of Hidden Forest because of powerful human weapons. But long ago, he ransacked castles and fortresses for their treasures. What they didn't know was that the last time he journeyed outside the forest his mate was brought down to earth by a large boulder flung by a catapult. Her wing was broken. The villagers pierced her body with sharp blades and she bled to death. He could do nothing for her as he watched her die in agony.

"The elves have been destroying our tunnels when they dig for their precious fake gold," snorted Snoot. "Not once have they apologized for ruining our passageways." During the elves' excavation of the mineral pyrite, also known as fool's gold, the moles' tunnels were often completely demolished or partially caved in.

When the rabbit commander from the first regiment requested their help in concealing the dragon's treasure, the moles did not hesitate to oblige. The moles did not like the dragon eating their rabbit friends. They hid the dragon's riches in a deep cavern, which was only a short distance from the dragon's lair. The moles had to choose a place close to the dragon's lair because of the amount and weight of the treasure. Since the dragon had looted from humans for hundreds of years, he had accumulated a massive amount of treasure.

Commander Lapin had left his post to be at the meeting. He put Poppin in charge of the eighth regiment during his absence.

Lapin stood on his hind legs as the other nine commanders listened to him. The rabbits leaned forward and strained their ears because Lapin talked in a low voice. The Black Dragon was in his lair along with the two young elves.

"We can demand that the Black Dragon leave, but we must have an idea of where he can go," said Lapin. "Otherwise, he will resist."

"Do you have a place in mind, Lapin?" questioned the commander from the fourth regiment. Of all the commanders, he was the most timid.

"Yesterday I spoke to the human girl—Shauna—who was rescued from the Malum. I asked her if there was a safe place in the human world for unique creatures. Somewhere they never go hungry and would not bother others." The other rabbits bent their ears closer to the commander, eager to hear the young girl's suggestion. "She told me that, indeed, such a place did exist. It was called a zoo. She said the animals there were well-cared for and never hunted."

The commander of the fifth regiment scrunched up his button nose. "A zoo? I have never heard of such a place."

"I, too, had not heard of a zoo until yesterday. But does it not sound like the perfect place for the Black Dragon?" beamed Lapin.

"It sounds like the perfect solution to our problem," chimed in the commander from the second regiment.

"How do you know the dragon won't hunt rabbits at the zoo?" questioned the commander of the seventh regiment. "I do not want the dragon to dine upon our cousins in the nonmagical world."

The commanders began murmuring among themselves that eating any rabbit on the planet was disconcerting.

"I was told that the dragon used to catch sheep and goats from farmers' fields when he used to hunt in the human world," said Lapin. "I do believe that he would find those animals more abundant and appetizing than our kind." There were no sheep or goats in Hidden Forest.

"Can we count on the elves to let the Black Dragon leave Hidden Forest?" The leader of the third regiment looked around the cavern. "They like to trade their gold for his riches. They have been bargaining with each other for countless ages."

"The elves have been trading fool's gold," said Erde, butting into the conversation. She had overheard the rabbits' every word because of her excellent hearing and she was upset with the elves' deceit.

"Fool's gold! How very interesting!" said Lapin. "And how devious of the elves."

"If the Black Dragon learns of the deceit, he will attack and destroy the elves," said the commander of the first regiment. "There might not be enough time for the Little Peepers to mount a defense against such an irate dragon in flight."

"We should not tell the dragon of the treachery," said Lapin. "However, he has imprisoned a couple of young elves. I hope they do not let it slip that he has been tricked."

All of them looked up in the direction of the dragon's lair, imagining the dragon prodding, if not torturing, information out of the young elves.

"One of the elves is Queen Rossen's son," said Erde. "The elf queen will make a swift bargain to free him."

"I do not trust Rossen or her negotiations," Lapin said matter-of-factly. "Though, I want this nasty business to end quickly. The faster we can banish the dragon, the better for us."

"The moles do not trust the elf queen, either," said Erde. "If she can trade fool's gold to the dragon, what other things will she trade away?"

"Her mate," said the commander of the ninth regiment. "When was the last time she tried to free King Koning from the Pit of Despair? Everything is renegotiable."

"But, has any of us attempted to speak with the Dark Shadow?" piped up the commander of the fourth regiment.

No one had approached the Dark Shadow.

"In all honesty, the Dark Shadow is a frightening creature," said the commander of the fourth regiment. "It doesn't appear to have a mouth or ears. Wherever it goes, it casts a gloomy shadow and leaves behind a deep sorrow. You'd have to be a fool to get near it."

"Are you saying that Queen Rossen is a fool for getting in touch with it?" asked the commander of the tenth regiment.

"No. But it does makes me wonder if the queen actually brokered a deal with the Dark Shadow," replied the commander of the fourth regiment. "Or did she make a deal to benefit herself?"

"A very good question," said Lapin. "We will keep an eye on the dragon as well as the elves. And we will cooperate with the Little Peepers. They will not turn their back on us, and we will not turn our back on them."

"Here, here," said the commander of the sixth regiment.

The commanders raised their glasses of carrot juice high into the air and downed their drinks.

Erde returned to Rooter and Snoot to continue their watch over the dragon's loot. The commanders finished their meeting and went back to their individual regiments. The rabbits kept up their vigilant patrols watching for trespassers. They were especially on the lookout for the Malum. They would not drop their guard because the Noble Rabbits prided themselves on being loyal.

☐ ☐ ☐

Rupin and Prince Massen were imprisoned in treasure chests that the Black Dragon had stolen back in the day when pirates ruled the high seas. The dragon was no fool. He realized that the shapeshifters could easily escape from him as mice, bats, or other creatures. Thus, he locked up the elves in separate chests and then secured the chests with locks and chains. He had no proof that the elves had pilfered his coffers. But who else loved shiny objects as much as he? It had to be the elves.

The young elves only called out for help once. The dragon threatened to burn them inside their wooden boxes if they made another peep. Ever since then, his prisoners have been quiet. He hoped they were still alive. He had no intention of killing them. He just wanted his treasure back.

Both Rupin and Massen had shapeshifted inside their treasure chest. Otherwise, they would have been dead from lack of oxygen.

Both of them transformed into squirrels and fell into a deep state of hibernation. They barely breathed. This also avoided any panic attacks caused by their tight confinement. Elves tended to be claustrophobic.

The Black Dragon once had a name but it had been mostly forgotten over time. He thought it was something like *Kveikja*, which meant "ignite" in a language spoken in a bitterly cold place. His mother had given him this name shortly before she was struck down by humans. His father moved him and his two siblings to Hidden Forest. They continued to hunt in the human world because they did not want to anger the local creatures. Eventually, his father and two siblings also succumbed to human weapons. For many years, he was alone and lonely. As he was out hunting one day for sheep, he came across another black dragon. She was as beautiful as the night sky and her scales shone as brightly as the stars. Her name was Agir, which meant fire in her language. She came from a place where wars were often fought. He was instantly smitten by her. They spent fifty-nine years together before she was killed. To this day, he grieved her death. The day after Agir was brutally murdered, he began hunting solely in Hidden Forest. He refused to die from human hands. Next to the loss of his family, his greatest sorrow was that he no longer hunted for treasure in the human world. His only remaining pleasure in life was trading his riches for the elf's gold. And now, the elves had even taken that simple joy from him. He had already lost so much.

He went to the lip of the cave and shot an angry fireball toward the mid-afternoon sun. But still, he found no solace or comfort in lighting up the sky.

He still missed what he had lost.

□ □ □

Auralia decided to shadow the search party all the way from Zeldar's backyard to Queen Wista's treehouse. Perched on a branch outside Wista's home, she was disguised as a barn owl. Inside were Queen Wista, Queen Rossen, Counselor Nirva, Counselor Herona, Advisor Baruk, and Tark, who seemed to be Rossen's favorite spy. Auralia eavesdropped on them as the other taxi birds flew by her, paying her no mind. If she was discovered listening, she would only be in trouble with Queen Rossen. Auralia was told that Queen Wista was the type of individual who invited strangers to her home for a cup of tea and asked for their opinions on a wide range of subjects. As she eavesdropped, a fairy landed alongside her, also interested in what was taking place in the queen's treehouse. Auralia had to turn her head to look at the fairy because owls cannot move their eyes. They're fixed in their sockets.

"My name is Sparkles," the fairy whispered to Auralia. "And you are an elf beneath those feathers."

Evidently, Auralia's disguise did not easily fool the fairy. "How long did it take for you to see through my disguise?"

"Only a moment. Your concealment as an owl is quite good. But, currently, there are no barn owls working as taxi birds. All the barn owls have been reassigned as patrol owls, under Queen Wista's orders."

"Evidently, I need to work on my espionage skills. By the way, I'm Auralia." She scanned the taxi birds who were roosting in the trees. Only a few of them were carrying passengers. At this hour, most of the Little Peepers were out patrolling for danger or gathering food. "Do the other birds know that I am not really an owl?"

"Of course, they do. But the owls don't mind that you're eavesdropping. They do it all the time, just like the Little Peepers. They are not keepers of secrets, like the elves."

"What do you mean by that?"

Abruptly, Sparkles put a finger to her mouth to indicate silence. There was a slight edge of impatience in Queen Rossen's voice. "Listen closely, Auralia, if you want to be a spy." Her whisper sounded like a faint breeze tickling Auralia's tiny ears.

As an owl, Auralia had better hearing than a fairy, but she did not point that out to Sparkles. Unless, of course, Sparkles was telling her to pay attention to *what* was being said.

"We cannot leave my son and Tark's brother with the Black Dragon," said Rossen, her voice carrying out the open window. "We need to get the treasure back from the rabbits at once."

"We should make the exchange before the dragon leaves his lair to hunt," declared Counselor Nirva. "He'll probably hunt *rabbits*, which will make it that much harder to resolve the matter."

"We could make a rescue attempt while the dragon is out hunting," pointed out Counselor Herona.

"The risks are too high. What if we fail to rescue the captives?" said Advisor Baruk.

"The risks are too high if we don't make an attempt," countered Tark.

Queen Wista looked troubled. She poured a round of herbal tea for everyone. "After we finish our tea, I will go speak with Commander Lapin. We have been great friends for a long time." She stopped pouring and observed them sitting around her table. "You do see the problem we're facing, do you not?" No one replied. "If we banish the Black Dragon from Hidden Forest, the Malum will track him down and convince him to carry them back to our forest. Naturally, the Black Dragon will agree to join their side because he, too, wants to return to Hidden Forest. Not even the air patrols will be able to bring the dragon down. Not when the Malum have regained their magic. So, you see, we cannot afford to make an enemy of the Black Dragon until we first deal with the magi. Of course, our first priority is having a face to face conversation with the rabbits." She served everyone a cup of tea as the room remained deathly quiet.

"Queen Wista is right," said Counselor Herona. "We need to speak with Commander Lapin and the other commanders and work something out before confronting the Black Dragon."

"If time drags on and the prince and Rupin are not rescued," continued Wista, "I promise that the Little Peepers will use our mindbending skills and force the Black Dragon to free them."

An expression of relief crossed Tark's face, but he said nothing. He waited for Queen Rossen to weigh in first with her thoughts on the matter.

"Do you want me to go and speak to the rabbits with you, Wista?" asked Rossen.

"If you don't mind, I would prefer to only take Tark with me," replied Wista. "He is well-acquainted with Commander Lapin and will seem . . . well, less intimidating." She peered over at Tark, who was sitting three chairs to the right of her. "You are good friends with Lapin, are you not?"

Tark nodded tentatively because Rossen seemed displeased to be left out of Wista's proposed plan. "I have spoken to the commander on numerous occasions. He has always been friendly to me."

"I thought so," said Wista.

Queen Rossen traded looks with both her counselor and advisor. "I suppose this will have to be acceptable. We will leave for Glenhaven after our tea. However, tomorrow morning we expect to hear about your meeting with the rabbit commander. The dragon's prisoners are my subjects," she reminded Wista.

"It has not slipped my mind," replied Wista. "And surely, Tark will not let me forget."

Outside Wista's treehouse, Sparkles whispered to Auralia, "We shall tag along with Queen Wista and Tark. But first, let me collect my cousins. They are in the home of Vorte and Berruga."

"Cousins?! But fairies have no parents."

"We share a relationship with each other. That makes us cousins."

Auralia nodded and almost sighed, wishing that she had the freedom of the fairies. They didn't have a queen or live in a hierarchal society. They all acted like princesses, yet showed equal respect to each other. They never ordered one another around or assigned tasks to others. They voluntarily offered their services. There were times they refused to help without offering a reason or making a weak excuse. They never felt guilty about turning down a request. Most importantly, no one ever held the fairies accountable or grew angry because of their choices. After all, fairies were known to be free-spirited and not mean-spirited.

"Your spirit appears to be on the low side, Auralia," said Sparkles. "I will put a little spark into it." Unexpectedly, she flew up and sprinkled a little gold dust over Auralia's head. "Feel better?"

"Much better." Auralia did feel much better. Her troubles seemed to be lifted away.

"It is only a temporary fix to whatever is bothering you. Someday you will have to face your troubles head-on, even if it is yourself or your queen. Now, come with me, my new elf friend."

Sparkles and Auralia flew off together.

Chapter Fifteen

Warlock Highbrow and His Magic

Warlock Highbrow proudly displayed his shiny .40-caliber handgun to Witch Blackheart. He had been staying in her apartment because his place was in the big city. He was the only one of the Malum who moved away from the small town and escaped to the city. For the past thirteen years, a hundred eighty miles separated Highbrow from the other Malum. He had a very good reason for living in the city—Renee Beckles, the mother of Ruby and Shauna. He shot her in cold blood for a good reason, too.

"Is that the gun you used to shoot the mother of your brats?" questioned Witch Blackheart, while admiring the handgun.

"It is. It only took a single bullet to end her life. I have developed pretty good aim from all those years of pointing my wand at others. I miss shooting down owls and rabbits and conducting experiments on them." He paused and grinned wickedly. "We should use human weapons to kill our enemies instead of wands."

"We would only get a few rounds off before the Little Peepers would either force us to put down our weapons or make us turn the guns on ourselves. No, we need black magic to defeat our enemies."

"Still, I plan to bring my guns with me to Hidden Forest."

"What we need is to get our new wands from Spellbinder before entering Hidden Forest," said Blackheart. "I don't trust that he made the wands equally. I imagine he kept the best one for himself."

"A wand is only as powerful as its owner," Highbrow reminded her.

"But still, I would like to test it out before confronting our foes. What if our wands do not work properly?"

"Spellbinder wouldn't risk giving us faulty wands. He needs us to win." The warlock ran his index finger against the barrel of the gun. "Nonetheless, if he does betray us down the road, I will shoot him dead when he's not looking."

Blackheart gave a smile of approval because she didn't care much for Spellbinder. She stole a look at the large duffle bag that Highbrow had brought to her apartment. "What's in your bag, anyway? It weighs too much to be clothing."

"The largest item is a container of rodent poison that Zeldar gave me. I plan to use it on the rabbits after we return to the forest. Zeldar also provided me with three cat skulls that I will need to make a special potion for the Little Peepers. One by one, I will force the potion down the throats of those who don't succumb to our wands."

"Do you have to grind up the skulls?"

"No, the potion must be made inside a cat skull."

Blackheart hid her mischievous smile from him. "What kind of special potion is it?"

"Thanks to Serpentine, I discovered that his neighbor is a Wiccan, who keeps spell and potion books in her basement—"

"Nonsense! Wiccans are fake witches!" hissed Witch Blackheart.

"No doubt they are. Nevertheless, the Wiccan possesses about a hundred magic books. I figured that at least one of them might be authentic, so I broke into her house a few weeks ago when no one was home. I happened upon an ancient book full of spells. It contains a potion to return beings to their natural form. There is also a transformation spell."

"So, you believe this concoction or spell will turn the Little Peepers back into frogs?"

"I believe so. I can't wait to begin experimenting on the forest creatures again," he said gleefully. "I miss those days."

"How do you know for certain the potion will work? Without your magic, you cannot try it out first. The book could be a fake."

Wizard Highbrow smirked. "I am not an idiot, Witch Blackheart. I can recognize an authentic book of enchantments when I see one."

"No, you are not a complete idiot. You always have some clever trick up your sleeve, like Sorceress Underhand." She and Sorceress Underhand had always been at odds with one another. "So, after all these years, are you going to tell me why you abandoned us for the big city?"

He shrugged nonchalantly, as if he hadn't intentionally kept it a secret for thirteen years. But Blackheart clearly remembered him being sneaky about it.

"Hell's Bells, Highbrow, just spill it!" she said, frustrated.

"I saw my fate on the day of our banishment. As soon as I realized there was no chance of defeating the Little Peepers and reentering Hidden Forest, I knew that I had to find a human in a hurry."

The witch cocked her head and gave the warlock a baffled look. "Why did you seek out a human?"

"Because I realized I wouldn't have magic for long before it would disappear in the nonmagical world. So, I had to act quickly. Since the Little Peepers forced us to break our wands, I snapped a branch off from an elm tree. I hastened toward the human village. It was there I spotted her on the street."

"Spotted whom?" asked Blackheart, regarding him much like a curious cat eyes a goldfish.

"Renee Beckles. But, of course, I didn't know her name then. I saw a young, human female heading toward her car. I still had some fairy dust in my pocket—"

"Fairy dust that you stole from the fairies." Blackheart and the rest of the magi captured fairies and took their fairy dust from them to be used in potions.

"I approached the young woman and tossed the fairy dust into her eyes as I said the incantation for obsession. She swore at me before the love charm took hold of her. Then, she couldn't take her eyes off me," he said with disgust, visibly shuddering. "Next, I pointed the elm branch at her and transferred my magic into her."

Witch Blackheart was keenly observing him, as if seeing him for the first time. He was more cunning than she had originally estimated. And yet, he was careless. "Why did you think it was safer to keep your magic inside a complete stranger than yourself?" she asked, incredulously.

"Can you not feel your magic pressing against you, wearing you down? Both of us are aware the magic needs to be recharged. If not, it saps away our energy."

Blackheart had to admit that Highbrow did seem more vigorous than the rest of them. But she assumed he received his zest for life from cheating humans. How else did he get his money, expensive car, and numerous guns? "So, just like that, you got inside Renee Beckles' car and the two of you drove off to the city?"

"What other choice did I have? I wasn't about to risk losing track of my own magic. I had to follow it, which meant I had to follow her."

"Then, you produced a couple of offspring with her, so later you could kill them for their blood."

"Indeed, I did. You have to admit it was rather clever of me. That poor, silly woman would have done anything for me because of the obsession potion. Even when I sent her away, she came looking for me. Finally, I ordered her to get a husband, so she would quit pining for me so much. If I didn't need to keep my magic safe, I would have gotten rid of her years ago."

"But you waited until a week ago or so to collect your magic from her because you thought we would be returning soon to Hidden Forest."

"Unfortunately, I did." A flash of anger appeared on his face. "However, those snooping patrol rabbits messed up our plans. As it turned out, I did away with Renee Beckles too soon."

"So, did you get your magic back from the human after you murdered her?" All magi knew that magic will quickly find a new host if its first host is killed. Magic cannot die. It will go somewhere else. "And, if it did, isn't it fading away?" Magic of the magi, or the fairies, for that matter, did not completely vanish when they crossed into the human world. Its power shrank inside them, making it unusable, like a dead battery.

He frowned, feeling deeply sorry for himself. "She had no magic in her. My spell must not have worked in the first place. Using the elm branch as a wand was a bit of a stretch, even in an emergency situation."

Witch Blackheart broke out in raucous laughter, almost doubling over.

Highbrow's face turned a dark shade of red. "What's so hilarious?"

"Haven't you figured it out by now?" smirked the witch, shaking her head. "Your plan backfired on you. Your magical powers were passed onto your two offspring. You gave your magic away to your two brats!"

"That can't be! The human female didn't have my magical powers because the tree branch didn't work. My magic has not been claimed by others!"

Witch Blackheart stopped chuckling and eyed the warlock in his black cloak, which needed a good washing. "Maybe so, Highbrow.

You shall find out the moment you step into the forest if your magic is or isn't working. Nonetheless, my bet is that your two daughters have your powers. And who knows what you have created? Those daughters of yours might be more powerful than you can imagine, if your magic has been reborn or renewed. Lucky for me, my magic will return to me once I enter the forest because I did not foolishly give it away."

"If I don't have my magical powers, I will shoot the girls and reclaim my magic," said Highbrow without any emotion. "It won't be hard to get it back." He brandished the gun in his hand. "Magic cannot be destroyed, but human flesh can be purged from this world."

"A magus can be destroyed, as you very well know."

"As I said, I do not think my spell worked on the annoying female," he said, scowling. "I saw no change in her."

"In case you are wrong, I advise you not to tell the others of what you just told me. Otherwise, one of them might murder the girls and obtain their magic . . . I mean, your magic, enabling him or her to be the most powerful of all. Subsequently, you will be left powerless and vulnerable."

"Do you intend to be one of those thieves, Witch Blackheart? Or, are you concerned the others will beat you to my magic? Maybe that's why you do not want me to mention to the others how I stored my magic in a human." He looked himself over. "I mean, how I failed to transfer my magic."

"I still think your brats inherited your powers. But no, I have no intention of stealing from you, Warlock Highbrow. It's Sorceress Underhand you should be concerned about. She blames you for not properly securing your children in the garden shed. Besides, she has never cared much for you. She thinks you're pretentious."

"And Sorceress Underhand is as sneaky as a fox. Fortunately, I have extra bullets in my canvas bag to put an end to her scheming ways," he sneered. "If she gets any funny ideas, I will do the same to her as I did to Renee Beckles."

"If our wands are working properly, your bullets will be useless against her."

"I'll shoot her when she has no wand in her hand."

"Any one of us can turn your guns into snakes as soon as we step into Hidden Forest. We just need our wands."

"You're impossible to reason with. Once more, I am quite positive that my magic is still inside me. I have grown old like the rest of you."

"Losing our immortality ages us."

"Do you have to counter my every word!" he said, exasperated.

"Yes. Besides, did you ever once feel your magic diminishing inside you?"

Highbrow clenched his jaw and made no reply.

"You haven't experienced the pain of losing your magic little by little."

"As soon as I stepped out of Hidden Forest, I felt the same painful loss as the rest of you."

"But your pain stopped as soon as you gave away your magic." She closely observed him. He once was built like an Olympic athlete, but now his shoulders were stooped from old age. The locals gave the Malum a wide berth because of their "mysterious illness" that rapidly aged them, as if it was contagious. In return, the Malum kept their distance from the townspeople because they didn't care much for humans.

"I want to change the topic," Highbrow muttered.

"I want you to drive me over to Spellbinder's place." Blackheart had neither a car nor a driver's license. Highbrow had a fancy car and a fake driver's license. "We are going to convince Spellbinder to give us our wands now. I don't want to wait any longer for them."

"I suppose we ought to make certain that Sorcerer Spellbinder made quality wands," he conceded. "We should not blindly trust him."

"Of course not."

As they drove over to Spellbinder's home, Highbrow relived the day of his banishment in his mind. It was Spellbinder who started the downfall of the magi, which took place years before the Great Banishment. He was the one who created the Little Peepers from frogs. He was the one responsible for letting them escape into the wild, where they grew in number and prospered. No matter how hard the Malum tried to corral or kill the Little Peepers, they managed to escape. It was a great blow to the magi when they discovered the Little Peepers had the ability to control minds. It didn't take long for the Little Peepers to establish a community. The Malum continuously tried to get rid of them. They created frog-snakes to kill them with venom.

The Little Peepers fought back with their minds. They were aided by the other forest creatures. Then, one day, Prince Cobias was unexpectedly dropped on Spellbinder's doorstep. That changed everything.

"What are you scowling about?" asked Blackheart, interrupting old memories.

"I was recalling how the Little Peepers retaliated against us after we killed King Hoppit." He continued dwelling on that time. That night, the Malum retired to their separate huts, assuming no one would dare go up against their powers. They were horribly wrong. In the middle of the night, the Little Peepers surrounded each Malum's hut. They forced the magi out of their beds and made them snap their own wands in half. The broken pieces of the wands fell to the ground. Using only their minds, Little Peepers drove the Malum out of the forest. Highbrow remembered how powerless he felt against them. His body involuntarily marching out of the woods. He noticed that the other magi were just as helpless resisting the mindbenders. As soon as they crossed the border, the Malum attempted to reenter, but the Little Peepers kept their minds trained on them. Realizing that the Little Peepers wouldn't ease up their control until the magic was drained from the magi, he headed straight for town and found Renee Beckles. That changed everything, too.

"Do you have any specific plans for the elves?" questioned Witch Blackheart, sitting in the passenger seat. Her feet were braced against the dashboard because riding in cars terrified her. She preferred riding on a broom, which she deemed a much safer way to travel.

"What do you mean?" Highbrow glanced at her black boots. "Put your feet down. You are scuffing up my car. This car is not cheap like your boots."

She rolled her dark eyes and reluctantly removed her feet from the dashboard. "What kind of punishment do you intend to unleash on the traitorous elves? After all, they refused to come to our aid during our exile, even though we never wronged them in the past. Well, except for the times Spellbinder transformed them into animals."

"I haven't decided yet. I am still weighing the options."

"I know what I aim to do with the elves. I will strip them of their lovely gems and silken clothing. I will have them march naked in front of the forest creatures and then have the Black Dragon burn them alive as the onlookers are forced to cheer their deaths."

Highbrow peered out of the corner of his eye. "Remind me not to tick you off."

"There's a good reason I am called Blackheart—"

"Because you charred the hearts of your enemies," interrupted Highbrow, half-kidding.

"Well, that. Plus, I never forgive and always even the score."

"And that's why you're my favorite witch," he said in an amused voice. "How will you convince the Black Dragon to set the elves on fire?" He pulled into Spellbinder's driveway. "The elves and the dragon get along well enough. They trade riches with one another."

"I know a secret of the elves," Blackheart said gleefully.

Highbrow turned off the car and observed Blackheart. Once, she was more beautiful than the other two witches Zeldar and Mortify. "What is this secret of theirs?"

"A few days before the Little Peepers launched their attack against us, I treated a deep cut on the Black Dragon's foot. In exchange for my service, I requested a gold nugget for this potion I was working on. To my dismay, the potion blew up the cauldron. After conducting my own research, I discovered the gold wasn't real gold. It was fool's gold. And that's why it exploded." She pouted her lips. "That happened one too many times."

"You should learn how to safely mix ingredients," he smirked. "How many cauldrons have you blown up? Twenty? Thirty?"

"Would you prefer to listen and learn or make fun of me?"

He shrugged off her remark. "Do you think the Black Dragon knowingly gave you fool's gold?"

"I don't believe so. After a little digging around, I learned that the elves have been exchanging fool's gold for the dragon's gold jewelry, chalices, precious gems, and whatever else he hoarded over the many years. Apparently, the dragon has no idea that he was the fool in the fool's gold. Unfortunately, we were banished before I could use this information to our advantage. It's a shame that the dragon hasn't hunted in the human world ever since his mate was killed. We could've used him to fly us back to Hidden Forest."

Highbrow whistled under his breath. "Evidently, the dragon has gotten sloppy with his treasures ever since his mate dropped dead. Agir would not have fallen for fake gold."

"I remember when Agir was killed. The Black Dragon stopped eating until we offered him the local rabbits," she said merrily. "We couldn't have a magical forest without a dragon in it, could we?"

"No, we could not. And we can't have an enchanted forest without us in it, either," he said fiendishly. He had parked squarely in front of the garage door that, like the house, was painted black. The magi loved the color black.

HIghbrow and Blackheart got out of the vehicle at the same time, slamming their door behind them. Hearing noises in his driveway, Sorcerer Spellbinder rushed over to his front window and swore. He assumed Highbrow and Blackheart were there to find out if he had received any news from the raven leader. *Warlocks and witches are so impatient,* he thought. He also thought sorcerers and sorceresses were superior to warlocks and witches. In his opinion, they were better at casting spells and transforming objects into animals and vice-versa. He had to admit that the Little Peepers were his best creations—and worst, of course.

Briefly, Spellbinder watched his uninvited guests march toward his front door, as if on an urgent mission. He answered the door before his company could knock. "What an unexpected pleasure," he said, holding the door wide open for them. "Please come in and make yourself comfortable."

HIghbrow and Blackheart walked through the door before greeting Spellbinder. Even though they regarded warlocks and witches to be superior to sorcerers and sorceresses, this was not the time to talk down to Spellbinder or mention his devastating blunder, the Little Peepers.

"I am afraid you are wasting your time coming here. I have heard nothing from Gavran since we left Zeldar's," Spellbinder said bluntly. The Malum had become gruffer since their recent failure to regain their magic.

Blackheart gave Spellbinder a look that could have melted a glacier. "We came here to claim our wands, Sorcerer Spellbinder. We want to practice with them before facing our enemies in combat."

Spellbinder raised his bushy, gray eyebrows. "Do you not trust me?"

"Over the years, you have given me plenty of reasons not to trust you." She put out her hand. "I want to see the wands—all of them—*now*."

Spellbinder turned on Highbrow. "I suppose that you are having your doubts, too."

"There is no harm in asking for our wands earlier than planned," said Highbrow.

"You were supposed to bring them to Zeldar's last night," Blackheart reminded both of them.

"What good is a wand if you have no magic?" said Spellbinder.

"What good will it do you if you continue to keep them from us?" said Blackheart in a threatening tone.

Sorcerer Spellbinder feigned a small smile to break the tension. He knew better than to challenge a witch. The three witches might bicker among themselves, but they would come together against any sorcerer or warlock. The witches had never been fond of males, in general. Furthermore, Blackheart wouldn't think twice about performing dark magic on him. And black magic was her specialty. "I will fetch the wands for you. Wait here." He went to his bedroom closet and pulled out the wands. He had them stuffed in an old golf bag. These wands were made from a strong oak tree that grew up leaning into the wind. His special wand, made of ancient olive wood, remained hidden in the closet.

While Spellbinder was retrieving the wands, Highbrow and Blackheart examined the sorcerer's living quarters. There were a dozen cages crowded with all sorts of birds. The birds appeared defeated and forlorn. The room stunk of bird poop.

Spellbinder reappeared with the wands. "I brought them all out, so you can see that they are all exactly alike."

"You better not let Gavran or any other raven see or smell these cages," warned Blackheart, motioning at a sad-looking parrot. "The ravens have never cared much for caged birds."

Meanwhile, Highbrow took the wands from Spellbinder and began to inspect each one. When he was finished, he handed the wands to Witch Blackheart who examined each one under a light. After she approved of them, she took the best one for herself. Both Highbrow and Spellbinder scowled, but said nothing. Highbrow selected his favorite. Then, they departed. The moment they shut the car doors, Highbrow rounded on Blackheart for taking the best wand for herself.

"Calm down, Highbrow," hissed Blackheart. "I was testing Spellbinder, which he failed, I might add. Besides, he lied about the wands being equal. You should know by now that Spellbinder doesn't believe in equality."

"What test do you speak of?"

"Spellbinder would never have let me walk out of his place with the best wand unless he has fashioned a better wand for himself. Probably stashed away under his pillow."

Warlock Highbrow swallowed his anger because Witch Blackheart was right. Spellbinder would never have given away his best wand.

"What is he up to?" Highbrow muttered to himself.

"Evidently, he doesn't want to share the forest equally with us."

"We will have to watch our backs."

"And our heads," said Blackheart, remembering how Highbrow shot Renee Beckles in the temple. None of the male magi could be trusted. She intended to speak to the witches, Mortify and Zeldar, about the untrustworthy behavior of both Highbrow and Spellbinder. It was obvious she needed to form an alliance with them before stepping into Hidden Forest. The warlocks and sorcerers could not be trusted. And the sorceresses, Hexla and Underhand, were not much better, either.

"Maybe I will have to shoot Spellbinder in his sleep once we are back in the forest," sneered Highbrow.

"You can try, but Spellbinder sleeps with his wand."

"I'll use magic to stop him."

"But don't forget that any wand in your hand is useless if you don't have your magic," she said, wearing a mocking grin. "You said yourself that a wand is only as strong as its possessor."

Clenching his jaw, Warlock Highbrow squealed his tires as he backed out of the driveway. He had to track down his offspring before the others did. Gavran and his flock of ravens had better come through for him.

Chapter Sixteen

Changing Course

Queen Wista rode on her magnificent northern hawk owl, Spruce, and Tark changed into an elf owl. They passed by Skit and Kreen on their patrol owls, acknowledging them with a simple wave. The young pilots kept a steady eye on their queen and the elf spy as they dropped down from the sky. They landed squarely in front of Commander Lapin's warren. The rabbit patrols observed the two owls, but did not signal the alarm when they noticed it was Queen Wista and Tark in disguise. Upon hearing the noise occurring aboveground, Commander Lapin and most of the rabbits of the eighth regiment popped out of their rabbit holes and gathered around Wista, Spruce, and Tark. Meanwhile, not far away Auralia, Golden Belle, Sparkles, Glitter, and Dazzle settled on a high pine branch. Both the owl and rabbit patrols caught sight of them, but were unconcerned about their presence. Four fairies and a barn owl were regarded as harmless.

Commander Lapin bowed to Queen Wista, who responded by placing her hand on Lapin's nose to show her respect. Tark gave a little bow and changed into his true form.

"I know why you are here," said Lapin. "And I would prefer to speak privately about this matter."

Rabbits and Little Peepers were similar in their curiosity. The rabbits were leaning in to better hear the conversation between their commander and the Little Peepers' leader.

"Follow me," said Lapin. Wista, Tark, and Spruce went with him to the edge of eighth regiment territory. A short distance away two patrols of the seventh regiment were watching them, bending their ears to catch their words.

"It's a lovely day," said Wista. "Though, I hardly imagine Prince Massen and Rupin are enjoying the day as the Black Dragon's prisoners." Lapin and Tark glanced at the top of Misty Falls, the highest point in Hidden Forest.

"It's apparent you came here to discuss the dragon's treasure," stated Lapin.

"You must be well aware by now that the dragon assumes the elves have stolen his treasure," said Wista.

"It's a terrible misunderstanding." Lapin peered at Tark. "I am sorry about your brother. It was not our intention to draw the elves into our argument with the Black Dragon. Before we had a chance to negotiate with the dragon, our patrols spotted him flying off in a rage toward Glenhaven and returning with two elves dangling from his claws."

"How long have you been planning the robbery?" questioned Wista.

"The other commanders have been wanting to remove the dragon from the forest ever since our population began declining. Our forest is ill."

"I am aware of it," said Wista. "Yesterday a Little Peeper was born with a missing arm. The parents were very distraught."

"We can no longer sustain the dragon's appetite," said Lapin. "He has to go! Otherwise, the rabbits will die off." A soft breeze was ruffling his gray coat. "The girl, Shauna, mentioned that there is a place in the human world for creatures with voracious appetites. It's called a zoo. According to her, the creatures are well-fed and well-cared for. I was hoping that we could send the dragon there."

"I do not know anything about this place called a zoo," said Wista. "I was wondering if the Black Dragon would allow himself to be shrunken to the size of a raven. In that way, he wouldn't require so much food. Perhaps one or two mice a night."

"I think he likes being big," cut in Tark.

"That's because he has never experienced the benefits of being small," said Wista. "You are right, Commander, the forest can no longer support a giant dragon. On the other hand, the human world is no place for a dragon, big or small. He does not belong there. We must convince him of the benefits of being reduced to a smaller, maintainable size."

All of a sudden, Auralia sprang from the branch and swooped down to the ground, alighting gently in front of Queen Wista and the others. She changed back into an elf. At the same time, Golden Belle looked at her three cousins, wondering if they should follow Auralia's lead.

"Auralia, you shouldn't be here," Tark said in shock. "If the queen knew you were here—"

"But the queen is here and I am fine with your presence," interrupted Wista. She squinted her eyes upward at Auralia. "I remember you. You carried Ruby to Arborville."

She bowed awkwardly before addressing the queen.

"There is no need to bow," said Wista.

"I heard you debating about what to do with the Black Dragon. May I suggest that you find him a new mate. I can see in his eyes that he is lonely. It is said that dragons exist in the far north where volcanoes melt the ice . . . but that was said a long time ago."

"I am doubtful there are any other dragons left in the world," said Wista. "The humans would have hunted them to extinction. Also, the Black Dragon hates the cold. That's why he hibernates during the long winter."

Auralia looked unhappy with herself. "I am sorry. It was a stupid suggestion."

"It was not a silly suggestion. You are right about the dragon being lonely. He spends too much time alone with his treasures and memories," said Wista. "It was thoughtless of us to ignore this conflict between the Black Dragon and the rabbits for so long. At least, you are trying to come up with a solution." She turned her head and gave Lapin an apologetic look.

"It has been hard on us," said Lapin. "By us, I mean the rabbits."

"King Hoppit once told me that he was detained by a dryad who sang a lengthy ballad to him. The song was about the great sadness that a ferocious dragon felt after his mate died at the hands of humans," said Wista. "I had forgotten about that until now." The Little Peepers came into existence centuries later than the rest of the species of Hidden Forest. They had to learn the early history of the forest from the others. Sometimes it was sketchy or incomplete information. And rarely did anyone take the time to consult with Sawwhet because she would rather write it down than speak of it.

The four fairies appeared, hovering between Commander Lapin and Tark.

"We have not forgotten the history of the dragons," said Golden Belle, who was older than any of them. The oldest fairies were just slightly younger than the Malum. "The Black Dragon once was called Kveikja. His father came here with him and his two other siblings. They also were killed by the humans. One day, Kveikja met his mate, Agir. The two of them seemed happy together. Then, Kveikja came home alone. He never hunted in the human world again. From then on, he became known as the Black Dragon."

"How come you never mentioned this before?" Wista asked Golden Belle.

"No one ever asked us anything about the Black Dragon," replied Golden Belle. "He wants nothing to do with us—or anyone else since Agir died."

"I recall that the dragon tried to starve himself to death after his mate died," added Sparkles. "It was the Malum who convinced him to feed on the rabbits in Hidden Forest. For some reason, they wanted to have a dragon in the forest."

Lapin's hind foot was thumping madly. "Those evil magi! They should have encouraged him to go. The Black Dragon offers nothing to the forest."

"But why would it be so important for the Malum to have a dragon in the forest?" questioned Auralia. "They don't care about anyone other than themselves."

"That is a very good question, Auralia." Queen Wista's gaze fell on Misty Falls. "The Black Dragon must have something they desire. It's the only logical explanation."

"But what could the dragon possibly have that they need from him?" asked Spruce. The northern hawk owl was shaped more like a falcon than an owl. "They did not ask him to fight for them during the Great Banishment."

"He does have gems and other riches," said Lapin.

"He can exhale fire," said Tark.

"He has scales," said Auralia.

"There is only one way to find out," said Wista. "We must ask him ourselves." She turned to face Lapin. "Commander, we need to speak with the Black Dragon. Do you want to go with me?"

Lapin exhaled through his nostrils, while stomping his back leg. "I will go and tell him that we stole his treasure. If he wants it back, he will have to quit killing us. We will find a solution for him."

"Yes, we shall," said Wista. "We have to get Prince Massen and Rupin back from him."

"Do you want the rest of us to come along?" questioned Tark, hoping to see his brother in the dragon's lair.

"It is better that Commander Lapin, Spruce, and I speak to him alone," said Wista. "However, is it possible, Tark, that you could give Commander Lapin a lift to the top of Misty Falls?" She shot a glance at the rabbit leader. "If you don't mind. It's a long way to the dragon's den."

Tark nodded and transformed into a harpy eagle. Harpy eagles have the strength to carry off a monkey from a tree.

"I will ask the rest of you to notify the rabbit commanders of our plans," said Wista.

"If we don't come back by morning, come looking for us," said Lapin.

"This is for good luck." The fairies sprinkled flecks of gold upon Wista, Spruce, Lapin, and Tark.

Wista thanked them and then set off for the Black Dragon's lair. Tark gently picked up Lapin with his talons and lifted him up in the air. They flew low to the ground, hoping to keep out of sight. Nonetheless, Gavran and his messenger ravens, who were roosting in a tree, spotted them during their flight.

□□□

Sorcerer Serpentine had a good idea of where to look for Jackie Jubilee and their children. When he and Jackie were first dating, she mentioned that her aunt and uncle had a cabin in a remote area of Montana. In her youth, she spent the month of July there. She fished for trout in the stream that snaked past the cabin. As much as he hated to admit it, he found Jackie interesting during their courtship. By the time their third child was born, he was ready to strangle her. However, he could not do so. Someone had to raise their children until they were big enough to be sacrificed. It seemed like it took forever for the children to grow to a suitable size. Although he had no feelings for his brats, he was relieved to hear that Warlock Highbrow's two girls were ready to be sacrificed. The thought of plunging a knife into his three children would be a messy affair. It would also require him to kill Jackie. She would never let him take the children from her.

When the youngest child was six months old, Serpentine suffered a major setback. Jackie asked him to watch the children while she went to the grocery store. While he was changing a dirty diaper, the baby peed on him. He smacked the child across the face. His oldest child, who was almost five at the time and already traitorous toward him, reported the incident to their mother. Consequently, Jackie watched him like a hawk. Their relationship soured and life became miserable with her and the kids. Two years later, he lost his temper again. He hit the boy for pooping his pants. Jackie Jubilee moved him out of the house and placed a restraining order against him. This complicated his life. From then on, he had to spy on the children. Every week, he would sneak a peek at them behind Jackie's back. Most of the time, he snooped on his children while they were at the school playground or the local library. The cat that resided at the library watched him suspiciously, though. *There was something not right with that orange cat.* So, needless to say, he was glad to learn Highbrow's children had grown to an appropriate size to fulfill the blood ritual. He was tired of constantly checking up on his kids. If only Zeldar had not dropped the ball and let the girls escape. He cursed the existence of witches.

He stepped harder on the gas pedal as he continued on toward Montana.

□ □ □

Queen Wista and her group set down a short distance from the dragon's cave. Wista asked Tark to remain there because Lapin would need a ride down from the top of Misty Falls.

"Because you're an elf, I think it is best that the dragon does not see you until we straighten out this misunderstanding," explained Wista. "But I promise you that we'll check on the welfare of your brother and the prince."

"I hope the Black Dragon isn't hungry," Lapin said under his breath, as they headed toward the dragon's den.

After Tark watched them take their leave, he rested on a boulder. All the surrounding rocks were covered with moss due to the mist from the eighty-foot waterfall. In the distance, he could make out two sky patrols. Below him he pictured the Dark Shadow with his latest souls in the Pit of Despair. The thought alone made Tark cringe. His father's soul was in the pit. His soul had been there for thirteen years. Often, Tark wondered if there was a way to free his father and the rest of the souls from the Pit of Despair. He imagined it would take a strong spell to release the Dark Shadow's grip on the souls. Perhaps Ruby or Shauna would become powerful enough to cast a spell upon the Dark Shadow and free his father. What he needed was a spellbook from Madame Papulose's basement.

While Tark thought about freeing his father, Queen Wista, Spruce, and Lapin stood at the mouth of the Black Dragon's cave. Stunned by their presence, the Black Dragon choked on his own acidic spit upon seeing them. No one had ever paid him a visit.

"Greetings, Black Dragon! We were hoping to discuss the terms of your proposal," Wista said brightly. She entered his dark, damp den with Lapin hopping behind her. The only light in the cave was provided by the sun shining through the opening of the cave. Spruce remained at the cave entrance. He refused to get any closer to the dragon because his breath was as foul-smelling as rotten eggs. Besides, he hoped to melt into the background without being set on fire. "Let us introduce ourselves. I am Queen Wista, leader of the Little Peepers. And this is Commander Lapin, leader of the Noble Rabbits of the Eighth Regiment." She gestured at Lapin and then at her owl companion behind her. "That's Spruce over there, one of the best owl flyers in all of Hidden Forest. Graduated top of his class."

The dragon's glare was as sharp as his pointed teeth. "I know who and what you are. Did you come here to bore me to death or bring back my treasure?" His gaze traveled past Spruce. "I do not see my treasure. This makes me very unhappy. When I become unhappy, it makes me hungry." He greedily eyed Lapin. "By the size of you, you must be well-fed."

Lapin flinched. He had to make a conscious effort to stop his hind leg from beating the stone floor of the cave.

"We came here to make everyone happy," said Wista. She glanced around the dragon's den. There was a mound of fresh pine boughs on the floor, which apparently was his bed. In one corner of the cave was a pile of rabbit bones. Nearby the bones were two trunks wrapped in heavy chains and locked for good measure. Obviously, the elves must be trapped in them since they were nowhere to be seen. "To get directly to the point, the rabbits, not the elves, took your treasure."

The Black Dragon appeared ready to scorch Lapin with fire. The commander stepped back from the dragon's mouth.

"The rabbits have every intention of giving you your treasure back in exchange for the two elves and a promise to refrain from hunting them," said Wista.

"I don't feed on elves," said the Black Dragon.

"Quit eating rabbits!" said Lapin, barely able to contain his temper. "Don't make light of this. I have lost many of my friends because of you."

"I will starve to death if I take that deal," said the Black Dragon.

"The rabbits will continue to die if you don't make that deal," countered Lapin.

"Surely, we can come up with a solution to everyone's problem," Wista said cheerfully.

"I could eat all three of you," smirked the dragon. "Then, all of *my* problems would truly be gone."

"You still would not have your treasure back," pointed out Wista. "And, if any of us are harmed, the Little Peepers will use their mindbending abilities and force you to leave Hidden Forest."

This threat caught the dragon's attention. He had the ability to set a handful of elves on fire in one breath, but he could not torch a thousand Little Peepers simultaneously, despite their diminutive size.

"The fairies told me that your name is Kveikja—"

"I thought so!" the dragon interrupted Wista. "I had almost forgotten it," he said, lowering his voice. Wista noticed that his tough demeanor softened just a hair. "Kveikja means 'ignite' where I came from. My mother gave me that name because I used to spew hot ashes at my siblings, trying to set them ablaze. My mother scolded me, but I told her that I was just trying to warm them up because of the cold." He grinned at his own mean shenanigans. "My parents claimed my siblings and I were quite the handful. Setting the villagers on fire, burning down castles, torching farm fields. I do miss the taste of their farm animals—sheep, goats, pigs, cows, and horses. They were all sumptuous. Their gems, gold, silver, all of their riches were just as pleasing."

Lapin shared a look with Wista.

"I can see why the humans were peeved at dragons back then," said Lapin.

"The fairies also told me that your mate was killed by humans a long time ago," said Wista, picking up right where she had left off.

"Her name was Agir. I will never forget her name." He sighed deeply, peering once again past Spruce, who kept scooting further away from them.

"That's a lovely name," said Wista. "I'm sure she was just as beautiful as her name."

He gazed toward the radiant sun, recalling the beauty of Agir. Her black scales were as glossy as his, but her teeth were whiter and sharper. "When we were out hunting, she shot out fifty-foot-long fireballs, roasting her prey alive. Agir means 'fire.' She used to enjoy burning things, like entire villages. Some of the villagers managed to get away, though." He shook his large head. "I cannot return to the human world. They will hunt me down."

"What if the fairies reduced you to the size of a crow or a raven?" questioned Wista. "You could live off mice. The owls do it."

"Oh, good heavens!" exclaimed Lapin. "The mice would be in an uproar!" He thumped his foot as hard and fast as a woodpecker pounding on a tree. "I recommend we find you a mate, Kveikja, in the human world—"

"Do not call me by my forgotten name! I will ignite you, just as my name suggests I should do with rabbits who get in my way."

Lapin cleared his throat, as if he found the dragon's words too distasteful to swallow. "After you find a lovely mate, the fairies could shrink both of you to a size that could be easily concealed from the humans. Perhaps the size of bats. And may I suggest that you don't burn down villages, so you won't draw attention to yourselves."

"That's a good idea," said Wista.

"It's a terrible idea!" roared the dragon. "And quit moving your foot, rabbit! It makes me all jumpy, like I want to pounce on something."

"Well, I think that's an equally terrible idea," said Lapin, keeping his foot as still as the pile of bones stacked in the cave.

"Why is it a terrible idea?" Wista asked the dragon. She noticed he was beginning to drool.

"First off, there are probably no remaining dragons in the world, aside from me—"

"I didn't say your mate had to be a dragon," interrupted Lapin.

The Black Dragon looked heatedly at the commander, as if tempted to roast him in the next breath. But he managed to swallow his anger and locked his eyes on Wista. "Secondly, the Malum would come after me if I left the protection of Hidden Forest."

"Why?" asked Wista.

"After Agir died, I made an agreement with the magi. I would give them three of my black scales a year so they would no longer pester me."

"Do you know why the Malum wanted your black scales?" asked Lapin.

The Black Dragon shook his head. "They would not tell me."

"That is very interesting," Wista said to herself. Then, she looked up at the dragon. "We need more time to work this out. However, the two elves that you have imprisoned in your chests cannot survive much longer. Please let them go."

"I will let you have them as soon as my treasure is returned," he said stubbornly. "It's the only thing I have left to remind me of my Agir. I will not give up my treasure for anything."

Queen Wista could see in his yellow eyes that his love for riches had made him unreasonable.

"Will you promise to stop eating the rabbits if we give you back your loot?" interjected Lapin.

"I cannot make that promise because I will not hunt beyond Hidden Forest. This is my home now. I will eat whatever or whoever I choose."

"The Malum are not here to protect you," Lapin reminded him.

"Give us the two elves now and we will give you your treasure tomorrow," insisted Wista. "We can negotiate later about the rabbits."

Commander Lapin shot Wista an appalled look. "I do not trust him."

"I do not trust you, Commander Lapin," said the dragon. "I don't trust anyone."

"If those two elves die, then you will start a war with the elves," said Wista. "If you continue to dine on the local rabbits, then you will start a war with the rabbits and the Little Peepers. Is that what you want?"

The dragon grinned maliciously and then licked his lips. "I believe that I might develop a taste for seared elves."

"Do not make me come back here with a thousand Little Peepers," Wista warned him.

"You will not come back here *ever again*," he smirked. He opened his mouth wide to blow out fire. However, just as he was about to incinerate his unwelcome company, he yawned. He had a strong desire to take a nap. He lay down and closed his eyes.

Commander Lapin looked over at Queen Wista, who had her eyes fixed on the dragon. He could tell that Wista was putting the dragon to sleep with her mind. He dashed over to the treasure chests. As he had expected, he was incapable of unfastening the locks. He began to frantically search for the keys. Meanwhile, Spruce flew off to retrieve Tark. The nimble hands of elves were desperately needed in this situation.

Tark flew into the cave as a harpy eagle, but quickly transformed into his elf self. Lapin was searching through the mound of rabbit bones. Half of them had been gnawed on. As he dug around the pile, he was cringing, certain that he had once known some of these rabbits. At last, he discovered two keys stashed in the jaw of a large-sized rabbit. Most likely, the rabbit came from the fourth regiment because they were bigger-boned rabbits than the other regiments.

"I found the keys," Lapin whispered to Tark. He did not want to wake up the dragon. Wista still had her mind trained on him.

Tark rushed over to the bone pile and snatched the keys from the skull. He darted over to the chests. After a moment of fumbling with the keys, he popped open the first chest. Curled up on its bottom was a squirrel. The creaking of the box hinges woke Prince Massen from his hibernation. He appeared a bit drowsy. Hastily, Tark opened the next chest. Rupin also awoke when the lid flew open. He blinked rapidly to adjust to the dim lighting in the cave.

"Change into owls quickly!" Tark said to them with a low, urgent voice.

Both Massen and Rupin noticed the sleeping dragon and shapeshifted in a hurry. Tark changed back into a harpy eagle and grabbed Lapin by his thick fur coat. Queen Wista quickly hitched a ride with Spruce. And off they went.

The Black Dragon slept until nightfall. After he awoke, the entire forest soon learned the dragon was angry. He roared furiously and sent a fireball high into the sky. A heated message sent to the creatures in Hidden Forest. He would seek his revenge.

□□□

Ruby and Shauna were fast asleep while Vorte and Berruga prepared for bed. Every night before going to sleep, Berruga opened the bedroom window and gazed up at the moon and the stars. In the Peep language, stars were known as "peepholes," where the dead looked through to see their loved ones on earth. The moon was considered a "keyhole" where the dead waited to receive nightly key messages sent up by their loved ones.

"Good night, Pip," she whispered toward the moon. Pip was the name of her son who was killed by the frog-snake many years ago. This time she did not move away from the window.

"What's wrong, Berruga?" asked Vorte. He was already in bed. Their mattress was stuffed with feathers and their sheets were made from plant fibers.

"I am worried about the girls. Don't you think there is too much pressure on them? They have gone through so much lately."

"We are doing our best to watch out for them. The fairies will be helping them with their magic, Oide offered to give them private flying lessons, Swift volunteered to watch over them from the sky . . . and they have us."

Berruga smiled faintly at her husband as the Black Dragon discharged a fireball into the night sky. She did not see the dragon's angry message because her eyes were on her husband.

"Come to bed, Berruga. You need your sleep."

She crawled into bed with him. She rested her head against the pillow and stared up at the ceiling. "But we are asking them to cast a

160

spell upon the Malum. Are they powerful enough to stand up to the magi, even with the aid of our mindbending skills?"

"This afternoon, I went to speak with Queen Wista and asked that very same question," confessed Vorte.

Berruga sat up in bed, surprised. "What did she say?"

"She believes the girls' magic is incredibly powerful, and that their magic was most likely jumpstarted when the fairies shrank them."

Berruga could hear the worry in Vorte's voice. "And what else?"

"Wista is concerned that their little bodies cannot contain so much magic. Their father is a full-grown warlock with incredible powers."

"What does Wista think will happen to the girls?"

"If the girls remain this size, they might . . . well, explode in the same manner as a star."

Berruga gasped.

"Queen Wista thinks it might be best if they return to their original human size," Vorte continued uncomfortably.

"That means they won't be able to stay with us," Berruga said miserably.

"It just means they can't stay in our treehouse," said Vorte. "Or ride on birds."

Tears began to slide down Berruga's cheeks. "I like having them here with us."

"Please don't cry. Queen Wista suggested that a new, large house could be built. We can still be their guardians in the new, larger place." He clasped her hand. "You have mentioned more than once that you wished our kitchen was bigger."

Berruga smiled at Vorte. "For the girls' sake, we must do what is right for them. They must change back into their original size and we will build a new place for ourselves . . . with a big kitchen."

Vorte returned the smile. "That's what I thought you would say. Otherwise, the girls could go live with the elves. But I don't feel right about that, especially with all their rules about what individuals can and cannot be."

"The elves are too rigid in their ways."

"Tomorrow I will go with the girls to Tinsel. I will explain to them the situation. The fairies will have to change them back."

"I will go along," said Berruga. "They will miss flying," she added after a lengthy pause.

"They will not have to stop flying. They are the children of Warlock Highbrow. They can learn to fly on a broomstick or change themselves into birds. With the proper training, they'll be as powerful as the magi, according to Wista and the fairies."

"You are right, Vorte. And it will be our responsibility to keep this power from going to their heads." She squeezed Vorte's hand. "It will be all right, won't it?"

"We will make it work."

Berruga lay down again, pulled the top sheet up to her chin, and closed her eyes. She would do whatever it takes to save those motherless children—her children now—from their warlock father and the rest of the magi. The Little Peepers were strong in their own way, too.

Chapter Seventeen

Caught Off Guard

The elves armed themselves with bows and arrows while four hundred Little Peepers and all three hundred forty-two fairies came to protect Glenhaven from being burned down by the Black Dragon. The sky was crowded with air squadrons.

Ruby and Shauna were shuttled over to Glenhaven instead of Tinsel to practice their magic for the day. Vorte and Berruga traveled with the girls. However, before they set out for Glenhaven, Berruga and Vorte informed the girls that they must return to their original size. Eventually, their little bodies would not be able to contain the warlock's powerful magic. At first, the girls took the news hard. They wanted to fly on birds. But Berruga and Vorte informed them that they would be able to turn themselves into any bird their heart desired, like the elves. After they assured the girls that the Little Peepers would build them a bigger treehouse, Ruby and Shauna asked if they could decorate their own room. The girls seemed to accept their new circumstances better than Berruga and Vorte had anticipated. Afterward, Swift arrived on their doorstep. The peregrine falcon notified them that the two kidnapped elves had been freed by Queen Wista and Commander Lapin. The Little Peepers were now being asked to defend Glenhaven from a dragon attack. The fairies had already been summoned to the elf village. The peregrine falcon had orders from Queen Wista to take the girls to Queen Rossen's royal residence, where the training session would be held.

"We appear to be at an impasse," Queen Wista said to Queen Rossen. They were in Rossen's private quarters. "The rabbit commanders refuse to give back the dragon's treasure unless the Black Dragon is kicked out of the forest. I speculate that he won't leave until there are no more rabbits left to eat."

"The Black Dragon locked up my son and his best friend in wooden boxes without food, water, or fresh air. If it weren't for you and the others, they would be dead," said Rossen, seething.

"Thank goodness, they were clever enough to change into squirrels."

The elf queen's face was as crimson as the rubies and garnets in her necklace. "Maybe it's time to slay the dragon."

Wista's protruding eyes bulged a bit further. "Kill the dragon? Surely, we can come up with a better solution than that."

"Like what?"

"I would like to discuss it over another cup of tea," said Wista.

Rossen nodded, stood up from her chair, walked over to the door, opened it, and asked her hand servant to bring them two more cups of tea.

□□□

In a private guest room in the queen's palace, Golden Belle and Flicker were training Ruby and Shauna to perform magic with wands. Vorte and Berruga were watching the training session. It was decided that Ruby and Shauna would remain small until their treehouse was built. Back in Arborville, there was a large group of Little Peepers beginning to construct it as the girls trained.

"I have the amnesia spell," said Counselor Nirva, as she entered the room. She was clutching a sheet of paper. "It looks complicated." She did not like to admit that she could not read a single word of it. She called Ruby and Shauna over, interrupting their training session.

All of them gathered around the sheet of paper.

"What does it say?" asked Berruga.

"For the spell to work, the tip of the wand must be touched by a dryad, a unicorn, and a witch, in that order," Ruby said, reading Mister Barnaby's handwritten notes. She cast an astonished look at all of them. "This can't be for real?"

"Amnesia spells are difficult," said Golden Belle. "As far as I know, not one of the Malum has successfully cast one. Unless, it was spun upon me, then I wouldn't remember it." She winked at Ruby to let her know she was teasing.

"We met a tree nymph the other day," said Shauna. "And we can find a unicorn on Unicorn Trail."

"Finding a witch will be more difficult," said Flicker. "Hidden Forest is currently out of them."

"I hope we don't have to track down Witch Zeldar and make her touch our wands," Ruby said frightfully.

"There are two other witches—Mortify and Blackheart," said Golden Belle.

"Are they as mean as Witch Zeldar?" asked Shauna, shuddering.

"Yes," answered Berruga. "Witch Blackheart has a reputation for her black magic—"

"And accidentally blowing up cauldrons," noted Golden Belle.

"Witch Mortify is known for performing humiliating experiments on the forest inhabitants," continued Berruga.

"She tortured owls the most," said Flicker.

"Well, one of the witches will have to fulfill the requirement of the spell," Nirva sighed.

"It won't be easy. We would have to use our mindbending skills on one of them," said Berruga. "It would require dozens of Little Peepers to force a witch to touch your wand. The bigger problem is that we would have to enter the human world. We would prefer not to be seen by humans, even if our miniature size reduces the chances of being spotted."

"Is there anything else needed in the spell?" questioned Vorte. He was not liking this amnesia spell.

Ruby continued reading. "The wand must be made from an ancient elm tree."

"Elm and mulberry trees are the choice woods of the elves," Nirva explained to the girls. "Both woods are hardy and resistant to rot. We believe they bring us luck and give us strength. We can provide the elm wood for the new wands."

"But the two wands should be carved by fairies," said Golden Belle. "It will strengthen the wands' magical power. We'll also sprinkle each wand with gold dust."

"The spell doesn't call for that," said Ruby. "But I think it's a good idea."

"Better safe than sorry," said Vorte. He couldn't help but be concerned for the girls' safety.

"They will have to be much bigger than this wand," said Shauna, displaying the one-inch wand in her hand. "It's the size of a pine needle. When we become full-size again, fairy wands will be way too small for us."

Flicker leaned over Ruby's shoulder. "What else does the spell require?"

"To recite the following, 'Qui olim fuerunt et erit in perpetuum,' while pointing the wand at the intended target," said Ruby.

"What does that mean?" asked Nirva.

"According to Mister Barnaby's note, it's Latin for 'Who you once were shall be nevermore,'" said Ruby, looking closely at Mister Barnaby's small writing. "That sounds like something the executioner would say to his victims right before chopping their heads off." The others, except for Shauna, were giving her an odd look. "Our mom used to tell us fairytales."

"We don't tell those kind of tales," declared Golden Belle, wincing at such a gruesome thought. "Human children must suffer from nightmares."

"Sometimes I wonder if we're not in one of Mom's fairytales," piped up Shauna, peering at her wand and then at the fairies.

"This is no fairytale," said Nirva. "Our world is as real to us as yours is to you."

"We are part of your world now," pointed out Ruby.

"Yes. Therefore, for the sake of all the good creatures of Hidden Forest, we are counting on you to finish off the Malum, once and for all," said Nirva. "We only have one opportunity to get it right."

"Those Latin words are a mouthful to say," Ruby said anxiously. "I'm not sure I will remember all of them when facing the Malum."

"Why don't you continue your lessons," suggested Berruga, "while we discuss how to carry out the amnesia spell."

Ruby and Shauna went with Golden Belle and Flicker to practice using their wands. As soon as they were out of earshot, Berruga said to Counselor Nirva, "They are only children. We need to build up their confidence, not frighten them out of their wits." She could tell by Nirva's expression that her advice was not well-received. She understood the reason, too. The top advisor to the elf queen viewed her as a simple commoner.

"Look at our girls perform, Berruga," said Vorte to diffuse the tension.

They watched Ruby and Shauna make themselves grow taller until the top of their heads touched the ceiling and then they reshrunk themselves. Golden Belle and Flicker were ready with their wands in case the girls overdid their magic and banged their heads against the ceiling or on the floor.

Suddenly, there was shouting from outside. They rushed out to see what was causing the commotion. The crowd gazed upward. The Black Dragon circled overhead. The patrol squadrons backed away from the enraged dragon. On the ground, four hundred Little Peepers focused their minds on the dragon, demanding him to leave. The fairies had their wands aimed at the dragon, hoping to shrink him. But the dragon was flying too high for their magic to reach him. The dragon shot out a long plume of fire, wheeled once in the air, and then abruptly flew off. Flycatcher, Hummer, and their owls, Tuft and Dots, barely avoided being hit by the dragon's fire.

"He seems to be taking pleasure in terrorizing the villagers, like he did in the old days." Queen Rossen remarked to Queen Wista. Both of them were watching the Black Dragon from the royal courtyard.

"I hope the rabbits are hiding," Wista said tensely. "He will kill them just for the sake of killing them."

"I wonder where the rabbits are keeping his treasure," mused Rossen.

Although Wista had a pretty good idea, she made no reply as she watched the dragon vanish from the sky.

□□□

Miss Whiskers enjoyed beginning her day reading the morning newspaper before the start of her busy day. Today's headline caught her attention, *Another Local Man Goes Missing.* She quickly skimmed the newspaper article and then let out a heavy sigh. Two local men in their sixties had disappeared under mysterious circumstances. The first man was the bank president and the second man was the town mayor. There were currently no suspects. Miss Whiskers turned the page. Just as she began reading the advice column about a divorcing couple suing over the custody of their pet dog, Mister Barnaby barged through the cat door.

"Did you read about the missing men, yet?" blurted out Mister Barnaby. He noticed the newspaper laying in front of Miss Whisker's nose. "Madame Papulose was taken into custody by the police early this morning."

"I see that you've dispensed with your usual greeting this morning, Mister Barnaby. So, please tell me, why was Madame Papulose arrested?"

"Because she's a Wiccan. I overheard some of the neighbors saying that Madame Papulose caused the victims to disappear using magic."

"But she has no magical powers."

"It doesn't matter to her accusers." Mister Barnaby jumped onto the librarian's desk where Miss Whiskers was seated and said in a low voice, "Opal and Edward are planning to break Madame Papulose out of jail if she isn't released." After recovering from the initial shock of two ghosts in her house, Madame Papulose had decided to let Opal and Edward stay in the basement because they got along splendidly.

Miss Whiskers put aside her newspaper and gave Mister Barnaby a thoughtful look. "What evidence do the police have against Madame Papulose?"

"There is no evidence against her because she didn't do it. We both know it was the big, frightening shadow from Hidden Forest that nabbed the men. But the locals are pointing their fingers at Madame Papulose. I tell you, it's a witch hunt . . . or a Wiccan hunt."

"The police can't arrest Madame Papulose if there is no hard evidence against her. Humans have laws they must abide by, Mister Barnaby."

"Madame Papulose has been accused solely because she is different from everyone else in town. Have we not learned that from books?"

Miss Whiskers twitched her whiskers. "You are a clever one, Mister Barnaby, using books to persuade me. How do you suppose we can assist Madame Papulose?"

"We must locate the fairies in Hidden Forest. They'll be able to shrink Madame Papulose, so she can escape through the cell bars. Once out, an owl can fly her to the magical woods. She will be safe there, hidden away from her accusers."

She rubbed her right cheek with the back of her paw as she deliberated. "It's possible that Madame Papulose might not like the magical world. You might want to ask her first before whisking her away."

"The magical forest has to be better than jail," retorted Mister Barnaby.

"I suppose that's true, Mister Barnaby. However, I can assure you that Madame Papulose was just brought in for questioning. She'll be home soon."

"If she is locked up in jail, Opal and Edward have offered to fetch the fairies in Hidden Forest," said Mister Barnaby, not reassured by Miss Whiskers' words. "They can easily slip into the enchanted forest without being seen."

"If I remember correctly, the fairies are unable to shrink people out here in the nonmagical world. Their magic weakens." She gazed down at the newspaper again.

Mister Barnaby looked disappointed. "I just wish these magical creatures could get rid of that creepy shadow. It's enough to have ghosts lurking around the local cemetery and one's basement."

"I prefer ghosts creeping around town than those terrible magi."

"I don't understand why *those terrible magi* aren't accused of the kidnappings. They wear black cloaks and pointy boots! Poor Madame Papulose doesn't deserve to be treated like this!"

"The police have probably heard the rumors about Madame Papulose's growing collection of spellbooks and that's why she is under suspicion. Or, it might be that she wears a black, pointy hat in public—just like the magi."

"But she doesn't wear pointy boots like them."

"Well, there's your proof that Madame Papulose is innocent of these kidnappings," Miss Whiskers said sarcastically.

Mister Barnaby didn't look reassured. "Madame Papulose uses a walking stick which closely resembles a wand. That could work against her."

In the meantime, a frantic Opal and Edward were making their way to the cemetery. It was time to call on their old friends in their time of need. Or rather Madame Papulose's time of need. They would not let the coppers lock up sweet Madame Papulose, who provided them with a new home. Both Opal and Edward enjoyed living in her basement. A roof over their heads kept them out of the weather and there were plenty of books there to read. Last evening, Madame Papulose came down to the basement and kept them company. Mister Barnaby joined them for a short while.

As Opal and Edward approached the entrance gate to the graveyard, events went from bad to worse. They spotted Jackie Jubilee. She was standing alongside the front gate. Her children were not with her. As the ghosts drew nearer to Jackie, it became apparent that she was a ghost like them.

"Oh, good heavens, sweet Edward, something is horribly wrong." Opal grabbed Edward's hand and they floated swiftly over to Jackie.

Jackie began wailing when she spotted them. Naturally, Jackie's loud cries caught the attention of the other spirits in the cemetery. A handful of ghosts, including Opal and Edward, were at Jackie's side.

"What happened to your head, Miss Jackie Jubilee?" asked Opal. Jackie's head sat crookedly on her neck. "And where are your children?"

Between her sobs, Jackie poured out the story of how Serpentine had tracked down her and their children to a remote cabin in Montana. On her way to the outhouse this morning, she felt a tremendous blow to the back of the head. After collapsing to the ground, she saw Serpentine out of the corner of her eye. He stood over her, sneering triumphantly. The stock of his rifle was bloody. He had whacked her with the butt of the rifle instead of shooting her.

"Probably did not want the sound of a gunshot waking up the children inside the house," Edward reasoned.

"I suppose so, dear. A gunshot can wake up the dead."

Jackie continued on with her story as if she did not hear their comments. "Before I lost consciousness, I felt him dragging my body down to the river. Then, he rolled me into the river and the current pulled me under . . . all I can recall is a cold blackness. The next thing I remember was waking up in bed at my house here. It took me only a few moments to realize that I was a ghost, but it has taken me much longer to accept that I am one. Since I couldn't go to the police, I came over here for help. I didn't know what else to do!" she moaned. "He probably killed my kids, too!" She cried without tears. Her entire body shook from agony.

"Your children are still alive," Edward assured her.

"You don't know that," spluttered Jackie.

"Yes, we do," said Opal. "We know what is happening. Isn't that right, my dear Edward?"

"Of course, my love."

Opal and Edward began relating the story of the magi from Hidden Forest. The other ghosts were transfixed. It had been a long time since anything this frightening had occurred in their town. The ghosts did not consider themselves terrifying because they did not harm anyone. In their opinion, living beings were much scarier than ghosts. Some of the ghosts were downright frightened of people. After Opal finished her account, the other ghosts promised Jackie that they would find a way to save her children from Sorcerer Serpentine and the rest of the magi.

As the ghosts developed a plan to rescue the children, they did not notice the three ravens, perched on a tree limb above the old grave of Jackie's grandfather, listening in. This was their first big break in learning the whereabouts of Sorcerer Serpentine or his children. They flew off to report to their leader Gavran.

Chapter Eighteen

The Forgotten Past

Tark and Auralia unexpectedly found themselves at the same molehill. All around them molehills dotted the lush meadow. They were surrounded by leafy trees with thick trunks, heavy bark, and gnarled limbs. Overhead, the sky was a brilliant shade of blue with white, wispy clouds. But dark clouds were gathering over the distant hills.

"What are you doing here?" they asked simultaneously.

"You know I am the queen's spy," replied Tark.

"But she didn't send you here," said Auralia. "Coming here was your own decision."

"Why did you come here? Shouldn't you be at the orchards?"

She shrugged. "Maybe I want to be something other than a beekeeper."

Both stared down at the molehill and then looked up at each other.

"If you find the dragon's treasure down there, what are you aiming to do?" Auralia asked Tark.

"I could ask you the same question." He didn't want her to know he had a premonition the treasure would trigger a major struggle in Hidden Forest.

"I came here just because I am curious where the treasure is hidden." Auralia wasn't entirely truthful. She thought if she recovered the dragon's loot, it would increase her chances of becoming a spy for the queen, like Tark. "Do you want to look for it together?"

"You can come along with me. I'm good friends with Rooter, Erde, and Snoot."

"I am, as well. If not, even better friends," she tacked on for good measure. She would not let Queen Rossen's top spy get the better of her.

Once more, they stared at the hole. Both of them unwilling to admit that claustrophobia was hindering them from changing into moles and entering the pitch-black tunnel.

Just then, Erde stuck her head out from the entrance. "Ah, it's you two who are making all the racket up here." She slid back into the tunnel. "Don't worry, it's only Tark and Auralia," she shouted, her voice echoing through the long tunnel. She reemerged. The bright midday sun hurt her eyes. "I have a strong suspicion why you are here."

"You are hiding the treasure for the rabbits, aren't you?" said Tark.

"Lately, I have learned a thing or two about the elves," stated Erde. "For instance, I have discovered that the elves have been trading fool's gold for the dragon's gold bricks, goblets, and gems. In my opinion, that's cheating."

Auralia stole a glance at Tark. "Did you know about this?"

Tark's cheeks reddened. "I was aware of it. There is no real gold to be found in all of Hidden Forest, only fool's gold."

"And fairy gold," added Erde. "But the fairies don't trade their gold because it's only useful coming from their wands." Fairy gold will dissipate after a purchase is completed. It's worth less than even fool's gold.

"Do Commander Lapin and the other rabbits know about the fool's gold?" asked Tark.

"I mentioned it to him," replied Erde. "I am afraid that we and the rabbits do not trust the elves anymore. What other creatures of the forest have they betrayed?"

"We go back a long way, Erde," said Tark. "You were friends with my mother."

"Aye," said Erde. "How much I miss your mother. It's still hard to believe she died from ingesting hemlock. She was so knowledgeable about plants and potions."

Tark felt a sharp twinge in his heart. He had lost both of his parents within a short period of time. Most elves did not suffer the loss of their parents.

"Have you lost your faith in all elves?" Auralia asked. For the most part, the moles and the elves had always shared a good working relationship. The elves allowed the moles to trespass on their land with the benefit of the moles breaking up and aerating the soil. The tilled soil improved the production of the crops. Though, she had to admit, there were times the elves inadvertently destroyed the moles' tunnels and instances where the moles accidentally ruined some of the elves' plants. Every so often, this caused tension between the two species.

"I have not lost my faith in all elves." Erde scratched the dirt below her sharp claws, as if searching for her next words. "But there are certain events that have always bothered us about the Great Banishment. Things that have never been properly explained."

"What hasn't been explained?" asked Tark.

"Why would the Dark Shadow choose King Koning, Prince Cobias, and Tark's father?" questioned Erde. "Why would Queen Rossen agree to have her mate imprisoned in the Pit of Despair? It makes no sense whatsoever."

Tark and Auralia had no answer.

"And now, we discover that the elves have been deceiving the dragon with fool's gold," Erde continued, after the elves made no reply. "There's something fishy going on."

"Perhaps there is an explanation . . . but I don't know what it is," admitted Tark.

"Certainly, there's an explanation. One that we may well not like." Abruptly, Erde sniffed the air. "It is going to rain soon. I suggest you seek shelter from the storm."

"But what about the dragon's treasure?" asked Auralia.

"I promise you that it will not get wet," replied Erde. "I must return to the darkness because the sunlight is hurting my eyes." She bade them a good day and disappeared into the tunnel.

Tark and Auralia remained there, staring at the tunnel.

"So, what do you want to do next?" she asked him.

"Sit down and think."

"You cannot stand up and think?"

"I have slept little since Ruby and Shauna have entered the forest. I'm groggy from lack of sleep."

"Lately, all of us are feeling more exhausted." She glanced around before leveling her eyes on Tark. "The forest is unwell. I think its magic is dying."

"And we grow weaker with it."

"Yes. Yesterday my father told me that the bees are producing less honey."

"Come and sit with me." He walked over to a boulder that sat squarely in the meadow. Auralia followed him and seated herself alongside him.

"The magi were here before the elves," said Tark. "No one really knows much about the Malum's history. Or where the magi came from."

"Or how many there were," said Auralia.

Tark gave her a funny look. "What do you mean by that?"

"We're assuming there's only been nine magi. How do we know there weren't more of them at the beginning? The bad magi might have destroyed the good ones. You know how the Malum are bent on destruction. And it is quite possible that the good ones who were eliminated might've created Hidden Forest. Otherwise, how did it get here?"

"It might've always been here."

"How did the elves get here?" asked Auralia. "And why do we have shapeshifting abilities while the other creatures of the forest don't?"

"Are you suggesting the magi created us?"

"Maybe."

"I don't believe the Malum created us," Tark replied quickly. "Or, at least, I hope they didn't create us."

"We know nothing of our history, as if it's a big secret."

"Sorcerer Spellbinder did create the Little Peepers," mused Tark. "And they have mindbending abilities . . ."

Their conversation was abruptly cut short by the appearance of Commander Lapin and First Officer Poppin. They did not conceal their surprise upon seeing Tark and Auralia in the meadow.

"Are you out searching for the dragon's treasure?" Lapin questioned them.

"We are out seeking answers," Tark answered truthfully. "I don't want to see anyone else harmed. My brother and Prince Massen are still healing from their brush with the Black Dragon."

"I hope that you do not blame me for their capture," said Lapin. "It was not my intention for anyone to be harmed."

"Commander Lapin," said Auralia, hopping off the boulder, "were the rabbits here before the elves?"

"Yes," said Lapin. "All the animals were here before the elves, except for the Black Dragon." He shifted his gaze from the two elves to the molehill. He was in a rush to speak with the moles.

Auralia and Tark drew closer to Lapin and Poppin.

"Has there ever been more than nine magi in Hidden Forest?" asked Auralia.

Auralia's question made Lapin and Poppin stop in their tracks. They wiggled their long ears and tapped their hind legs, reflecting on ancient stories told by their elders.

"There is an ancient tale of a head magus that was defeated by the other nine," replied Lapin. "But I believe it's just an entertaining story to tell during the long, cold, winter nights."

Tark and Auralia knew the rabbits handed down their history orally from generation to generation. They did not write anything down on scrolls, parchments, or cave walls.

"Perhaps the owls know more about the history of the Malum," said Poppin. "Why don't you go speak with the elder owl, Sawwhet. She might be able to answer some of your questions."

"We need to get going," said Lapin. "I would appreciate it if you did not tell anyone that you saw us here."

"We won't," said Tark. "Likewise, please don't tell anyone that you spotted *us* here, either."

The two elves and the two rabbits nodded, acknowledging their mutual understanding.

Sawwhet lived in a tall, broad western cedar tree that bordered Unicorn Trail. She spent most of her days roosting or recording the history of Hidden Forest onto parchment with her beak and talons. At night, she hunted mice and voles. She was never a patrol bird or even went to Aviation School. She considered herself a historian and preferred not to get caught up in current political affairs. She was one of the oldest birds in Hidden Forest and much older than the elves.

Auralia stole glances at Tark as they trod along Unicorn Trail. She was hoping to catch a glimpse of a unicorn, but it was highly unlikely because Tark was with her. Unicorns, typically, only revealed themselves to young maidens, although there were exceptions. Auralia had to admit that Tark was quite handsome. Nonetheless, he would've been more appealing if he wasn't smitten with Counselor Nirva. "I have never met Sawwhet," she said, as a red hummingbird zipped across the path. "I have heard stories about her, though. It is said her parchment of our history is so big and heavy that it could smother the Black Dragon or fill the Pit of Despair." She grinned at Tark. "Maybe we could use her parchment to suffocate our enemies."

Tark smiled, despite his worries. Rupin suffered a nightmare early this morning. His brother dreamt that he had fallen into the Pit of Despair. He landed on top of their father who had become a skeleton.

As they approached Sawwhet's cedar tree, they spotted the small, rufous-colored owl roosting on a branch outside her cavity. She was not alone. Queen Wista was there along with Swift, King Hoppit's peregrine falcon. The three of them appeared to be engaged in a serious conversation. Tark and Auralia halted, wondering if they should interrupt them. The two elves stood on the path and debated what to do. Suddenly, Swift took off from his perch and flew toward the elves. Within seconds, he landed at their feet.

"Queen Wista desires your company. She wants to speak with you." In the blink of an eye, Swift flew off and returned to his place on the branch.

"I wish I could fly as fast as Swift," said Tark.

I can, thought Auralia.

As Tark and Auralia drew closer, Wista greeted them cheerfully while Sawwhet, who was only half the size of Swift, appeared displeased to have more company. Sawwhet preferred to be alone. Introductions were made quickly because urgent business was at hand.

"Elves," said Sawwhet, eyeing Tark and Auralia from head to toe. "I recall the very first time I laid eyes on your kind."

"How long ago was that?" asked Auralia, looking up at the branch.

"During the one hundred forty-second eclipse of the moon," Sawwhet replied. "This cedar tree had not even sprouted yet. I have the exact date noted in my records."

"Sawwhet was just sharing the story of the Malum with us," said Queen Wista.

Tark observed Sawwhet. Saw-whet owls closely resembled elf owls and pygmy-owls. All three species had yellow eyes, lacked ear tufts, and were on the smaller size in comparison to most owl species. "Did the magi live in Hidden Forest before the owls, Sawwhet?"

"The saw-whet owls came after the magi," explained Sawwhet. "According to my ancestors' stories, the owls were created for the enjoyment of the magi. But they turned mean and harmed the owls. They only wanted to capture them and use them in their experiments."

"Who created the owls?" asked Auralia.

"Mem," replied Sawwhet. "She is the mother of the magi." The others were shocked at the news. "She is the one who created Hidden Forest and most everything you see around you."

"How come we've never heard of this before?" asked Tark.

"It is written down in a couple of my scrolls," Sawwhet replied matter-of-factly.

"I can't read your language," Tark retorted. "And even if I could, your scrolls are hidden away in your tree."

"I have to keep them in a safe place because I do not want them to be pilfered," explained Sawwhet. "They are precious to me and need to be guarded from others."

"You protect your scrolls like the Black Dragon protects his treasure," Swift pointed out.

"Where is Mem now?" Wista broke in, after noticing Sawwhet's ruffled feathers.

"She vanished many years ago," replied Sawwhet. "I would like to know myself what happened to her, so I can put it down on record."

"What else do you know about the Malum?" Wista asked again.

"I was not born yet when the magi came to the forest," said Sawwhet. "But as a wee youngster I heard tales from my elders. However, they were all eventually slain by the Malum. According to them, the Malum's story began with a single deity with great powers. Mem created the magical inhabitants of Hidden Forest to keep her company. Yet, she was still lonely. Therefore, she created a child for herself. She named the child Zeldar. But Mem's loneliness wouldn't go away. She created eight more offspring. But none of them turned out right. Their magic eventually corrupted them. Then, Mem vanished from Hidden Forest. She was never seen or heard from again."

"What happened afterwards?" asked Auralia.

Sawwhet shrugged. "That's no mystery. The Malum increased their trapping of owls and rabbits and using them in their potions and spells. I recall the magi tried to go after the elves at the very beginning, but they couldn't capture the shapeshifters, except for the wee ones. As a result, the elves closely guarded their youngsters. Eventually, the magi left the elves alone because they were incapable of eliminating the elves' shapeshifting ability. The magi were stuck with the elves."

"Why can't the Malum remove the elves' shapeshifting ability?" asked Tark, craning his head to see the small owl. She was so small that he could easily cup her in both hands.

"It was Mem who gave the elves their ability to shapeshift. And only she who could take that ability away." She looked pointedly at Tark and Auralia. "Not even black magic can take your powers away."

This was the first time Auralia and Tark had heard this story. They assumed elves had always been shapeshifters.

"The elves cannot lose their shapeshifting abilities because Mem created them," said Wista, mostly to herself. "However, Spellbinder created Little Peepers. If he is canceled out for good, I do not know if Little Peepers will continue to exist. I don't believe anyone will know until it happens."

Tark and Auralia were disturbed by Wista's statement.

"There is one thing I know for certain—none of us will be safe if the Malum return," said Sawwhet. "They will go back to their old ways and put owls and rabbits in their cages and cauldrons again. I might have to hole up in my tree and never come out again."

"That reminds me," said Wista, staring down at the elves. She never got tired of looking at the physical beauty of the elves and fairies. "Tark, Auralia, I need to ask a huge favor of you." They gave the leader of the Little Peepers their full attention. "I want you to go with Skit and Kreen to the basement of Madame Papulose's house . . . do you know where it is? It's across from Sorcerer Serpentine's house?" Neither one knew its location. "Skit and Kreen will show you the way. With the help of Madame Papulose's housecat, Mister Barnaby, I want you to search through Madame Papulose's spellbooks. I want you to find a spell that calls for three dragon scales, memorize it, and then report directly back to me." The two elves gave her puzzled looks. "It's important that you carry out this errand. The spell might reveal a vulnerability of the Malum. Skit and Kreen will be leaving at sunset." She glanced over at the darkening skies on the western horizon. "The owls might not be able to fly tonight. You might have to travel in another disguise."

"Queen Rossen might not let me go," said Auralia.

"I will have a message delivered to Queen Rossen," said Wista. "She will agree to my request, especially when four hundred Little Peepers are protecting Glenhaven from the Black Dragon. However, I suggest that you come with me to Arborville and not return to your village until your mission is accomplished."

Auralia and Tark knew something was upsetting Wista by the way she said Queen Rossen's name. They could only guess Sawwhet revealed something earlier about Queen Rossen that disturbed Wista.

Sawwhet yawned. "It is time for my afternoon nap. I must ask all of you to leave." She offered a simple goodbye and then flew into the cavity of her tree and vanished from sight. She had always preferred her privacy over the company of others. In many ways, she was like a unicorn. One of the reasons she lived alongside Unicorn Trail was that she realized the unicorns would never bother her. They had a mutual understanding.

The others traveled together to the village of the Little Peepers. Once they reached Arborville, Swift went out to hunt for his midday meal.

Chapter Nineteen

Menacing Skies

Opal and Edward escorted Jackie Jubilee to Madame Papulose's house. A summer thunderstorm was forecast for late afternoon and she desired protection from the rain and the lightning. Jackie did not want to remain in the cemetery because she wanted a roof over her head. However, she did not want to live in her own house since there were too many memories of her children in it. Her physical body, though, was still exposed to the weather. It was back in the river in Montana, lodged on a sandbar. No boater or fisherman had discovered it yet.

"Madame Papulose is currently detained," said Opal, as they passed through the front door, as ghosts do, without having to open it. "But Mister Barnaby should be here." She glanced around the front parlor. "Mister Barnaby!" she called out. "Are you home?" A black cat jumped down from the windowsill. "Well, there you are, Mister Barnaby!"

"I see that you brought home a graveyard friend," said Mister Barnaby. He noticed that the head and body, of the unfamiliar ghost, were misaligned. It looked like the head had been hit hard from behind. Another murder victim, he assumed.

"This is Jackie Jubilee," Opal said. "Sorcerer Serpentine murdered her and now she is a ghost." Jackie began to sob. "Please don't cry, dear."

"I can't even produce tears!" Jackie sobbed harder. "I don't like being a ghost . . . my children will be frightened of me. How will I be able to rescue them?"

"*We* will rescue them," said Opal.

Mister Barnaby's green eyes grew wide. "We will?"

"We will," said Edward.

"Have you heard anything lately from Madame Papulose?" Edward asked Mister Barnaby.

Jackie stood with her mouth hanging open. "Can all cats communicate with ghosts?"

"We can, if we choose to," replied Mister Barnaby. He shifted his attention to Opal and Edward. "Renzo stopped by to let me know that

Madame Papulose is still being held in custody." Renzo was a black-and-white tomcat who lived in the jailhouse. "So, how are you planning to rescue the children?"

"We intend to get help from the creatures in Hidden Forest," said Edward.

"Miss Whiskers thought Madame Papulose would be released from jail soon. But, evidently, she's wrong." Suddenly, his ears and tail shot straight up as he looked up at Jackie. "Holy Cat! Will Madame Papulose be blamed for you and your children's disappearance, too?"

"The police will suspect Serpentine. I had a restraining order against him and he is currently out of town," said Jackie, scowling. "In another state."

"Witches are *always* blamed," insisted Mister Barnaby. "Haven't any of you read *The Crucible*?" The others stared blankly at him. "It's a story based on actual events. The townspeople in a small community falsely accused their neighbors of being witches and then put the accused on trial. They were always found guilty and received a death sentence. This defies logic. If they were real witches, they would have killed their accusers and everyone else in the courtroom."

Jackie was tapping her foot just like Commander Lapin. "We must leave right away for this Hidden Forest! I must save my children from Serpentine! Most likely, he has them locked up in the house. They must be terrified!"

"Where are they?" asked Mister Barnaby.

"In Montana," replied Jackie.

"Holy Cat! It would require an airplane to get there in time," said Mister Barnaby.

"We do not need a flying machine! All we need are peregrine falcons," exclaimed Edward. "Remember how the Little Peepers told us that they rode all sorts of birds! They could fly there on falcons and tie up Serpentine in the same fashion as the Lilliputians did to Gulliver in *Gulliver's Travels*."

"Going to Hidden Forest would be an adventure similar to the ones Gulliver had," mused Opal. "So, who is willing to venture to the forest with Edward and me?" Opal was looking straight at Mister Barnaby.

"Not the black cat," said Mister Barnaby. "In spite of our camouflage, black cats can be spotted at night. Or in a dark forest. Our eyes glow in the moonlight."

"Ours, too," said Opal. "Nonetheless, Mister Barnaby, I suppose it makes more sense if you remain here, in case Madame Papulose returns home before we do. We do not want her to fret over us."

"I guess that means the three of us will have this exciting adventure without Mister Barnaby," said Edward, indicating himself and the other two ghosts in the room. "Perhaps a kind creature from the forest will show us the way to the village of the Little Peepers."

"Do you think the magical forest has unicorns, my dear Edward? I have always wanted to see a unicorn."

"For your lovely sake, I do hope so."

As they ironed out their plan to recruit the Little Peepers, they were unaware that the Black Dragon was launching his own plans for the forest creatures.

□□□

"Amorite lives in this tree over here," said Golden Belle, pointing her wand at a laurel tree. "It's the only laurel tree in the entire forest. She guards it with her life." Amorite was a tree nymph.

Ruby and Shauna were carrying their new, full-sized wands. Golden Belle and her cousins Sparkles, Glitter, Dazzle, and Flicker, had changed the girls back to their original size. During their practice session in the elf village, Ruby's and Shauna's magic grew too powerful for them to remain so small. After they blew a hole in the palace wall with their tiny wands, practice was temporarily put on hold. It did not take long for the fairies to carve the girls' new twenty-inch long wands from the elm wood that the elves provided. The girls and their wands were taken back to Arborville. It was there that the girls were returned to their human size. While Ruby, Shauna, and the five fairies were fulfilling the requirements of the amnesia spell, the Little Peepers were putting the final touches on their new treehouse. Vorte and Berruga returned early to Arborville to move their possessions from their old treehouse to their new place. They were not too worried about the girls' safety because they were in the company of fairies.

Everything is happening so fast, thought Ruby, as they drew closer to the laurel tree. Not long ago, she was living with her mean stepdad, who scared her half to death, and now she was expected to put a spell on the nine powerful magi. She had to make so many adjustments. Yet, the need to protect her younger sister had not changed at all. She would have to find a way to perform the spell herself and leave Shauna out of it. She would not let the Malum hurt her only sibling.

"Amorite is not quite as shy as the other dryads," Flicker explained to Ruby and Shauna. "She will gladly touch the tip of your wands. Finding a unicorn will be the challenge for today."

"I believe getting a witch to touch the wands will be our biggest challenge," said Ruby.

"Let's focus on accomplishing our first step," said Golden Belle.

"What if Amorite isn't in her tree?" asked Shauna.

"Tree nymphs don't leave their trees," said Golden Belle. "Amorite will be in her home."

"I can hear you!" a singsong voice called out from the laurel tree. A beautiful, young woman with long, dark locks and piercing green eyes appeared before them. She began to sing and dance about a young nymph who fell in love with a vain god. He rejected her. Brokenhearted, the dejected nymph turned the god's mistresses into apple trees.

After Amorite finished the last note and dance step, Shauna and the fairies applauded her performance. Ruby considered it rather unfair that the god's mistresses were turned into apple trees while the god got off scot-free, but she kept her opinion to herself. She needed the dryad's help.

"Bravo! Bravo!" cheered the fairies.

"Your performance was even more magnificent than the last time you performed it," stated Sparkles, who had seen the same act over two hundred times.

Amorite showed her appreciation by curtsying.

"We came here to ask a small favor of you, Amorite," said Golden Belle. "To carry out a spell, the tips of the girls' wands must be touched by a dryad. Ruby and Shauna, show her your wands."

Ruby and Shauna held out their wands. Instead of examining the wands, Amorite inspected the girls. "Your skin is the color of a chestnut and your hair and eyes are the same shade as a black walnut. You are definitely not an elf. Elves are as white as the wings of a moth." She reached out and brushed her hands against the girls' forearms. "You are human. And not human."

"Their father is Warlock Highbrow and their mother is human," explained Golden Belle.

"I never cared for Warlock Highbrow," said Amorite, making a face. "Once, he attempted to cut off my limb to make a wand from it."

"Your arm or leg?" asked Shauna.

"A tree limb," said Amorite.

"I am sorry," said Ruby. "My sister and I had little involvement with Warlock Highbrow. The only time we ever had any interaction with him was when he handed us over to Witch Zeldar. She proceeded to lock us up in a garden shed."

"Word has spread through the forest about the blood ritual," said Amorite. "The other nymphs and I are aware that the Malum are determined to come back to the forest. Even if they return, they will eventually die like us."

"What do you mean?" asked Shauna.

"Nymphs live a long life, but we are not immortal."

The fairies exchanged perplexed glances.

"Doesn't the forest give the Malum immortality?" asked Golden Belle.

"It provides them with a very long life," said Amorite. "But they must take a potion to give them immortality."

Once more, the fairies wore bewildered expressions.

"This is the first time we've heard of this," admitted Flicker.

"What kind of potion must they take to get immortality?" asked Ruby.

"I do not know," said Amorite. She cast a longing look at her laurel tree. "I must return to it. It is calling to me. Quickly, show me your wands again."

Ruby and Shauna did as she requested. Amorite put a finger to the tip of each wand and vanished as fast as she appeared.

"If the nymphs weren't so shy and stayed around longer, we could learn so much more from them," said Golden Belle, shaking her head.

"We need to report Amorite's information about the Malum to Queen Wista," said Glitter. "Their mortality could be used to our advantage."

"We will," said Golden Belle. "But first, we must locate a unicorn."

High above them, the Black Dragon was circling the dark, thick storm clouds while exhaling fire.

□ □ □

While Ruby, Shauna, and the fairies headed toward Unicorn Trail, Sorcerer Serpentine was putting dog food into bowls. He could not afford for his children to go hungry and lose weight. He did not think the blood spell would work well if they were anemic, so he fed them canned dog food that he purchased on sale at the local market. He hoped the canned meat, which he assumed came from a dog, would provide the iron the children needed for their blood.

He had locked the children in the bedroom. He could never remember their names. Therefore, he referred to them as the Redhead, Bedhead, and Big Head, respective to their physical appearance. His eight-year-old daughter had a thick mop of unruly, red hair. His six-year-old daughter refused to run a brush through her bushy, brown hair, so it stuck out in all different directions. The head of his youngest was too big for his four-year-old body.

He unlocked the door to the bedroom and slid the bowls toward the children, who were bawling for their mother. He yelled at them to pipe down and then slammed the door shut, locking it again. He hated children, especially his own.

□ □ □

Gavran was roosting in a cedar tree near the border of Hidden Forest with the rest of his flock when he received news of the whereabouts of Sorcerer Serpentine and his children.

"Where is Montana?" questioned the raven leader.

No one perched in the tree had heard of Montana.

"It doesn't matter. The magi will know of this place," said Gavran. "Now that Witch Zeldar's garden shed is stocked with bags of

186

corn, we'll pass this information on to the other eight magi. It's going to be a particularly cold winter this year. I can feel it in my gizzard. The promise of perpetual seed corn will see us through every winter henceforth."

"What if the Malum are defeated by the other creatures?" asked the raven three branches over from Gavran. "Then, we won't get any more corn and will be tossed out of Hidden Forest by the other creatures."

"We are only guilty if we are caught," said Gavran. "If we are caught, then we must lie and feign ignorance."

"The Little Peepers will not believe us," said a raven from the top limb of the tree.

"If we're tossed out of Hidden Forest, we won't be able to obtain the corn in the shed," pointed out another raven perched from a middle branch. "The patrol rabbits will make sure of it."

"That's enough dissent!" Gavran cawed sharply. "Have any of us suffered at the hands of the magi? No! I have kept every one of you from being a caged bird! None of your feathers were plucked and used in a spell. So, you must trust my judgement."

The ravens suddenly grew quiet when they spotted a few ghosts passing by their tree. It struck them as odd until Gavran said, "Perhaps they are the souls that have escaped from the Dark Shadow. We do not have time to be concerned with spirits. Instead, keep a sharp eye on the Black Dragon flying above us. He has been blowing out plumes of fire and hot steam all afternoon. I don't want any of us to get burnt feathers." He took flight and the rest of his flock followed him. They were heading to the apple tree in Witch Zeldar's backyard.

Opal, Edward, and Jackie did not enter Hidden Forest unnoticed. Commander Lapin and Poppin, who were returning home, had spotted the three ghosts. The two rabbits began trailing them. They also were being careful to avoid the Black Dragon. They kept to the underbrush. In the meantime, the three ghosts seemed unaware of the danger looming over them. Then again, thought the two rabbits, the fiery breath of a dragon might not have any effect upon ghosts.

"This is a scary place," said Opal, as a huge, dark shadow blanketed them. Her first thought was that they had crossed paths with the Dark Shadow. However, when she looked up, she saw a giant, black dragon soaring over them. He was spitting out fireballs. "Oh,

Fiddlesticks, Edward! I wanted to see a unicorn, not a ferocious dragon."

"Are you sure this is a good idea?" said Jackie Jubilee. "I haven't seen any other creature in the forest, aside from the dragon."

"The Little Peepers have to be around here somewhere," said Edward. "The young girl Ruby told us that Little Peepers lived high in the trees in little treehouses."

"Perhaps we need to be looking higher in the trees," suggested Opal, craning her neck upward. "All I can see above us is a dragon. He is beginning to frighten me, Edward."

They stopped dead in their tracks when two rabbits hopped out in front of them, blocking their way.

"I am Commander Lapin, head of the Eighth Regiment of the Noble Rabbits." He nodded his head at Poppin. "This is my cousin, Poppin, who is second in command. State your purpose in the forest."

"They have talking rabbits, Edward!" said Opal. "How adorable is that!"

"Yes, I see that, love," said Edward.

"I am Jackie Jubilee," said Jackie. She wished to get down to business because of the dragon flying overhead and the desperation she felt for her children. "We are looking to speak with the leader of the Little Peepers."

"We are friends with Kreen and Skit and their owls, Trill and Peck," Opal said. "And we met the fairy Golden Belle and a shapeshifting elf . . . what was his name, dear?"

"His name was Tark, my sweet."

"Sorcerer Serpentine murdered me!" blurted Jackie. "And he has my three children."

"He murdered Jackie in the most ruthless way, I might add," said Opal, clutching her bodice. "Almost as callous as our own murders on our wedding day! Isn't that so, Edward?"

"That is so, my love."

Lapin and Poppin looked sideways at each other.

"We will take you to the Little Peepers at once," said Lapin. "Follow us."

"Have I not always said, my love, that rabbits are sweet and thoughtful creatures," said Opal. "So, you see, it was wrong of your mother to poison them in the garden."

"Goodness gracious!" said Poppin. "Was this woman a mean witch?"

"Edward's mother was called many things," said Opal. "I don't recall that 'mean witch' was one of them. If she had been called that name, she would've taken it as a compliment."

"Now, my sweet Opal, Mother was not a witch. Just difficult."

"Do they always talk this much?" Lapin asked Jackie.

"Yes," she replied bluntly. "I am still getting used to it."

"Why is there a dragon circling above us and shooting fire from its mouth?" asked Opal.

"He is very angry," said Poppin. "His treasure has been stolen."

"Who took it?" questioned Opal.

"We did," replied Lapin.

"Oh, dear," gasped Opal, stealing a glimpse at Edward. "Do you suppose we should even be following these talking rabbits?"

"I suggest we move quickly," said Lapin. "And perhaps talk a little less."

Lapin and Poppin glanced at each other again. They did not know what to make of these ghosts, but they seemed harmless enough. Besides, they knew the whereabouts of Sorcerer Serpentine and his offspring. Coincidentally, Opal and Edward were wondering why a couple of rabbits would dare steal a dragon's treasure. Jackie's thoughts, however, were solely on rescuing her children from the hands of Serpentine. Lapin and Poppin kept scanning the sky, not wanting to be snatched by the dragon's talons.

□ □ □

After Vorte and Berruga finished moving into their new treehouse, they became concerned about Ruby and Shauna. The girls had not returned home, yet. Even though the girls were with Golden Belle and four of her cousins, Vorte and Berruga couldn't stop worrying. The Black Dragon had been circling the skies all afternoon and a storm was fast approaching. They decided to check on the girls and their fairy chaperones. They sought out the fastest flyers, Swift and Chase, both peregrine falcons. Vorte and Berruga did not have their own companion owls because they were never patrol pilots. Luna, a veteran patrol pilot, and Oide, the flight instructor, offered to go with Vorte and Berruga because it took an experienced pilot to stay upright on a peregrine falcon flying at top speed.

"If there's trouble in the skies," said Luna, "our falcons can outrace the Black Dragon." A peregrine falcon flew four or five times faster than an owl. The swiftest owl in the forest clocked in around fifty miles per hour.

"That's why we chose these peregrine falcons," said Vorte. He clambered on top of Swift and sat behind Oide. "Because we're sensing trouble."

"I hope that we are not the ones in danger," said Berruga, cautiously eyeing Chase. She preferred flying on slower birds.

"I have never lost a passenger," Oide reminded them.

"Me, either," said Chase.

"Good to know," said Vorte. "I have a feeling the Black Dragon might take a swipe at us."

Berruga peered upward at the dragon and then mounted Chase. Luna was already onboard.

"We will have to fly quickly," said Luna. "I felt a raindrop on my arm."

The falcons spread their wings and flew off.

In another part of the forest, Ruby, Shauna, and the fairies spotted a unicorn in a small meadow, located a short distance from Unicorn Trail. The unicorn had been drinking from a fresh spring when they came upon it.

"We mean no harm," Golden Belle called out to the unicorn.

The unicorn did not flee. Instead, she remained still while they approached. She had dark, soulful eyes. Her coat and horn were pearly white as was her long tail and mane.

Golden Belle explained their reason for being there and then gestured to the wands in Ruby's and Shauna's hands. "Please help us satisfy the requirements of the amnesia spell."

The unicorn came closer to them. Ruby and Shauna displayed their wands. The unicorn touched the tip of each wand with the tip of her spiral horn. Then, the unicorn silently slipped back into the woods without saying a single word.

"Well, that was easy," said Glitter. "I thought it would be more difficult—" Before she completed her sentence, the Black Dragon, who was hiding above a dark, low-lying cloud, swooped down from the sky and grabbed Ruby and Shauna with his claws. Ruby and Shauna screamed. Luckily, they managed to cling onto their wands. It was their only protection. The fairies shot golden specks at the dragon with the intent of shrinking him, but they missed. The dragon was moving too fast. There wasn't much the fairies could do for Ruby and Shauna, except cry out for help. The unicorn did not reappear. It had no magical powers that would help. Unicorn tears and horn contained medicinal properties that could be used in potions. Therefore, it hid away from the magi and perhaps the elves.

Swift and Chase heard the girls' screams. They flew faster toward the disturbance. However, by the time the fairies explained what had happened, the Black Dragon was too far away to chase down.

It began to hail and lightning flashed across the sky. They were grounded until the storm passed.

☐ ☐ ☐

The news of Ruby's and Shauna's capture by the Black Dragon spread to Arborville just as Opal, Edward, and Jackie arrived. Commander Lapin and Poppin did not venture into the village of the Little Peepers because of the dragon's attack. The Little Peepers would have been furious with Lapin and Poppin for angering the Black Dragon in the first place. Lapin and Poppin decided to call another meeting with the other rabbit leaders. Never in the history of Hidden Forest had the Little Peepers been upset with the rabbits. All the woodland creatures could feel the tension building between the different communities. Queen Wista was among them. After speaking with Sawwhet, not even a cup of tea decreased her level of anxiety.

"Counselor Herona," said Wista, who was pacing back and forth in her treehouse. "Bring Tark, Auralia, Skit, Kreen, and their owls to me. I will meet them at the base of my tree. I want us to speak to the ghosts before the searchers set off for Madame Papulose's house. The ghosts might be helpful in their search to find a spell requiring three dragon scales."

"It's a shame the ghosts can't go with our scouting party," said Herona. "They are familiar with the human world and they can read the human language."

"They came here because Jackie is desperate to rescue her children."

"It's difficult when we are being pulled in different directions," said Herona.

"I believe our community in Hidden Forest will continue to break apart before we are able to come back together."

"Unfortunately, that is true. Should Queen Rossen be notified of the ghosts and the knowledge of Serpentine's whereabouts?"

"Not yet," said Wista, screwing up her eyes. "But we will notify her of the abduction of Ruby and Shauna. Most likely, she has already heard the news."

"Just in case Rossen isn't aware of the girls' kidnapping, I will have a patrol bird deliver the message." Herona knitted her brow. "Are we going to mount a rescue for the girls? And Serpentine's offspring?"

"We will shortly. But first, there is something I must do. And I would like you to join me. It will not be an easy task."

"What is it?"

"We must go to the Pit of Despair after the Dark Shadow leaves for his nightly hunt. I suspect there is something lying at the bottom of the pit that the Malum do not want us to find."

"What is it?" Herona repeated.

"You will see tonight."

"Are you sure we shouldn't go after the girls right now?" questioned Herona, sounding reluctant to wait any longer. "The Black Dragon might harm them."

"He won't harm them. He needs them for the sake of trading for his treasure. Besides, the girls have their magic . . . and their wands. The wands seem rather unwilling to leave their masters," said Wista. "The fairies are confident that the girls could set the dragon on fire if they so desired. Or make his teeth fall out. It's the dragon that's in trouble, but he doesn't know it yet."

"I don't believe that will bring much comfort to Vorte and Berruga. They are worried sick about the girls."

"I will speak with them after I've finished with the ghosts and the others," said Wista, sounding a little exhausted. "It won't be easy keeping both Highbrow's and Serpentine's offspring out of danger."

"No, it won't," sighed Herona.

Unbeknownst to either Wista or Herona, Vorte and Berruga had already left the village on the back of two taxi owls. They had departed as soon as the hailstorm passed through Hidden Forest. They were heading straight for the Black Dragon's lair.

Chapter Twenty

Revelations

The storm rolled past Hidden Forest, spitting out hailstones and raindrops here and there. Since the threat of heavy rain was over, Skit and Kreen rode on their owls while Tark and Auralia traveled as boreal owls. They flew straightaway for Madame Papulose's house.

Mister Barnaby was on the windowsill, looking out the living room window for Madame Papulose, who had not yet returned. He watched as four owls and two Little Peepers landed on the front steps of the house. He hopped off his perch and opened the front door. He invited the guests in, hoping they brought news of Opal, Edward, and Jackie. He also hoped they would help him free Madame Papulose from jail.

"Mister Barnaby," said Tark, as he changed back into his elf self. Auralia did the same. "We require your assistance. We are searching for a special spell."

"I'm hoping that you can help me, too," said Mister Barnaby, appearing distressed. "Madame Papulose is sitting in jail for the crimes that the big, ugly shadow committed."

"What's a jail?" asked Auralia.

"It's like a cage." Mister Barnaby could clearly see that they needed his assistance in the nonmagical world. "Did you encounter Opal, Edward, and Jackie on your way over here?"

"They are currently in our village," said Kreen.

Immediately, Mister Barnaby looked relieved. "Well, at least, things are going well for them." He wagged his head. "Poor Madame Papulose. She hates being cooped up."

It was at this moment they heard a car door slam followed by human voices.

"Have a good night, Daisy," they overheard a female voice say.

"You, too, Violet," replied Madame Papulose. "Thanks for the ride to the hospital and back."

Mister Barnaby ran to the front window and peered out. He watched a car back out of the driveway and then park next door. It was their neighbor Violet Vane behind the steering wheel. Meanwhile,

Madame Papulose was walking toward the house. She had a cast on her right wrist. "Go hide in the basement!" he said to the others in the room. "I can't explain your presence here because she doesn't speak our language." He pointed to the basement door.

Tark and Auralia and the others were on their way to the basement when the front door flew open. People in town never locked their front doors, even after the mysterious disappearance of the mayor and the bank president.

"Mister Barnaby, I can't tell you how happy I am to see you again!" exclaimed Madame Papulose. She was a tiny woman with a loud voice. She had wild, bushy, gray hair and bright, blue eyes. "It was the most awful day of my life!" She spoke to the black cat, not expecting him to fully understand. After she shared her day with Mister Barnaby, she intended to repeat her story to Opal and Edward. She expected nothing less than sympathy from the ghosts. After all, they knew how it felt to be unfairly victimized.

Mister Barnaby sat quietly and stared without blinking at Madame Papulose to let her know that it was well past dinnertime. Actually, he had missed all three of his daily meals since the police hauled Madame Papulose off to the jailhouse at daybreak.

"Oh, you must be absolutely starving, Mister Barnaby."

He watched her as she struggled to pull the lid off the can of cat food with only one hand. "I broke my wrist after I left the police station. I tripped on the sidewalk. It was such a bad break that I had to go to the hospital." She gave up on opening the can and pulled out a bag of dry cat food from the kitchen cupboard. "Well, Mister Barnaby, this town doesn't have a hospital or an ambulance. So, I had to find someone to drive me to the nearest city that has a hospital. Violet was the only one who had the time to make the trip. It was a three-hour drive and Violet said about ten words during the entire car ride there. She told me that she wasn't much of a morning conversationalist. Then, I had to wait another three hours in the emergency room. Violet didn't have much to say there, either, because hospitals gave her the willies, according to her. It didn't really matter, though, since the ER waiting line was practically backed up to the parking lot. The loud complaining and moaning from patients made it impossible to hold a conversation. On the way back, Violet broke her silence and couldn't stop talking. At that point, I was so tired that I wished she would close her mouth and give my ears a rest."

She placed food in the food bowl and added water to the water bowl. "The only good thing that came out of the accident was that the police no longer suspect that I am responsible for the disappearance of those two men. Captain Hollander said I wasn't capable of witchcraft if I couldn't even fix my own broken wrist. Of course, I didn't correct him and say that magic doesn't work quite that way. Besides, I didn't have my wand with me. And I don't know of a spell to mend broken bones . . . I wonder if one of the spellbooks in the basement has such a spell? Maybe Edward and Opal can help me search through the books for a quick cure—" Her voice suddenly broke off and she looked at Mister Barnaby. "How come you're not eating? Are you feeling okay?"

Mister Barnaby began to eat, despite not wanting dry cat food. He preferred the canned food. He had to fight the urge to walk away from his bowl.

"You must be upset with me," said Madame Papulose. "You haven't made a peep, or a meow, since I got here." Suddenly, there was a loud noise in the basement, as if a pile of books had toppled over. "What's that racket downstairs?"

Mister Barnaby pushed away his food bowl with his paw, catching Madame Papulose's attention.

"You don't like your food?"

He glared at his food while giving the bowl another shove. Next, he turned his back on his food, snubbing it.

"Let me see if I can't pry open the canned food with a pickaxe. Or maybe Violet can help me. I'll be right back." Madame Papulose left the house with a can of cat food.

Meanwhile, Auralia restacked the books that she had just knocked over. There were books everywhere in the basement. The problem wasn't just that there were too many books to read, but none of them could read them. And it looked like Mister Barnaby would not be able to help them. He was too busy keeping Madame Papulose occupied upstairs.

"Miss Whiskers knows how to read books," said Kreen. "Perhaps Trill and I could fly over to the library and bring her back here."

"She told us that she doesn't like to leave the library unattended," said Skit.

"Trill and I will have to be persuasive," replied Kreen. "Can someone pop open the basement window?"

"I can," said Auralia. As quietly as she could, she pushed open the small basement window.

Kreen and Trill left through the window after Madame Papulose returned with an opened can of cat food.

"While Kreen and Trill are gone, let's search through the books for pictures of dragons," suggested Tark. "It might make our search go faster since the spell calls for dragon scales."

Meanwhile, Mister Barnaby was distracting Madame Papulose by demanding her attention. He rolled over and she rubbed his belly. Next, he chased after a laser dot that Madame Papulose flashed across the room, which he swore was the most boring game in the world. When she sat down to rest, he jumped into her lap and curled up.

"Wow, you must have really missed me today, Mister Barnaby. I've never seen you need so much attention."

The whole time he was hoping the creatures in the basement would quickly find the spell they needed and leave. He couldn't keep this up much longer.

It wasn't long before Miss Whiskers arrived with an army of mice. As much as Miss Whiskers claimed to dislike the library mice, they were rather fond of her. Not once did she set a mousetrap or put out rat poison. Miss Whiskers introduced the mice as "little readers who had consumed pages and pages of reading materials over many years" and told them not to fear the two owls eyeing them. She put the mice to work. "Skit and Kreen told me that you are searching for a spell that requires dragon scales." The mice were frantically flipping through the spellbooks. "Be gentle with the pages," she directed them. "Ignore the potions that call for a mouse or its head or tail. No one in this room is going into a cauldron. If you see something that you can't read, give it to me to read." She looked at the others. "Their Latin isn't very good. Where is the girl, Ruby, who can read English?"

"She is detained at the moment," Auralia replied evasively. She didn't have the heart to tell them that Ruby and her sister were being held captive in a dragon's den.

"Where is Mister Barnaby?" asked Miss Whiskers.

Tark gestured up the stairs. "He is entertaining Madame Papulose to keep her from coming down here."

"We must hurry then. Mister Barnaby isn't known to be very entertaining." She broke out in a wry grin and then turned her attention to the spellbooks.

Tark, Auralia, Skit, Kreen, and Peck had made a pile of books that had images of dragons on their covers. A handful of mice were already skimming through them.

Upstairs, Madame Papulose was itching to get downstairs and find a spell for her fractured wrist and speak with Opal and Edward. She gently pushed Mister Barnaby off her lap. As she moved closer to the basement door, Mister Barnaby jumped on the drapes to stop her. She spun around and marched over to Mister Barnaby. "Good heavens, Mister Barnaby! What has ever gotten into you? You know better than to claw the drapes."

As Madame Papulose pulled Mister Barnaby off the drapes, a mouse squeaked, "I found it, Miss Whiskers! A potion that requires three black dragon scales. It's a potion for immortality."

"No wonder they are desperate to return to Hidden Forest," said Peck. "They need the Black Dragon to save their lives."

"Their potion is wearing off quickly," added Tark.

"Are there dragons in your world, Miss Whiskers?" asked Kreen.

"Only in books," responded Miss Whiskers.

A crowd had gathered around the little mouse, who was beaming proudly at his accomplishment.

"I can't read the potion ingredients," said Trill. "But I can count them. Fourteen things are required."

"Queen Wista asked us to memorize the potion, but we don't have time for that," pointed out Skit. "Any moment now, poor Mister Barnaby is going to run out of ideas for distracting Madame Papulose."

"We have to take the book with us," said Auralia. "Ruby and Shauna can read it to us . . . once they have returned." She shapeshifted into a great gray owl. The mice impulsively backed away from her. "I won't eat any of you." She landed on top of the spellbook. "We promise to bring the spellbook back when we no longer need it."

"Please take it," said Miss Whiskers. "Or else, Mister Barnaby will have to start performing headstands and cartwheels for Madame Papulose."

"Thank you, Miss Whiskers and library mice, for your help." Tark transformed into a barred owl, identical to Peck. Once again, the mice recoiled. "Let's go."

Skit and Kreen hopped onto their companion owls. Once more, they thanked the cat librarian and her librarian mice for their assistance. The owls flew out the basement window. Auralia was carrying the spellbook with her talons. A few moments later, Miss Whiskers and the mice also made their departure through the same window. Before heading back to the library, Miss Whiskers knocked on the front door to notify Mister Barnaby that the coast was clear.

"Who could that be at this late hour?" Madame Papulose cautiously answered the door, expecting a nosy neighbor to be on the other side of it. The neighbor would want to know about today's events. But no one was there. "Well, that's odd." She decided to lock the door. Lately, there were too many unexplained things happening in town. After returning to the living room, she spotted Mister Barnaby curled up on the sofa, napping. Since her cat appeared to be drained of energy, she made a beeline for the basement. She was determined to have Opal and Edward scare creepy strangers and snooping neighbors away from the house. But she didn't hear any response when she called out to them. The basement was eerily quiet and the spellbooks had been rearranged into new piles. She assumed Opal and Edward repositioned the books. The absence of her ghostly tenants did not worry her because they occasionally visited their friends at the cemetery. However, there was one thing that did concern her. There were mice droppings scattered all over the basement floor. She would have to encourage Mister Barnaby to do a better job of catching the rodents. If not, she would have to set out mousetraps. She did not want mice messing with her books.

As Miss Whiskers and the library mice were making their way back to the library, they spied the Dark Shadow moving across the town square. They quickened their pace.

Back at Misty Falls, Ruby and Shauna had the Black Dragon pinned against the cave wall. He could not move or even open his mouth. He got himself into this situation by threatening to set the girls on fire.

"You shouldn't be so mean . . . what is your name, anyway?" said Shauna. "It can't be Black Dragon."

Ruby heard the crankiness in her sister's voice because she was hungry and thirsty. "He can't talk unless we lower our wands," she reminded Shauna. Their wand lessons from earlier in the day had helped to save their lives. They learned how to control an object with a wand, even a large dragon. She eyed the dragon in a threatening manner. "We will lower our wands. But if you make any sudden movement toward us, we will make certain that you never fly again. Do you understand me?"

"He can't talk until you lower your wand." This time Shauna reminded her.

"Oh, that's right." Ruby lowered her arm, but kept a steady grip on the wand.

"My name once was Kveikja," said the dragon, after working his jaw. He had been immobilized for quite some time. "It means ignite. My mother gave me that name."

"Where is she now?" asked Shauna.

"She is dead."

"Ours, too," said Ruby. "Do you miss her, Kveikja?"

"What a strange question to ask," muttered the dragon. "And do not call me by my old name."

"Why are you so mean?" Shauna asked him. She did not dare take her eyes off him after what he had done to Ruby and her. He had dangled them high above the ground and then dropped them onto the cold cave floor. Before the dragon knew it, the girls had their wands pointed at him. At first, he laughed at them. Then, he threatened to incinerate them in one fiery breath. Within the blink of an eye, he was thrown against the cave wall, unable to move.

"I am protecting myself because the world is out to get me."

"My stepdad used to say the very same thing," said Ruby. "He didn't give a damn about anyone because the world didn't care about him. That's why he stole and made other people's lives miserable."

"I have not forgotten how the human world works," said the dragon. "The rich lived in castles and the poor lived in huts. Which ones were you?"

"We were poor like everyone else in the neighborhood," said Ruby. "Do you mind if we sit down? I am tired of standing."

The Black Dragon motioned for them to sit on the floor. Ruby and Shauna sat near each other, clutching their wands. They did not drop their guard.

"Do you have anything to eat beside rabbit meat?" asked Shauna.

"You can gnaw on rabbit bones." This time the dragon pointed to a big pile of rabbit bones.

Ruby noticed the two treasure chests. "Did you imprison the two elves in those chests?"

"I certainly did. There was plenty of room for them because the chests were empty. My treasure was looted by the rabbits."

"I will not be going in your treasure chest," Shauna said adamantly.

"Where do you suggest I put you then?" The dragon's yellow eyes were full of amusement. "In my empty belly?"

"You can put me back in Arborville," said Shauna without having to think twice about it. "However, I would prefer to go back there under my own free will."

"Why would I do that?" the dragon said smugly.

"Do I have to remind you that Shauna and I have the ability to shrink you to the size of a frog and feed you to a frog-snake," warned Ruby.

Ruby's words made him flinch. He sensed the girls were more powerful than any one of the Malum. Initially, he had captured the girls, knowing they were a valuable asset to the Little Peeper community. He had intended to use them for bargaining. He did not realize they possessed powerful magic until they put a chokehold on him. He struggled to breathe until they put their wands down. He wasn't even sure the girls knew the full strength. However, he would not be the one to test their magical powers by attempting to shove them into a wooden box.

"Why don't we figure out a solution to your problem, and then we can go home," suggested Ruby.

"I want my treasure back," the dragon said irately. "The rabbits won't return it until I promise them that I will no longer eat them."

"I must admit it's not an easy problem to solve," said Ruby.

"What else do you like to eat besides rabbits?" Shauna questioned him. "Personally, I like hamburgers. But they don't serve them here."

"I like all sorts of meats," he admitted. "But the problem is the humans will kill me if I hunt in their world. They won't tolerate a dragon killing their livestock. Or, even tolerate a dragon."

"Well, I suppose Hidden Forest could be stocked with animals that you might like to eat from the human world," said Ruby.

"Do you like pigs?" asked Shauna.

"Rooting pigs can damage the forest floor," Ruby cut in. Last year she watched a documentary about wild pigs destroying Hawaii's natural environment.

Shauna narrowed her eyes, thinking. "You could put the pigs in pens."

"The creatures in Hidden Forest frown upon pens and cages because the magi were notorious for using them," said the dragon. He, too, appeared to be putting some thought into the matter.

"There are too many rats in the cities," said Ruby. "Maybe there is a way that you could hunt them and decrease their population."

"There are also too many people in the city," pointed out Shauna.

"That's true. But I don't think it would go over very well to have a dragon consume them," said Ruby.

The dragon's huge eyes swiveled back and forth from sister to sister during their discussion. How many years had it been since he heard the voices of his own siblings? When was the last time his mother scolded him and his siblings for talking with a full mouth? It was ages ago. And he would not hear their voices again.

"Why can't we put a spell on the magi forcing them to trap rodents in the human world and then drop them off at the edge of Hidden Forest?" said Ruby, sounding excited by her own idea. "I remember Witch Zeldar saying that she likes catching mice in her mousetraps and poisoning them for good measure."

"Poison can't be used," said the dragon. "Eating poisoned rodents would eventually poison me. I remember this one time a farmer put poison in a sheep carcass to kill Agir and me—"

"Who is Agir?" interrupted Shauna.

"My mate. She was killed years ago by the humans." Ruby and Shauna saw the sadness in his face. Puffs of smoke wafted from his nostrils. "Anyhow, Agir snatched up the poisoned carcass and dropped it on the thatched roof of the farmer's hut. The carcass fell right through the roof and landed squarely on a table where their family was eating. Agir and I laughed for days over the incident." The memory brought a fleeting smile to his face.

"I remember a time when our stepdad forced Ruby and me to eat rotten food," said Shauna. "We were throwing up all night! He was a mean man."

"That's terrible!" said the dragon. He seemed genuinely concerned. "My father was always kind to my siblings and me, even when we tried to toss each other out of the den. He put a stop to it by warning us that we needed to protect each other in this world and that we should not harm one another. We had to depend on each other . . . our mother had already been killed by humans."

"Our father is Warlock Highbrow," admitted Ruby. "Supposedly, he's horrible to everyone."

"The magi are about as wicked as they come. They like to be in control of others. Even the Dark Shadow avoids them," said the dragon.

"Have you ever spoken to the Dark Shadow?" asked Shauna.

"Of course not. No one approaches it."

"What exactly is the Dark Shadow?" asked Ruby.

"A dark shadow is the soul or the shadow left behind of a murdered victim from the human world," the dragon explained. "This is not the first time I've seen a dark shadow. Dark shadows used to be more common in the olden days . . . when there were other dragons in the world."

"Why does it go out at night?" asked Shauna.

"It is probably looking for revenge against its murderer or murderers. But after many years of searching, it grows tired. It just wants to be left alone down there in the cavern, just like I want to be left alone up here in my cave."

"It sounds lonely," said Shauna. "You sound lonely."

"Both of us are outcasts," the dragon admitted. He was no longer glaring at them. In fact, his pent-up anger seemed to have dissipated.

"There are probably no others like us in the world. We are misunderstood."

Ruby considered the matter. "Why does the Dark Shadow occasionally come out of its hibernation and snatch others?"

The dragon lowered his enormous head and stared straight into Ruby's eyes. "I don't know. Like I just said, I have never actually spoken to the Dark Shadow. I assume it doesn't want to be bothered, like me."

"That makes no sense," said Shauna. "It wouldn't abduct others if it wanted to be alone."

"It might be a little bit lonely for company," admitted the dragon.

"Why doesn't it allow itself to die?" questioned Ruby. "Or move on to the afterlife?"

"Because it is still looking for revenge or solace, like *someone else* I know," answered Berruga, who was listening near the mouth of the cave. "And that individual has taken my girls from me!"

Vorte stood alongside Berruga, pulling himself to his full height of four inches. Their taxi owls were behind them, ready to take flight if necessary. Both Vorte and Berruga were stunned to find the girls engaged in a friendly discussion with the dragon.

"That's my new mom," Shauna said proudly. "And my new dad."

Berruga began to tear up because it was the first time one of the girls referred to her as "mom." Vorte's round cheeks were as red as cherries.

"Are you okay?" asked Berruga, stepping closer.

"We're fine," replied Ruby. "We were just problem-solving."

Vorte raised his brow. "*Problem-solving*?" He also inched closer to the girls and the dragon's fire-breathing mouth.

"I think there might be a way to cast a spell upon the magi to supply the Black Dragon"—Ruby gestured to the dragon—"with rodents from the human town. We just need to find the right spell. Madame Papulose has all sorts of spellbooks in her basement. Maybe there's one that could make the magi fetch mice or turn them into awesome mousers."

"You mean, turn the magi into cats?" asked Berruga.

Ruby shrugged. "Sure, why not?"

"I have to admit it would make them more useful than they are now," noted Vorte.

"Cats also have nine lives, so they could fetch mice for a long time," Shauna pointed out.

"It's great that you have figured out what to do with the Malum," said the dragon, sarcastically. He didn't see how changing the magi into cats was a very good idea. "But what about returning my treasure?"

Berruga exchanged a look with Vorte. "I think we can work something out with the rabbit commanders. Your treasure will be brought back to you by midday tomorrow. That is, if you agree to release the girls right now." said Berruga. She could not imagine that Wista would be upset with her for making this bargain. No one wanted the dragon to harm the girls.

"I have learned not to trust anyone," said the dragon.

"That sounds reasonable. So, we'll be on our way to carry out your request. Then, you will learn to trust us," said Vorte, as his eyes flicked over to the mound of rabbit bones. He didn't see any skeletons of Little Peepers, but he didn't want to be the first of his kind in the pile.

"Not so fast!" said the dragon. "I need assurance that you will follow through on your word."

Ruby flicked her wand at the treasure chest that had held Prince Massen prisoner. The chest turned into gold. "There you go. You can rest well tonight, knowing that you have some gold to keep you happy."

"Fair enough," said the dragon. His eyes were gleaming from seeing the shiny gold. "I will expect my treasure to be returned by noon tomorrow."

Shauna walked over to the dragon and placed her hand on his shoulder joint. His scales were sharp as knives. "You are not a bad dragon. Just misunderstood, as you said yourself."

Ruby and Shauna exited the cave with their guardians as the dragon watched them go. Since Ruby and Shauna had never transformed themselves, they decided to walk down the hillside as they were. Vorte and Berruga rode on their shoulders while the taxi birds returned to Arborville. The owls would deliver a message to Queen Wista's treehouse that the girls were on their way home.

"You turned the treasure chest into fairy gold, didn't you?" Vorte questioned Ruby.

"Yes. Golden Belle told us that fairy gold will disappear once a transaction is completed. So, the treasure chest will return to wood once the treasure is given back to the dragon."

"That was quick thinking back there," said Vorte.

"Thank goodness for our lessons this morning," said Ruby. "Otherwise, Shauna and I would not be here—"

"I cannot bear to think of such an unfortunate outcome," interrupted Berruga, her eyes welling up. "I am just glad that you didn't drop your wands as the dragon was carrying you back to his lair."

"We're safe now," said Shauna.

"Yes, you are safe for the moment," Berruga sniffed.

"My wand wouldn't leave me anyway," said Shauna.

"Mine, either," chimed in Ruby.

"Your wands seem to have a mind of their own," Berruga stated. She didn't know much about wands, but she recalled that the magi were greatly distraught when their wands were destroyed during the Great Banishment. Snapping their wands in half seemed to break their will to fight back. Or, at least, it weakened their resolve.

"The Black Dragon will leave them alone from now on," Vorte said with confidence. "It even appeared that he was enjoying the girls' company."

"It's not the dragon I am worried about," said Berruga. She didn't need to remind them that it was the Malum she feared most.

"We will keep practicing our magic," said Shauna to cheer up Berruga. "Golden Belle told us that we were quicker with our wands than the magi because we're much younger."

"They are getting up there in years," said Vorte. "But they are immortal. Age will not stop them from aiming their wands."

"Not according to the woodland nymph, Amorite," said Ruby. "The Malum have to drink a potion to give them immortality. Amorite told us this today. It was the first time the fairies had heard this."

"Why have I never heard this?" said Berruga, surprised by the news.

"Because nymphs are shy," answered Shauna. "They don't talk much. Mostly, they communicate with nature, according to the fairies."

"We better hurry along and share this information with Queen Wista," said Vorte. "There is a good chance, however, that the fairies have already mentioned it to Wista." Mostly, though, he was in a rush because he was afraid of encountering a frog-snake on the trail. Though, typically, frog-snakes slept at night, keeping warm in their dens.

Coincidentally, as Berruga and Vorte were discussing the queen, Wista and Herona flew over them. The queen and her counselor did not spot Berruga and Vorte and the others as they made their way to the Pit of Despair.

Chapter Twenty-One

The Pit of Despair

Wista and Herona made certain the Dark Shadow had departed for the night before entering the cavern with their owls. While they stood at its mouth, their apprehension was as deep as the cavern. The queen and her counselor took a deep breath and pushed onward. The roar of the waterfall drowned out their footsteps. Their owls were always silent in their flight. The cave was as black as coal. Luckily, the moon cast enough light so they could see each other. They communicated through facial expressions and hand gestures until the roar of the waterfall grew quieter.

"It's not a very nice place to live," stated Herona, glancing around.

"I would rather live at the top of a tree than at a bottom of a pit," said Rings.

"Let's hope this cavern has a bottom to it," Wista replied.

All four of them peered down into the deep cavern. It looked bottomless. If it wasn't for the fairy wands they had borrowed, which provided a little light, they would have been incapable of seeing anything down there. Even the owls, Spruce and Rings, seemed hesitant to enter such a dark place. Since the Little Peepers did not sport wings, the northern hawk owl and the grey gray owl knew it was necessary to fly Wista and Herona to the bottom of the Pit of Despair. Wista suspected that the greatest secret of Hidden Forest would be found at the bottom. She felt that a resolution to the problem of the Malum was also there. They had no choice but to enter the pitch-black pit. Or so, they thought.

As they descended deeper into the cavern, it became chillier. The summer heat did not penetrate so far underground. Sometimes they could hear water drip from the ceiling and splash on the cavern floor. It seemed to take a long time to reach the bottom. As usual, Spruce and Rings landed softly. Wista and Herona dismounted their owls and flashed the fairy wands around the large room. Long stalactites dangled over their heads. They looked like dragon's teeth.

"What are we looking for?" asked Herona. Her pupils were huge in the low light as were the owls'.

"Mem," whispered Wista.

"Who is Mem?" Herona whispered back.

"The mother of the magi. I don't believe she just vanished from Hidden Forest. I think her children attacked her, blasted her into pieces, and threw her remains down here."

A cold wind swept around them. "Your speculation is correct," they heard a haunting voice, but saw no one. "I intended to take their magic away because they became so cruel to my other creations. They fought amongst themselves and they would not listen. But they ambushed me before I could remove their magic. My body was torn apart, but my magic remained intact. Magic can never be obliterated. It lives on forever." They felt a blast of icy air on their necks. "I had given up all hope of returning aboveground and seeking my revenge. But then, the Dark Shadow, comprised of a dozen murdered souls, came here. It encouraged me to continue on. These tortured souls renewed my hope and willpower."

"Did you ask the Dark Shadow to bring you company?" asked Wista.

"Yes." Another shot of icy air swirled around Wista.

"Is my son Cobias here?"

"Cobias," repeated Mem. "If he is your son, then you must be Queen Wista of the Little Peepers."

"I am his mother." Eyes squinting, Wista scanned the cavern. "Is he here?"

"Yes. Did the queen of the elves not tell you about our deal?"

"I know only of the bargain she made with the Dark Shadow."

"The elf queen made the deal with me. The Dark Shadow communicates to no one but me."

"Will you let my son, King Koning, and Rowl go?"

"I cannot. It is not safe for them to go."

"Why not?" asked Wista, sounding devastated. "I miss my son."

"It is not safe," Mem repeated. "I will release them when I've become stronger."

"What do you need to grow stronger?" asked Herona, who felt Wista trembling next to her.

"Gold. I need to consume lots of gold. I need it to heal myself."

Wista, Herona, and the owls traded looks.

"The elves have gold," said Herona. The air in the cavern became so cold that she was shivering.

"I do not want the elves' false gold!"

"Did the elf queen bring you fool's gold?" asked Wista, her brow lifted.

"Only once." Mem's voice was as chilly as the cavern.

"Can the Dark Shadow bring gold to you?" asked Herona.

"It can only carry souls."

"I certainly know where to find gold," said Wista. She was trying hard to keep her temper under control. It didn't require much thinking to put the pieces together. Rossen could not part with the gold she had obtained from the dragon through bargaining. All this time Cobias could've been back with her, if it hadn't been for Queen Rossen's love of gold. Rossen was just as bad as the Black Dragon. To make matters worse, Rossen's own husband was stuck down here, along with the father of Tark and Rupin.

"Do not bring me fool's gold," Mem warned them. "The elf queen tried to fool me once. She is not welcome here anymore."

"Do you think I could talk to my son? Please. It's been so long since I've seen him."

A cold wind gust swept through the cavern room and then Prince Cobias stood before them. He was exactly as Wista remembered him. She put her hand out to touch him, but her hand went right through him. "Cobias?"

"I am here, Mother," he said.

"I miss you."

"I miss you, too."

Numerous times she had rehearsed all the things she would say if she had the opportunity to see him again. Now that the time was here, however, her mind went blank. "I will free you from this place," she said, at last.

"I know you will."

"Are you doing okay?"

"Mem is good to us," Cobias said. "But I do want to come home with you. Please bring Mem the gold." Abruptly, he vanished.

"Cobias, come back!" Wista cried out.

"He will come home after you bring me the gold," Mem whispered into Wista's ear. "Do not disappoint me like the elf queen. The forest depends on it." All of a sudden, a wind swirled around them and then the cavern fell quiet.

"We now have the answers," said Herona, breaking the silence. She glanced over at Wista and noticed that the queen's face was wet with tears.

"Let's go home," Wista said softly. "The three ghosts are waiting for us. And Tark's search party should be back by now."

"And we need to get our hands on some gold," said Spruce.

"We might need the moles' help to accomplish that," said Wista. "Oh, and we still have to free the girls from the dragon and return our wands to the fairies." She breathed out deeply. "We have a long night ahead of us."

"Let's go before the Dark Shadow returns," said Rings, giving a little shudder.

Wista and Herona climbed on to their owls and took off for the surface. They quickly flew over the dragon's den, but did not spot Ruby, Shauna, or the dragon.

"Where could they be?" questioned Wista, speaking to herself.

Moments later, a couple of owl patrols swooped down from the night sky and informed Queen Wista that Ruby and Shauna were on their way home. "They are traveling by foot."

"Berruga and Vorte are with them," said a pilot on an eastern screech-owl. "The patrols are watching over them. The Black Dragon left his den, too."

"Is he out hunting?" asked Herona.

"No, we have learned that he is at the grave of his mate," replied the patrol, whose companion was a barn owl. After Agir died, the Black Dragon retrieved her bones from the humans who had slain her. The human wouldn't give up the bones easily. It cost the man his life. "In the past, we often saw him go to the same pile of rocks. We never knew what he was doing there until today. We didn't know that his mate was buried there."

"We really ought to learn more about the history of the forest," said Wista. "It is not enough to know how to ride on birds."

"Should we go see Berruga, Vorte, and the girls?" Herona asked after the pilots left.

"Yes, I am curious to learn what occurred between the dragon and the girls," replied Wista. "Let's go look for them."

☐☐☐

It was very late when Queen Wista returned to Arborville. She had left with her advisor and two owls but now returned with a bigger party. Opal and Edward introduced themselves to Shauna. Edward shook her hand and Opal kissed her cheek. Both the handshake and kiss felt cold against Shauna's flesh.

"Oh, my dear, how you have grown since the last time I saw you!" Opal said to Ruby, marveling at her change in size. "You were only three inches tall! And now, you must be well over five feet!"

"The fairies returned me to my original size," Ruby replied.

Opal eyed the wand in Ruby's hand. "And what is with the wand?"

"I perform magic with it. Shauna can do the same with hers."

Shauna nodded and then yawned loudly.

"Off to bed, you two," Berruga said to Ruby and Shauna. "It's almost the witching hour."

The girls did not put up much of a fuss because they were exhausted by the day's events. Vorte and Berruga also turned in for the night. In fact, everyone was exhausted but the ghosts. While everyone slept, the ghosts offered to look through the spellbook that Tark and Auralia brought back. Their objective was to find a spell that could be used against the Malum.

Before Queen Wista parted from the company of the ghosts, she promised Jackie that the Little Peepers would rescue her children. "The magi will keep them alive until the next full moon," Wista said to Jackie. "Though, we will attempt to free them as soon as possible. However, I have one more task that I must accomplish tonight before we can begin the rescue."

Jackie nodded solemnly and thanked Wista for her help.

☐☐☐

Back at Zeldar's house, eight of the nine magi were sitting around the dinner table, debating what to do about Serpentine and his offspring.

Earlier in the day, they learned from Gavran the location of Serpentine and his children, as well as the whereabouts of Highbrow's offspring. With additional investigative work, the magi located the cabin of Jackie Jubilee's late grandparents.

"We should bring Serpentine and his brats back here," said Sorcerer Underhand. "I don't trust him."

"Now, now, Underhand. I don't believe he will keep the children to himself," said Sorceress Hexla. "He needs us as much as we need him."

"There's no need for us to stay here in Witch Zeldar's house," said Witch Blackheart. "We can drive to Montana now, perform the blood ritual there under the full moon, and later fly our brooms back to Hidden Forest."

"It had better not be cloudy on the night of the full moon. We cannot afford to lose any more time," huffed Zeldar, sounding as if she was at her wit's end. "I cannot waste any more time! I need to get my hands on some dragon scales!"

"Calm down," said Warlock Gloominus. "We all need to drink the immortality potion." Several body joints cracked when he moved in his chair.

"We're in a race against time!" Sorceress Underhand retorted. "Is your mind as dull as your personality, Gloominus?"

"Enough with the insults," said Blackheart. "We should be concerned about Highbrow's girls. Now that we know they have been in the forest and practicing their magic with the fairies, we have to be prepared for them."

"They are just young girls," scoffed Highbrow. "Their power will not be able to match our own."

Witch Blackheart shot Highbrow a skeptical look. "You don't know that for certain, Warlock Highbrow. Your daughters might've inherited more magic than you think."

Highbrow's face turned bright red.

"But still, there are nine of us versus two of them," said Sorceress Hexla. "If we could overcome the all-powerful Mem, then we can defeat a couple of little witches."

"Half-witches," Sorcerer Spellbinder corrected her. "Besides, we should not speak of Mem. It might jinx us."

"You are forgetting about the Little Peepers," said Blackheart. "The little half-witches will have them on their side."

"I have good news," announced Highbrow. "I discovered a spell *and* a potion that could change the Little Peepers into frogs. It would be easier to cast a spell upon the Little Peepers, though, than force them all to drink a potion. I intend to eventually poison all of them."

"I'll assist you, Highbrow," Zeldar said excitedly. The mere thought of poisoning her enemies lifted her mood. "We'll poison the rabbits and moles, as well."

"We have been trying for centuries to turn the Little Peepers into frogs," Sorceress Underhand said dubiously. "Where did you learn of this spell?"

"From a spellbook that belonged to a Wiccan," said Highbrow. "She lives across the street from Serpentine."

"I know of her. She is a fake witch," said Sorcerer Spellbinder. "Her spellbooks are useless."

"She is not the one who wrote the spellbooks," retorted Highbrow, irritated. "They are ancient books. They were probably written when kings and queens lived in castles and took advice from warlocks."

"And sorcerers," said Sorcerer Spellbinder.

"And more importantly, witches," said Witch Blackheart.

"Enough of this competition!" hissed Witch Zeldar. "We don't have time to listen to jealous squabbling. The clock is running out on us!"

"How come you didn't mention this until now, Highbrow?" Sorceress Hexla questioned in an accusatory tone. "Why should we trust you or any of those spells? The books come from the human world. They might be fakes, like the Wiccan and the wand that I've seen her carry to the park, pretending it's a walking stick. It appeared as if she was attempting to cast a spell on a squirrel. The squirrel just looked at her like he was looking at another nut."

"I knew you would have your doubts," snarled Highbrow. "We cannot be this way. If you want to live forever, we have to trust one another. Or, at least, depend on each other." Not in a million years, though, would he ever trust Hexla, or any of them, for that matter.

Witch Blackheart nearly broke out in a fit of laughter. She would never completely count on Highbrow for anything. Nonetheless, she must put her doubts aside. To survive, she needed her magical powers back, as well as the dragon potion for immortality. The Little Peepers stood in their way. "What harm is there in at least trying to cast new spells upon the Little Peepers? Does anyone have a better idea to deal with them?"

No one replied as Highbrow gave Blackheart a look of gratitude for defending him.

"As I said before, we must do a better job of working together this time around," said Zeldar, who woke up this morning looking ten years older than yesterday. "And we must keep our promise to the Black Dragon. We will continue to show our respect to him if we want him to keep providing us with his scales."

"As long as the dragon continues to feed on rabbits and has his treasure, nothing else concerns him," pointed out Spellbinder.

"I suggest we all pack up our wands and brooms and go to Montana," said Blackheart. "I heard that it is a lovely place for a summer visit."

"I recommend we leave now," said Sorcerer Hexla. "I highly doubt that Serpentine can keep his offspring alive for a month. The frogs for his experiment didn't even live that long."

"We can rent a van," suggested Highbrow. "Since I have the most experience, I'll drive."

"I can drive, too," said Mortify.

"No, you can't," said Highbrow. "I saw you drive over your neighbor's dog."

"It was on purpose," hissed Mortify. "I hated it yipping at me."

"That's enough arguing!" Witch Zeldar snapped again. "I do not want to grow old listening to more of your bickering! We will leave as soon as Warlock Highbrow has a van for us. Now, go retrieve your possessions. Highbrow can pick us up from our homes."

The other magi fell silent as they watched new age spots and deeper wrinkles pop up on Zeldar's face. Then, they looked at each other. Their skin was beginning to decay. All of them were rapidly deteriorating. It was a wake-up call for how little time they had left to live. They stopped their quarreling and hurried back to their homes and collected their personal items, including their wands.

□ □ □

Queen Wista had one last task to undertake before retiring for the night. Only she and Spruce would go on this mission. Her destination was the tunnel leading to the home of Rooter, Erde, and Snoot.

Their flight to the tunnel's entrance was uneventful. Most forest creatures were asleep. Wista hopped off her hawk owl when they reached the tunnel entrance of the three moles. She shouted down into the tunnel for them to come to the surface because she needed their assistance. Within several minutes, the three moles emerged from their tunnel.

"What is it, Queen Wista?" asked Erde. The last time Wista came for a visit was when she needed them to rescue the two girls from Witch Zeldar.

"I need a great favor from you. It will be just as dangerous as the last rescue mission I requested," said Wista.

"Is it more dangerous than digging a tunnel to Witch Zeldar's garden shed? Or stealing the dragon's treasure?" asked Snoot. Though, it was Commander Lapin who sought out their assistance to pilfer the dragon's loot.

"It's possible. I need you to steal all the gold from the elves' underground treasury," said Wista.

Snoot's tiny eyes went big. "Whoa! That is more dangerous than stealing from the dragon! The elves love their gold as much as the dragon loves his riches. The elves' treasury is well-guarded."

"In all probability, only the entrance is guarded," said Rooter. "I can't imagine that there is a guard in the treasury room. We'll just have to be quiet when we remove the gold from the room."

"Can it be done by morning?" asked Wista.

"If we round up all the moles, I believe so," replied Erde. "Working together, we can dig a new tunnel that links up an old tunnel to the treasury room."

Wista thanked them.

"May I ask you what the gold will be used for?" asked Snoot.

"It'll be used as a healing remedy for the mother of the magi," replied Wista.

"Holy Moley!" exclaimed Snoot. The moles almost fainted.

"News of the magi's mother was a shock to me, as well." Wista shared the day's events regarding Sawwhet and Mem with the moles, who were listening attentively. Their hearing was always acute and they never forgot a word of gossip. "If it wasn't for Sawwhet, I would not have learned of Mem's existence. But apparently, Rossen learned of her presence when she went to negotiate with the Dark Shadow right after the Great Banishment. That's a long time to keep a secret."

"Well, my goodness," said Erde. "Mem has been keeping your son down there! How terrible is that!"

"If I give the elves' gold to Mem, I will have Cobias back," Wista said determinedly. "And the others as well."

"Is gold all she demands?" asked Snoot.

"She asked for nothing else," Wista answered. "After the gold restores her strength, she intends to destroy her children."

"It sounds like a win-win situation for all of us," said Rooter.

"Except the elves will lose their gold," pointed out Wista. "And Rossen's secrets will be exposed."

"Why would Rossen sacrifice her husband to the Pit of Despair?" asked Erde, wearing a puzzled expression. "Not to mention your son and Rowl?"

"Those are questions that only Queen Rossen can answer." Wista peered up at the night sky, speckled with stars. "I must get some rest. Tomorrow will be a long day, too."

"You go rest, Queen Wista," said Rooter. "We will have that gold before you wake up."

She showed her gratitude by touching their pink snouts and then boarded Spruce, who had not spoken a word during their time with the moles. But on their return flight, the hawk owl did not stop talking because he had to keep his passenger awake. Upon reaching home, Wista immediately crawled into her bed without changing into bedclothes. She fell into a deep sleep where even dreams of her son could not penetrate her subconscious.

□□□

Oide was on his favorite owl, Blizzard, a snowy owl. Since Blizzard was an older white male, he was pure white with no dark spots or bars. Blizzard received his name because of his coloring and because he moved across the land as swiftly as a blizzard. He was gliding close to the ground when they came upon Commander Lapin. The commander was just returning home to his warren after a long night of guarding the forest.

"Oide," said Lapin, surprised to see the flight instructor. Oide usually did not patrol the forest. "Are you patrolling the skies at this wee hour?"

"I am here as Wista's messenger," said Oide, who remained seated on Blizzard. "I offered my services because we are short on numbers. Four hundred of us are protecting the elf village and another three hundred are patrolling the skies tonight. Some of us are also watching over our children."

"I noticed the large number of patrols. However, I have not seen the Black Dragon."

"A tentative agreement has been reached with the dragon," said Oide. "He will stop hunting rabbits if his treasure is returned by midday."

"Why wasn't I told of this?" Lapin began stomping his foot.

"We have just learned of this agreement ourselves. Queen Wista sent me here to tell you. It was Berruga and Vorte who made the deal with the dragon while they were rescuing the girls. As it turned out, the girls didn't need any rescuing. They held their own against the dragon."

Lapin's tapping slowed down. "What guarantees do we have that the dragon will keep his word?"

"So far, none. But I highly doubt he will go back on his word with Ruby and Shauna in the forest."

"I am glad to hear they were not injured," said Lapin, softening his tone. "I would have blamed myself if something would have happened to them."

"There is another matter . . ." Oide said tentatively, his words breaking off.

Lapin scrunched up his face and twitched his whiskers. "What is it?"

"Tark and Auralia brought back a spellbook from the human world. It has a transformation spell in it."

"What does that have to do with me?"

"As you know, I was born a frog," said Oide. "However, I've been a Little Peeper for such a long time that I have almost forgotten what it was like to be a frog."

"I don't understand where you are going with this."

"I believe that you were once an elf," said Oide. "One of the magi changed you into a rabbit; most likely it was Spellbinder. It only makes sense. You have by far outlived all of the other rabbits in the forest. You have the strong sixth sense of an elf. You despise the Malum more than any rabbit I know." He took a deep breath. "I think that your transformation occurred such a long time ago that you have nearly forgotten what it was like to be an elf, just like me barely being able to remember what it was like to be a frog."

A lengthy pause stood between them.

"You are correct. It was Sorcerer Spellbinder who did this to me," Lapin said quietly. "I was here long before most of the other elves." His face was still scrunched up as his mind went back in time. "It happened when I was a young boy . . . I was picking elderberries in the woods the day Sorcerer Spellbinder, who was a youngster himself, accidentally stumbled upon me and turned his wand on me. I will always remember his cruel laughter as I hopped away, escaping from his clutches. I tried to shapeshift back into an elf . . . The spell was too strong. I was so embarrassed to return home as a rabbit that I did not go back. For weeks, the other elves searched for me, but I never showed myself. Eventually, they assumed that one of the magi had killed me. The only thing they ever found of me was my berry basket."

"If you could change back into an elf, would you?" asked Oide.

"I don't know. Would you change back into a frog?"

"I don't believe so," answered Oide. "This is who I am now."

Lapin gave him an understanding nod. "If Spellbinder dies, then I might not have a choice in the matter. I could become an elf again."

"If Spellbinder dies, Wista and I might change back into frogs. I don't know what will become of the others."

"Perhaps the girls' magic will be needed to keep us as we are," said Lapin.

"Perhaps."

"I saw firsthand how the magic destroyed the Malum over time. Queen Rossen is not completely wrong about the girls. Their magic will eventually influence them in one way or another . . . whether we like it or not."

"Berruga and Vorte will watch them closely. They won't let the magic go to the girls' heads." He ended his sentence with a peep. His face turned a darker shade of green. "I haven't felt this anxious since the Great Banishment."

"Thank you for telling me about the transformation spell, Oide. The Little Peepers have always treated the rabbits with respect."

"Well, think it over, Commander. I must tell the other nine commanders about returning the dragon's treasure at midday. In the worst-case scenario, the dragon's loot can always be stolen again if the dragon doesn't keep his promise." Oide grinned at Lapin and then flew off with Blizzard.

Lapin remained frozen to his spot until he spied the Dark Shadow moving through the forest. He moved away from it and then hurried off to his burrow of many years. As an elf, he was a gatherer of fruits. Queen Rossen would return him to that position because his family worked in the orchard fields. Now, he was the Commander of the Eighth Regiment of the Noble Rabbits.

He would not go back to being an elf. Though, he realized, he might not have a choice if Sorcerer Spellbinder was eliminated. The spell might be broken.

Chapter Twenty-Two

The Race to Montana

After catching some shuteye, Queen Wista woke up with a clearer head and a clever plan to rescue Jackie's children from Sorcerer Serpentine. It would require a team effort, and include the assistance of the Black Dragon. Feeling calmer, she had tea and blackberries for breakfast while the reports came in from her messengers. In the midst of her morning meal, Wista received a message from the moles. They had taken every piece of gold from the elves' underground vault. It had taken all night. The gold was squirreled away, deep in a mole tunnel, and guarded by the moles. She hoped that she could deliver the gold before the elves discovered it was missing. After finishing her breakfast, she took a taxi bird to see the three ghosts, who had been patiently waiting throughout the night to speak with her again. Opal, Edward, and Jackie spent the night discussing various ways to rescue Jackie's children, Elli, Freyja, and Mani. They were named after Norse deity. Jackie was appalled by Serpentine because he always had trouble remembering the names of his own children. He had never been a good father. Nonetheless, she never foresaw that he had sired offspring with the sole intent to eventually murder them for his benefit. Jackie shivered every time she thought of the sorcerer's cruelty toward their children.

"I am sorry that I've not given you the appropriate time you deserve," Wista said to the trio of ghosts. "I've been busy putting our plans into action. And I'm happy to report that we have made some good headway since we last spoke. This morning I was informed that the rabbits have agreed to return the Black Dragon's treasure. If we win over the dragon, there is a good chance that we can persuade him to fly us out to Montana and back. The children can ride on his back."

Jackie's eyes widened. "Isn't that dangerous?"

"They will be riding along with Little Peepers and their trained owls," said Wista. "Our pilots are the very best. At least a couple of fairies will go along on this rescue mission to watch over them."

"Are the little fairies strong enough to catch them if they fall off the dragon?" asked Jackie, skeptically.

"They will use the strength of their magic wands," explained Wista.

"Will my children be able to perform magic like Highbrow's girls?" asked Jackie. "I was told the girls have amazing wizarding skills."

"If your children have magic, their magical abilities might kick in once they enter Hidden Forest," explained Wista. Jackie whistled under her breath. "On the other hand, they might take after you and not be magical at all."

"Oh," said Jackie, sounding a bit disappointed.

"Even if your children have magic, they cannot bring you back to life," Wista said to her.

"Oh," said Jackie, sounding even more disappointed.

Opal reached over and patted Jackie's hand. "Your children will love you no matter what."

"What if this dragon chooses not to go?" Edward asked Wista.

"We Little Peepers can use our mindbending abilities to convince him to go," said Wista. "I would prefer the dragon choose to go of his own free will. Forcing individuals to do something against their will just causes resentment."

"Can we come along for the ride?" asked Opal. "We barely weigh anything. Or perhaps nothing at all."

"Sure," said Wista. "Jackie will have to come along to show us the way."

"What time do we leave?" asked Jackie.

"Tonight. Under the cover of darkness," said Wista. "The Black Dragon won't enter the human world if he is seen."

"Does the Black Dragon have a name?" asked Opal. "Black Dragon is so plain. Don't you think, dear?"

"A dreary name, indeed, my sweet," replied Edward.

"His mother named him Kveikja," said Wista. "But he no longer uses it."

"I assume others gave him that horrid name, Black Dragon. He should pick out a name for himself," said Opal. "One that is more fitting. He would feel better about himself."

"You can suggest that to him"—Wista gave her a warning look—"after our rescue mission. He is very sensitive and has a fiery temper."

"Of course, he does. He's a fire-breathing dragon," said Opal. "I would expect no less from him."

Jackie noticed that the Little Peepers milling around them were eavesdropping on their conversation. "How do we pass the time until tonight?"

"Is it possible that you could help Ruby and Shauna with the pronunciation of the words used in the spells?" asked Wista. "Nearly all of them are written in an old language."

"Certainly," Opal and Edward said together. "It will be our pleasure to do so."

"I suppose I could rewrite the script into block lettering," said Jackie. "Kids today struggle to read cursive handwriting. My kids can't read it—" She burst into tears before she could complete her thoughts.

"Now, dear, don't cry," said Opal. "We will bring them back here. They will soon be freed from the magi and riding on the back of a dragon. How exciting is that!"

"They will be terrified of me," Jackie cried harder. "Look at me! I'm a ghost!"

"At first, they will be scared of you," Wista said candidly. "However, you are still their mother and they will adjust quickly to their new situation."

Jackie lowered her head and sighed heavily. "But they cannot live with me in the human world."

"You can stay here with them in Hidden Forest, if you choose," offered Wista.

Jackie lifted her head and noticed that the Little Peepers were beginning to crowd just around her. They offered her words of comfort. Suddenly, the Little Peepers turned their heads toward the commotion occurring at the other end of the village. A long line of gnomes entered Arborville, in the same manner as a string of ants. The gnomes carried baskets of nuts, mushrooms, fruit, fruit pies, and all sorts of melons. Gnomes love melons and grew them in their own patches.

"Heard you have your hands full," said Groppy, the leader of the gnomes. "Thought you might need some help at feeding time." He ran his hand through his long, white beard, trying to make it look presentable. Most of the gnomes dressed as plainly as the Little Peepers, except for Groppy. He wore a bright red hat, a red shirt, and red knickers. He had on a pair of striped red-and-white socks and large, wooden shoes.

"Thank you, Groppy," said Wista. "Why don't you stay and eat with us. Maybe do some bartering." She knew the gnomes enjoyed nothing more than trading with the other creatures in the forest. As she watched the gnomes swapping their wares with the villagers, she decided that she would ask them to help carry the dragon's treasure to the top of Misty Falls, where the Black Dragon was waiting for its return. Commander Lapin and the other rabbits would not be joining them at the dragon's den. They decided it was best to stay clear of the dragon for a while.

▢▢▢

Queen Rossen was frowning at Tark and Auralia in her private quarters. Counselor Nirva was also there.

"Yesterday, Queen Wista sent me a message that your scouting services were required," said Rossen. "You did not return until early this morning. What were you scouting? And where?"

"We were searching for a spellbook in the basement of a Wiccan," replied Tark. "Ruby and Shauna were in need of one."

Rossen focused on Auralia. "What makes you think that you can be a spy, Auralia? You have not received any special training in the field."

"It's what I am supposed to do," replied Auralia. "I do not want to follow in my parents' footsteps and become a beekeeper. The Little Peepers get to choose their own destinies. Why can't we?"

"We are not Little Peepers," retorted Rossen. "We did not descend from frogs."

"What did we descend from?" questioned Auralia.

"We have always been here," lied Rossen. "This is not the time for such questioning."

Both Auralia and Tark could see in the queen's eyes that she was not being truthful. She knew where the elves originated. She was one of Mem's original creations. Rossen had no parents, like the older elves in the community.

"If you want to be spies," continued Rossen, "then tell me what Queen Wista and the Little Peepers are up to. They seem so secretive lately. And they are not the secretive type." She shot a look at her counselor, who stood stone-faced alongside her. "Do either of you know if Queen Wista learned something of importance from the Black Dragon? Something that she is not telling me?"

"The last thing I heard was how Ruby and Shauna freed themselves from the Black Dragon," said Tark. "They were unharmed," he added for good measurement.

"Of course, they were unhurt. Most likely, they performed black magic on the dragon. I am going to recommend to our council that we bring the girls here. They need to be examined. It's possible they could hurt us if they are not carefully monitored." Rossen crossed her arms over her chest, as if she was convinced that the girls possessed dark magic.

"You don't intend to lock them up, do you?" asked Auralia.

"Not yet," Rossen replied sharply. "Counselor Nirva, I believe we should visit Arborville today."

"Also, no one has spotted the Black Dragon since he departed in a huff from our village yesterday," pointed out Nirva. "I suspect he is up to no good. Or perhaps the girls killed him during their escape."

"The girls did not slay him," Tark said adamantly. "From what I heard, the dragon and the girls got along splendidly."

"We will see," said Nirva. She cast Tark an angry look. He should not have doubted her in front of their queen.

At that moment, Tark's romantic interest in Nirva faded away. Her hair seemed less lustrous and her aquamarine eyes and smile no longer appeared as bright.

Suddenly, Advisor Baruk rushed into the queen's quarters and announced that all the gold had been stolen from the treasury.

Queen Rossen narrowed her eyes. "The moles must have taken our gold and given it to the rabbits for use as a bargaining chip to appease the Black Dragon! The rabbits and the moles are so conniving! How dare they plot against us at our expense!" She stood up from her elm chair. "We will go speak at once with Commander Lapin about this treachery! Counselor Nirva and Advisor Baruk, come with me. Tark and Auralia, go and inform Queen Wista what the rabbits have done. We will meet up later in Arborville. Do not forget whose side you are on. Do not make any decisions without my approval. Most importantly, do not disappoint me again." The last part was issued as a strong warning.

Rossen and her two advisors whisked out of the room while Tark and Auralia followed behind them. The two groups parted in different directions, flying away as different birds.

□□□

Tark and Auralia arrived in Arborville shortly after dozens of moles and all the gnomes departed for Misty Falls. The gnomes agreed to haul the treasure to the dragon's den for a year's worth of blueberry tarts. Meanwhile, other moles were digging a new passageway from an abandoned tunnel to the Pit of Despair. The elves' gold would be taken through the new shaft to the cavern and given to Mem.

Opal was admiring a ruby necklace when Tark and Auralia changed from red-tailed hawks into their elf forms. "Oh, you startled me! I wasn't expecting to see you until later this evening."

"Why is that?" asked Auralia.

"We are leaving tonight for Montana to rescue Jackie's children," she replied, as she picked up a diamond tiara. "This must have belonged to a rich princess." She made a face, peering at the two elves. "I wonder if the princess was wearing it when the dragon snatched it from her. I hope he didn't remove her entire head with it. I suppose these lovely items will be given back to the dragon . . . although he is incapable of removing my head." She placed the tiara on top of her head.

"The tiara looks lovely on you, my princess." Edward was drifting toward them.

"Where is the rest of the treasure?" asked Auralia.

"It's hidden away in a cavern near Misty Falls. The gnomes and the moles are returning the treasure as we speak." Opal placed the ruby necklace around her neck. "The mole named Erde brought these jewels here." She pointed to the tiara and necklace. "It was Queen Wista's idea to keep a few of them to make sure that the dragon will come tonight. How do I look, Edward?"

"Like the Queen of England. You would be even lovelier wearing opals, my sweet Opal. On second thought, you couldn't become any lovelier, even if you were draped in jewels."

"You are quite fond of each other," Auralia remarked to the ghosts. "Like the dryads are fond of their individual tree. In contrast, elves only speak words of devotion to their leaders but not to their loved ones."

"You can never take your loved ones for granted," replied Opal. "In an instant, they can be taken from you forever."

"I would never leave your side, my precious," said Edward.

"And I, you, my love."

"Are all humans like you?" questioned Auralia.

"Sadly, no," responded Opal. "Death gave us a fresh perspective on life. Isn't that so, Edward?"

"It is so, dearest. Life should be lived to its fullest."

"I shall do so," said Auralia. She was more determined than ever to become a spy.

Queen Wista spotted Tark and Auralia and flew over to them on a taxi bird. "Did you tell Queen Rossen that a settlement has been reached between the rabbits and the Black Dragon?"

"May we speak in private?" Tark asked Wista, glancing around.

"Of course," said Wista. "Follow me."

Tark and Wista went to the meadow, giving the trees a wide berth and reducing the risk of the dryads overhearing them. Meadowlarks sang their songs from the tall meadow grasses, while swallows swooped back and forth over a small pond to catch insects. There were six ravens perched in a maple tree, their backs to the gentle breeze. A light wind stirred the meadow grasses and wildflowers, as well as the bulrushes and cattails that surrounded the pond.

"Put me on your shoulder, so I can hear you better," said Wista.

Tark bent over and lifted Wista onto his right shoulder. There were times Wista wished she were tall. She could have asked the fairies to make the Little Peepers a little taller, but it would have devastated their culture. They liked living high in small treehouses and taking to the skies on birds.

"It's a beautiful day, isn't it?" she asked, taking in the lovely surrounding from this new viewpoint.

"It is a beautiful day."

"What did you want to say privately to me?"

"Like all elves, I sense things that cannot be seen. However, my visions are stronger than most. Lately, I've been having a very disturbing vision . . ." Tark's voice began to falter.

"What is this vision of yours?"

"That Hidden Forest disappears. I've had this vision once or twice a day since the last full moon."

"How often do your visions come true?" asked Wista.

Tark turned his head to look at Wista. "Almost always."

"I see." Wista waited a few seconds before speaking again. "I must ask you again, did you tell Queen Rossen that we are giving back the dragon's treasure today?"

"No," said Tark. "I had another vision where I saw Queen Rossen's hand reaching out for gold. I didn't want to take the chance of her snatching it back."

"She wouldn't take the gold we are returning to the Black Dragon," said Wista. "It's fool's gold."

Tark arched his eyebrow at her. "You know about that?"

"I think everyone knows about it now, except the dragon. I don't believe anyone will tell him with that temper of his."

"It was discovered this morning that the gold in our treasury was missing. Queen Rossen believes the moles took it and gave it to the rabbits. She left this morning to speak with Commander Lapin about the matter. She is coming here afterward."

"The dragon will have his treasure back before Rossen arrives here. The gnomes are taking it to him as we speak." She didn't tell him about the plan to hand over the real gold to Mem. It was too soon to reveal that information to others.

"According to Opal, the moles are helping the gnomes."

"That is true. The gnomes need the moles to guide them underground. I think it's best we don't mention the moles' role in this to Queen Rossen."

"I won't. I hope that you do not think I am being traitorous to Queen Rossen. I just had to say something to relieve my conscience," Tark said uneasily. "My visions are becoming stronger."

"I am glad that you spoke up," replied Wista. "Will you and Auralia be staying with us today?"

"Queen Rossen instructed us to stay until her arrival."

"It's good that she is coming. I need to speak to her about tonight's rescue plan for Jackie and Serpentine's offspring."

"There's a lot going on."

"Yes. But there will be a lot less to do once we win over the Black Dragon by returning his treasure. In a way, the rabbits have unintentionally helped us all. It brought secrets out into the open, which forces us to address old wounds." Wista did not elaborate. "Do you mind giving me a lift back to the village? It's a long way to go with short legs."

Tark smiled at the leader of the Little Peepers. He wished his queen was more like Queen Wista.

□□□

Dozens of curious fairies flocked to Arborville to look over the spellbook that was brought back from Madame Papulose's home. They also came to teach magic lessons to Ruby and Shauna. Their primary focus was to instruct the girls in casting the amnesia spell and then the obedience spell. The plan was to first strike the Malum with the amnesia spell. From this spell, their minds would go blank. Next, Ruby and Shauna would order the magi to stay out of the forest. It was a tall order for the girls. Wista did not tell the fairies or the girls about Mem and her intent to destroy her offspring. Other than her owl Spruce and the moles, no one else knew about Mem's vengeful plot against her children. If Mem was successful, then the girls' magic would not be needed.

"I'm not sure how Miss Whiskers, Mister Barnaby, and the other local cats will feel about having the Malum remain in their world," Ruby said to Golden Belle. They were in the midst of practicing the amnesia spell again.

"The Malum won't live much longer," stated Shauna.

"That's true," replied Golden Belle, sounding distracted.

"What's wrong?" asked Ruby.

Golden Belle lowered her wand and let out a little sigh. "We still don't know what will happen to the Little Peepers when Spellbinder dies. Will all of his spells die with him, too?"

"Will Ruby and I die if Highbrow dies?" asked Shauna.

"No, you're safe because you have his magic. Magic cannot die. On the other hand, the Little Peepers are the creation of a spell. Spells can be undone," Golden Belle replied gloomily. "Queen Wista and Oide are most vulnerable because they were made directly by Spellbinder's wand. They might change back into frogs."

"What should we do?" asked Ruby, worriedly.

"After training with our wands, we'll search through the spellbook for a spell that will prevent Spellbinder's spell from being undone," replied Golden Belle.

A spark flew out of Shauna's wand and almost singed Golden Belle, who ducked to avoid it.

"It's best we keep our focus on our wands for now," said Golden Belle.

"But our wands aren't fully able to cast the amnesia spell. A witch is needed to touch the tips of our wands," said Ruby.

Golden Belle grinned broadly at them. "You haven't figured it out yet?"

"Figure out what?" asked Ruby.

"You are witches," said Golden Belle, wagging her head in amusement. "Your father is a warlock."

"But we are only half-witches," insisted Ruby.

"It does not matter. You have the magical abilities of a full-bodied witch," countered Golden Belle. "If it makes you feel better, both of you can touch the tips. That would add up to the strength of a full witch. The requirements of the amnesia spell would be met. But once you do this, please be careful where you point your wand. I don't want to lose my mind."

Ruby peered curiously at Golden Belle. "How come you didn't tell this to us earlier?"

"Queen Wista asked us not to mention it until you had more control over your wands. It's a bit dangerous if you unintentionally shoot off your wand . . . like you did a moment ago. Please pay attention to your wand at all times. None of us wants to lose our memories or be transformed into mice."

The girls promised that they would be more careful and touched the ends of their wands.

Occasionally, Vorte and Berruga would sneak a peek at the girls while they practiced. Out of the corner of his eye, Vorte caught a glimpse of Queen Wista standing at the edge of the village. She was speaking with Erde, whose head poked out of a molehill. They saw Wista nod her head, gaze over at Misty Falls, and nod once more at Erde. The mole disappeared into the hole while Wista returned to the village center. Vorte and Berruga assumed Wista had wrapped up the entire affair between the Black Dragon and the rabbits. Hopefully, it was all behind them and everyone could now fully concentrate on the Malum problem. For starters, they had to rescue Serpentine's children. Therefore, Vorte and Berruga were not surprised when Wista gathered the community around her and asked for volunteers to go on the rescue mission.

"We need to rescue the children of Sorcerer Serpentine and return them here. The Black Dragon has agreed to fly us to Montana and back," Wista said, as she stood on an old stump. Counselor Herona was at her side. "Nonetheless, we should take a fair number of Little Peepers with us, in case the Black Dragon changes his mind during the trip."

"Where is Montana?" asked Luna, the veteran pilot.

Wista's gaze wandered over to Jackie, who stood by Opal and Edward. "Jackie will answer that question."

"It's hundreds of miles from here." Seeing that the Little Peepers wore puzzled expressions, she replied, "It will take all night to fly there."

"It is, by far, the longest rescue mission we have ever undertaken," noted Wista. "It is not for the fainthearted."

"We have already agreed to go," spoke up Golden Belle. She gestured at her cousins, Sparkles, Glitter, Dazzle, and Flicker. "We might be needed to make Serpentine fall asleep," she said to the crowd.

"And use fairy dust to make the children understand our words," added Dazzle.

"And lift their spirits," said Sparkles, sprinkling fairy dust on a couple of nearby Little Peepers. Within moments, they were grinning from ear to ear.

"Your assistance is appreciated," Wista said kindly to the fairies. "Your services always come in handy."

"What about us?" asked Ruby. "Shauna and I could use magic on Serpentine."

"We need you here," said Wista. "We still have to watch out for the other eight magi." It was not necessary to explain her reasoning to the onlookers. They realized that Ruby and Shauna were still in danger from the Malum. At least until Mem was healed. Wista had no idea how long it would take for the gold to mend the magi's mother. Nothing was guaranteed right now. "Besides, I want the two of you to continue your magic lessons."

Ruby was secretly relieved to stay behind on this mission, despite missing an opportunity to ride on the dragon. She hoped there would be other opportunities down the road. She just wasn't ready to face down a magus. She could tell that Shauna was relieved, as well.

"I can go on the mission," offered Oide.

Within a short amount of time, Skit, Kreen, Flycatcher, Hummer, and Luna also volunteered to go.

Berruga and Vorte were tempted to go along, but they knew that Ruby and Shauna would be too worried about them. They had already been traumatized enough by the recent loss of their mother.

"We're joining the mission, too," Opal announced to the crowd. She gestured at Edward. "Aren't we, dear?"

"That is correct, my sweet Opal," said Edward, beaming at the spectators. "We will not get in your way because you can go right through us."

"Naturally, I have to show the way," added Jackie. "And my children will need me to be there for them."

"Do you want elves on this operation, Queen Wista?" asked Auralia.

"You should be asking *me* that question," said Queen Rossen. "I am your queen." She pushed past the onlookers, with Counselor Nirva on her heels. "I need to speak with you privately, Wista."

Everyone in the crowd heard the anger in the elf queen's voice.

232

"We may speak alone in my house, Queen Rossen." Wista called for a taxi bird. A small hawk, a Cooper's hawk, swooped down from a tree. After she climbed aboard, the hawk flew up to Wista's treehouse. Meanwhile, Rossen changed into a yellow finch.

The three ghosts were clearly impressed by the performances.

"Never seen anything quite like it before, my love," said Opal.

"They certainly do things differently here, my sweet," replied Edward.

After entering the treehouse, Wista asked Rossen if she wanted some tea before they got down to business.

"No, thank you," said Rossen brusquely. "I just spoke with Commander Lapin. He emphatically stated that neither he nor the other rabbits stole the gold from our treasury. If the rabbits did not take it, I presume the Little Peepers did. Did you give the gold to the Black Dragon?"

"I did order the gold to be taken from your treasury," admitted Wista. "But I gave the gold to Mem."

Rossen's face turned paler than ever and she plopped down on a chair, as if her legs could not support her weight any longer. "You should not have done that."

"When were you planning on telling me about the existence of Mem? And about the deal you made with her? You are preventing my son from returning to me!"

Rossen had never seen the leader of the Little Peepers so furious until now. "Please let me explain. As you know, I went to the Pit of Despair to speak with the Dark Shadow about freeing the captured souls. Once there, the Dark Shadow beckoned me to speak with Mem. I swear to you, Wista, I did not know of her existence until that moment."

Wista slumped in a chair directly across from Rossen. "What did she tell you?"

"She wanted to make a trade. She would free all the souls, except for King Koning, your son, and Rowl. She told me that she wanted their souls because she enjoyed their company. I suspected she kept them because they had the most influence over us." She fiddled with the gold bracelet on her left wrist. "In return for the release of most of the souls, she wanted me to bring her gold. She said the gold would heal her. Then, she proceeded to tell me the entire story about how her

233

children destroyed her. Her spiritual body was ripped apart by their magic."

"She shared that part of the story with me, too."

Rossen gave a tired nod. "Did she also tell you that she intended to annihilate her children once she was healed?"

"Yes."

"Did she also mention that she was planning on destroying Hidden Forest, as well? She wants to start over. She made a promise that she would spare the lives of the elves and give us a new place to live. But I did not believe her. After all, she created her evil offspring. Why should I trust her?"

Two little, red circles popped up on Wista's pudgy cheeks. "No, she did not mention this to me."

"Ah, I didn't think so. I couldn't let Mem get her hands on the gold. So, I brought her fool's gold. She released all but three of the captured souls. After Mem discover the gold was fake, she sent the Dark Shadow to warn me about breaking our agreement. She threatened to take our shapeshifting abilities away from us once she was whole again. That was the end of our arrangement. It is best that we keep Mem in the Pit of Despair and not let her return to destroy us."

Wista sat there, speechless. She did not know whom or what to believe. Until now, the elf queen had not been forthcoming about her interaction with Mem. She knew, though, that it was too late to return the gold. The moles already delivered it to Mem.

"Where is the gold?" Rossen asked her.

"Would you like a cup of tea?"

"Did you give Mem the gold?"

"She has it."

Rossen rested her chin in her hands. "We are doomed."

"No, we are not doomed. After Mem eliminates her children, we must convince her to protect Hidden Forest and not annihilate it. It will have to be a joint effort, though."

What?" Rossen felt her head spin. "No matter what happens to the Malum, Mem will massacre the elves because I gave her fake gold. Magical beings are never kind to their betrayers."

"Your apology will have to be heartfelt. I suggest you get down on your knees and appeal for forgiveness."

Rossen felt her head spin again. "You should not have taken the gold from us without permission!"

"You should not have kept Mem a secret from me. You know we Little Peepers hate secrets. Also, you made this deal with Mem without first discussing it with me."

"You were so distraught over the death of King Hoppit and the capture of your son, I didn't think you would be thinking straight. I was afraid you would have agreed to anything to free Cobias from the pit."

"Poppycock!" Wista blew air out through her nostrils like an enraged bull. "Besides, how do I know for certain that you are telling me the truth? Perhaps you could not part with the gold. And that is why my son is stuck in the Pit of Despair."

Insulted, Rossen rose from her chair. "This is madness! I need time to figure out how I am going to fix your mistake!"

"Tark and Auralia are going on tonight's mission," said Wista, after taking a calming breath. "If the rescuers run into trouble, they might need a couple of shapeshifters."

"Take them with you," said Rossen, infuriated. "All of us will eventually wind up dead anyway." She walked out of the treehouse and flew down to the ground, joining up with Counselor Nirva. The elf queen and her advisor left in a hurry, leaving Tark and Auralia behind with baffled expressions. Several Little Peepers and the Cooper's hawk had eavesdropped on the conversation between the two queens. Word spread quickly through the forest about Mem's existence and her plans to put an end to Hidden Forest. Fear in the forest ran as deep as the roots of the tallest tree, penetrating all of Hidden Forest.

Chapter Twenty-Three

Road Trip

The magi did not depart for Montana until the sun dropped below the horizon. Warlock Highbrow sat in the driver's seat while Witch Blackheart occupied the passenger's seat. The other six magi were crammed in the seats behind them. As their black van passed Madame Papulose's house, Highbrow suddenly slammed on the brakes. His passengers jerked forward.

"Holy Hades!" swore Witch Mortify. "Is it your intention to kill us?"

"I want to get my hands on more of those spellbooks," Highbrow announced. "We might need them down the road."

"Why can't we get them later?" asked Witch Blackheart.

"I want those spellbooks now because I have no intention of returning to the human world once I leave it," said Highbrow, as he turned off the ignition. "I'll be back in a moment."

"What if the Wiccan is home?" asked Sorceress Underhand from the backseat. She sat between Sorceress Hexla and Warlock Gloominus.

Highbrow showed the handgun he had tucked away in his cloak. "We will be long gone before anyone finds her dead body. Better yet, I'll take it with us and dump it on some lonely highway."

"Don't be a fool, Highbrow!" snapped Blackheart. "We are so close to achieving our goals."

"That's right! We don't have time for such foolishness," snarled Witch Mortify.

"What does the loss of a few minutes and the death of a human matter when we can obtain valuable spellbooks? Besides, you should've stolen them years ago." Highbrow opened the door, got out huffily, and slammed the door shut.

"Sometimes he can be a pain in the rear," muttered Warlock Gloominus.

Warlock Highbrow did not bother to knock on the front door because he knew it would be unlocked. No one locked their door in town, even after the disappearance of its three residents, because people were creatures of habit. Madame Papulose was in the basement with Mister Barnaby, sorting through the spellbooks. Even though the piles of books appeared disorganized to others, Madame Papulose had her own system. She was disturbed that her spellbooks were neatly stacked. She counted the books and, sure enough, two books were missing. She still assumed Opal and Edward were the ones responsible for rearranging the books, as well as taking a couple of spellbooks to show her friends at the cemetery. She was disappointed that they had not returned yet.

"Well, Mister Barnaby," said Madame Papulose, as Highbrow turned the knob on the basement door, "I've put the books back into their original places."

Mister Barnaby peered at the book piles. They were still as untidy as ever. Miss Whiskers would have rolled her eyes at Madame Papulose's organizational skills. Suddenly, they heard footsteps on the basement stairs. When they turned around, they saw a wizened man in a black cloak creeping down the steps. He looked a lot like Serpentine. In fact, they could have passed for brothers.

"Who are you?" asked Madame Papulose, as she jumped to her feet. She had been kneeling over a mound of spellbooks.

"I came here to get your spellbooks."

Madame Papulose backed away from him. "They are not for sale."

Highbrow removed the gun from his cloak pocket and pointed it at her. "You misunderstand me. I came to take your books, not buy them."

"You can't!"

"Yes, I can."

"I will call the police!"

Mister Barnaby shook his head. Madame Papulose just gave the gun-wielding man a good reason to shoot her. Sometimes humans weren't very bright.

"You are irritating me," Highbrow said coldly. "You give me no choice but to eliminate you from this world." Just as he was about to pull the trigger, Mister Barnaby lunged at Highbrow. The cat's claws dug deep into Highbrow's right ankle, which was not protected by his cloak. Next, the cat bit his ankle. Highbrow howled and dropped his gun. Madame Papulose had the sense to pick up the gun and then began shooting wildly at the strange man. Highbrow ran up the stairs empty-handed and out the front door. He did not stop running until he jumped inside the van and sped off.

Madame Papulose chased after him with the gun in her hand. She fell down the front porch steps, landing on her broken wrist. After the van raced off, Madame Papulose looked down at her feet and saw Mister Barnaby there. "I would've hit him if it wasn't for my broken wrist. My aim was off. Let's call the police and then the doctor. My wrist is killing me."

Unfortunately, Madame Papulose did not think of reading the van's license plate number because of the pain shooting up her arm. In fact, she nearly went into shock from facing the armed intruder and reinjuring her wrist. She fainted on the front lawn. Luckily, the neighbors heard the gunshots and were rushing over to come to her aid. One of them called the police chief.

Meanwhile, Highbrow was getting an earful from the other magi in the vehicle.

"I warned you, Highbrow," hissed Blackheart, "to stay away from there."

"I should have shot her first," Highbrow said regretfully, "and grabbed a few spellbooks. The damn cat scratched and bit me and prevented me from shooting the fake witch."

"Well, next time shoot the cat first," snorted Blackheart.

The other magi chuckled and the matter was soon forgotten. The Malum were actually in a good mood. And the more distance they put between themselves and the town, the lighter their moods became.

In the meantime, Madame Papulose recovered from fainting and was being helped to her feet by her neighbor Violet. The police chief began questioning Madame Papulose in her front yard. He believed she had concocted the entire story because no one off the street would walk into someone's house to steal a spellbook. He thought Madame Papulose was a crackpot.

"You have the suspect's gun!" Madame Papulose said in disbelief to the police chief. "Get fingerprints off the gun or run a check on the gun's serial number."

"Small police departments don't operate like police shows on TV, Madame Papulose," the police chief stated impatiently. "These things take time." He pulled out a stick of gum from his front pocket, slowly removed its wrapper, and stuck the gum in his mouth. "We'll get to the bottom of this—eventually."

"Three people are currently missing from our town!"

"No need to get hysterical, Madame Papulose. We're closing in on a suspect." He looked at her suspiciously. "We have the situation well in hand."

"Well, I reinjured my wrist. I need medical attention."

Once more, Madame Papulose was driven to the city hospital by Violet Vane. She was in physical pain from her broken wrist but also suffering emotionally since the police doubted her story. Violet did her best to cheer up Madame Papulose.

Mister Barnaby had listened to the police chief's interrogation of Madame Papulose. Afterward, he sought out Miss Whiskers. The spellbooks had to be hidden away from the man in the black cape. In all probability, he was an associate of Sorcerer Serpentine and one of the nine magi that the creatures from Hidden Forest mentioned. Perhaps it was the father of Ruby and Shauna. That thought made Mister Barnaby shiver, all the way from the tip of his black nose to the tip of his black tail. He felt that the malicious warlock would not think twice about shooting his own children. Also, this business with the Dark Shadow had to come to an end. It was too terrifying to go out at night, even though he did.

□ □ □

Ruby and Shauna were looking out the window of their new and much bigger treehouse. It had two stories. The Little Peepers built wooden steps for them to reach the top floor, which was the girls' bedroom and bathroom. The first floor was the kitchen, living room, and the bedroom and bathroom for Vorte and Berruga. Their treehouse stuck out against all the other tiny treehouses, but no one criticized its unsightliness. As a matter of fact, another giant treehouse was in the process of being built for Serpentine's children. The fairies were presently carving them wands, not knowing for certain whether the three children inherited their father's magical powers. In the meantime, Ruby and Shauna were memorizing spells as fast as possible. The spellbook was with them in their new bedroom, which was a little cramped. However, they did not complain because it was much safer to be high in the treetops than sleeping on the bare ground, where the frog-snakes could slither pass them at night.

From their room, they watched the rescue crew prepare for their mission. The Black Dragon was just below their window. The Little Peepers were scrambling around him to make sure that the dragon and the crew had packed enough food and water for their voyage. The owls had even brought in a deer that was killed by a car. The accident happened on a road just outside Hidden Forest. The six strongest owls tore the deer carcass into large chunks of meat and fed them to the dragon.

"Do you wish you were going with them, Ruby?" asked Shauna.

Ruby shook her head in a tired manner. "I think we already have our work cut out for us."

"What day do you think it is?"

"I don't know. It might be June."

"Do you think we can raise Mom from the dead?" asked Shauna.

"Golden Belle said that we couldn't. Even the blackest magic cannot bring back the dead."

"Mem is rising from the dead," countered Shauna.

"She's not dead. Just badly wounded. And she's not human like Mom, either."

"Do you think Mem will destroy this place and start over again?" asked Shauna.

"I don't know."

"We'll have to leave before she does," said Shauna. "I'm not sure where we would go."

"We can't believe everything that Queen Rossen says is true."

"I don't trust her, either," admitted Shauna. "She thinks our magic will make us evil. It won't, will it?"

"Of course not."

"Mom raised us to be good," said Shauna.

"She did."

"But she couldn't protect us from bad people, like our dad and stepdad."

Ruby let out a little sigh. "The Little Peepers will protect us. They can bend minds."

"Including ours," noted Shauna.

"That won't be necessary. We won't go bad."

"We have to be careful."

Ruby glanced at the wand held in her sister's tight fist. Shauna was rarely seen without her wand. "Be careful of what?"

"Just be careful that others won't harm us or we won't harm others."

"We won't become like the Malum," Ruby said sternly. "Do you hear me?"

Shauna gave a little nod.

They watched as Kreen, Skit, Flycatcher, Hummer, Oide, and Luna climbed on top of the dragon's back. Subsequently, Golden Belle and her four cousins hopped on behind the Little Peepers. Then, Tark and Auralia changed into Little Peepers. It would have been exhausting for them to fly all night. At last, Jackie sat right behind the dragon's neck and played the role of the navigator. Opal and Edward sat behind Tark and Auralia. Wista instructed the ghost couple to sit near the dragon's tail, so they wouldn't bother the Black Dragon with their ghost stories and romantic poems of yesteryear. Furthermore, Opal began referring to the dragon as "Smolder," which did not sit well with the Black Dragon. Ruby and Shauna liked the name, though, because it suited him perfectly. He had a fuming temper, discharged fire and smoke from his mouth, and exhaled ashes through his nostrils.

Queen Wista and a large crowd wished the rescue team success while the fairies sprinkled gold dust all over the dragon for good luck. The Black Dragon sneezed and then grumbled that the fairy dust got into his eyes, nearly blinding him. As he blinked his enormous eyes furiously, he managed to take flight straight off the ground without a running start. The dragon was a skillful flyer with hundreds of years of navigating the skies.

"The dragon flies like an owl," said Oide, clearly impressed. "Only a bit louder."

The riders clung carefully to the dragon's sharp scales that ran down his spine, while the onlookers waved and shouted goodbye. Still standing at the open window, Ruby and Shauna recited an incantation and flicked their wands. Fireworks shot out high into the air. The spectators cheered. Berruga and Vorte, who were watching the events from their first-story window, were not as amused as the crowd. They did not like seeing the girls show off.

The sisters stood there until the dragon was no longer in sight. Then, they returned to memorizing more spells. They had found a spell that would prevent Sorcerer Spellbinder from reversing his spells. It was written in Latin and almost impossible to recite.

□□□

Miss Whiskers was surprised to see Mister Barnaby so soon. Last night the book club held a meeting, which he attended. Their book for the month was *Old Possum's Book of Practical Cats* by T.S. Eliot, which was a collection of poems about cats, of course. She had just started her second chapter of *Miss Tails and Her Tales* when Mister Barnaby sauntered through the cat door as if he owned the place. *I really ought to start locking that door.* She was about to scold Mister Barnaby for barging in during her writing session when Renzo stepped through the door, too. She was taken aback to see the debonair tomcat, who lived at the jailhouse. Renzo had never been to the library. As far as she knew, he was not a book reader. Instead, he sent most of his time courting the female cats. He was the cat's meow among the felines, so to speak. Miss Whiskers had to admit that the black stripe over his upper lip made him appear as if he had a dashing moustache.

"What brings the two of you here?" asked Miss Whiskers, as she moved the computer screen away from them. She did not like anyone reading her writing before a thorough editing.

Mister Barnaby told her how a man in a black cape attempted to steal Madame Papulose's spellbooks from her basement and how the police did not believe her story.

"The police refer to Madame Papulose as a 'loose cannon', a 'nutcase', and a 'looney', to name a few," Renzo interjected. "They crack jokes about her down at the station."

"That's not very nice," said Miss Whiskers. "I've heard people say the local police are incompetent, but I don't poke fun at them."

"Well, Madame Papulose does at times," admitted Mister Barnaby. "She said the police chief and his deputy"—they were the only two on the police force in their small town—"couldn't find the end of their noses if it weren't for a mirror."

"The police certainly can't find the three missing townspeople. They are way over their heads," said Renzo. "They come up with all kinds of cockamamie ideas. I have overheard them say that Madame Papulose and anyone who wears a black cape in town is involved in the kidnappings. They believe they are dealing with a cult that sacrifices their victims."

"Included on their list of suspects are eight of the nine magi," added Mister Barnaby, "and Madame Papulose."

"The police are unwilling to confer with other departments to help with the case," said Renzo.

"Interesting," purred Miss Whiskers. "Do you want me to help the police with their case or remove those spellbooks from Madame Papulose's basement?"

"Remove the spellbooks," replied Mister Barnaby. "The magi will come back for those spellbooks. And next time, they will most likely kill Madame Papulose."

"Probably so," replied Miss Whiskers.

"Also, there's the matter of this big, night shadow kidnapping humans," said Renzo. "It's true the shadow leaves us cats alone. However, the thought of a shadow hunting for its next victim is just plain creepy."

"I've been conducting research on dark shadows," said Miss Whiskers. "According to ancient texts, dark shadows roaming the earth are the souls of the dead. As people, they were viciously murdered or unjustly put to death. Their assailants were never brought to justice, and the murdered souls never had a funeral rite to help them get to the next world. Because of the huge size of our particular dark shadow, it probably consists of victims who were massacred at the same time. Their dead souls bonded together, forming a dark shadow that is very much alive."

"Is there a way to get rid of it permanently?" asked Mister Barnaby, shuddering.

"Yes," replied Miss Whiskers. "The lost souls can be helped to the next world. Or, a dark shadow can be destroyed by the midday sun. A dark shadow will not come out on its own accord when the sun is out. So, we can either hold a memorial service for the Dark Shadow to send it on its way or lure it out during the daylight hours to destroy it."

"I think it would be easier to hold a memorial service for it," said Mister Barnaby. "Our book club could arrange it."

Renzo snapped his tail to get their undivided attention. "Why does this Dark Shadow keep collecting souls, though?"

"That's a good question," said Miss Whiskers. "I believe it must be collecting souls for another spiritual individual. The Dark Shadow lives in Hidden Forest. Did Mister Barnaby tell you about the magical forest?"

Renzo nodded. "It's quite a story. And all of it happening practically under our noses."

"I sense our Dark Shadow is gathering souls for another spirit," continued Miss Whiskers. "That's pure speculation on my part, though."

"The three ghosts in my house went to Hidden Forest to get help for rescuing Jackie's children," Mister Barnaby explained to the other two. "Perhaps they will have the answer from the forest creatures when they return. Meanwhile, we should remove the books when Madame Papulose isn't home or is sound asleep."

"I can ask the library mice to go retrieve them tonight," offered Miss Whiskers. "In return, I'll give them old newspapers they can use to make nests. I hate encouraging them to have more babies, but this is an emergency. We have to save those ancient spellbooks and prevent them from falling into the wrong hands."

"What about the Dark Shadow?" asked Renzo. "When should we hold a memorial service for the murdered souls?"

"It's too late to round up club members for a memorial service tonight," said Miss Whiskers. "If the Dark Shadow comes back tomorrow night, the book club members should be prepared to put on a heartrending service."

"Renzo and I will notify the book club members of our plans," said Mister Barnaby.

"I know some other alley cats who would be willing to help out," said Renzo. "I know they would like to get that frightening shadow off our streets."

Miss Whiskers flicked her ears and looked at them. "Don't invite any cats that could scare off the Dark Shadow."

Renzo looked deep into her green eyes and felt his heart flutter. He told himself he should come to the library more often. There were more than books to check out.

"Are you okay, Renzo?" asked Miss Whiskers.

"Of course. I'll bring as many cats as I can who aren't ruffians."

"We do need to get going," Mister Barnaby said with a tone of urgency. "There are many cats we need to track down tonight."

"My grandfather used to say there is a grand adventure waiting around every street corner. But he was an alley cat who lived on the streets." Renzo winked at Miss Whiskers. "I will see you tomorrow night."

Mister Barnaby and Renzo went to inform the other cats in town of their plans, while Miss Whiskers went to the basement to ask the mice to collect more books for the library. She enticed them with a bundle of gossipy tabloids. She did not care if the mice chewed through flakey stories. She caught herself smiling while thinking of Renzo. She found that more disturbing than the Dark Shadow.

◻◻◻

On the night flight to Montana, the Black Dragon stopped once along the way to feed on a fresh elk carcass. It appeared that it had been shot solely for sport and left to die on the side of the road. While the dragon refueled on elk meat, the others, except for the ghosts, dined on raw berries and drank water. The ghosts watched the others enjoy their food, while recalling their last meal. They missed sitting at the dinner table and sharing a good meal and conversation with others.

Before long, the rescuers hopped back on the dragon and resumed their journey. The passengers took turns resting. Half of them fell asleep while the others remained awake, making certain that the sleepers didn't fall off the dragon. Once more, the ghosts stared with envy at those who slumbered. Though, Jackie imagined she could not have dozed off even if she were alive. She was too overcome with worry for her children to rest her eyes for long or enjoy the night ride.

The hours dragged on. The Black Dragon grew tired. Jackie encouraged him to push onward.

"Soon I will need to rest my wings," said the dragon, breathing heavily.

"There it is!" said Jackie elatedly. She pointed to the river below, which was wedged between mountain ranges. "The family cabin is down there!" The Black Dragon glanced down and saw a small, gray, wooden building surrounded by trees. "I drowned in that river," she said, her excitement fading away like the stars above them. It was almost daybreak.

"You must be exhausted," Kreen said to the Black Dragon, stifling a yawn. She had been sound asleep until Jackie's shrill voice woke her up.

"I'm exhausted." However, truth be told, the Black Dragon hadn't felt this exhilarated since he freely roamed the countryside and raided stone fortresses. Being trapped inside Hidden Forest felt like a prison.

"Let's set down by the river, behind that patch of trees," said Oide. "The sound of the river should muffle our landing. We need to take Serpentine by surprise."

"We need to stretch our legs before barging in," said Tark.

"And loosen our wings," said Golden Belle. She and her cousins did not flutter their wings once during their journey.

As soon as the Black Dragon landed, his passengers hopped off his back. They refreshed themselves at the river's edge, splashing water onto their faces. They noticed a bull moose watching them from the wide, clear river before loping off.

"I used to love this river," Jackie said morosely, watching the river flow around a large boulder.

Opal flung both arms around Jackie's shoulder and gave her a comforting hug. "We'll get your darling children back." She removed her arms, which were weightless, from Jackie and walked up to the dragon. "Smolder, how much time do you need to rest before taking off again?"

"Smolder isn't my name," he growled. "It's Kveikja. It means 'ignite.' My mother gave it to me. The others call me 'Black Dragon', but I go by no name."

"When did you stop using your rightful name?"

"When I stopped being Kveikja," he said tersely.

"I shall forever be Opal. I would refuse to answer to 'White Ghost'. Isn't that so, Edward?"

"You shall forever be my precious Opal," Edward answered adoringly.

"We need to make a plan," interrupted Auralia, rolling her eyes at the sappy exchange between the ghost couple. Then again, she wished Tark would look at her the way Edward and Opal looked at each other.

"I suggest we knock on the door," said Glitter. "When Serpentine opens it, we hit him with fairy dust. It should put him to sleep."

"We could shapeshift into wild beasts," said Tark, "and attack him, if he doesn't fall asleep."

"We could also use our mindbending skills on Serpentine and force him to let go of the children," said Luna.

"Whatever we decide to do," said Hummer, "we have him greatly outnumbered."

"I like all the ideas," said Jackie. She reflected on all the options. "Let's try fairy dust on him first." Abruptly, she gave them a strange look. "What are we going to do with Serpentine?"

"We'll have to leave him here," said Golden Belle. "We don't have the ability to shrink him in the human world. Without shrinking him, he is too big to bring back with us."

"You're not going to harm him?" asked Jackie, tentatively.

"As in, kill him?" asked Flycatcher.

"That's exactly what I mean," replied Jackie.

"Queen Wista specifically ordered us not to unjustifiably end Sorcerer Serpentine's life," said Luna. "She does not want Serpentine becoming a dark shadow or a vengeful spirit and haunt Hidden Forest for eternity."

"She has a good point," Jackie conceded. "After today, I don't ever want to come across him again in any lifetime."

Auralia and Tark changed back into their true selves. They would transform into ferocious beasts only if the situation called for it. Otherwise, they did not want to unnecessarily frighten Jackie's children.

As they emerged from the trees and drew nearer to the cabin, Jackie spotted a black van parked alongside Serpentine's car. As she opened her mouth to warn the others, Serpentine and Highbrow rushed out the front door of the cabin with guns blazing. The first bullet struck Auralia's thigh. She shrieked in pain. Tark grabbed her and pulled her behind a tree. They retreated and took cover in the woods. The bullets were coming fast and furious. Unfamiliar with guns, they didn't know that Serpentine was shooting with a shotgun and Highbrow with an assault rifle. Highbrow gave the shotgun to Serpentine after Witch Mortify spotted the Black Dragon in the sky. It so happened that

Mortify was exiting the outhouse when she saw the dragon and warned the other magi.

The fairies' wands were useless against bullets, and there weren't enough Little Peepers to bend the minds of the two sorcerers. Occasionally, they could make Highbrow or Serpentine lower their weapons, but the sorcerer and the warlock were able to fight back with their minds as well as their guns. The three ghosts attempted to scare the shooters away, but it was a futile attempt. The magi did not fear ghosts. So, the ghosts looked for things to throw at them. However, there was nothing large enough to cause bodily damage to them. The van and the car were too heavy for the ghosts to lift.

"I'm going inside to find my children!" Jackie shouted to Opal and Edward.

"No!" Opal yelled back. "You will scare your children to death! They can't find out that you're dead at a time like this. They will lose all hope."

Jackie stayed put, realizing Opal was right. It was not the right time to show them she was a ghost, nor for them to find out what the magi aimed to do with them.

The Black Dragon had remained by the river. His entire body jerked when he heard gunfire. *Human weapons.* He was torn over what to do, so he waited to see if the Little Peepers and the others could escape on their own. However, as the gunshots became louder, he knew the shooters were closing in on his—*friends?* He had never had friends in his life, not counting his mate Agir. Suddenly, he felt the need to protect them. The last time he wanted to safeguard someone was when Agir was alive. Oh, how deeply he had cared for her.

Serpentine and Highbrow were making headway. They had their victims pinned down behind the trees, unable to escape. The fairies could have escaped from an ordinary handgun, but the rapid fire of an automatic and the blast from the shotgun were too much for them. The bullets traveled faster than peregrine falcons. The group was trapped. From the cabin window, the other Malum watched the incident unfold. They were cheering, but Elli, Freyja, and Mani covered their ears and cried in the locked bedroom.

The Black Dragon lifted off the ground and landed in front of Serpentine and Highbrow, blocking the bullets from his new friends.

Serpentine and Highbrow were astonished as the dragon blew fire at them. They ducked and ran into the cabin.

"Don't set the place on fire!" Jackie shouted at the dragon. "My children are inside!"

The Black Dragon closed his mouth. He had intended to burn down the cabin.

In the meantime, Luna was bleeding from the abdomen. "I've been hit," she moaned to Flycatcher.

Flycatcher saw the wound and realized that Luna would die if they did not return to Hidden Forest. She needed a healing potion made by the elves. Tark was not a potion maker like his parents nor was the rescue party carrying potions with them.

Noticing that the dragon had no intention of incinerating the cabin, Highbrow and Serpentine began shooting again from the open windows.

"Get on!" the Black Dragon shouted over his shoulder.

The rescue party darted over to the dragon and got on his back. Flycatcher carried the bleeding Luna while Tark assisted the limping Auralia. The elves morphed into hummingbirds as the smaller creatures tucked in between the dragon's hard scales, shielding themselves. The ghosts screeched at their assailants. The dragon took flight within seconds. About twenty feet in the air, the riders felt the dragon's body jerk. Then, the dragon flew off with great speed.

Highbrow and Serpentine swore as they watched the dragon escape.

"You fools!" Witch Blackheart hissed behind them. "You could have killed the dragon! We need him for our immortality!"

Serpentine whirled around, his face beet-red. "What does it matter? Dead or alive, his scales will still work in the potion!"

"But dead dragons don't grow new scales," snapped Blackheart.

"He has enough scales until we find another dragon," Serpentine retorted irately.

"When was the last time you heard reports of a dragon sighting?" snarled Blackheart.

"I'll make one out of magic," growled Serpentine.

"You can't make a magical dragon and then use its scales in a potion," said Gloominus, angrily marching up to Serpentine. "That's double-dipping. It won't work."

Spellbinder stepped in between Serpentine and Gloominus. "I think it would work—"

"Be quiet all of you!" yelled Witch Zeldar. "And someone go check on those brats in the bedroom. We can't afford to have dead children." She shot a scathing look at Serpentine and Highbrow. "They need to be alive when we perform the ceremony. Just like we need a living and breathing dragon. When we return to Hidden Forest, we will have to capture and cage the Black Dragon. He won't cooperate with us after this."

"We will deal with the dragon later. Right now, we need to find a new hiding place," said Warlock Gloominus. "The Little Peepers and the others will come back for us. And next time, I suspect there will be more of them. Too many Little Peepers will doom us."

"We're a long way from Hidden Forest. Queen Wista will not risk sending the Little Peepers far from the safety of the forest," said Sorcerer Spellbinder.

"No matter how far we go, they will come as long as we have the brats," pointed out Witch Hexla.

"Next time, we'll be better prepared for them," said Sorceress Underhand. She had just returned from looking in on the children. They were huddled in the closet of the back bedroom, very much alive. The boy had peed his pants. She told him to clean up his mess because he stank.

"We know the creatures of Hidden Forest can be defeated with human weapons," said Warlock Highbrow proudly. He thought highly of himself for bringing the bag of weapons and stopping off along the way to purchase more ammunition from a big chain store.

"We can mow down the elves, no matter what shape they take," added Sorcerer Serpentine.

"But we can also die from those guns," Witch Blackheart reminded them all. "The Little Peepers can force us to turn on one another. That is why it is so important we find a new place that is more difficult for the Little Peepers to locate. We cannot go on the offense until we have our magic back."

They all agreed this was prudent. They began to think of a new place to conceal themselves.

□□□

The fairies tried to stop the bleeding with their wands. They sprinkled fairy dust over Luna's and Auralia's wounds. But their magic was beginning to fade in the nonmagical world. Auralia, who was no longer a hummingbird, could not move her injured leg without flinching. Although the pain was excruciating, her injury was not life-threatening, unlike Luna's situation. Luna's face was as pale as an elf's. Every time the dragon jerked up or down from air turbulence, the veteran pilot winced in agony. Kreen and Skit were holding onto Luna, while Oide was helping to direct the dragon back to Hidden Forest. Near the dragon's tail, Opal and Edward were comforting Jackie, who was wailing for her children.

"We must go back for my kids," moaned Jackie.

"We will," said Opal. "But not today. We must take the injured back to Hidden Forest."

"We will bring back reinforcements," said Edward, patting Jackie's hand.

"Hang a right by the big cloud over there," Oide said to the dragon.

"I know the way back," panted the Black Dragon. "But I must land now."

"You cannot keep going?" said Dazzle, who dowsed Luna with more fairy dust.

"I must rest. And I cannot fly during daylight. The humans will shoot me down." He aimed for an open patch of land near a small lake, which was surrounded by tall pine trees. He landed so hard that his passengers almost tumbled off.

"What's wrong?" Oide asked the dragon. He leapt to the ground, like the frog he once was. The rest of the passengers clambered down from the dragon's back.

The Black Dragon rolled over on his side, revealing his underside. It was pockmarked with bullet holes that pierced all the way through his scales. Oide quickly counted eleven wounds. He surmised the dragon was hit when they took off from the ground.

Quickly, the fairies went to work on the dragon's wounds, but their magic was diminishing swiftly. Hardly any gold dust fell from their wands.

"Tark, can you make an herbal potion for these injuries?" asked Golden Belle.

"I'm not familiar with the plants in the nonmagical world," replied Tark.

"I know the woods," said Opal. "Isn't that right, dear?"

"It is true," answered Edward. "We will go with you to the woods and assist you, my dearest elf friend."

Tark squeezed Auralia's hand for reassurance. "I will be back soon." He had transformed back into his original form. It took some concerted effort for elves to remain in an alternate form. Both elves were growing tired as time wore on.

Opal glanced around her new circle of friends. "Will someone please comfort my dear friend, Jackie Jubilee, while I am away? She is in a great deal of pain, too."

Flycatcher went over to Jackie, while the fairies tended to the dragon's wounds. Kreen and Skit were at Luna's side, as Hummer and Oide looked after Auralia. All of them were within earshot of each other.

Before Opal left with Edward and Tark into the unfamiliar forest, she looked back at the dragon. Puffs of smoke emanated from his flared nostrils. "Kveikja, you are a brave dragon." She vanished into the woods before waiting for the dragon's reply. She assumed that he would stave off death just to protest her use of his former name.

"She is very peculiar," said the Black Dragon, while gritting his teeth in discomfort.

"Give it enough time and Opal will grow on you," said Jackie between loud sobs.

"You must be quiet, Jackie Jubilee," said the dragon. "The magi will be looking for us, particularly me."

"Why you, in particular?" asked Flicker. "Is it because you're easier to spot due to your large size?"

"No, they want my scales," he answered, sounding exhausted. "They need my scales for their immortality potion. Queen Wista recently told me that was the reason the Malum wanted my scales."

"It was stupid on their part to shoot you," Jackie pointed out. "I believe dragons are hard to come by."

"It was brave of you to risk your life for us," Kreen said to him.

"I think Serpentine and Highbrow wanted to ground me," said the dragon. "The last time I saw them they were young and full of life. They have grown very old without my scales."

"I noticed that they have grown much older since the last time I saw them, too," remarked Glitter. "Their hair was not gray when they were banished."

"Serpentine was young and handsome when I first met him. Now, he looks as if he already has one foot in the grave," said Jackie. "And I should know about such matters. Just look at me! I am a picture of death!" Her voice was full of rage and sorrow. "He did this to me!"

"But the magi haven't died from old age, yet," Hummer noted. "They still can reclaim their youth." He gestured at the dragon.

"Even if I'm capable of returning to Hidden Forest, they will come after me first," said the dragon, who did not see Hummer point to him. "The forest will not restore their youth. Only their magic."

"If the Malum return to the forest, that means my children had been sacrificed!" howled Jackie. "Oh, we mustn't let that happen!"

"Please don't shriek," said Flycatcher. "We cannot afford to draw attention to our whereabouts."

Jackie nodded and wiped her eyes, even though there were no tears. "I must be strong for my children." Once more, she dabbed her face and lifted her head to regard the others. "If the dragon is too weak to fly, how will we get home?"

No one responded because they had no solution.

"We must stand guard against the Malum," said Auralia, breaking the silence. Her leg wound felt much better after Glitter sprinkled gold flecks on it. "The Malum might want to obtain dragon scales before entering the forest."

The Black Dragon let out a little snort. "I can still set them on fire."

"Their bullets can travel a long way," said Tark, scanning the horizon for signs of danger.

"But the Malum do not know the dragon is severely injured," pointed out Dazzle. "For all they know, we're on our way back to Hidden Forest."

"Unless the ravens have spotted us," said Golden Belle, "and report our presence to the magi."

"Even so," said Auralia, "the Malum are quite aware that our new dragon friend will not fly during daylight in the human world."

Once more, the group fell quiet, mulling over their perilous situation. The fairies gazed upward, scanning the skies for ravens.

Golden Belle shook the last of her fairy dust on the dragon's last wound. Afterward, she placed her tiny hand between the dragon's nostrils, showing her respect. "We will see how you feel by the end of the day. Meanwhile, please get some rest." She flew over to Luna, whose single wound was more serious than any of the dragon's eleven bullet wounds. Nonetheless, it was the fairy dust that was keeping both Luna and the Black Dragon clinging to life. The fairy dust decreased the bleeding, but it did not heal their wounds. They needed a medicinal potion.

"I hope Tark remembers what his parents taught him about herbs," said Auralia. Her hand was pressed against her leg injury. Although her wound was no longer bleeding, she felt tired and weak. "His parents were celebrated potion makers," she explained to Jackie. "Tark was young when they met their misfortunes. He was supposed to have followed in his parents' footsteps, but Queen Rossen made him a spy."

"What happened to his parents?" asked Jackie.

"His father is stuck down in the Pit of Despair and his mother died from hemlock poisoning," replied Auralia. "However, neither incident was ever fully explained." Despite her pain, she grinned. "I could get in trouble for starting rumors." Her smile faded in and out like Jackie's ghost form. "Little Peepers are so open about things. I suppose that's why I like them so much."

"Who do the elves spy on?" asked Jackie. She was familiar with the Pit of Despair and the inhabitants of Hidden Forest because the Little Peepers had entertained the ghosts with their stories back in their village.

"The elves spy on ravens, the Dark Shadow, and the Malum," answered Auralia. "And they keep a close eye on the gnomes and the moles."

"And me," said the Black Dragon, lifting his head to look sideways at Auralia. "The elves were always checking to make sure that I only traded gold with them, and not the gnomes."

"You should rest," Golden Belle reminded him. The talk of gold was unsettling to her since she and her cousins could not produce any more gold dust. They had nothing more to offer the victims, other than soothing words. Furthermore, the elves had cheated the dragon out of his gold. It appeared as if he was the only one in the forest who was unaware of it.

In the meantime, Tark, Opal, and Edward were striking out in the woods. They could not find any of the medicinal plants that Tark had learned about from his parents. He had to admit his knowledge of plants was limited. Opal was much more familiar with these woodland plants. "My father used to take me into the woods and point out plants that would kill me if I ate them. For instance, this is a black nightshade. It grows in the cemetery. Doesn't it, my dear Edward?" She pointed to the tall, sprawling plant with purple flowers.

"It certainly does, my sweet."

"Its ripened berries are used in pies and jams, but its unripe berries and leaves are deadly to consume," said Opal. "And there was a fellow in the cemetery who died from eating poisonous mushrooms. Isn't that so, my love?"

"He had poor eyesight," Edward explained to Tark.

"Even the moles have poor eyesight, but they don't eat plants that kill them," said Tark.

"He wasn't a very bright fellow, either," said Opal. "Isn't that right, dear?"

"That is sadly true, my sweet Opal. That's why his grave is in the back row of the cemetery and his headstone is shaped like a dunce cap-"

"Do you know of any *healing* plants?" cut in Tark, who was growing more desperate by the moment. He was losing patience with the ghost couple. They chatted about everything, especially about their time spent at the cemetery. He did not want to think about death at this moment.

"Why, of course, there are hundreds of plants with medicinal properties," said Opal. "Wild ginger, ferns, garlic, nettles, lavender, mints, chamomile—"

"I mean . . . do you see any healing plants before your eyes?"

"Oh, look, there's broadleaf plantain right over there! It's used for wounds." She hastened toward the plant that her eyes were fixed on. "The plant leaves are pressed against the wound for healing purposes and to prevent infection." She leaned over the plant and began tearing off its leaves. "Start searching for more plants, my sweet Edward and my dear elf friend, Tark."

Tark's attitude softened toward the ghosts when Opal called him a "dear elf friend." How could he be upset with them? They were doing more for their injured friends than he was. At that moment, he regretted not paying more attention to his parents when they pointed out plants to him. Thereafter, he realized he couldn't care less if Opal talked all day long. He was full of gratitude for her knowledge. As they plucked leaves off different plants, she explained that her grandparents emigrated from Europe, bringing their knowledge of medicinal plants to America. "They were too poor to afford medicine in glass bottles," she explained. "Therefore, they grew their own healing plants and searched in the woods to find cures for themselves. Usually, they got better. The gout in Grandpa's foot never completely went away. It usually acted up before bedtime. He said that he never got a good night's sleep. There were times he was tempted to cut his bad foot off with a hacksaw. Surgery was done differently back then . . ."

Tark nodded repeatedly, although he didn't understand half of the things she was saying. His mind was mostly focused on healing their friends and getting back to Hidden Forest. If the Black Dragon could no longer fly, he would have to change into a long-distance bird and retrieve help. No matter how fast he flew, it would be a long flight home.

□□□

After Tark and the ghosts returned from the woods, their medicinal plants were applied to the wounds. Opal took charge of tending to the injured. As the patients were being cared for, Golden Belle pulled Tark aside, out of earshot from the others.

"Our wands weren't strong enough to remove the bullets from their flesh," said Golden Belle. "They cannot be moved until we extract the bullets." She caught his eye. "Ruby and Shauna are powerful enough to remove the bullets and heal the wounds. We need them here. It is the only way we will be able to make it home, particularly the Black Dragon."

Tark glanced up at the sky. It was approaching midday. "I will fly back to Hidden Forest and bring back help."

"Do you need someone along as a rider?"

He shook his head. "I need to fly as light as possible." In front of her eyes, he changed into an albatross. He didn't want to tell her that he was losing his strength. He noticed lately all the elves seemed to have lost some of their vigor. "Tell the others I'll be back with help as soon as possible."

"Be careful, Tark. I cannot sprinkle you with fairy dust for good luck."

"You be careful, too, Golden Belle. Don't let your guard down."

"We will keep an eye out for trouble." She did not want him to know that she and her cousins were rapidly growing weaker. Soon, they would not have the strength to fly.

He flapped his wings and became airborne. Golden Belle returned to the others when Tark was out of sight. She did not want him to see her struggle trying to take flight.

Chapter Twenty-Four

Dangerous Encounters

Berruga was with Ruby and Shauna as they made for Sawwhet's tree. She rode in the front pocket of Ruby's shirt. She had spent the night before sewing it on, so the girls could carry her from place to place. The pocket was an easier way of traveling than balancing on top of one of the girl's shoulders.

"Do you think the rescue party will return tomorrow morning?" Ruby asked Berruga.

"I expect so," replied Berruga. "The dragon won't fly during the daytime, so they will take flight tonight. Right now, they are probably resting comfortably under the protection of the trees. I imagine Jackie has her children back. Serpentine is probably sound asleep because of the fairy dust. He'll be surprised when he wakes up and sees the children are gone."

"I hope so," said Ruby.

"I hope Elli, Freyja, and Mani are nice," said Shauna. "Do you think they will be more powerful than us? That is, if they are magical at all," she added as an afterthought. In her right hand, she was swinging her wand. Last night, she had set it beneath the bed. However, it flew back to her, placing itself alongside her body. The same thing happened to Ruby and her wand. The wands seemed more reluctant than ever to leave their owners.

"I can't say for certain if Serpentine's children are stronger than the two of you. I guess it all depends on how much magic they inherited, if any," said Berruga, thinking it over. That was one of the things the girls liked most about the Little Peepers—they never dismissed or ignored questions. "All I know about magic is that it can be used for good or evil and that it cannot be destroyed."

"Yesterday we came across a spell that reverses spells," said Shauna.

"Oh, dear," said Berruga. "I hope the magi don't discover that spell."

"We also came across one that blocks spells, so spells cannot be reversed," said Ruby. "There are spells for everything. And potions, too."

"It can be confusing," admitted Shauna. "Without a spellbook, it would too hard to remember all the spells. Even with a spellbook, we can't pronounce all the words right."

"But we have to memorize the spells because we won't have time to look them up when we need to cast one against the Malum," Ruby said to her sister.

"Remember, if you do encounter the Malum, do not let them fool you. It doesn't matter if they beg for forgiveness or make false promises. They will feed you lies," said Berruga.

"Maybe Mem is lying, too," pointed out Ruby. "It's possible she intends to destroy everything in Hidden Forest once she is well again. She might want to start over . . . I guess I couldn't blame her. Her kids didn't turn out too well."

"I don't want to start over," Shauna said defiantly.

"Me, either," admitted Ruby.

Berruga peered at both girls, noticing their tenseness. "I guess that we will have to keep our guard up like everybody else in the forest. In the meantime, we will gather as much information as we can. We'll be prepared as much as possible."

The afternoon sun was hot upon the back of their necks. At last, summer had pushed out spring. There would be no more cool mornings until autumn. Since Unicorn Trail was muddy from the latest storms, the girls left behind a trail of footprints. Berruga's shoes remained dry in Ruby's pocket. Above them, there were only a few patrols out because the Black Dragon was with the rescue crew. The Little Peepers protecting the elf village had returned to Arborville the evening before. Actually, Queen Rossen ordered them to go home. This was the first time there was tension between the elves and the Little Peepers. While that thought weighed heavily on Berruga's mind, a unicorn stepped out in front of them. They stopped dead in their tracks, as though they had slammed into an invisible wall. The unicorn was pure white. The sun reflecting off her coat was so bright that Berruga, Shauna, and Ruby had to squint to see her. The unicorn walked up to them and rubbed her long, spiral horn up and down both of their wands. She vanished as if by magic.

"What was that about?" asked Ruby, astounded.

"She gave healing powers to your wands," said Berruga, who appeared just as thunderstruck as the girls. She looked off into the distance. "Unicorns sense things that we cannot. They can hear the trees whispering among themselves. News is carried on the wind."

"So, did something good or bad just happen?" asked Ruby, who appeared truly baffled.

"I'm not sure," said Berruga, still stupefied.

"A good thing happened to our wands," said Shauna. "But a bad thing might be happening somewhere else—"

"Like a warning sign," Ruby finished.

Berruga called to a sparrow in a nearby tree. The sparrow flew over to her. "Please deliver a message to Queen Wista in the village of the Little Peepers that Licorne has given healing powers to the girls' wands."

The sparrow nodded and flew off.

"Do you know Licorne well?" asked Ruby, still confused.

"Only the unicorns know each other well. Licorne is the matriarch of the unicorns. She is ancient and as mysterious as the surrounding hills," replied Berruga. "Let's continue on our way. I am just as curious as you are to meet Sawwhet."

"How come no one spoke to Sawwhet until recently?" asked Shauna.

"She's rather peculiar," replied Berruga. "Individuals tend to stay away from unusual beings."

"She must be like Madame Papulose, who you or the others mentioned, Ruby," said Shauna. "People think she's a crackpot, too. But all this time she had those amazing spellbooks in her basement."

"What good insight you have, Shauna!" said Berruga, taken aback by the nine-year-old's perception. "Sawwhet has been keeping amazing historical records, but no one has taken the time to learn from them. She is different, which makes her an outcast like your Madame Papulose."

Shauna was beaming the rest of the way to Sawwhet's evergreen tree. In the meantime, a couple of ravens followed the sparrow to Arborville. They were curious about the interaction between the unicorn and the girls who carried the wands. The ravens noticed that the dryads glanced at the girls when they passed by their trees.

Something was happening in the forest. This time around the ravens did not want to be on the wrong side. Even though they claimed neutrality during the Great Banishment, the other forest creatures did not see it that way. As the two ravens tailed the sparrow, the peregrine falcon, Swift, trailed behind the ravens. Swift wondered why the ravens were spying on the sparrow.

Sawwhet was perched on a limb, catching a fresh breeze. She had spent the morning putting the final touches on her account of Ruby and Shauna's escape from Witch Zeldar's garden shed. Therefore, she was very surprised to see the same two girls staring up at her.

"Hello, Sawwhet. I am Berruga. And this is Ruby and Shauna—"

"Beckles," said Ruby.

Berruga gave Ruby a strange look. "You have two names?"

"Humans usually have more than one name," Ruby explained.

"It seems a bit of an overkill when you only need one." Berruga shrugged at Sawwhet, who shrugged back. "I suppose all species have strange customs."

"Did you come here for a *short* visit?" asked Sawwhet. Her round eyes darted over to the hollow trunk of her cedar tree, where her scrolls were stored. "I have much work to do."

"We came here for information about Mem," said Berruga.

"Ah, yes. Queen Wista was just here yesterday collecting old knowledge to gain new insight. Before yesterday, no one was interested in the history of Hidden Forest. What precisely do you need to know?"

"Is Mem good or evil?" blurted out Shauna.

"Stop waving that wand in your hand. It's making me nervous," Sawwhet scolded Shauna.

"The wand is moving my hand around," Shauna replied. "It's jumpy today."

Sawwhet looked toward the Pit of Despair. "Maybe Mem is more active today."

"Do you know what Mem is?" asked Berruga. "And where she came from?"

"Everything I know of Mem has been passed down from my ancestors. According to them, Mem is a powerful magical being who had been banished from a faraway place. Her loneliness drove her to create this magical forest. It is also said that she thrives on loyalty but will perish from disloyalty, which I imagine is not uncommon among divine beings."

"Well, it appears that the Malum's disloyalty did a real number on Mem," Ruby pointed out.

"What number is that?" asked Sawwhet.

"It's just an expression we have in the human world," Ruby explained.

"Numbers have significant meaning in our world," said Sawwhet. "The number nine signifies hierarchy. It explains why the nine magi were constantly fighting with one another. They were trying to establish a hierarchy amongst themselves."

"They might still be doing that," remarked Berruga.

"Maybe Mem should've made ten kids," suggested Shauna. "Is ten a good number?"

"Zero would've been the best number of all," remarked Ruby.

"There's only one way to learn the truth about Mem," said Sawwhet, ignoring the girls' comments. "And that is to speak to her in person. I recommend that you go talk to her *before* she emerges with all her power intact."

"But we would have to get past the Dark Shadow to speak with her," Berruga said apprehensively.

"Take these girls with you," said Sawwhet, gesturing at Ruby and Shauna with her right wing. "They are more powerful than the Dark Shadow. Probably not Mem, though. I would strongly suggest you go at once. And remember not to agitate Mem. Don't ask her why she made nine children . . . or made any of them, for that matter." She looked sternly at Ruby and Shauna. "Now, I must return to my writing. Good luck."

"Wait!" cried out Berruga. "How do we know for sure that your information is accurate?"

"Because owls never lie." Sawwhet returned to her cavity in the tree.

Berruga turned her head to size up the girls and their situation. "How well do you know your spells?"

"We have, maybe, one-tenth of them memorized," said Ruby. "There are a lot of spells and potions. It will take years to remember them all."

Berruga chewed on her bottom lip while plotting their next course of action. "Since Queen Wista is occupied with the rescue of Serpentine's children, we will deal with Mem ourselves. And I believe Licorne rubbed your wands for a good reason. We can't ignore what happened with her. . . that would be insulting to all the unicorns. On the other hand, she might have been signaling us to turn around and hurry back to Arborville."

"She was definitely strengthening our wands," said Shauna.

"You're right," said Berruga, throwing back her shoulders. "We need to straighten this matter out . . . both queens managed to return from the Pit of Despair unharmed . . . do you think we should go?"

"How else will we know what we are up against?" pointed out Ruby. "We don't know her true intentions."

"We don't know Mem at all," added Shauna.

Both Ruby and Shauna felt their wands pulsating in their hands.

"Okay, we'll go do our part." Berruga said, still sounding a little reluctant. "If there is any sign of trouble, I want you to aim your wands at it and then run away."

The girls nodded in agreement.

□ □ □

Berruga clung onto the top seam of Ruby's pocket as they made haste for Misty Falls. Along the way, they debated what they would say to the Dark Shadow if it awoke from its nap. Addressing Mem was another thing. They had no idea what awaited them.

The Pit of Despair was hidden behind Misty Falls. Thousands of years of pounding water had carved a gigantic hole in the rock, forming a cave. They entered the cave. In the middle of the cave, there was a hole hammered out by dripping water. Over many years, this hole had become a deep shaft, leading down to a gigantic cavern. At the bottom of the cavern was Mem. Between the top and the bottom of the cavern was a sleeping Dark Shadow.

"We might be able to slip past the shadow," whispered Ruby, doubtfully. She was gazing into the dark pit and using her wand as a giant glow stick. "I can't even see the bottom."

"We could change into bats and fly past the Dark Shadow," suggested Shauna, who was using her wand as a torch. Even though a flame was burning at its tip, the wood did not burn. "One of us can carry Berruga down with us."

"Why don't we holler down into the hole and ask her to meet us here?" said Berruga. "She might be well enough to float up here."

"But the Dark Shadow might meet us first," said Ruby.

Berruga peered down into the cavern again. "I might be willing to take that chance. I can't see the bottom."

As they debated what to do, they heard a thunderous yawn.

"I believe the Dark Shadow is awake," Shauna said in a low voice. "I think we were talking too loudly."

Cautiously, the three of them peeked into the shaft. A blast of cold air hit them squarely in the face. Their hair was blown backwards. The Dark Shadow appeared before them, floating directly above the hole. It did not address the trespassers, but hovered above the cavern floor. The Dark Shadow filled up half the cave.

Berruga politely introduced themselves and asked if they could speak with Mem. Momentarily, the Dark Shadow lingered and then abruptly vanished into the shaft.

"I don't believe Queen Rossen could have bartered with the Dark Shadow," said Berruga. "It doesn't talk. She must have made her bargain with Mem."

Ruby peered down at her pocket. "The bargain that kept her husband down there?" She gestured at the shaft.

"That's the one."

"She must not like him very much," noted Shauna.

Another icy blast of air shot up the chute and circled the cave before a translucent spirit stood before them. Mem was the same color as Opal and Edward, only much bigger than either one. Mem swept over Ruby and Shauna. "I sense magic. It is more powerful than a fairy's." Mem had no mouth, or a face, for that matter. Her words came from her inner core. "And the wands have healing powers . . . who are you?"

"These are the children of Warlock Highbrow," replied Berruga. Once more, she introduced herself and the girls and explained their reason for coming to visit. "So, you see, many half-truths have been told about the nine magi. We would like to know the full truth. Ruby and Shauna must be prepared to confront them. Otherwise, they will kill Serpentine's three offspring and destroy many of the forest creatures."

"They will kill my sister and me," Ruby added anxiously.

Mem sighed. It sounded just like a spirit's wail. Out of nowhere, the cavern filled with light. "Lower your wands," she said in a kinder voice. "I will not harm you."

"You must be getting stronger, your magic is back," remarked Berruga. "The gold must be healing you."

Mem laughed bitterly. "The gold did not heal me. It was the loyalty of your little queen. You resemble her." She was looking at Berruga. "I do not care for the tall queen. The elf queen's disloyalty almost destroyed me."

"I do not understand," said Berruga.

"I do," interrupted Shauna. "Don't you remember what Sawwhet said about loyalty and disloyalty? Loyalty makes Mem stronger and disloyalty makes her weaker."

"Who is this Sawwhet?" asked Mem. Her interest was obviously piqued by her visitors, especially when two of them carried magic wands with healing properties. The girls were unaware their wands were renewing her strength.

"Sawwhet is a little, reddish owl who records the history of Hidden Forest on scrolls," answered Ruby.

"I have always liked owls," said Mem. "My children were cruel to them."

"Is that why you tried to kill them?" blurted out Shauna.

"Shauna!" gasped Ruby. "Don't say that! Mem is their mom."

"It's not a lie, is it?" Shauna shot back, unwilling to take back her words.

"It is partially true," Mem said, not the least bit offended. "I attempted to take back my children's magic. They didn't like the idea of losing their magic, so they tried to destroy me. They blasted me with their wands, rendering me unconscious. When I awoke, I found myself in this cavern. I was in a thousand pieces, like a scattered cloud in the sky. I was broken in more ways than one. Many years I lingered down here, too weak to heal myself. One day, I felt a shadow entering the cavern."

"It was the Dark Shadow," whispered Shauna, her eyes as beautiful and almost as big as a doe's.

"It saved my life. To heal, I needed its loyalty. However, the loyalty of a shadow is not the same as the loyalty of a living being. It would not be enough to completely cure me."

"But why does it collect souls?" asked Berruga.

"I was lonely down here in this pit. So, I asked it to bring me souls to keep me company. Periodically, I released some of them over the years. I planned on freeing the rest of the souls once I left this place. However, not so long ago, bodies were thrown into the cavern. I knew immediately it was the doing of my children because they had tossed my body down here and left me to wither away in the dark. Soon afterward, I heard a voice calling down. Then, suddenly before me, I see a light and a figure. This figure introduced herself as the queen of the elves."

"Queen Rossen," said Shauna.

"Yes, it was Queen Rossen. She offered me a deal. I could keep three souls if I would release all the others. Also, the Dark Shadow had to agree to only take the corrupted souls of humans. In return, she would bring me what I requested. As I said, only loyalty would heal me. But loyalty needs to be tested. Thus, I demanded what she loved the most-"

"It was gold!" This time it was Ruby who interrupted.

"Yes, it was gold. But she brought me fake gold, which cost her nothing. I began to weaken. Her betrayal almost destroyed me."

"I've been told that the Dark Shadow is made of murdered souls," said Ruby. "Is that true?"

"It is true. Their souls come from the human world," said Mem.

"But doesn't the Dark Shadow collect human souls?" questioned Ruby, appearing confused.

"It collects humans. With my remaining magic, I turn them into souls," replied Mem. "Living beings cannot survive down here for very long."

"Do the corrupted human souls provide good company?" asked Berruga, sounding doubtful.

"It is better than being alone," said Mem. "However, the souls from Hidden Forest are far more interesting than humans."

"You mean, King Koning, Rowl, and Cobias?" asked Berruga.

"Yes."

Berruga visibly shivered from the cold. "But the freed souls returned as themselves. They don't even remember their time spent in this pit."

"Before freeing the souls, I erase any memories of their time spent down here. I never want them to leave here with any memories of this place. I never harmed them, either."

"That's why the freed souls have no memory of your existence," Berruga said to herself.

"I imagine the Dark Shadow is not very good company," said Shauna.

"It is often asleep, exhausted from seeking solace on an earth where there is none to be found," said Mem. "Sometimes I cannot even wake up any of its souls."

"The murdered souls want to go to the afterlife, but they don't know how to get there," said Ruby. She paused, waiting for someone to praise her insight.

"That is very good," said Berruga.

Ruby wore a wide smile.

"I have one last question," said Berruga. "Who chose the three souls that would remain here? You or Queen Rossen?"

"The queen. Now that you know the truth, what do you intend to do about it?" asked Mem. Before Berruga could answer, Mem swirled around Ruby and Shauna. They felt as if a cold blanket was being wrapped around them. The girls' wands tingled in their hands. Ruby and Shauna could feel Mem's power. It was beginning to suffocate them. Their wands began to jerk in their grip. Abruptly, Mem released them from her grasp.

Mem moved slightly away from the girls, as if scrutinizing them from head to toe. Ruby and Shauna caught their breath while Berruga attempted to put a protective hand on each of the girls. Her short arm could not reach Shauna, who stood closely to her sister. "I have decided to help you, but I need a little more time to regain my full strength. Come back in two days. Or, I might find you before then." With a swish, she vanished into the cavern.

"She leaves like Sawwhet," remarked Shauna.

"Apparently, they don't like long goodbyes," said Berruga.

"Mem prefers long, forceful hugs," said Ruby.

"Did she hurt you?" asked Berruga.

Both girls answered no.

"What do we do next?" asked Ruby.

"Leave the cavern," said Berruga. "We'll report our findings to Queen Wista."

"Do you think Mem will destroy Hidden Forest?" asked Shauna.

Berruga shook her head. "I think Queen Rossen has been lying about many things."

"I think it's Queen Rossen who is destroying Hidden Forest," said Shauna.

"I think so, too," replied Ruby.

"Well, I bet if we hurry back we can still make it to the Noble Rabbits' celebration in time," Berruga said. "We need to have some fun after a visit to the Pit of Despair. Besides, we shall find Queen Wista there. She never misses a festival."

"What kind of celebration is it?" asked Ruby.

"It's their annual festival. All ten rabbit regiments are throwing a party to celebrate the coming of summer. The Little Peepers are invited to it."

"Who'll be there?" asked Shauna.

"You'll see when you get there," Berruga replied with a twinkle in her eye.

"I hope the gnomes show up," Shauna said excitedly. "They're funny."

"The gnomes turn up wherever there is free food," said Berruga, smiling. "I suppose the Little Peepers tend to do the same." She patted her potbelly.

The girls returned their guardian's smile.

□□□

Commander Lapin gave a speech before the festivities began, thanking everyone who was involved in providing food for the rabbits over the long winter. "From this day forth, we shall no longer be served as food for the dragon!" Thousands of spectators cheered, including Ruby and Shauna who made it to the party in time. Lapin bowed to his audience. He then proceeded to make the rounds of the crowd and individually greet guests.

All ten rabbit regiments of the Noble Rabbits were there, except the rabbits on patrol. The gnomes provided the music with their homemade instruments. The gnomes, Little Peepers, and the fairies danced, jigged, and swayed to the music. The elves did not come. Queen Rossen was still furious with Queen Wista for stealing the gold from the elves' treasury. Lapin learned this from Erde, Snoot, and Rooter. They and the other moles came to the surface and joined the party.

"We were amazed by all the gems that were stockpiled in the treasury," Erde said to Commander Lapin. "I have no idea where all those jewels came from."

"Certainly, not from the dragon's loot," added Rooter. "We all have seen what happens when the dragon's riches go missing. The Black Dragon would have burned down the elf village if his gems had been pilfered."

"How many gems did you see in the elves' treasury?" asked Lapin, twitching his nose.

"We don't have the best eyesight, but we could tell there were mounds and mounds of precious gems," answered Snoot. "The treasury was overflowing with rubies, emeralds, sapphires, pearls, amethysts, garnets—"

"There you are, Commander Lapin!" said Queen Wista, rushing over to him. She smiled at the commander and the three moles. "Hello, everyone!"

The moles scrunched up their long, pink noses and squinted at Wista. The late afternoon sun was shining in their nearly blind eyes. The moles could not stay at the party much longer because the sun was too bright for them.

"Hello, Queen Wista," all three moles replied in unison.

"I am pleased the rabbits did not call off their celebration, despite recent events," said Wista.

"Well, the matter was debated," replied Lapin, "but we decided to go ahead and have our celebration since the forest is dragon-free. At least, for now."

"So right you are," said Rooter. "Besides, the forest community needs a break from all this tension."

"When do you expect the return of the rescue crew?" Erde asked Wista.

"Hopefully, they will be back by tomorrow morning."

"On patrol last night, it was strange not seeing the Black Dragon circling over Hidden Forest," said Lapin.

"I suppose he plays a part in Hidden Forest as much as the rest of us," stated Wista. "We're still working on a reliable way to keep him fed. The owls have offered to supply him with mice until we have another feeding system in place."

"I'm not offering to feed him," remarked Lapin. "The rabbits have done their fair share."

Out of nowhere, an albatross suddenly dropped down in the middle of the meadow, startling the merrymakers. The albatross transformed into an elf.

"Tark?" questioned Wista.

"Climb onto my back, Queen Wista," said Lapin, crouching to the ground. After Wista scrambled on top of him, he hopped over to the commotion. The crowd parted for them. There, sprawled out on the ground, was an extremely exhausted Tark. The fairies were already showering him with gold flecks.

"Bring him nectar!" shouted Wista. "And some herbal tea!" She moved closer to Tark. "Where are the others?"

Tark pushed himself off the ground into a sitting position. Already the fairy dust was reviving him. "They need our help." He told them what took place at the cabin in Montana.

Wista wagged her head woefully after he had finished telling his story. She was clearly distressed. "So, the magi shot them with human weapons," she said, almost in disbelief.

"The fairies cannot remove the bullets with their wands," said Tark, after drinking a full glass of nectar. "Now, the fairies are stranded without their magic."

The fairies at the party gasped.

"We need to rescue them at once," Commander Lapin said in a panicked voice. "The fairies will crumble to dust if their magic isn't rejuvenated."

"And the wounded will die without our aid," added Wista.

Ruby and Shauna pushed through the spectators with Berruga still in Ruby's pocket.

"My sister and I will go," said Ruby.

"If they go, then I must go," said Berruga.

Wista scanned the onlookers' faces. There were thousands of individuals looking back at her, waiting anxiously for her advice. She wished Counselor Herona was there with her. But she had remained in Arborville in case any messages were received from the rescuers.

"Excuse us, Queen Wista," said Berruga. "May we have a private word with you?"

"Yes." Wista looked out at the crowd again. The ears of the rabbits were bent toward her, while Eide, Rooter, and Snoot were straining their eyes to see what was happening. She glanced at Lapin and then Tark, who was now up on his feet. "Let me gather more information. I will let you know our course of action soon."

"I will handle the crowd for now," offered Lapin. "Go speak with Berruga and the two girls."

Wista nodded gratefully. "Follow me," she said to Berruga, Ruby, and Shauna.

They only walked as far as the edge of the meadow. As soon as they were out of earshot of the others, Ruby removed Berruga from her pocket and placed her on the ground, alongside Wista. Ruby and Shauna sat cross-legged across from Berruga and Wista. Berruga revealed to Wista about their visit to Mem earlier that day. Wista paid close attention to every word.

"Are you absolutely sure the Dark Shadow does not speak?" asked Wista.

"Absolutely," answered Berruga.

"That's interesting because Queen Rossen told me that the Dark Shadow had delivered a message to her. I was under the impression it was a verbal message." Wista was positive that Rossen had told her the Dark Shadow had relayed a message from Mem, threatening to take her shapeshifting abilities away. Rossen had also stated that she negotiated the deal made with the Dark Shadow, which was a baldfaced lie. The elf queen could have only spoken with Mem. *What is Rossen hiding?*

All of a sudden, Wista caught sight of a frog-snake hurling through the air.

"It was sneaking up on us," explained Shauna. She had flicked the snake away with her wand.

"Thank you, Shauna," said Wista, her heart beating fast. "We will need your skills to bring back the rescue party. I see no other choice but to have the girls help rescue the injured. If the fairies cannot remove the bullets with their wands, then it will have to be the girls. I see no other way around it."

"Girls," said Berruga. "Vorte has a surprise for you waiting at home. I wasn't going to tell you until he showed it to you. However, the time to tell you is now. All day Vorte has been working hard crafting broomsticks for you. Since you can't ride on birds, you need your own method of transportation. Besides, you are witches. And witches ride broomsticks. It is only proper."

Ruby and Shauna did not know how to react for they were worried about falling off their broomsticks.

"Little Peepers do not tumble from birds and witches do not fall off broomsticks," said Berruga to reassure them. "You can put a spell on your broomsticks, so you can't tumble off. You probably can even cast a spell on Little Peepers to keep them from falling off birds . . . or dragons. Why didn't I think of that earlier?"

"Because we have a lot on our minds," replied Wista, rising to her feet. "We should be returning to the party. We need to put together another rescue team as quickly as possible to save our wounded. Also, it is apparent we will need an army to free Serpentine's children from the Malum."

The others followed her back to the party, though the celebration had died down. The partygoers wore grim faces and they spoke of a final showdown against the Malum. The Little Peepers had not forgotten that they might lose. Ruby and Shauna had not mastered, or even attempted, a spell that would uphold Spellbinder's spells. Wista and the Little Peepers saw no choice but to risk their lives to save the others.

Chapter Twenty-Five

The Most Precious

Queen Rossen stared sourly at the empty spot where her gold used to be stacked in the treasury. All around her were piles of precious stones.

"We can replenish the missing gold," Counselor Nirva said to cheer up her queen. "We can send out spies tonight." The elves had two types of spies—the inner spies and the outer spies. The inner spies kept tabs on the woodland creatures. All the elves were aware of inner spying. It was known in the elf community that the outer spies kept an eye on the Malum in the nonmagical world. In actuality, the outer spies often stole valuables from the humans as the dragons had done in the past. Only a handful of well-heeled elves knew about these activities. Tark was an inner spy. He did not know that Queen Rossen let the outer spies keep a small share of the stolen gems. One day, Tark's mother, Ukai, stumbled upon this knowledge. Because stealing was a crime, Ukai confronted Rossen. A day later, it was discovered that Ukai had died from accidentally consuming hemlock. Nirva also knew Rossen was jealous of King Koning's deep fondness for Ukai. They had once been paramours. Their relationship was broken off when the council arranged the marriage between Koning and Rossen. Nirva kept her suspicion of Queen Rossen to herself, though. If she had mentioned it, she would have lost her position and would not presently be standing in the treasury with the queen, consoling her over the loss of the gold.

"Replenishing the gold is a good idea," said Rossen. "We also need to spy on Mem. I have received word that her health is quickly improving. I also received a report that the two human girls and their guardian went to the Pit of Despair today. We must learn what they are up to."

"We must keep in mind that the two girls are also witches. The fairies have said more than once they appear to be more powerful than Warlock Highbrow himself."

"How is that possible?" fumed Rossen. "For years, we've tried to gain magic through our potions."

"They are born with their magic," Nirva reminded her for the hundredth time. "Ruby and Shauna came into this world as witches. As far as Serpentine's children, the fairies tell me they have a fifty percent chance of inheriting their father's magic. They will learn of the children's abilities as soon as they are brought here."

Rossen stopped staring at the place where the missing gold had been stored and focused her gaze on her advisor. "Can the children's magic be stolen from them?"

"I don't know. The fairies once told me that magic is alive and can never be destroyed. If the host is killed, the magic will look for a new host."

Rossen mulled this over for several seconds. "So, it might be possible to take Mem's magical powers from her. Or perhaps we could steal the power of the little witches?"

"I wouldn't know how that could be accomplished . . . unless they were terminated." Nirva nearly choked on her last words.

"I think there is another way, Counselor." Rossen gave her a clever grin. "Tark and Auralia brought back a spellbook from the human world and left it in Arborville. While I was there, I saw those ghosts flipping through it."

"Reportedly, there are more spellbooks in Madame Papulose's basement."

"Who is Madame Papulose?"

"She's the fake witch I mentioned—"

"Oh, that's right," interrupted Rossen.

Nirva noticed that Rossen seemed more distracted lately, as if something was weighing on her mind. If the queen had been a commoner, Nirva would have used the term "scatterbrained" to describe Rossen. But since Rossen was her queen, she chose "preoccupied" to explain the queen's behavior to others who had noticed it, too.

"We need to get our hands on those spellbooks," stated Rossen. "I want a few of our outer spies to retrieve them tonight. But we must keep it a secret from the commoners." She looked shrewdly at Nirva. "Do you suppose this witch keeps any gold in her house?"

"I don't know."

"Have our spies search her house for gold or other valuables. If the fake witch has something of value, they are to bring it back along with the spellbooks." Rossen quickly dismissed Nirva. She had to act fast in order to stop Mem's recovery and reemergence in the forest.

□□□

Miss Whiskers stood in front of her neatly stacked spellbooks, admiring her handiwork. The mice promised not to touch them anymore after moving them to the library basement from Madame Papulose's house. The books appeared to be fakes, except for one. She asked Mister Barnaby to look at it.

"These spells are similar to the ones in the book that was taken to Hidden Forest. I am guessing they both have the same author," Mister Barnaby's black nose was buried between the pages.

"Look on the back page. There's the signature, Merlin the Wizard."

"So, you think Merlin the Wizard was the book's author?"

"It's quite possible . . . or maybe, Merlin's cat."

"Madame Papulose had exactly one hundred spellbooks—"

"There are ninety-eight here. I counted twice," interrupted Miss Whiskers. "We know one of them is with the little froglike creatures. Do you know who has the other book?"

Mister Barnaby shook his head. "Madame Papulose has already contacted the police about the missing books." He motioned toward the spellbooks. "The police told her they were too busy searching for missing persons to search for missing books."

"Once those magi are no longer around, we'll return the spellbooks to Madame Papulose. We will put them back in neat piles, arranged alphabetically, of course. Maybe leave behind a thank-you note for letting us borrow the books. It ought to make her a little more forgiving of the theft."

"She is having a difficult time with everything going on right now."

"I imagine so," said Miss Whiskers. "Are the cats prepared to give the Dark Shadow a good sendoff to the afterlife?"

"Yes, we will be gathering in the town park in fifteen minutes." It was almost nine o'clock. "Will you be there?"

"I wouldn't miss it for the world. I'll find a way to put this into my novel. Perhaps in chapter five, right after Miss Tails saves Paris from burning down."

"Doesn't Miss Tails also save New York City from incinerating?"

"Yes. She saves the residents of New York from a devastating fire."

"There's a difference?"

"Yes," she huffed.

"We ought to leave for the park," said Mister Barnaby. "I don't want to be late. Renzo is meeting me there." He cast a sideways look at her and noticed the little smile hidden behind her stern expression. "I must admit Renzo is quite the dandy, but he's also a Casanova, as the ghost Opal would put it."

"I hope this memorial service works," replied Miss Whiskers, ignoring Mister Barnaby's remarks.

They climbed up the stairs to the main floor and then exited through the cat door. It was a clear night and the half-moon and stars were shining brightly. They only had to cross the empty street to reach the park. People were not out and about, but staying home because of the recent kidnappings. As soon as Miss Whiskers and Mister Barnaby stepped into the park, they were met by dozens of other cats. Every cat in town knew Miss Whiskers and Mister Barnaby by name.

"Hello, Mister Barnaby, you look very handsome under the moonlight," said Miss Katze, a white, short-haired cat with orange ears. "Your black coat is glistening like obsidian."

"How nice of you to notice, Miss Katze!" beamed Mister Barnaby, looking down at himself with admiration. "It is said my family and I inherited luxuriant coats from our ancestor Bastet."

"Only you say that," Miss Whiskers remarked in a low voice to Mister Barnaby.

"Centuries ago, my royal family made the claim, which still makes it true today."

"All cats come from royalty," Miss Whiskers reminded him for the thousandth time. "Everyone gather around me!" she shouted. To the human ear, it sounded like a cat yowling.

The cats bunched around Miss Whiskers.

"We must get this memorial service right," Miss Whiskers exclaimed. "This is not the time for flimsy excuses—"

"Miss Whiskers," interrupted Mister Barnaby, "may I remind you that we are at the park, not in the library."

"I am just driving home the point, Mister Barnaby, about the importance of performing this memorial service in a suitable manner"—she looked sharply at her onlookers—"so I am expecting the saddest wailing, caterwauling, and mewling from all of you. We want to give this shadow, and all its souls, a proper send-off."

"Won't that wake up the humans?" asked Mademoiselle Lait. She was a wealthy French cat with a blue fur coat.

"They'll be too scared to come to the park with all the racket going on," said Miss Whiskers.

"But still, they might try to shoot us from their windows," Renzo pointed out.

"Perhaps it's best we keep it simple then," said Miss Whiskers.

"I recommend we sing *Amazing Grace*," said Sir Rex, who was a Cornish Rex from Britain. He had a curly, cinnamon coat and spoke in a British accent. "And then, at the end of the song, we gaze upward at the sky. If these poor, lost souls don't pick up the hint, we point toward the heavens and wave goodbye."

"Let's go with that idea," said Renzo. His bright smile seemed to light up the darkness around him. The nearby female cats swooned.

"I agree with Sir Rex, too," said a tabby named Putty. She recently lost her mate to a car accident. "We should let the poor souls know they will be missed on earth, but their families are waiting to embrace them in the afterlife."

Everybody agreed this was a very fine idea. And they began their wait. They did not have to wait long. Mem sent the Dark Shadow out earlier than usual because she decided to release the souls of the three townspeople in exchange for the soul of another. She told the Dark Shadow to bring back someone more interesting this time.

The cats in the park looked interesting to the Dark Shadow, but they were not human souls. Nonetheless, some of the murdered souls had cats while they were alive. Cats made good pets. Perhaps this was what Mem needed to finally cure her loneliness. With its interest piqued, it approached the group of cats. There must've been over a hundred of them. And they came in all shapes and colors. The Dark Shadow noticed that the cats seemed pleased to see its presence.

"It's coming toward us," said Mister Barnaby, almost breathless.

"Commence singing," commanded Miss Whiskers. "In an octave C."

The cats began belting out *Amazing Grace*.

The Dark Shadow stopped moving and began listening.

"It appears to be working," Mademoiselle Lait said to an ancient cat. The old cat was tempted to follow the dead souls to the afterlife. "I hear the sound of falling tears and the mending of broken souls." She was known to be sentimental and regularly read poems to the book club members. "I sense the restless souls will find refuge in the hereafter and live glorious and peaceful lives."

"Sing louder!" said Miss Whiskers, raising her voice. Never in her life had she raised her voice. She was a librarian, after all. "This is not the time to recite poetry, Mademoiselle Lait! Sing loud enough for the angels to hear us!"

The Dark Shadow remained quiet, letting the sweet music sweep through all the souls. After the song was finished, Miss Whiskers gave the memorial speech. She spoke of finding peace in the afterlife and how their cherished family members were waiting for them to join them. "They have been waiting for you for a very long time. It is time that you unite with them and bring joy to them." Then, all the cats looked up at the heavens in unison with their tails pointed toward the closest star. "It is time for you to leave this earthly place and, at last, achieve the solace that you seek."

A man opened his window and shouted at the cats to shut up. "I'll shoot if you don't stop that yapping!"

"It is time to go yonder," continued Miss Whiskers. Her eyes slid toward the man. In the morning, he would find his newspaper chewed and shredded by mice with their droppings covering the front page.

The Dark Shadow contemplated grabbing a couple of cats and bringing them back to the cavern as pets. But the idea of having eternal peace was too tempting. The cats watched as the Dark Shadow rose toward the sky like chimney smoke on a cold day and then suddenly vanished like a hot balloon.

"Now we can rest, too," said Mister Barnaby. The cats decided to stay in the park that night to celebrate their success, except for Miss Whiskers and Mister Barnaby. Miss Whiskers returned to the library to make sure the mice weren't making new nests from the library books. Mister Barnaby went back home to check on Madame Papulose. She was very distraught over the recent events—the loss of her books, her broken wrist, and the man who broke into her house.

As Mister Barnaby walked up to the cat door at the rear of the house, he spotted three great gray owls escaping out an open window. Each one had a gold necklace clutched in its beak. He shouted at the owls to stop, but they quickly flew away. He raced through the cat door and up the stairs to Madame Papulose's bedroom closet. Sure enough, her jewelry box had been emptied of its three gold necklaces. The jewelry belonged to Madame Papulose's late mother, who had been from a distinguished family. Mister Barnaby was concerned this might be the final straw for Madame Papulose. She might wind up in the mental hospital like the neighbor down the street, who believed the devil was after his soul. *Maybe the man wasn't crazy after all,* thought Mister Barnaby. *It might've been the Dark Shadow that chased the poor man.* After the frightening episode, Madame Papulose's neighbor saw shadows wherever he went.

But owls stealing from Madame Papulose made no sense at all to Mister Barnaby. He left the house to fetch Renzo. He wanted Renzo to accompany him to the edge of the forest, so he could speak with the patrol rabbits about the robbery. Madame Papulose would not bear losing her mother's jewelry. The loss of the spellbooks was already causing her too much grief. To make matters worse, *he* was mostly responsible for her recent troubles. He had to make things right again.

□□□

Queen Wista brewed another cup of tea for Counselor Herona. It was just the two of them sitting in her treehouse. She was so grateful to have her counselor with her. It had been another long, stressful day in a string of long, stressful days. Having Herona near her had a calming effect on Wista. Almost as calming as a cup of tea.

"Shauna suggested we call the police and have the Malum arrested for kidnapping the children," said Wista, seating herself on a comfortable chair. "But Ruby said Jackie wouldn't want her children to be turned over to the State. I had no idea what they were talking about."

"If Serpentine's children have magic, it would be best to bring them here to Hidden Forest." Herona was sitting in her favorite chair in Wista's home. It was carved out of birch wood.

"That's what I said."

"How much longer do you think Queen Rossen will be angry with us?" Herona asked. She was stunned to hear that Rossen refused to send help to the stranded rescue party.

"I don't know. What I do know is that she is keeping secrets from us. The holes in her stories keep getting bigger and bigger."

Herona took a sip of tea and raised her eyebrows at Wista. "What holes?"

"For starters, she could never have negotiated a deal with the Dark Shadow because it's incapable of speaking. I am positive that Rossen spoke directly to Mem and intentionally did not tell anyone. Second, it's impossible that it relayed a message to Rossen from Mem, threatening to take away the elves' shapeshifting abilities. I believe Rossen made that up. Nonetheless, she does fear that Mem will retaliate against her for trying to fool her with the gold. Third, Rossen never explained how the elves accumulated so much gold in the first place. There was more gold in the elves' treasury than what the dragon could ever have stolen from the humans. Furthermore, the moles told me that the treasury was also stocked with gems. Those riches—both the gold and the gems—had to have come from the human world. Last and most heartbreaking, Berruga found out from Mem that it was Rossen who chose to leave Cobias, King Koning, and Rowl behind in the Pit of Despair!"

"Why would she leave them behind? Her own husband, no less! And Cobias was just a boy!" said Herona, appalled. "That's something only the Malum would do to a child!"

"That is the question that needs to be answered. Rossen did not choose randomly."

"Maybe they knew something that would damage Rossen's reputation," said Herona.

"Yes, indeed, and she wanted to keep them quiet about something she had done." Wista narrowed her eyes, remembering her son's last day before he was kidnapped by the Malum. He was returning home from the elf village with three other Little Peepers when they were attacked by Spellbinder. Only Cobias was taken by the sorcerer.

Suddenly, she buried her face in her hands and began to cry. "I miss my boy."

Herona came over and put her arms around her. "I know. We can still get him back. Mem said she would release him as soon as she was healed."

"She will," Wista said, wiping her eyes. "I sense her truthfulness. I believe she would have let him go while I was there, but she needed to test my loyalty."

"The gold should heal her." Herona returned to her chair and her cup of tea.

"The gold will have nothing to do with her healing. She needed my loyalty to heal and free herself from the Pit of Despair. Though, she hinted that she had been protecting Cobias these past thirteen years, probably from Queen Rossen."

"That makes sense." Herona puckered her face, replaying recent events over in her mind. "I will ask around and see if I can find out more information about Rossen. Someone must know more about her doings than we do."

"Off the top of my head, I can come up with a couple of names— Counselor Nirva and Gavran."

"The raven leader?" said Herona in a surprised tone.

"Gavran and his messenger birds know about most things. Word travels with them."

"I'll get right on it," said Herona. She thanked Wista for the tea, opened the door, and climbed aboard her great gray owl, Rings.

Meanwhile, Wista stood at her window, gazing out in the direction of Montana. The second rescue crew had already left. It was too late for Queen Rossen to interfere with the mission. Wista looked up at the moon and poured her heart out to King Hoppit. She swore that he whispered their son's name to her. *I will save him*, she promised King Hoppit. *I will save our son.*

□ □ □

Herona decided to track down Gavran. Most likely, he would be roosting in a tree with his fellow ravens. Before the Great Banishment, the ravens usually roosted in the territory of the Malum. There was a huge tree that the ravens favored because its long branches could hold a great number of birds. The ravens preferred to stick together, particularly during their night roosting. Herona headed straight for this tree, which was close to Sorcerer Spellbinder's deserted hut. She flew past Sorceress Hexla's old hut, which looked beaten down by time and the weather. A half-mile later, she noticed Sorceress Underhand's abandoned home hadn't fared any better. No creature dared to move into any of the magi's huts.

"I see Gavran in the tree," said Rings. "He's on the fourth limb on the right."

Herona leaned forward, craning her neck. "I see him. There might be room to squeeze in next to him."

"They'll make room for us." Common ravens were large birds, measuring two feet in length. Although the great gray owl was only slightly larger than a raven, its sharp talons could tear into a raven's flesh. The ravens on both sides of Gavran scattered when they saw Rings coming in for a landing.

"Hello, Gavran," Herona greeted him cheerfully. "You remember me, don't you? We met during the Great Banishment."

"I know who you are, Counselor Herona."

"I thought so. The last time we spoke I came and asked for your help in ridding the forest of the Malum, but you refused."

"We ravens remain neutral when it comes to conflicts between the species."

"Is that so?" scoffed Herona. "Isn't delivering messages for the Malum showing support for them?"

Gavran ordered the other ravens to leave because he did not want them to overhear his discussion with Herona. "Fly farther away!" he shouted at them when they moved one tree over. Reluctantly, they flew fifty yards away and settled on the branches of a pine tree. "The problem with Hidden Forest is that we all like to eavesdrop on one another because we don't completely trust each other."

"True," replied Herona. "But, occasionally, snooping around can be beneficial. Did you unintentionally see or hear something that was meant to remain a secret?"

"Like seeing the gnomes sneaking fruit from the elves' orchards to make their famous tarts?"

"No."

"Then, what do you mean?"

"Do you know anything about the kidnapping of Cobias? For instance, why did Sorcerer Spellbinder only take the prince and not the other Little Peepers who were with him?"

"What will you give me if I told you something of importance?"

"What do you want?" asked Herona.

"A guarantee that the Little Peepers won't use their mindbending skills to force us out of Hidden Forest."

"The problem with Hidden Forest is that everyone is making deals with each other." Herona met Gavran's gaze. His irises were so black that she could not make out his pupils. "I'll agree to your terms, but only if you provide me with something worthwhile."

"You will like what I have to say."

"Let me be the judge of that. Plus, I would like to remind you the Malum enjoy caging birds. They intend to sacrifice their offspring. I am keenly aware that these acts are offensive to ravens." She could see that her words had an effect on him.

"On the evening Prince Cobias was kidnapped, I was in this very tree. Suddenly, I spotted Sorcerer Spellbinder rushing toward his own hut. He was gripping something small. Next, he placed the little object on his own doorstep and knocked on the front door."

"That's peculiar."

"It was so bizarre that I moved closer to get a better look. Meanwhile, Spellbinder dashed off behind those trees over there, leaving the little gift on the doorstep." Gavran gestured at a nearby grove of evergreens. "He stood behind that big tree, watching his own hut."

"That is truly bizarre," remarked Herona.

"It gets stranger. It was Sorcerer Spellbinder who opened the door from the inside."

"You just said Spellbinder was behind the tree."

"I did. But there's another Spellbinder standing in the doorway. He glanced around and then looked down at his feet. He looked surprised. He bent down and scooped up the unconscious Prince Cobias. Of course, this was a great gift for the magi. They had the son of King Hoppit and Queen Wista in their midst. They now had a way to lure King Hoppit to their neck of the woods, where he would be vulnerable to an ambush."

"Since there could not be two Sorcerer Spellbinders, it must have been an elf in the form of Spellbinder," said Herona. "It had to have been an elf who kidnapped Cobias."

"Does that information help you?" Gavran asked smugly.

"Very much," said Herona. "Our agreement stands. Thank you for your time, Gavran."

"Remember, Counselor Herona, the ravens are neutral and swear allegiance to no one."

"You might change your mind when a magus has a wand aimed at you. Good night, Gavran. And may you sleep with a clear conscience." She got on Rings and they took off for the elf village, even though they were not welcome there.

□ □ □

In another part of the forest, Commander Lapin and Poppin were approached by their young cousin Lop.

"There are a couple of cats who want to speak to someone in charge," said Lop, who was born with a short, floppy, left ear. His right ear was two inches longer than the left and stood straight up. Birth defects and abnormalities continued to occur among the younger rabbits. "They are waiting at the forest's edge. It has something to do with the magi, spellbooks, and stolen jewelry. The black cat was so distraught I couldn't catch everything he said. But he rambled off the names of Queen Wista, Tark, Kreen, Skit, and so forth. He said the ghosts—Opal, Edward, and Jackie—were in the forest—"

"So, he's believable," Lapin cut in.

"Yes."

"Poppin and I will go see what he wants."

All but the youngest rabbits were out on patrol that night because there were no owl patrols. The pilots and their companion owls were needed for the rescue operation. It would take many Little Peepers to fight the magi, using their mindbending skills.

Commander Lapin and Poppin were a short distance from Mister Barnaby and Renzo, who did not dare enter the forest. Two rabbit patrols kept a wary eye on the cats since they were known to prey on rabbits. Nevertheless, the commander dismissed the guards once he saw the distress on the black cat's face.

Quick introductions were made and then Mister Barnaby launched into his tale about Madame Papulose, the spellbooks, and her pilfered jewelry. He did not say where the spellbooks were currently hidden. "Her three gold chains were taken by three owls. Owls in our world do not steal jewelry. When Madame Papulose discovers that her jewelry is missing, she will die from fright or a broken heart."

"I'm guessing you came here to ask us to track down Madame Papulose's jewelry and bring it back to her," stated Lapin.

"Yes. But please bring it back to me. I think Madame Papulose would suffer a heart attack if a rabbit showed up on her doorstep with her missing jewelry," said Mister Barnaby.

"I suppose so," said Lapin.

"You could have the ghosts return it," Mister Barnaby said in a tone as if he had hit upon a bright idea. "They came to your forest a couple days ago. They should be coming back soon . . . I hope. You have seen the ghosts, haven't you?"

"I know whom you speak of." Commander Lapin did not reveal that the ghosts were already back in the human world. Montana, to be precise. Or that they were in trouble. "I will have our rabbit patrols look for these owls who stole the gold necklaces. They will be returned to you as soon as possible."

Mister Barnaby thanked him.

"We, also, did you the favor of getting rid of that dark shadow who lived in your forest," interjected Renzo. "All the local cats gathered together and gave it a memorial service, and it floated away into the next world." He was beaming from cheek to cheek. "Some of your troubles have hopefully vanished with the shadow."

"The Dark Shadow is gone?" said Poppin in disbelief.

"I hope Mem will not be saddened by the loss of the Dark Shadow," added Lapin. "We can't afford to have her grow weaker."

"It wasn't a good thing to get rid of that giant shadow?" asked Renzo, appearing baffled. "And who is Mem?"

"You did a good thing," said Lapin. "Mem is the creator of Hidden Forest. It's a long story."

"Oh, Mem is a deity like Bastet," said Mister Barnaby. "My ancestors are descendants of Bastet."

"Which ones?" asked Lapin.

"All of them," Mister Barnaby replied proudly. His tail suddenly stood taller.

"Can you perform any magic?" asked Poppin.

"Sadly, I cannot," said Mister Barnaby. "Neither can Madame Papulose. After purchasing a hundred different spellbooks, two cauldrons, and a broomstick, she still can't do a lick of magic. She can't even do a card trick. If I had magic, I would give her a little bit of mine, just to make her happy."

"That's a very kind thing to say," said Poppin. "Madame Papulose must mean a great deal to you."

"Oh, she does. When I was a kitten, she saved my life," said Mister Barnaby. "The witch Zeldar set out poison in her yard to kill as many cats as she could. My mother was a street cat raising four kittens on her own. She was always hungry. Unknowingly, she ate the poison and died in front of my siblings and me. Eventually, my siblings became sick and died, as well. That left me to fend for myself. I didn't do well. Madame Papulose found me half-starved and shivering on her front steps. She took me in and made me well again."

The rabbits were clearly moved by Mister Barnaby's story.

"I promise you we shall immediately look for Madame Papulose's jewelry," Lapin said again.

"Won't it be difficult to track down owls who can stash stolen objects high up in a tree?" questioned Renzo.

"Owls do not collect riches," replied Lapin. "But shapeshifting elves do. I know precisely where to look for Madame Papulose's stolen jewelry." Although it had been a long time since he was an elf, he had not forgotten the desire elves have for shiny objects. They shared the same affliction as dragons—the need to collect treasure. And apparently, people desired riches, too. "Poppin and I will contact you when we have the gold chains in our possession. We know how to find you because we know where you live."

"You already knew who I was?" asked Mister Barnaby.

"Of course, we are patrol rabbits. We track everything around us," replied the commander. Of course, this was an exaggeration, but he wanted to impress the cats by showing strong leadership. "Also, we'll notify the others in our forest that the Dark Shadow has left this world."

"By the way, how did you know a memorial service would help the Dark Shadow move on from this world?" asked Poppin.

"Our cat librarian, Miss Whiskers, knew," replied Mister Barnaby. He stole a look at Renzo, who lit up when he heard Miss Whiskers' name. "She likes to read books and conduct research. She is almost as curious as I am."

"And she is writing an adventure novel about cats," boasted Renzo.

"She sounds smart," stated Poppin.

"She is certainly a clever cat," smiled Renzo.

"We knew the midday sun could incinerate the Dark Shadow," added Mister Barnaby. "But that would've been cruel. We didn't want to murder the souls again. They deserved another chance at happiness."

"Don't we all," said Lapin.

"Well, I must return in case Madame Papulose wakes up and discovers her jewelry is gone. If that happens, you will hear her screaming or sobbing from way out here." Mister Barnaby grinned.

"I hope not," said Renzo. "The police will arrest her for disturbing the peace."

"The police are bumbling idiots. The town should hire you, the patrol rabbits, and we would all sleep better at night," said Mister Barnaby, smiling. "Good luck and good night, Commander Lapin and First Officer Poppin."

The rabbits and the cats bade each other farewell.

□ □ □

Herona had been good friends with Counselor Nirva for many years. Often, they were present for the same meetings with their queens. They doled out advice and spilled their disappointments to one another. Therefore, Herona and Rings went directly to see Nirva. Silently, Rings swooped by the night guards undetected. The great gray owl landed on the windowsill of Nirva's private room, which was situated in the east wing of the royal palace. Queen Rossen's private quarters were in the west wing. Herona had heard Rossen was a sound sleeper. Rings pecked on the windowpane.

The pecking on the window startled Nirva, jerking her out of a dream. She got out of a bed and lit the candlestick on her nightstand. Cautiously, she approached the window. When she spotted Herona and Rings, she opened the window and let them in. Rings flew over to Nirva's desk, made from the finest elm wood, and rested there. Herona jumped down onto the desk.

"You shouldn't be here, Herona," she said.

"No, I had to come here. The truth lies here in Glenhaven."

Nirva's breath caught in her throat. She did not want to be confronted by the truth. "You shouldn't be here," she repeated. "If the Queen found you here, both of us would be in trouble."

"Your queen's stories are unraveling."

"What stories?"

"Listen to me, Nirva. The moles saw all the precious stones in the treasury. The dragon would never have traded away that many stones. Those gems came directly from the human world to the elf treasury. We also discovered that it was Rossen who chose the souls that remain in the Pit of Despair. Furthermore, tonight I learned that the raven leader, Gavran, spotted two different Spellbinders on the day of Cobias' kidnapping. The first Spellbinder left the unconscious prince on the doorstep of the real Spellbinder. Obviously, the first Spellbinder was really an elf."

Nirva pulled out her chair and fell into it, as if her legs had given out beneath her. The overstuffed chair absorbed her weight, but not her misery.

"We have been friends for a long time, Nirva. I understand you. And I know that you want to unburden yourself of all this deceit."

Nirva lifted her aquamarine eyes to meet Herona's amber ones. "The elves have been stealing from the humans and stockpiling the riches in the treasury. Most of the community is not aware of the thievery."

"And what about Cobias' kidnapping?"

"I will tell you everything I know. On the day of the kidnapping, Cobias and three of his friends were in the courtyard playing games with Prince Massen and some of his friends. I was in Queen Rossen's chambers along with King Koning. All of a sudden, Rowl burst through the door, shouting at Rossen for killing his wife, Ukai. Quickly, Rossen ordered me out of the room."

"Why did Rowl think Rossen killed his wife?"

Nirva sighed heavily. "Koning was in love with Ukai before he married Rossen. To be truthful, Koning never stopped loving Ukai, and Rossen knew it. Ukai was a gifted alchemist. It's inconceivable she died from hemlock. I think Rowl believed Rossen got rid of Ukai to make her husband forget his ex-love."

Herona cocked her head. "Do you think it's possible Prince Cobias overheard Rowl's accusation? He could have been standing near the open window. Maybe she spotted him and feared that Cobias would tell his parents—"

"And Little Peepers are not known to keep secrets," Rings cut in. He had been silently listening, noting every word. Someday he would share this story with Sawwhet. All the written history of Hidden Forest came from owls. "To be accused of murder is a terrible thing."

Herona nodded in agreement. "Queen Rossen would have been dethroned if there was any truth in Rowl's allegation."

"I've gone over that day countless times in my mind," said Nirva. "I can't rule out Rossen having a hand in Cobias' kidnapping. Or in Ukai's murder." Her body went slack in the chair. It was very difficult for her to admit that her queen could be a murderer. Stealing riches was one thing, but murder was indefensible. In the morning, she would resign her position as first counselor to the queen.

"Thank you, Nirva." Herona went over and placed her tiny hand on Nirva's nose, showing her deep respect. She sat on top of Rings again.

"Herona," Nirva said quietly.

"Yes?"

"Queen Rossen is not here. She told me she had to attend a late-night meeting. And not to tell anyone."

"Where do you suppose she went?"

"I think we both know."

"The Pit of Despair," answered Herona, barely hesitating. "She needs to stop Mem from returning to the forest, and to keep Cobias, King Koning, and Rowl in the Pit of Despair unable to reveal the truth."

"Do you want me to come with you?"

Herona shook her head. "Queen Wista must be the one to stop her. Mem must see Wista's loyalty, enabling her to fully heal from

Rossen's betrayal. And we need Mem to defeat the Malum. It is the only way."

Nirva nodded slightly. "I wish you success. I will address the village at first light. No more lies will be told, Herona. The truth will come out."

Herona returned the nod. Rings flew out the open window.

Chapter Twenty-Six

Revelations

Ruby and Shauna were wide awake on their broomsticks. It wasn't the night air that kept them awake. It was the No-Snooze Spell they had cast on themselves and everyone else in the rescue party. All the owl squadrons, a total of three hundred, were on this mission with them. Each Little Peeper rode his or her own owl. Tark accompanied them. He was the navigator because he was the only one who knew where the Black Dragon and the others were waiting. Ruby had the spellbook stored in a compartment beneath her seat that Vorte built specifically for this purpose. Vorte rode on Ruby's broomstick while Berruga rode with Shauna. Their job was to make certain the girls guided their broomsticks in the right direction. Although it was a warm summer's night, the riders dressed in warm clothes. It was cold and windy high above the earth.

The rescue party had two goals. First, Ruby and Shauna had to use magic to heal the wounded. Second, their party had to track down and remove Elli, Freyja, and Mani from the magi. Hopefully, the Black Dragon would be able to fly the three children home, along with Auralia and the ghosts. Tark and the girls were also planning to hitch a ride with the dragon. The smaller passengers, such as the fairies, would ride on the owls. Both rescue crews would fly home together. They were hoping the Malum would chase them back to Hidden Forest, where Mem, her strength restored, would be waiting for them. That was the plan, anyway. It came with a lot of "ifs" and depended on good luck and good weather. Even though they were protected by the cover of darkness, they hoped they would not be detected by human eyes. Nor did they forget the magi had dangerous guns. With the help of the Little Peepers, Ruby and Shauna would have to disarm the magi. The Little Peepers and their owls hoped the girls had better aim than the Malum.

□ □ □

"Queen Wista," said Herona.

Wista jolted awake. "Cobias?" She was dreaming about her son.

"No, it's Herona. We must go to the Pit of Despair. I believe Rossen is already there trying to stop Mem from recovering." She quickly explained the situation.

"I will call for Spruce." Her northern hawk owl did not go on the rescue mission.

In no time, Wista and Herona were at Misty Falls with their owls. The waterfall did not flow as heavily during the summer. Wista, Herona, and their owls barely got wet as they passed through the drapery of water falling from above. They entered the cave with only traces of water upon them. They immediately spotted Rossen speaking with Mem, who had risen to the surface. Surprised to have company, Rossen whirled around. Her mouth dropped open, but no words came out.

"Hello." Wista bowed slightly to each of them. Herona also greeted them in the same manner.

"Where is the Dark Shadow?" asked Mem in a fury. "Queen Rossen said you killed it because you want me to die from loneliness!" Rossen had learned of the Dark Shadow's demise from her outer spies. They had witnessed the cats performing the memorial service at the park. Rossen knew she could present it to Mem as a betrayal.

Neither Wista nor Herona had known of the Dark Shadow's death. Before they could speak, another voice broke the silence.

"It's not true!" Commander Lapin darted into the room with Poppin right behind him. "Cats in the human world gave the Dark Shadow a memorial service, so its murdered souls could go to the afterworld. The cats wanted the Dark Shadow to have peace. They meant no harm."

"Liar!" hissed Queen Rossen. "The Little Peepers destroyed the Dark Shadow."

"How could they accomplish that?" said Lapin. "It is nighttime. Only the midday sun could have destroyed the Dark Shadow. Besides, most of the Little Peepers are gone on a rescue mission. They hope to bring back Serpentine's children. Your grandchildren, Mem."

"Who are you?" asked Mem.

"Commander Lapin, head of the Eighth Regiment of the Noble Rabbits."

"And I am Poppin, First Officer of the Eight Regiment of the Noble Rabbits," piped up Poppin.

"Noble Rabbits? I don't recall creating noble rabbits," Mem stated.

"You created rabbits. We made ourselves to be noble creatures," Lapin declared proudly.

Mem suddenly swirled around the rabbits and then through them Lapin and Poppin felt a cold chill run through their bodies. "Only one of you is a true rabbit. You, Commander Lapin, were once an elf."

The others looked at Lapin in shock.

"It's true. A very long time ago, I was an elf. But Sorcerer Spellbinder cast a spell on me and changed me into a rabbit. I knew the elves could not change me back. So, I remain a rabbit to this day."

"Do you want to become an elf again?" asked Mem, clearly intrigued by Lapin.

"No. I would like to remain a rabbit."

Poppin was staring openmouthed at her commander.

"Then, why did you keep your true identity a secret?" asked Mem.

"Over time, I became a true rabbit," replied Lapin. "I decided there was no shame in being a rabbit. In fact, I quite like it. As an elf, there were too many rules to follow. But as a rabbit, I was free to run through the woods on my own. Of course, the rabbits always had to keep a wary eye on the Black Dragon."

"I did not create this dragon," said Mem.

"No, he moved in after—well, after you were disposed of down here," said Lapin. His back leg was beginning to thump. He tried his mightiest to make it stop.

"Why did you come here, Commander Lapin and First Officer Poppin?" asked Mem.

"To tell you what happened to the Dark Shadow," replied Lapin. "We did not want you to think that the Dark Shadow betrayed you."

A wind swirled around the cave again. But this time it was not as cold. "You came all this way because you were concerned about me? Or, did you come here because you were afraid the betrayal would weaken me?"

"I thought you would want to know what happened to your longtime companion," Lapin stated honestly. "Not knowing is a terrible thing. There were times my fellow friends did not return from the forest. We waited and waited for them to come home. Finally, we had to accept that the Black Dragon killed them."

"I know how that feels," chimed in Wista, eyeing Rossen. "Waiting for a missing loved one to come home is a horrible thing." She noticed Rossen backing away from them. She was moving closer to the mouth of the cave. "You kept my son from me to hide your crimes! King Hoppit died because of the events you triggered by kidnapping my son and leaving him on Spellbinder's doorstep."

"How dare you accuse me of such a thing!" Rossen turned herself into a bat and flew off toward the exit. Within moments, she hit the floor of the cave. Mem had knocked her to the ground. Then, Mem changed Rossen back to her elf form.

"From now on, you cannot hide from your true self," Mem said to the helpless elf leader. Rossen could not move, as if pinned to the floor.

All of them stared at Mem, astonished by her magical abilities. Once more, Mem swirled around the cave and briefly invaded Rossen's body. Moments later, she reappeared in front of them.

"The thoughtful and selfless rabbits have completely healed me. To come here for my benefit is indeed a noble act because I know you were afraid of me," Mem explained. She stared down at Rossen, who looked back at her with terrified eyes. "And you, elf queen, have not weakened me with your recent lies. Don't you think the souls of King Koning, Prince Cobias, and the potion-maker Rowl have told me their stories regarding you after all these years? I know everything there is to know about you. When you came here to cut a deal with the Dark Shadow, I knew you were lying. But your husband begged me to give you another chance to redeem yourself. So, I tested you by asking for the one thing that you loved most in the world, which was gold. Not your son, Prince Massen. You love riches more than you love your family, and you chose treasures over friendships."

Rossen tried to deny it all, but she couldn't shake her head.

"When I was inside your mind, I saw every despicable act you ever committed during your life. I saw how you plotted to get rid of King Koning's true love. I saw you spot Prince Cobias peeking in the window as Rowl accused you of murdering Ukai. I saw you change into a peregrine falcon and snatch Cobias from his owl as they returned home. I saw you transform into my no-good son Spellbinder.

I saw how you coldly left the unconscious prince on Spellbinder's doorstep. You thought you were being clever. If my other children spotted you as Spellbinder, they would have thought nothing of it. You were hoping that my son would experiment on him and turn him into a frog. But your plans did not go as intended. You didn't foresee my children killing King Hoppit during the rescue effort. However, it all worked out in your favor. You eliminated the three individuals who knew about your crimes. Or so you thought. You did not know of my existence. And now, I will free the souls of the prince, the king, and the potion-maker." She stared down at Rossen. "You will replace their souls and remain at the bottom of the pit. You will be alone and lonely, as I once was."

A flash of light illuminated the cave, followed by a loud boom. The onlookers shrank back from Mem. Suddenly, standing before them were Cobias, Koning, and Rowl. They were no longer just souls. They looked exactly like they did on the day they were abducted. Rossen was gone from the cavern.

"The elf queen has taken my place," Mem said quietly.

Cobias ran over to his mother and hugged her. Both of them began to cry. Herona put her arms around them. Lapin and Poppin welcomed Koning and Rowl. In the meantime, Mem transformed herself into a beautiful, white witch.

"Much better!" she exclaimed, looking herself over. "So many years I spent in the pit, slowly dying. At last, I am well enough to leave it. Since I have no intention of ever going back there, there is one task I must do." She looked at the others. "Who wants to see me defeat my children?"

Wista, who still had her arms wrapped around Cobias, began to explain the current situation.

"This would go a lot faster if I just entered your mind," Mem said to Wista.

Wista nodded her approval. Mem swept through Wista's mind, learning everything she needed to know. In return, Wista felt Mem's warm gratitude. Both of them were whole again.

"I suppose I should let the human souls go, too." With a whish of her hand, three spirits rose up from the pit and flew out of the mouth of the cave. "They will have their human form again once they reach home. They will have no memory of this place." She stopped to regard her audience. "Do you wish for me to send you home?"

"No, thank you. It's a lovely night for a walk," said Lapin, unwilling to be spirited home at the speed of light.

The others agreed they would rather travel under their own power.

"Very well." In a flash, Mem was gone from the cave.

□ □ □

Opal sat next to the Black Dragon as his life slowly drained away. The fairies believed the bullets were poisoned by the magi. Most of the others were asleep under the half-moon. Luna was sleeping fitfully and Auralia had taken a turn for the worse. Opal hoped Luna would still be alive by the time the sun rose. Jackie tended to Luna, while Edward kept guard for the night. By the end of the day, the fairies without their magic had wilted like parched flowers. Earlier, Opal and Edward scared two hunters away from the campsite. They knocked off the hunters' camouflaged hats, but that didn't seem to frighten them. Next, they walked behind the hunters and breathed down their necks. Eventually, they wailed directly at the hunters, which, finally, caused them to turn around and run back to their jeep.

"I am afraid to die," Black Dragon said to Opal. "Was it painful?"

"The gunshot to my chest happened so fast that I don't remember a thing about dying. I do remember waking up, frightened out of my wits to discover that I was a ghost. But then, I saw that my dear Edward was also a ghost, so it lessened my fear."

"It's good you have Edward to lean on."

"I am certain that Agir is waiting for you to join her in the next world," said Opal. She patted the dragon's neck, unaffected by his sharp scales.

"How come you haven't moved on to the next world?"

"I suppose I have some unfinished business in this world. But, I don't know what it is yet. Perhaps it is to save you from dying." She looked deeply at him. "Agir might have to wait a little longer to be with you again." She gave him an encouraging smile. "Tark will soon bring the girls with their magic. Then, they'll fix you up properly."

"Opal?"

"What?"

"Don't leave me alone. I have spent too much of my life alone."

"I shall remain here with you. But when we return to Hidden Forest, I suggest you find a new home closer to civilization. Life doesn't have to be lonely for you." Opal pressed more medicinal leaves into the dragon's wounds, but the plants weren't working. The poison from the bullets was too much.

"Opal?"

"What?"

"You can call me Kveikja. You were right. The name Black Dragon is dull. The truth is I chose that name after Agir was killed because my heart was full of blackness. I wanted to forget whom I had once been."

"Well, I am glad to hear that you are finally listening to me. Now, I recommend that you get some sleep. It is very late. The morning sun will greet us before you know it."

Kveikja shut his eyes and soon Opal heard his snores.

The hours dragged on.

Kreen woke up and spotted Opal still sitting beside the dragon. Jackie still hovered over Luna, and Edward floated around their campsite. Edward was keeping an eye out for intruders, such as the Malum or grizzly bears. A short distance away, Kreen heard a series of short whistles. It was her western screech-owl, Trill, calling to her. She answered with a short trill followed by a longer one.

"Wake up, everyone!" shouted Kreen. "They're here! Our rescuers have arrived!"

Since it was still dark, they couldn't see the rescuers until they nearly landed on top of them. Over three hundred Little Peepers and their owls joined them. Ruby and Shauna didn't land as quietly as the owls. Although they were still wide-awake, their arms and legs were screaming for rest. They had to brace themselves during the entire ride on their broomsticks. Vorte and Berruga were exhausted from supervising the girls' safety.

Tark went over to Oide. "How is everyone?"

"I'm afraid it's not good. The fairies are fairly sure the bullets were poisoned. The injured are all running high fevers. The fairies are unwell. Their magic has been completely drained. They are even too weak to fly."

"Ruby! Shauna!" Tark called out. "The bullets need to be removed immediately!"

The girls removed their wands and the spellbook from their broomsticks. They rushed over to Tark.

"Which patient first?" Ruby asked.

"Luna," said Jackie.

"Kveikja is next," said Opal. Since the Black Dragon did not respond to his name, the rescuers silently wondered if the dragon was still alive.

"Auralia needs the poison removed from her, too," said Flycatcher.

"Okay," gulped Ruby. She and Shauna quickly went to work. They read the spell directly from the book to make certain it was performed accurately. In the meantime, others were discussing strategies to track down the Malum.

"Where could they go without being seen?" the Little Peepers asked.

As the Little Peepers discussed various possibilities, Tark held Auralia's hand. Elves did not sweat but became paler when ill. Auralia was as pale as the ghosts, who were floating from patient to patient. It seemed the ghosts were just as concerned about dying as the living.

It took Ruby a half-dozen attempts to pronounce all the Latin words correctly in the "Removal Spell." Berruga and Vorte were at her side supporting her. At last, the spell successfully removed the bullet from Luna. The next step was to cast the healing spell. Meanwhile, Shauna showered the lethargic fairies with golden flecks from her wand to revive them the best she could. It was decided that a few of the Little Peepers and their owls would take the fairies home as soon as they recovered from their long flight. They could not wait for the Black Dragon to recuperate from his injuries. The fairies would not last much longer in the nonmagical world, even with Shauna's magic to renew them. Besides, Shauna had to save her magic in case she had to protect the others from the magi. Already, Shauna and Ruby could feel the human world sapping their magical powers.

As Ruby recited from the spellbook, miles away, Witch Blackheart flipped through the same spellbook. Unbeknownst to anyone but Madame Papulose, the two spellbooks were the same. A third, matching copy was safely hidden away in the library and was currently being examined by Miss Whiskers and Mister Barnaby. Not only were the two cats fascinated by the strange ingredients required for the spells, but the writing on the last pages caught their attention. It was handwritten in Arabic. It described a family lineage. Miss Whiskers used a computer to translate the words. It stated that Nebeta was the half-sister of Bastet and Mem.

"I am only aware of the name Bastet because she's my ancestor," announced Mister Barnaby.

"For the last time, Mister Barnaby, all cats descended from Egyptian deity," said Miss Whiskers, shaking her head at his nonsense. "On the last page, there's a spell to summon Ra, the Egyptian sun god. Do you need to summon our ancestor?"

"Not at the moment."

"It appears that Madame Papulose was interested in Egyptian deity," said Miss Whiskers. "But why?"

"She's desperate to find magic in any culture," replied Mister Barnaby.

"By the way, how's Madame Papulose faring with the loss of her jewelry?"

"Not well. She looks unwell, too."

There was a knock on the basement door. Miss Whiskers and Mister Barnaby exchanged looks.

"Who could that be at this early hour?" asked Miss Whiskers. The library didn't open for another hour.

"It's me—Renzo."

Mister Barnaby noticed the faint smile on Miss Whiskers' orange face.

"There are some individuals who are looking for Mister Barnaby. Are you there, Mister Barnaby?"

"Yes, I'm here." He peered at Miss Whiskers, puzzled. "I wonder who that could be."

"Open the door and find out," replied Renzo from the other side of the door.

"The door is unlocked, Renzo," said Miss Whiskers.

"Oh." The door swung open and a dozen fairies flew into the room. They were carrying jewelry. To be precise, they were returning Madame Papulose's stolen gold chains.

Mister Barnaby's jaw dropped.

"Sorry, it took so long," said one of the fairies named Cheerful. "We first went to your house, Mister Barnaby, but you weren't there. We didn't want to startle Madame Papulose, as you requested. So, we searched around until we could ask someone where you could be—"

"Luckily, they came across me," Renzo finished. "If you weren't home, I assumed you were here in the library. And I was right."

The fairies placed the three gold chains on the table, near the spellbook. Then, they rested on the table, regaining their strength for the flight back home. The jewelry was heavy for them.

"There is other good news," said Renzo. "The three missing humans appeared in the middle of the night. They are talking to the police right now. They don't seem to remember anything about their disappearance, as if they suffered amnesia."

"That is good news," declared Mister Barnaby. "That means Madame Papulose is no longer considered a suspect in their disappearance. Unless, of course, the police believe Madame Papulose was responsible for their amnesia. They might accuse her of putting a spell on them."

"Let's hope not," replied Renzo. "I want to put this whole supernatural business behind us."

"What does this say?" asked a fairy named Silver. She pointed to the words in the spellbook with her wand. Little silver flecks fell from her wand to the page.

Instantly, Miss Whiskers swept the silver flecks from the book, worried that they would burn holes in the pages like cigarette ashes. "It says that Mem is the half-sister of the goddess Bastet. Mem felt betrayed by her own Egyptian family and vanished from sight. It was thought that she created her own world to live in, away from her family."

"It would explain her need for loyalty," said Silver. "And why she created her children. And why their disloyalty nearly killed her."

"We should bring this information back to Queen Wista," said Charm, who stood beside Cheerful.

"We should share it with Sawwhet," added Silver. "She'll want to note it in her scroll." Last night, the fairies had decided to share their knowledge with the small owl for history's sake.

"Who is Sawwhet?" asked Miss Whiskers.

"She is like you," replied Silver. "She is our keeper of history. She puts our history down in scrolls."

"And she likes to keep to herself," said Charm.

"I like her already," smiled Miss Whiskers. "And who is Mem?"

"She is the creator of Hidden Forest," replied Charm. "The Malum tossed their own mother down into a cavern."

"That's terrible," said Renzo. "I was always fond of my mother."

"And who is Nebeta?" asked Mister Barnaby.

"No idea," replied Silver.

"Have Jackie's children been rescued?" asked Mister Barnaby. "And if so, when are Opal, Edward, and Jackie coming back?"

"The children are in the midst of being rescued," replied Silver. "They are in Montana. Do you know where that is?" The cats nodded. "The ghosts went with the rescue party. Actually, the first rescue crew." She brought them up to speed on the current situation.

"What an adventure! I will have to put that in my novel," said Miss Whiskers, grabbing a pen. She scribbled words into a notebook.

"Sawwhet writes with her talons," said the fairy alongside Silver. Her name was Moonbeam. "She punches holes into parchment."

"Can anyone read it, besides Sawwhet?" asked Miss Whiskers.

"The other owls," replied Moonbeam. "But Sawwhet squirrels her scrolls away in a humongous cedar tree. She's afraid if she lends out her scrolls they won't be returned."

"I know how she feels," remarked Miss Whiskers.

"Perhaps, someday, you can pay Sawwhet a visit," said Silver, "if Hidden Forest remains as it is."

"What do you mean by that?" asked Miss Whiskers.

"Mem will be back in charge," said Silver. "We do not know what's in store for us."

"Does Mem seem like the destructive type?" asked Mister Barnaby.

"Queen Wista has a good feeling about her," said Cheerful.

"Cheerful is as optimistic as Queen Wista," noted Silver. "Now, however, we must return to Hidden Forest. It took a lot of the magic out of us to get the jewelry here."

"Where did you find the jewelry?" asked Mister Barnaby.

"It was in the elves' treasury," replied Silver. "King Koning is now in charge of the elves. He let us into the treasury to retrieve the stolen necklaces. But now, we must really take our leave."

The fairies zipped through the open basement door, up the stairs, and out through the cat door.

"I need to get going, too," said Mister Barnaby. "Madame Papulose will be pleased that I found her jewelry in the backyard. She'll want to pat my forehead for it." He wagged his head, as if he was making a great sacrifice. "Do you suppose you could help me put this jewelry on?" After Miss Whiskers and Renzo slipped the necklaces around his neck, he looked at himself. "If I don't want to be seen by other cats, I'll have no choice but to take the alleyways all the way home."

After Mister Barnaby departed, he realized that he left Renzo and Miss Whiskers alone together. He liked Miss Whiskers too much for her to fall for Renzo, even though he and Renzo were good pals.

□ □ □

After perusing the spellbook, Witch Blackheart knew she wanted the spellbook for herself. She knew whoever had the spellbook would become the strongest among them. It would take too long to memorize or copy the spells. Once they were back in Hidden Forest, she would have to steal the book away from Warlock Highbrow. She felt like she needed to take his guns from him, too. She noticed the expressions on Highbrow and Serpentine when they were shooting the Black Dragon and the others. From that episode she learned the guns kept the Little Peepers far enough away that they could not effectively use their mindbending ability on them. Then again, a village of mindbenders might have more force than a bagful of human weaponry.

After leaving the cabin by the river, the magi found an abandoned mining camp built by gold seekers. Four small, wooden cabins were still standing. The children were locked up in one of the cabins, while the magi divided themselves between the remaining three. The witches, the sorceresses, and the male magi split up into individual groups. The rental van was hidden in a grove of trees. The magi argued who would keep watch until they grew tired from bickering. They desperately needed the dragon scales and a good night's rest.

Blackheart heard male voices draw close to the campsite. Quickly, she stuffed the spellbook back into Highbrow's duffle bag, which also contained his guns and ammunition. She would come back to look at the spellbook another time. She overheard Highbrow and Spellbinder discussing food supplies for the children. They were only fed canned dog food. No one took the time to cook meals for "Serpentine's brats." The magi were beginning to notice that the children were becoming skinnier and weaker. Despite their own lives depending on the children's health, the magi were consumed with other matters. They worried the Little Peepers would launch an attack on them and that they would die from old age before the next full moon. The magi's deterioration was accelerating at a rapid pace. Their hair became whiter and sparser with each passing day. To keep their remaining strength up, Highbrow and Serpentine hunted for ducks and cooked them over an open fire. They kept themselves well-fed and healthy, despite the aches in their bones from old age.

▢ ▢ ▢

Cobias was drinking tea and eating chanterelles that his mother had fixed for him. Wista stared at her son, still in disbelief that he was with her again.

"Mother," he said, peering across the table at Wista. "I hope that you are not angry with Mem. She told me she wanted to return us, but it wasn't safe. She was too weak to protect us from Queen Rossen. She said the elf queen would attempt to keep us quiet, forever."

"I wish that I could've protected you."

"It cost Father his life trying to protect me," Cobias said sadly. "I didn't know he had been killed until King Koning and Rowl were thrown into the pit with me."

"What was it like down there?"

"Cold. Very cold. Mem tried to warm up the cavern, but she was too weak. We told each other stories to pass the time. However, we became bored with our repeated stories. Mem asked the Dark Shadow to collect more souls, so they could tell us their tales. Some of them told more interesting stories than others. She let the boring souls leave first."

"Did you like Mem?"

"Yes. She was good to us." Cobias wore a sad smile. "If you had not come along, Hidden Forest would have died along with Mem."

Wista leaned forward. "How so?"

"She said that not even her children were aware that Hidden Forest would die along with her. It's her magic that keeps the trees and flowers growing and the waterfalls and the rivers flowing."

"That could explain why our offspring lately have been born deformed or stillborn. And, the rabbit population took a nosedive over the past year." She glanced out the window. "I believe the trees have been trying to warn us. They sense things that we cannot."

"That's true, Mother."

"I guess that means the magi would've destroyed themselves if they had successfully annihilated Mem the first time around."

"Mem intentionally did not give them immortality because she wanted them to have a weakness, in case she might have to destroy them someday."

"She was right," Wista replied quietly.

Cobias glanced out the window. "Do you think the rescue party will be home soon? I would like to meet the rest of the Little Peepers." The village was extremely quiet with so many gone.

Wista glanced out the window and sighed. "I hope so. I'm running out of ideas on what to do."

"Mem will step in to help."

"I hope so. No one has seen her since she left the Pit of Despair. I don't know what she is planning for her children."

"It will not be a welcome homecoming," said Cobias. "She has been planning her revenge for a long time."

"I imagine so."

"Are you going to leave Queen Rossen in the pit?" asked Cobias.

"It's not up to me. Do you think it's the right place for her?"

"In a sense, she murdered Father and Ukai, and intentionally left King Koning, Rowl, and me to wither away in a sunless cavern." He shrugged. "I think it's the right place for her for the time being. But I feel sad for Prince Massen."

"I know. But he has his father now."

"And Rupin and Tark."

She took a couple bites from a toasted chanterelle and then put her fork down. "I can't figure out what to do about the Black Dragon. If he can't eat rabbits anymore, what is he going to live on? The owls can't keep feeding him mice forever."

"Mother, the answer is right in front of you."

She peered around. "I don't see it."

"Ask Mem or those girl witches to give him the appetite of a rabbit. There are plenty of mushrooms and other plants in the forest to eat, even for someone with the appetite of a dragon."

"Why didn't I think of that? You are your father's son! King Hoppit was as clever as they came."

"Mother, you were always as clever as father. I have not forgotten."

She reached over and squeezed his hand. His skin was warm to the touch. "I might need your help. If the rescue party doesn't return by tomorrow morning, I want you to locate Mem for me. She'll show herself to you."

Cobias heard the worry in her voice and in turn squeezed her hand. "I don't believe it will be necessary for me to search for her. She is out there, preparing for her revenge. I can feel it."

"How can you feel it?"

"She put a little bit of her magic in me, so no harm would ever come to me again. But her magic links me to her. I can feel her when she is nearby."

"Is she nearby?"

"She is moving away from here."

"I hope she is moving toward her children in Montana. Do you know what she intends to do to the Malum?"

"All I know is that she plans to get her magic back from them."

"I'll wait for her to do it."

"And I will wait with you."

Wista smiled at her son. He smiled back. And they waited together as they drank tea and ate their mushrooms. But both were silently wishing King Hoppit could be at their table, like he used to be before the Malum murdered him.

Chapter Twenty-Seven

The Change in the Air

Berruga and Vorte noticed the girls' exhaustion. The nonmagical world was depleting their magic and energy in the same manner as the fairies'. Ruby and Shauna managed to mend the wounded, thanks in part to the healing properties bestowed by the unicorns who touched their wands. However, removing poisonous bullets and healing an enormous dragon, an ailing elf, and a Little Peeper on the edge of death overtaxed the budding witches. They no longer had the strength to deflect the Malum's bullets with their wands. Their rescue plans were already "shot to hell," as Ruby's stepfather used to say to describe his failed endeavors, meaning his drug deals went bad.

The Black Dragon was encouraged to fly home carrying Auralia, the ghosts, and the girls with him, but he did not want to leave until everyone could leave together. Besides, there was no one else who could fly Jackie's children back to Hidden Forest. Even if Tark could shapeshift as a dragon, he did not have the strength to fly far with the weight of three children on him. Furthermore, Jackie did not want to abandon her children.

Ruby offered to drive Jackie's children in the Malum's van back to Hidden Forest, but that idea was quickly rejected when the rest of them learned that the twelve-year-old didn't know how to drive. Jackie also offered to drive. However, she was the first to admit that it would look strange to passing drivers seeing a ghost in the driver's seat. The other drivers on the road would notify the police at such a strange sight. To make matters worse, the chances of the Little Peepers getting close enough to bend the minds of the magi were looking close to nil without the magic of Ruby and Shauna.

"Maybe we should locate the Malum first before we lay out our tactics," recommended Berruga. The rescuers sat in a circle. An individual stood when he or she wanted to speak. "At least, we should know where they are." She sat down.

"I suggest we take the stealth approach," said Hummer, after rising to his feet. "We send the ghosts in to rescue the children. We race back home with the children in tow and do our best to outrun the magi. We have a dragon and three hundred owls."

"They have guns," Luna reminded him. "They might be able to shoot us down."

"Our dragon can blowtorch them," countered Flycatcher.

"The guns shoot farther than his flames," said Auralia. "Maybe Mem can deal with the magi after we get back."

"*If* we get back," piped up a voice from the front row.

Oide stood up. "In the worst-case scenario, the dragon must take the children back. In order to retrieve Jackie's offspring, we will have to risk our lives to fight the magi."

"We might die anyway if Spellbinder dies," Luna said, "if Ruby and Shauna are unable to prevent Spellbinder's spells from disappearing."

Before the audience could respond to Luna's words, the owls Trill and Peck landed in the middle of the circle.

"We owls have decided to do an aerial search for the Malum. We'll have to undertake the search without pilots since owls don't have pilots in the human world," said Trill. "Three hundred of us can cover a wide range. To speed up the process, we'll ask the local birds if they've seen individuals in black capes or a black van."

Oide popped up again. "Let's have a show of hands for Trill's idea."

Everybody voted for the idea.

In the meantime, Ruby and Shauna were resting by the Black Dragon. They grew weaker while the dragon became stronger.

"I will fly you back as soon as this is over," he offered.

"Thank you," said Ruby. "I'm not strong enough to hold onto a broom."

"I appreciate you saving my life. Humans are kinder than I had imagined."

"Some humans are nice. Some are not," said Ruby. It was hot in the sun, sapping more of her strength. She crawled into the dragon's shade. Shauna followed suit, staying near both Ruby and the dragon.

"I remember, a long time ago, a wizard in the human world had a spellbook just like the one you're holding," the Black Dragon said to Ruby.

"Do you remember the wizard's name?" asked Shauna.

"No. But I do recall he was a famous wizard who was known for his spells and potions."

"I feel like a failure today," admitted Ruby. "Having a powerful spellbook and wand made it seem possible we could take on the Malum. I will never be famous for my spells or my bravery."

"How long have you been practicing witchcraft?" the dragon asked.

"Not long," replied Ruby. "Several days, I think. To be honest, I've lost track of time."

"It took me weeks to learn how to fly. You are much too hard on yourself."

"Why is the nonmagical world so hard on us?" asked Shauna, as she squeezed in tighter to the dragon. The shade shrank as the sun rose higher.

"Your magic is your life force. The human world is short on magic. It's feeding off yours," he replied. "The nymph who lives in Misty Falls taught me that. That's the reason nymphs never venture into the human world."

Shauna had fallen asleep by the time Berruga and Vorte came over to speak with the sisters. Berruga and Vorte had just left the meeting. "It was decided at the assembly that the owls will search for the magi's hideout while we wait on the ground. If located, Opal, Edward, and Jackie will sneak in and try to get the kids out tonight. Can you make it until then?"

Both Ruby and the Black Dragon nodded. Shauna snorted in her sleep.

"I will watch over them," said the dragon.

"Not so long ago, you were trying to kill us," Ruby reminded him.

"A few days ago, I was killing rabbits and hating your kind. Elves are not the only ones that can change."

"I suggest that you get your rest," said Berruga. "No matter what happens, we will have a long day and night ahead of us."

◻◻◻

Mister Barnaby was approaching his house when he heard two voices drifting out of the open window. One of them belonged to Madame Papulose and the other was unfamiliar to him. He removed the three gold chains around his neck and hid them behind a flowerpot. He crept through the cat door and snuck toward the living room where he saw Madame Papulose speaking to someone wearing a falcon mask. Upon closer inspection, the woman had a falcon head and a human body. He had to stop himself from gasping.

"How was the family reunion?" the falcon lady asked Madame Papulose in a snarled tone. "I see that father hasn't returned your powers to you."

"He is not forgiving, as you know."

"That's why I never ask him for forgiveness. He is incapable of giving it," replied the falcon lady. "By the way, we have a visitor watching us." She moved her hand and Mister Barnaby found himself airborne and then landed in the center of the living room.

"That is Mister Barnaby," said Madame Papulose. "He has been a good companion to me. Haven't you, Mister Barnaby?"

Madame Papulose's question was different this time. She was actually looking at him, as if expecting a reply.

"Madame Papulose and I are good friends," Mister Barnaby said to the falcon lady sitting in the chair.

"Do you know who I am?" the falcon lady asked him.

"An Egyptian goddess?" he ventured. She looked like a dead ringer for the female version of Ra, the sun god.

"I am Mem, goddess of nature. This is my half-sister Nebeta, the goddess of truth. We share the same father, Ra. Our father disowned us and our names are stricken from history."

"I am a descendant of the Egyptian royal family," stated Mister Barnaby, puffing out his chest. "That makes us related."

Mem gave him a little bow. "It is nice to meet you, little cousin."

"Then, I am your cousin, too," said Madame Papulose.

Mister Barnaby locked eyes with Madame Papulose. "Have you always been able to understand me?"

"No. I can only understand you because Mem is here. Her magical powers make it possible. She also healed my broken wrist." She showed her right arm to Mister Barnaby. "It's as good as new."

"Why did your father disown you?" asked Mister Barnaby. "And why does Mem have magical powers and you don't, Madame Papulose . . . I mean, Nebeta?"

"Nebeta once was as powerful as I," replied Mem. "But our father Ra stripped her powers because she refused to marry his chosen suitor for her. The same fate was about to happen to me, but I fled and hid from Father before he removed my powers. I chose the spot where I created Hidden Forest, not knowing Nebeta was hiding nearby. But I felt strangely drawn here. Now, I know it was the bond that I shared with Nebeta that pulled me here. I did not even know of her whereabouts until I was freed from the Pit of Despair."

"Did you create Hidden Forest as a refuge from your father?" asked Mister Barnaby.

"Yes. I even created my own family. But, unfortunately, my children turned on me," Mem said bitterly. "And now, I will severely punish them for it."

"Mem came here today, wondering if I wanted the magic of her children after she destroys their bodies," Madame Papulose explained to Mister Barnaby. "I lost my powers so many years ago that I have forgotten what it feels like to cast a simple spell."

"Now, I know why you collected all those spellbooks," said Mister Barnaby, his tail shooting up. "And why you joined the Wiccans." He also understood why the drapes were drawn shut. Madame Papulose did not want the neighbors to see a woman with a falcon head sitting on the sofa.

"Every year since my suitor wed someone else, I have pleaded with Father to return my powers and each time he has turned a deaf ear to my pleas."

Mister Barnaby wrinkled his brow. "So, you never attended a national Wiccan meeting?"

"No, I went to Egypt to see my family."

"What about your mother?" Mister Barnaby asked. "Won't she take your side in this matter?"

"My mother was human. Father killed her in a fit of rage centuries ago."

"How awful!" exclaimed Mister Barnaby.

"If it hadn't been for my mother's jewelry, I would have died in the human world. For you see, my father gave the magic jewelry to my mother to stave off her mortal death. Nonetheless, Father tore the gold chains from her neck and strangled her with his bare hands. After Father stripped me of my powers, I ran off with my mother's three gold necklaces. That's why I was so devastated by the loss of my jewelry. It has kept me alive all these years. Today, just when I thought the end of my life was approaching, Mem appeared."

"I would have visited years ago if I had known you were here . . . before I was destroyed by my own children."

"I used my mother's gold chains to hide myself. I did not want Father to find me until his temper cooled, which could take centuries." She turned her attention to Mister Barnaby. "Each of the gold chains has a special property. One gives me immortality, the second one conceals me, and the third one produces gold nuggets to provide money for me. Father wanted Mother to hide from his jealous wife and other mistresses."

"Such as my mother," added Mem. "She desired Father's loyalty. We all deserve family loyalty. And disloyalty should be punished."

"Speaking of your mother's stolen necklaces, they can be found in the backyard. The elves took them and the fairies recovered them from the elves' treasury. It's a long story," gushed Mister Barnaby. He wanted to get all his thoughts out before Madame Papulose lost her ability to communicate with him. "And all but two of your missing spellbooks are safely hidden away in the library basement. I wanted to keep them safe from . . . well, it would be your nieces and nephews. One of the missing spellbooks is with the Little Peepers and the other is mysteriously absent—"

"Warlock Highbrow stole it," interrupted Mem. "I can sense his treachery. He has been in this house."

"You can sense it?"

"Of course, I am perceptive, except for the time I refused to acknowledge my children were plotting against me. I suppose I turned a blind eye to their hatred of me."

"It has been such a long time since I have been able to perform magic," Madame Papulose said softly to herself. "I often imagined it . . . dreamt of it."

"Come live with me in Hidden Forest," said Mem. "I can give you your own magic. You will no longer have to beg for Father's forgiveness or go to another family reunion and beg Father to return your magic. Bring Mister Barnaby to live with you. I would enjoy my little cousin's company."

Mister Barnaby wasn't so sure he liked this recent turn of events. He wanted to stay in town with Miss Whiskers and the other cats.

"But first, we need to retrieve my children's magic before you come live with me, Nebeta." Mem turned and looked at Mister Barnaby. "When the body is destroyed, the magic is not. The magic looks for the closest and most suitable host." She looked at Madame Papulose again. "Please join me, sister."

Madame Papulose gave a simple nod of consent.

"I need to retrieve the jewelry from the backyard," said Mister Barnaby. "I will be right back." He slipped out the cat door and picked up the necklaces with his mouth. One of the gold chains had a small, golden nugget lying beside it, as if it had a baby while he was away. He decided to come back for the nugget later.

Upon his return, the house was quiet. Mem and Madame Papulose were gone.

□□□

A patrol owl discovered a black van concealed in a thicket of woods about three miles away. It was just after sunset. The rescuers were preparing to set out on their mission. The Black Dragon and the owls carrying their riders would move in closer to the Malum's hideout. Jackie, Opal, and Edward were intended to creep into their hideaway and remove the kidnapped children from the Malum's grip.

After taking a long afternoon nap, Ruby attempted to stand. Shauna was still sleeping alongside her. The Black Dragon was no longer there to offer the girls shade. Ruby almost fainted when she stood up to her full height. Now, she knew how the fairies felt after losing their magic. The depletion of her magic was almost crippling. Perhaps it was how Mem and the magi felt when their magic was unavailable to them.

"Shauna," she said. "Wake up."

Shauna stirred in her sleep.

"Wake up!" she said a little louder. "The ghosts will need our wands."

Shauna opened one eye, wearily. "I am not handing over my wand."

"We have to. Jackie's kids will scream bloody murder when they see those ghosts coming for them."

"But . . . but our wands have no magic left in them," stammered Shauna.

"No, *we* have no magic left in us. Our wands still do," Ruby corrected her. "I can feel the wand pulsating in my hand. I think you can, too."

"I don't think I can let go of it even if I try. It wants to stay with me. It's protecting me from the nonmagical world."

"You will have to order it to leave you. For the sake of Serpentine's kids and everyone else's, we have to hand over our wands."

"How will our wands help the ghosts, anyhow?"

"I'm giving them the spellbook, too. There's a spell in there to silence people. It'll prevent the kids from screaming. The spell is written in an old language. I think Opal and Edward will have an easy time with it since they're old."

Shauna peered at her wand and began addressing it. "The ghosts need your help right now. I must put you in the care of another. Please work your magic for them. The ghosts need you."

Ruby told her wand the same thing with a reminder that it was only temporary. Shauna tried to stand up, but could not. She collapsed onto the ground.

"Hand me your wand," said Ruby. "I'll take them to Opal and Edward."

At first, Shauna's wand was a bit hesitant to leave its owner's grasp. But it did allow itself to be taken by Ruby. Some of the Little Peepers caught sight of Ruby staggering toward the ghosts who were taking last-minute instructions from Oide and Tark. Kreen and Skit jumped on their owls and flew over to Ruby, who was gripping the spellbook and the two wands. Ruby fell to her knees.

"You must rest, Ruby!" shouted Kreen, as she saw Ruby collapse. She hopped off Trill and ran to Ruby. Skit was right behind her.

"We need to move her back into the shade," Skit said to Kreen. "She's sweating heavily."

"Give the wands and the spellbook to Opal and Edward," Ruby said in a weak voice. "Tell them to use the 'Silence Spell' on the kids.

They'll know what I mean." Her eyes rolled back in their sockets, as she passed out.

Skit and Kreen yelled for help. Dozens of Little Peepers, including Berruga and Vorte, rushed over to Ruby's side. They dragged her to the shade of a wide tree.

"I think I know what's wrong with her and Shauna and the fairies," said Luna, who was gazing down at the unconscious Ruby. Although she had made a full recovery from her injuries, she stayed behind to help watch over the girls. "I sense a sudden change in the air. Now that Mem is liberated from her prison, she's out for revenge. Her powerful and vengeful magic is charging up the air. Probably sending currents of magic through the air and the wind. It's probably overcharging other magical beings since they draw their energy from the earth. Their bodies aren't used to absorbing or dealing with the full-fledged magic of an irate deity."

"That could be it, Luna. I sense we are dealing with black magic. It could be surrounding us," said Berruga. "These poor girls haven't been witches for long. They don't know how to repel such dark magic." She glanced at the rescue party, who were moments away from taking flight. "I hope they rescue those children quickly. We need the Black Dragon to save these girls, too. They are my children." She had to choke back her tears.

"If your theory is right, Luna," said Vorte, putting a comforting hand on his wife's arm, "that means Mem is close by. The girls cannot be absorbing Mem's magic all the way from Hidden Forest."

The small group surveyed the area but did not spot any disturbance.

▢▢▢

"Something is wrong," said Witch Blackheart. "I feel a zing in the air, like it's electrically charged."

"It's probably an approaching storm," said Witch Zeldar. "These parts are known for their thunderstorms, lightning, and hail. Have your pick."

"Your hair is standing up on end," said Blackheart. "I'll pick lightning."

"Yours is, too," said Zeldar, as she patted down her hair.

Secretly, Blackheart hoped she didn't look as old as Zeldar. In a few weeks, she reminded herself, I can reclaim my youth. The magi never mentioned how their mother had made them beautiful. Their looks began to fade soon after they assaulted her with their wands and left her to wither and die at the bottom of the cavern. Unbeknownst to them, by destroying their mother, they had destroyed themselves. Gradually, they began to age. If it hadn't been for the dragon and Spellbinder's discovery of an immortality potion, they would have died from old age. Once more, the risk of dying was at their doorstep.

"I don't trust Highbrow and Serpentine. They're the only ones with guns," said Witch Mortify, as she entered their cabin. "We need to arm ourselves. They might shoot us before the next full moon."

"I did see the pleasure in their faces as they shot at the dragon and the others," said Blackheart. "It concerns me, too."

"And I," added Zeldar.

"We really don't need them," whispered Blackheart. "There is a spell I found in the spellbook, which turns Little Peepers into frogs."

"Do you trust that spellbook of his?" asked Mortify.

"I do. It looks authentic," replied Blackheart.

"My suggestion to work as a team won't work if Highbrow and Serpentine have guns," said Zeldar. "They'll shoot us before we reach Hidden Forest."

"Then, why don't we sneak out with the spellbook and the children tonight," said Mortify. "It would be safer for us. Besides, I just got back from tossing food to the brats. They are not looking as good as they once did. They might be producing less blood or inferior blood. We might need every drop of their blood for the three of us."

"I think I could drive the van," said Blackheart, pursing her lips. "It didn't look too difficult."

"We also have our wands," said Mortify. "What else do we need?"

"Another hiding spot," answered Blackheart. "The rest of them will come looking for us."

Over in the next cabin, the sorceresses Hexla and Underhand had the same idea. They also wanted the spellbook, the guns, the van, and the blood of the children to themselves. Meanwhile, warlocks Highbrow and Gloominus and sorcerers Spellbinder and Serpentine were plotting to shoot the female magi in their sleep. When the magi met for dinner, the tension around the campfire was high. They barely looked each other in the eye. Luckily for them, it began to downpour and they sought shelter in their cabins.

The driving rain grounded the owls. They sought cover in the trees, while the dragon landed in a meadow. They were within a mile of the Malum's hiding place. The grass was too high for the Little Peepers to wade through. They decided to wait there and launch their rescue when darkness settled upon the land. No one spoke as they waited for nightfall. When it was time to go, Tark walked with the ghosts until they spotted the mining shacks. The ghosts would have to go it alone the rest of the way.

"I am frightened for my children," whispered Jackie. She had the spellbook in her right hand.

"The Malum will avoid harming them," said Edward in a low voice. "They need to keep them alive." He had Shauna's wand. It was cold to his touch, but everything felt cold to him.

Opal, who had Ruby's wand, didn't say much because she was rehearsing the Silence Spell. There was no time to read the incantation from a book. She hoped the girls were right about their wands still having some magic left in them. If the children screamed, their plan was doomed. The ghosts could not scare off the Malum.

It was still raining. The raindrops fell right through them and landed on the ground. Fortunately, the dark storm clouds made the night darker, obscuring the moon and the stars. Such darkness would help conceal the children.

They did not speak as they came upon the four mining huts. Three of them were lit up, making it easy to determine which shack the children were in. They floated over to the unlit cabin. The door was blocked with a pile of rocks and the only window was boarded up. There was a tiny slit between the boards to let light slip in. The opening also provided a place to shove in an occasional can of dog food or a bottle of water.

Opal, Edward, and Jackie worked together and rolled the heavy rocks away from the door. Even though the pattering of rain against the tin roof helped to drown out the sound, they could not do their work noiselessly. Opal and Edward wished they could flick the rocks away with their wands without waking up the dead, but they did not know how to perform a levitation spell. Besides, they wanted to conserve the magic in their wands for the silence spell.

At last, all the rocks were removed. Opal and Edward drew their wands, while Jackie drew a deep breath and cracked open the door. What they saw would have made the ghosts retch if they'd been alive. The children were covered in filth. Their eyes were hollowed out as if they were starving. Empty tin cans were covered with maggots. The wands were not necessary because the children were too traumatized to speak, much less scream.

"It's me, your mother," Jackie whispered to her kids, though she really wanted to shout out angrily at the world. "I am a ghost now, but I am still your mother."

"Where are you planning to go with our brats, Jackie?" snarled a voice behind the ghosts.

The ghosts wheeled around and saw Sorcerer Serpentine pointing a gun at them.

"Bullets won't kill us," Jackie said as calmly as she could.

"But they kill elves," said Warlock Highbrow, as he dangled a net in front of him. Tark, disguised as an elf owl, was trapped inside the net. "You left someone behind. I shall kill him if he transforms."

Instinctively, Opal and Edward aimed their wands toward the two magi. The magi's guns turned into frog-snakes. The ghost couple seemed more surprised than either Highbrow or Serpentine because the wands were operating on their own accord. The two magi jumped back dropping the snakes. The snakes struck at them with their fangs, but missed. The ghosts grabbed the children, as Tark, who changed back into an elf, freed himself from the net and tackled Serpentine to the ground. Highbrow went after the children. Meanwhile, the other magi heard the racket and came out of their cabins. They were too old to run, although they could still move quickly, if necessary.

"Put down your wands or I'll shoot the brats!" Witch Blackheart held a handgun that she stole from Highbrow's bag.

Opal and Edward lowered their wands, which seemed to have run out of magic. The children were too weak to run.

Blackheart snatched the four-year-old from Jackie's grasp. The witch pointed the gun at the child's head. "If you take the children, I will blow out the boy's brains. We don't need all three of your kids."

Of course, she was bluffing, but the ghosts were unfamiliar with blood potions. "We can afford to get rid of the puniest one."

Jackie wailed so piercingly that the coyotes on the far hills began howling in reply.

"Shut up!" yelled Blackheart, scowling at her in a threatening manner.

Tark let go of Serpentine, scrambled to his feet, and took a step toward Blackheart. "She's lying through her rotting teeth! They won't kill the children. They do need all three."

"But I don't need a useless elf!" snapped Blackheart. She aimed her gun straight at Tark's heart.

Suddenly, there was a loud crack overhead. Everyone ducked. When they stood up again, Mem was before them. Madame Papulose was at her side. They were in human form, so they wouldn't frighten the children. And they were stunning. Their clothes were made of gold, as if sewn by a fairy's wand.

"Did you miss me, children?" Mem said sarcastically.

The Malum began to back away, but Mem pulled them toward her with a simple flick of her wrist. She didn't need a wand to perform magic or chant an incantation. She was a goddess, after all.

"This is your aunt Nebeta," said Mem, gesturing at Madame Papulose. "She is going to take the magic that is lying dormant inside you." She regarded Highbrow coolly. "Except for you, my second son." A flash of jealous anger exploded onto the other magi's faces. "You have no magic. You gave it away to the mother of your two daughters. The mother passed the magic onto your daughters when they were born. Just as I passed on some of my magic onto you. Except . . . you gave all of your magic away."

"I told you so," Blackheart said from the side of her mouth to Highbrow. She looked pleased with herself for being right.

"And you," Mem addressed Blackheart. "I expected so much more from you. Of all my children, I expected you to stand up for me. To be loyal to your mother. You have greatly disappointed me. And I hate being disappointed." Mem flicked her wrist again. Blackheart flinched, but nothing bad happened to her. Mem had cleaned up the children, as if she had given them a long, soaking bath. "Take them to the Little Peepers. Wait for me there. I have some family business to attend to first."

Tark and the ghosts picked up the children and departed at once.

"While I was suffering in the cavern, I wondered where I went wrong with the nine of you," Mem continued. Sorceress Underhand attempted to sneak away again. This time Mem paralyzed their bodies, making it so they could never go anywhere again. "I gave you everything you needed to be happy, even a share of my magic. I created the animals in the forest for you and gave you the ability to speak with them. In return, you caged and tortured them. I gave you elves and gnomes to delight you, but you either neglected them or played cruel pranks on them. You schemed behind each other's back, always plotting to destroy one another. Even tonight, you conspired against one another. And when I threatened to take your magic away, you plotted against me. You attempted to murder your own mother. And you almost succeeded. What you did was unforgivable." Her children could not deny it, even if they could overcome their paralysis and shake their heads no. Also, Nebeta, the goddess and the protector of truth, was there to set the facts straight. "I spoiled all of you. My mistake was that I gave you everything that you desired. You became cruel. You murdered the things that you were supposed to love. And now your punishment will fit your crimes. When I remove your magic, it will hurt you. When I remove your heart, your body will crumble to dust. I will not waste any more of my time lecturing you. What is done cannot be undone."

The magi's faces and bodies remained frozen. They could not express their fear or escape their punishment.

With a giant flash, Mem pulled the magic from her children. Eight clouds of magic combined together and swirled once around Mem and then entered Madame Papulose's body. Of the Malum, only Highbrow did not feel the agony of watching their magic disappear from them. As the magic was yanked from Spellbinder's body, the Little Peepers and Commander Lapin could not breathe. Spellbinder's spells were being pulled apart. When his magic settled into Madame Papulose's body, the Little Peepers and Lapin regained their breath. The spells were not broken because Spellbinder's magic had a new host—a more powerful host. Meanwhile, the magi watched as their hearts were ripped out of their bodies. They toppled to the ground. Their bodies became dust as Mem said they would. Black capes and boots were all that remained.

"It is finished," Mem said to Madame Papulose. "Let us retrieve your spellbook from the cabin and bring all the wonderful creatures back to Hidden Forest."

Madame Papulose snapped her fingers and the spellbook flew out of the mining shack into her outstretched hand. "It feels good to produce magic again."

"It is good to have a loyal family member standing at my side," replied Mem. "Now, sister, let us save the others. There are two witches whose magic is suffocating them. It's Highbrow's black magic. They cannot contain it."

"They weren't always this evil, were they?" said Madame Papulose, clearly disgusted by what she had seen in the nine magi. Regaining her magic powers had returned her all-seeing ability.

"My children once were good until they weren't any longer," Mem replied sorrowfully.

Before they departed, Mem demolished her children's new wands that were left behind. There was no use for them anymore.

□□□

Tark, the ghosts, the dragon, and the Little Peepers and their owls were waiting where they had been grounded by the rain. It was no longer raining, but they waited there because Mem had ordered them to do so. There was no way they would disobey her. In a flash of light, they found themselves hurtling through space. They felt their breathing being constricted, as if they were sucking air through a straw. The same sensation occurred with the other group that remained behind to watch over the ailing Ruby and Shauna. Within a few seconds, the tightness in their airways went away. They could breathe easily once again. The ghosts were also affected by their speedy flight.

"What a strange sensation, my dearest Edward! The wind rushed through me!" exclaimed Opal. "My head feels as if we had ridden on a carousel. It has been a long time since I've been on a carousel. I miss those days."

"My head also feels like a spinning top, dear," said Edward, looking around. "It appears we're back in the forest. How strange."

They were all now back in Hidden Forest. In Arborville, to be precise. Queen Wista, Prince Cobias, Counselor Herona, and others who had remained in the village ran to their windows when they heard a thunderous sound. Wista realized at once that it was Mem who was causing this commotion. Sure enough, everyone had returned to their village, looking mystified.

Boom!

Mem and Madame Papulose stood before them. This time Madame Papulose looked like herself. She did not have on golden clothing and neither did Mem, who was dressed in the clothing of the Little Peepers.

Mem introduced herself to the crowd as the creator of Hidden Forest. "And this is my sister, Nebeta, goddess and protector of the truth." The onlookers were speechless. "Never again will you have to worry about the magi. They are no more."

The spectators cheered until Mem reminded them that they had been her children. She shared with them the history of Hidden Forest, beginning with her escape from Egypt. The crowd didn't make a peep, not even the Little Peepers. In the background, Sawwhet was listening. Somehow the historian had wound up here. One moment, she was writing her scroll in the cedar tree and the next moment she was perched on the branch of a pine tree in Arborville.

"Today, I watched your attempt at saving the children of Serpentine," said Mem. Jackie did not dare mention that they were more her children than his. "I was impressed by your concern for others. My children never learned to care about others." She gestured at Ruby and Shauna, who were in the front row, alongside the ghosts and Jackie's children. The audience was circled around Mem and Madame Papulose. "The girls acted unselfishly. They gave their wands over to the ghosts. Most magi would not turn over their wands to another. I have decided to let you keep the magic you inherited from your father."

"Thank you, Mem," said Ruby. "But I no longer want to have magical powers. I saw what having too much magic did to your children. It corrupted them."

"I don't want the magic, either," said Shauna. "The magic is too powerful. It almost killed me."

"And the responsibility is too much," explained Ruby.

"Are you certain of your decision?" asked Mem, who had not expected their responses.

"Well, on second thought, could we have a little less, like the amount the fairies have?" asked Ruby. She was hoping she wasn't pushing her luck too far with Mem.

Mem was genuinely surprised. She was insightful, but she did not see this coming. "I will retrieve some of the magic but leave a portion in both of you. Is there anything else you want?"

Ruby felt uncomfortable with everyone watching her, but pushed herself to speak up. "Would you remove the frog-snakes from the forest? I've been told Sorcerer Spellbinder created them to kill the Little Peepers."

"It will be done." Mem swept her hand in front of her, as though she was clearing all the wicked deeds from Hidden Forest. Next, she focused her attention on Jackie. "Your children were born without magic because Serpentine did not pass his magic onto you. Where would you like your children to live? I can erase their memories of all these recent events. What I cannot do is return your life."

"Come live with us, Jackie Jubilee," said Auralia, standing up. "King Koning and the rest of us would welcome you and your children into our fold."

"I would like to remain with my children," said Jackie. She gazed at her kids. "What do you want?" They wanted their mother, despite her ghostly appearance. "We will live with the elves."

"Very well." Mem looked over at the Black Dragon. "And now, we come to you, Kveikja. What do you desire most in this world? Is it treasure? Or it is something else?"

"It is something else," answered the dragon. "I believe you already know what I desire most in the world."

"I do." Mem clapped her hands and a burst of smoke and fire exploded around them. When the smoke cleared, there was another black dragon alongside Kveikja. The crowd was in awe. "I cannot return Agir to this world. But I can create a mate for you. What is that? Prince Cobias is sending me a message to make the dragons plant-eaters. I will honor his request. I owe him that much for the years he kept me company. The two dragons will no longer crave meat," she announced to the spectators.

Kveikja didn't argue because he was tired of catching prey. He was also pleased to have company of his own kind. Besides, he was beginning to like the other forest creatures. He didn't want to hunt them anymore.

"And finally, Opal and Edward," Mem said, turning toward them. "Do you want to remain in this world or go on to the next?"

Edward and Opal gazed at each other before answering, as if reading one another's thoughts.

"We would like to remain in Hidden Forest for a little while longer," replied Opal.

"That is acceptable." Mem looked out at all the different faces watching her. "Nebeta and I will live with you in Hidden Forest, too. I do not ask for your servitude. I solely ask for your company. After my time in the Pit of Despair, I do not care to be alone again. Even though I have lost my nine children, I have five grandchildren now, as well as my sister and all of you." She gazed out at the crowd. "We will live well and be joyful. That is all we can ask of life."

"If you don't mind, I'd like the cats from the human world to visit me on occasion," spoke up Madame Papulose. "For thousands of years, I have lived in the company of cats. I will not stop now." She would not force Mister Barnaby to take up residence with her. But she would request frequent visits from him. "I would also prefer to be called Madame Papulose."

Queen Wista flew down from her treehouse on a taxi bird. She thanked the two goddesses for rescuing their community members and permanently eliminating the Malum from their midst. "The fairies and the rabbits will want to throw a homecoming celebration. They like a good party."

□ □ □

The following day Miss Whiskers went down to the library basement and found a note where the spellbooks had been. Someone had removed them from the library. She picked up the note and read it:

Thank you for safeguarding my spellbooks.

Sincerely,
Madame Papulose

P.S. See you at the celebration!

Miss Whiskers smiled and tucked the note in a pile of her own scribbled notes for an upcoming novel. Next, she prepared for the celebration in Hidden Forest. Her escort was Renzo. She smiled. She had not foreseen a handsome, jailhouse cat in her own story. Nor had she imagined Mister Barnaby moving in with her and becoming a second library cat. She decided that she would no longer be spending her evenings alone.

□□□

As the villagers of Arborville stayed up all night celebrating the defeat of the Malum, Sawwhet returned to her cedar tree to finalize the story of the Great Banishment. Most individuals would think the story of Hidden Forest had a happy ending, she noted in the parchment with her talons. And perhaps it had a happy ending for those who survived this trying time. However, it did not end well for those who had been murdered because of the jealousy and spite of the Malum and Queen Rossen. Sawwhet wrote down the names of the dead in her book. Her list began with King Hoppit and his owl, Greystone, Renee Beckles, and Jackie Jubilee. She inscribed their murderers' names: Witch Zeldar, Warlock Highbrow, Witch Mortify, Witch Blackheart, Warlock Gloominus, Sorcerer Spellbinder, Sorcerer Serpentine, Sorceress Hexla, and Sorceress Underhand. She added that Ukai was murdered by the elf queen, who was still imprisoned in the Pit of Despair. Years later, Sawwhet would write in the same scroll that Jackie Jubilee chose to remain a ghost until the passing of her own children. They decided not to remain immortal. Opal and Edward then went with Jackie to the afterworld. Ruby and Shauna did not retaliate against their stepfather for murdering their mother. They did not want a dark shadow living in their hearts. They remained with Berruga and Vorte and practiced magic among the fairies. They healed the sick and injured with their wands and became good friends with Mem and Madame Papulose. The two sisters from the nonmagical world grew up but never grew old. As an afterthought, Sawwhet recorded the names of the individuals who were killed by the frog-snakes. Every night, Berruga gazed up at the night sky and whispered good night to her son, Pip.

Sawwhet continued to keep to herself in her great cedar tree, writing down the history of the enchanted Hidden Forest. Every word of it true because owls never lie.

THE END

Main Characters

Humans and Ghosts:
Ruby – 12 years old, her sister is Shauna
Shauna – 9 years old, her sister is Ruby
Jackie Jubilee – mother of Elli, Freyja, and Mani
Madame Daisy Papulose – human companion of Mister Barnaby
Edward and Opal – the ghost couple who live at Hillside Cemetery

Little Peepers and their Owl Companions:
Kreen – a first-year pilot, pilot patrol companion is Skit, owl companion is Trill, a western screech-owl
Skit –a first-year pilot, pilot patrol companion is Kreen, owl companion is Peck, a barred owl
Queen Wista – leader of the Little Peepers, spouse is King Hoppit, son is Prince Cobias, owl companion is Spruce, a northern hawk owl
Counselor Herona – first advisor to Queen Wista, owl companion is Rings, a great gray owl
Flycatcher – skilled pilot, pilot patrol companion is Hummer, owl companion is Tuft, a long-eared owl
Hummer – skilled pilot, pilot patrol companion is Flycatcher, owl companion is Dots, a western spotted owl
Vorte and Berruga – guardians of Ruby and Shauna, their son's name is Pip
Oide – flight instructor, owl companion is Blizzard, a snowy owl
Luna – veteran pilot, owl companion is Chase, a peregrine falcon

Rabbits:
Commander Lapin – leader of the Noble Rabbits from the Eighth Regiment
Poppin – First Officer of the Eighth Regiment, Lapin's cousin

Other Notable Animals:
Swift – King Hoppit's peregrine falcon
Sawwhet – northern saw-whet owl, the historian of Hidden Forest
Mister Barnaby – black cat who lives with Madame Papulose
Miss Whiskers – librarian cat

Renzo – jailhouse cat
The Black Dragon – lives on Misty Falls
Rooter, Erde, and Snoot – moles
Gavran – leader of the ravens
Licorne – leader of the unicorns

Fairies: Golden Belle, Sparkles, Glitter, Dazzle, and Flicker
Gnomes: Groppy, leader of the gnomes

Malum:
Witch Zeldar – the oldest of the magi, lives on Dead End Street, favors poisoning her victims
Warlock Highbrow – lives in the big city, away from the other magi, father of Ruby and Shauna
Witch Mortify – makes mortifying remarks to embarrass others
Witch Blackheart – expert on black magic, prefers to burn her victims alive
Warlock Gloominus – gloomy personality
Sorcerer Spellbinder – his spells are unbreakable, fashions wands
Sorcerer Serpentine – extremely deceitful, father of Elli, Freyja, and Mani, hates children
Sorceress Hexla – quick to put hexes on others
Sorceress Underhand – youngest magi, least trustful of the magi

Elves:
Queen Rossen – leader of the elves, spouse is King Koning, fourteen-year-old son is Prince Massen
Counselor Nirva – Queen Rossen's top advisor
Tark – talented spy, father is Rowl, mother is Ukai, fourteen-year-old brother is Rupin
Auralia – desires to be a spy, has secret crush on Tark
Advisor Baruk – second advisor to Queen Rossen